Mrs. Merritt's Remorse

BOOK TWO
LORD DERE'S DEPENDENTS

CHRISTINA DUDLEY

PROLOGUE

**If any other man...conceive of
a better course, let him speake.
—John Bingham, translator, *The historie of Xenophon containing the ascent of Cyrus* (1623)**

If ever a man knew precisely what he planned to do with his life, and which steps should be gained by what means at which time, that man was Philip Egerton. Born the first of six children to an Oxfordshire parson, he took after his father in choice of profession, but only there. Where Mr. Philip Egerton, Senior, was content to shift as he might on a limited income, his oldest son had greater ambitions.

"Imagine how different my father's life might have been, if he had only waited a few years before marriage," he told his sister Cassandra as she measured him for the plain subfusc shirt and trousers he would wear under his Oxford gown. "Nothing excessive—say, five years. Not only would he have had more time to save income from his fellowship, but there would consequently have been fewer of us to feed, house and raise."

"Which of us would you lop from the family tree, then?" she asked mildly around the pins in her mouth. "The oldest branches? If Papa and Mama waited to marry, you might not be here to congratulate them for doing so, and I might not be here to hear it. Or would you rather amputate the lowest limbs and remove Anna and Tim?"

"I'm not speaking of metaphysical questions but of practical matters," he rejoined. "Even after marrying too soon Papa might yet have risen, had he exerted himself to curry favor with the archdeacon and the bishop. Instead, whenever not positively *required* to be in the pulpit or performing some parish duty, he has always preferred to hide in his study. Who knows what more lucrative living might have come his way, not to mention plum positions or honors, had he done otherwise."

Unmoved, his sister jotted numbers down and switched the position of the tape. "In short, if Papa had not been Papa, he would have been someone else. One might say that of anyone."

"Think on it, Cassie. If he did not avoid the politics of the diocese—if he listened more to my mother's urgings, we might even now be living in a bishop's palace with an army of servants."

She laughed. "But then he would have been more like Mama than Papa. There's no doubt Mama would have been an archbishop by now. But never mind. Papa is perfectly content, Philip. It's *you* who would not be." Stepping back, she clasped her hands and regarded him with mocking admiration. "Speak, Mr. Egerton! Having seen the ship of your father's life run aground, as you embark on your own voyage, what will you do differently?"

Though he grinned at her teasing, he answered seriously enough, "In the first place, I will gain a fellowship as he did. But when I have, I will add to it as many curacies as I can scramble into, until I have gained the living Uncle Geoffrey promises or another of equal value. Only then will I marry."

"And suppose that takes ten years, Philip?"

"Then it takes ten years. But I do not think the present vicar of St. Lawrence can possibly last that long."

Now whipping stitches with admirable speed, Cassie shook her head fondly. "You always get what you want, so I imagine poor old Mr. Holden will give up the ghost the instant you think it convenient. Probably the moment you deign to look favorably upon some young lady."

But here Cassandra Egerton proved less prophetic than her storied namesake, for however accommodating life had been thus far to young Philip Egerton, it then began to "yeild to fickle Chance," as Milton phrased it. For the very week he matriculated at Christ Church, the vicar of St. Lawrence Church was prematurely gathered to his fathers!

Here was a to-do.

Though Geoffrey Cottrell fully intended the living for his nephew, the raw youth had only just begun at Oxford and was years from his degree. Mr. Cottrell therefore did the next best thing: calculating as carefully as an actuary at an assurance company, he chose a gouty, middle-aged successor who might safely be expected to expire within five to seven years. At the very least, if the selected man insisted on drawing out his existence, by that period he would certainly be infirm enough to require a curate, and Philip could begin there.

But another fickle Chance followed.

It came to pass that the new vicar Mr. Spacks took such a liking to the setting of St. Lawrence Church that he began to walk daily in all weathers, until he was as common a sight in the country lanes as the similarly attired blackbirds. With such habitual exercise, Spacks grew as slim as those same birds, his gout entirely resolving and the health of his youth returning. Very good news for the vicar, but less so for Philip Egerton once he had taken his fellowship and begun to look about him for the next rung on the ladder.

And finally, the third fickle Chance was the death of his uncle's dear friend, who in his will entrusted as ward to Geoffrey Cottrell one Miss Felicity Hynde. One glimpse of Miss Hynde's golden hair and round blue eyes—one enchanted evening in her company (in which she hung on his words with flattering fascination)—and the newly chosen fellow of Christ Church found himself cursing Mr. Spacks's endurance and rethinking how much money was absolutely necessary for a young couple to begin in life. Sweet, charming, innocent Miss Hynde, raised in isolation by a succession of severe governesses in the Devonian hinterlands! (The late Mr. Hynde had chosen Geoffrey Cottrell as her guardian, in fact, because Cottrell's spinster daughter Martha so reminded him of all those severe governesses.) What would it be like, Philip wondered, to claim such an angel for his own?

He was too hard-headed to cast practicality to the winds, however. Rather, he bit back any rash endearments which might escape him in the presence of his Ideal and began to seek opportunities to improve his situation. He haunted the senior common room to consult his colleagues; he accosted his father in his study; he wrote letters; he made himself agreeable. And soon his efforts yielded his first curacy.

"Look here," said the senior Philip Egerton one Sunday during the summer holidays as he read his post. "Old Terry says he and his wife plan to avail themselves of the peace and seek warmer climes until next summer. What would you say to taking his duties in his absence?"

"Where?" demanded his son, his head snapping up as if he would order his trunk packed at once.

"Church of St. Mary the Virgin in Iffley. A mere five miles from here and half as many from Tom Quad at Christ Church, so you might continue your fellowship duties," said his father. "Better yet, Terry offers the use of the rectory, saving you the cost of lodgings. It's only seven months, but—"

"But it's better than nothing," Egerton finished. "I'll take it."

"Yes, yes." His father sighed. "Poor Terry and his wife never did have any children, though the size of the rectory and the living would have allowed for both. Instead he has always taken in a few pupils. He writes that if you did not wish to teach, the 'two Tommies' might be sent to school in Oxford, but he would feel easier if they were not subject to such disruption."

"I will teach them," answered Egerton promptly. "Does he mention the pay?"

The senior Egerton peered at the letter in his hand through his spectacles. "He does. *With* the pupils he offers £50 for the seven months. Without them, £35. Quite unexceptionable of Terry. Even generous."

"Very," his son agreed, his normally intent gaze uncharacteristically distant. He was making calculations in his head, the columns of numbers shivering like fringe on a curtain, now drawing back to reveal...Miss Hynde. The peerless Miss Hynde, pacing steadily toward him, wreathed in bridal flowers.

"...Cassie might go with you to keep house," his father mused. "It would be almost a holiday for her, after tending your mother and Anna and Tim through their recent sickness. And then you might pool her little allowance with your pay and be almost wealthy people."

Shaking off his distraction, Philip immediately saw the sense in the suggestion.

Yes, Cassie should accompany him. If he could not yet claim Miss Hynde as a helpmate, Cassie would do very well.

Thumping a fist on the tablecloth, he lifted his chin. Here, at last, was his future resuming its orderly march!

"Shall you write to him, sir, or shall I?"

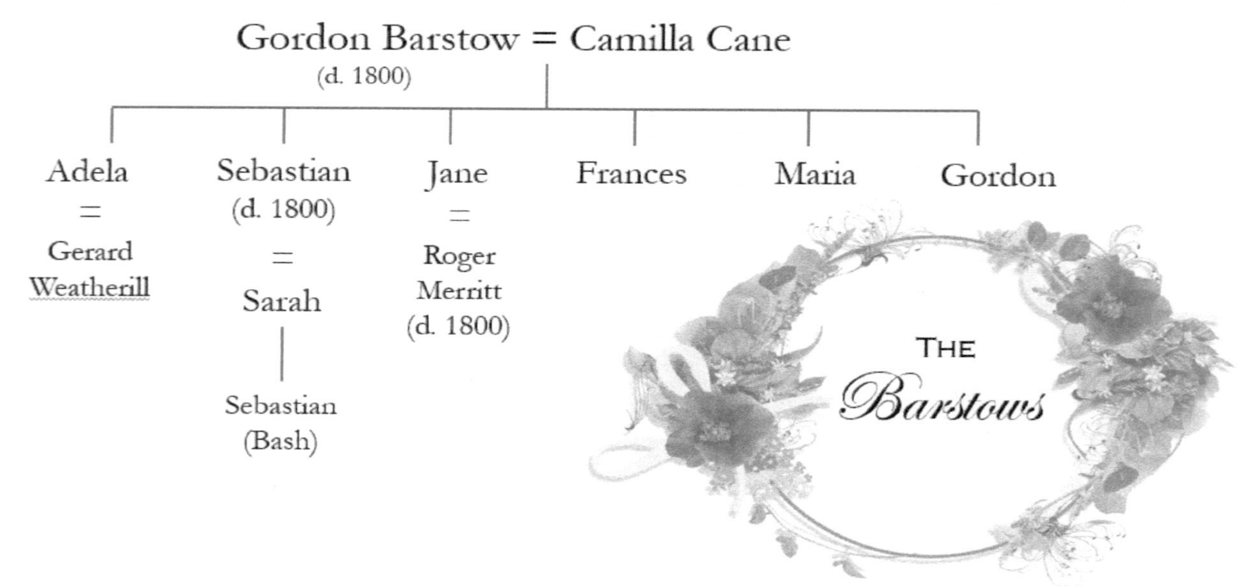

Gordon Barstow = Camilla Cane
(d. 1800)

Adela
=
Gerard
Weatherill

Sebastian
(d. 1800)
=
Sarah

Sebastian
(Bash)

Jane
=
Roger
Merritt
(d. 1800)

Frances

Maria

Gordon

THE
Barstows

CHAPTER 1

The fruit of our own ill doing is remorse.
—Richard Hooker, *Of the lawes of ecclesiasticall politie*
(1597)

Mrs. Gerard Weatherill, née Adela Barstow, vaulted—there could be no other word for it—over the low stone wall surrounding Iffley Cottage and dashed across the yard to the door.

"Why, Della!" cried her mother, when her oldest nearly collided with her. "What on earth are you doing here? We did not expect you, but do come in."

"I haven't time, Mama," she panted, holding on to her bonnet strings to prevent Mrs. Barstow untying them. "I only came to say that—that Mrs. Markham Dere told Gerard that, if he enrolls Archie Wilson at Keele's school, she will withdraw Peter!"

"Withdraw her son?" echoed Mrs. Barstow, having to raise her voice because all at once every other resident of Iffley Cottage, from her daughter-in-law Sarah Barstow, to her second-oldest daughter Mrs. Merritt, to seventeen-year-old Frances, to eleven-year-old Maria, to nine-year-old Gordon, to two-year-old Bash, to the servants Reed and Irving, crowded into the passage, most of them speaking at once.

"What's wrong with Archie Wilson?" asked Maria, plucking at Adela's sleeve.

"She can't take Peter from Keele's!" protested Gordon. "He and I do everything together, including ride back and forth to Oxford in Lord Dere's coach. Peter would never stand for it! He didn't say he would let her, did he?"

"Where would Peter go, if not to Keele's?" was Frances' question. "Would she hire another tutor?"

"Mr. Terry cannot do it," Sarah pointed out, "not if he and Mrs. Terry leave for the Continent soon. In fact, I thought he was going to send his own two pupils to Keele's as well."

Adela addressed herself to Sarah first because, after two years of assisting her husband and his mentor with the running of Keele's school, she tried not to reward blurting and shouting children. "That's my other piece of news: Mr. Terry sent a note to Gerard saying the Tommies would *not* be matriculating after all because Mr. Terry's new curate offers to teach them himself."

"My dear girl," breathed Mrs. Barstow, "if Mr. Terry's new curate keeps the Tommies, and Mrs. Dere removes Peter, can the school survive the loss of fees?"

Her oldest daughter met her worried gaze, but it was Frances who spoke first: "I daresay the baron would make up the difference, Della, if you apply to him."

This drew sighs from the older women. Apply to Mrs. Barstow's cousin Lord Dere, when he had already done so, so much for them? It was Lord Dere who provided Iffley Cottage when they had nowhere to go after the death of Mr. Barstow. It was Lord Dere who had allowed Gordon to share a tutor with his own heir and great-nephew Peter, and who now paid Gordon's school fees. It was Lord Dere who came to the family's rescue when Jane Merritt's husband ruined himself. It was Lord Dere who had recognized that Adela and the tutor had fallen in love and who then arranged for them to marry. And in between these monumental things, it was the baron who smoothed over the countless little difficulties between them and his niece by marriage Mrs. Markham Dere, despite being generally under the woman's thumb.

"It will only be a few more pounds and shillings for him," Frances tried to buoy them. "A mere drop in the bucket of the amount we already owe."

Unsurprisingly, they took no comfort from this, and young Maria, peering into her elders' faces, soon burst out again with, "But why should Mrs. Dere be so troublesome?"

"Now, now, Maria," chided her mother, "I suppose Mrs. Dere only wants the best for Peter."

"But what is wrong with this Archie Wilson anyway?" Maria persisted.

"He is—there is—" Adela fumbled. "Well, sweeting, he is someone's natural child."

"Natural child?" Maria repeated, perplexed.

"I will explain to you later, Maria," said her sister. "Or Mama will. But I must return to Oxford now, or Gerard will wonder what became of me. I only meant to go for a long, long walk to clear my head and try to think what must be done—but then I realized you all would be seeing the Deres at Perryfield tomorrow when you meet the new curate, and I thought—oh, I hardly know! That you might be able to sound Mrs. Dere and discover how in earnest she is and what may be done."

"Of course we will," Mrs. Barstow assured her. "And I will write to you directly if we learn anything, or even if we don't."

"Della—" It was the first word Jane Merritt had spoken since her sister's appearance. "Della, wait. I feel this is my fault. Mrs. Dere's objections to the boy, I mean. She would not be so touchy about it, if she did not feel she has already...tolerated enough irregularities."

Even in her hurry, Adela Weatherill stopped at this to grip her sister by the shoulders and look directly in her eyes. "No, Jane. This is not your fault. Archie Wilson has nothing to do with you, and I'll warrant Mrs. Dere was touchy before she ever heard the name of Barstow."

"But should I stay home from the dinner?" Jane insisted. "Will my presence vex her further?"

"Go, Jane. Go, and never mind her. Never mind all of this. It will sort itself out."

Then, with kisses for each of them, Adela scampered away as quickly as she had come.

A little silence fell in the passage which had been so noisy, and the servants, finding no excuse to linger, reluctantly withdrew.

"If I am not needed," said Jane after a pause, "I think I will lie down for a little while."

Iffley Cottage was small for the seven family members and two servants it held, but during the day privacy could be found in one of the three modest bedrooms, and it was to the one Jane Merritt shared with her sister-in-law Sarah that she now retreated.

"So much for time curing all," said Frances when they heard the door shut upstairs. Throwing herself upon the sofa beside the cat, she rubbed the favorite spot below its ears. "Now she will mope, and it will be a fortnight before we can persuade her to show her face in the village again."

"We cannot let her continue to hide, Mrs. Barstow," Sarah sighed. "I know the baron arranged tomorrow's dinner especially, so she might—we all might—meet the new curate and his sister before any of the tittle-tattle about us reaches them. So they might get their information 'from the source,' as it were."

"I know it," said her mother-in-law. "But what can we do, except add our encouragement to Adela's and try to persuade her if she resists going?"

"I wish she had never married Roger Merritt," Maria said stoutly, but this was so self-evident a sentiment that it drew no response. "Did you know I once asked her if she wanted to marry the next time in a church, instead of eloping, and she told me she would never marry again."

Mrs. Barstow drooped. "Yes. She has said that to me too."

"For now, never mind her marrying again," Frances said, throwing up her hands. "Let us begin with getting her to the Perryfield dinner."

"I do believe I have caught a little chill and had better stay home today," Jane announced at breakfast the following morning, not looking up as she diligently spread jam on Bash's toast.

Across the table, her family exchanged glances which said, You see? It is as we feared.

"Might I go in her place, then, Mama?" Maria asked artlessly. "I'm eleven now, and I don't see why I should stay home with Gordy and Bash as if I were a baby."

"You weren't invited," Frances said shortly, before turning on Jane. "You're perfectly well, and you know it, Jane," she accused. "You just don't want to see Mrs. Markham Dere because of the Archie Wilson business."

"No," returned Jane. "I have thought about Archie Wilson and see that Della is probably right. Mrs. Dere would have objected to him in any case."

"Then this is about meeting the new curate and his sister," Frances pursued. When Jane made no reply, Frances leaned forward and rapped on the table in her insistence. "But don't you see? If this Mr. Egerton is to take Mr. Terry's church for several months, you will see him and Miss Egerton every week, Jane, if not oftener, so it would be better to meet them now and have done with it."

Biting her lip, Jane gave the toast to Bash, who promptly smashed it against his face, smearing jam over his round cheeks.

The fact was, Jane considered herself the black sheep of the family. Nay—if there existed a deeper dye than black, she was that. For she, the daughter of a respectable Berkshire clergyman, had loved and eloped with a man of whom her father disapproved, only to learn too late the wisdom of the late Gordon Barstow's opinion. And though, with his good looks and dash and high spirits, Roger Merritt had been all that her twenty-one-year-old self thought desirable, their brief union led only to misery. After his aunt cut off his allowance in response to his imprudent match, Jane's husband soon regretted marrying her. Not that he ever said so, but his bitterness had been plain enough. And if she could not now recall his descent into drink and ruin without cringing in shame, much less could she bear to think of his ultimate confinement in the Fleet Prison for debt—!

Two slow years had passed since Roger's death brought that wretched chapter of her life to a close, two years in which her family never once reproached her for the jeopardy in which her misadventures placed them—but they had no need to. Jane was fully capable of administering her own punishment.

With the assistance of Lord Dere and of the man who was now Adela's husband, she had returned to the bosom of her family, taking shelter there from the storm and rarely venturing out. For the first three months she had not even gone to church, and for the next three she had gone only there, if she emerged from the cottage at all. And over time the practice which began in shame for her failures grew into habit. This, despite the fact that even the most horrifying affairs will lose their power to horrify through sheer familiarity. After two years, the repetition of her scandalous story grew so commonplace in Iffley that it ceased to scandalize. Contrarily, it was curiosity which grew, in direct parallel with her reclusiveness. Had Jane been a dowd, or closer in age to forty than twenty, she doubtless would have been forgotten by this point, but because she was still young and pretty, her reticence drew interest. Evoked sympathy, even.

Frances made an impatient movement, guessing what passed through her sister's mind. "The point is," she said again, "the new curate is coming, whether we like it or not, and Mr. Terry is going away, whether we like it or not. You know how Mrs. Terry worries over her husband's cough, and now that peace has come they may escape someplace warm. I envy them! Imagine Italy and the South of France!"

Sarah, who had lost her husband Sebastian in a naval action against the French, gave a shiver, but she reached around her son to pat Jane's shoulder. "Even without the children, there will be four of us to be introduced tonight at Perryfield," she observed. "And with Lord Dere, Mrs. Markham Dere, and the Terrys, we will be such a comfortable crowd! It is the Egertons who will be the strangers. Think, Jane. Suppose you did not meet them tonight—you would then have to be introduced on a later occasion, likely in the churchyard this Sunday, and when that happened you would be conspicuous as the only new acquaintance."

Jane straightened, her hazel eyes widening. "Oh! How true, Sarah. I did not—did not think of that." Picking up her teacup, she brought it near her lips, only to set it down again. Then she snatched up the toast on her plate and began to pull it apart. But seeing everyone at the table watching her, she made another effort and folded her hands in her lap.

"Yes," Jane said quietly. "I had better accompany you all, then. I should like to see what Mrs. Dere says of Archie Wilson, at any rate. And, as Sarah says, there will be safety in numbers."

While it would be an exaggeration to call Mrs. Markham Dere the Barstows' nemesis, she certainly was mistrustful of Lord Dere's constant kindnesses toward them, and who could blame her, when the oldest Barstow daughter had nearly carried the baron off as a matrimonial prize?

For Mrs. Markham Dere, to come so near being supplanted, to have her son Peter's position as Heir threatened—these things had left their mark.

The Dere coach which fetched the Barstows that afternoon was just one example of the baron's thoughtfulness, but as the women climbed in, settling upon the Morocco leather cushions and feeling their slippers sink into the Wilton carpets, Jane could spare a thought for neither the vehicle's elegance nor the owner's care. She was too occupied with what lay ahead. I will know everyone there but the Egertons, she reminded herself, and they might be more apprehensive than I, for they know no one. Yes. The Egertons would be the strangers in that gathering, not she. And truly, how frightening could one inexperienced curate and his younger sister be?

Curates were harmless, after all. Often colorless and uninteresting. Pitiable in their poverty. Take, as a specimen, her late father's curate Mr. Liddell, the one they once thought would marry Adela. Why, Mr. Liddell had been so ordinary in appearance and personality that recalling him was no easy task. He had been a curate's curate, as it were. Mouse-brown hair and eyes set close together. That was all she could remember. Oh, yes, and a tendency to clear his throat before every speech. If it had been Mr. Liddell she were being introduced to on this occasion, he would have said only, "Oh—hem! Mrs. Merritt? Ahem." And Jane would have known straight off whether he had been told her history by whether he blushed or not. He certainly would not have had the courage to refer to it, much less to disdain her for it. Please heaven, may Mr. Egerton prove just another Mr. Liddell!

Too soon the coach passed the long stone wall which enclosed the great house. Too soon they reached the windowless arch with leaded traceries which peeped into the grounds. Too soon the coach drew up before the symmetrical, three-storey, ivy-bearded stone house with its neat rows of mullioned windows.

And far too soon the footman Wood threw open the drawing room doors to announce, "Mrs. Gordon Barstow, Mrs. Sebastian Barstow, Mrs. Roger Merritt, and Miss Barstow."

Not raising her eyes above the semicircle of shoes and skirts confronting her, Jane allowed that Sarah had been right. With so many gathered, the Egertons might not even have caught her name.

Straightening from his bow, the slim and silver-haired Lord Dere raised an arm and opened his mouth to greet them, but his niece anticipated him.

"Ah, Barstows," Mrs. Markham Dere said coolly, striding forward. "You must allow me to present Mr. Terry's new curate, Mr. Philip Egerton, and his sister Miss Egerton. Mr. and Miss Egerton, may I present his lordship's cousin Mrs. Barstow? She and her family tenant Iffley Cottage in the village. I have already mentioned Mrs. Weatherill, who lives in Oxford and who is Mrs. Barstow's eldest daughter…"

Mrs. Dere had more to say—much more—but Jane scarcely remarked it over the rush of her pulse. For—oh, my!—Mr. Egerton was not a thing like innocuous Mr. Liddell. In fact, he was not a thing like any curate she had known or imagined.

It was not his good looks which made him stand out. Indeed, Jane hardly remarked his looks at all, other than to see he had light brown hair streaked with gold, eyes which were a paler, greener shade of hazel than her own, and a long nose with the slightest bump halfway down, which gave him the air of, if not a Roman, at least something near to one. No, it was not his looks which struck her first. It was…something else. Though she struggled to put her finger on it, it might be best described as the energy contained in him. A vigor carried in his person, though his build was neither particularly tall nor large. Some mysterious force, expressed without his needing to move or shout or otherwise draw attention. Was it confidence? Resoluteness?

Whatever one might call it, it was accentuated by a clear, clear gaze, beaming forth from eyes which had nothing to hide. And because Mr.

Philip Egerton had nothing to hide, when he looked at one in turn, one felt seen—and seen through—for better or worse.

And in Jane's case, it was definitely for worse.

Because did his sharp gaze not sharpen still further when presented with her, picking her out among the other Barstow women? *Mrs. Dere has told him about me. Or Mrs. Terry has. It could not have been Mrs. Lamb, though she is such a gossip, for how could he even yet know the postmistress, to speak with her?*

"Mrs. Merritt." He had murmured each name in turn, and the sound of her own made color bloom on Jane's face, making her feel gauche as a schoolgirl.

Thankfully no more was expected of her, and she retreated to the lee of Sarah's shoulder and then to take a seat between Sarah and Frances on the sofa.

"...Fortunate that Mr. Egerton is willing to take on the tutelage of Wardour and Ellis," the rector Mr. Terry was saying to the company. "The Tommies, you know. Less disruptive for them, as well as for Keele's."

"Disruptive for Keele's!" sniffed Mrs. Markham Dere. "After all the baron has done for the Weatherills, they would have shifted to take on your two pupils whether it was convenient or not."

Indeed, the building in Oxford where Jane's sister and brother-in-law both lived and ran a school had been leased to them by Lord Dere, and the Barstows all knew the Weatherills would have done whatever was asked of them, if it were the baron doing the asking. To have Mrs. Dere doubt their gratitude gave general offense.

"I don't doubt it, Mrs. Dere," the rector's wife intervened. "But for that very reason we did not want to force the Tommies upon them. Moreover, Mrs. Weatherill told me that they had just enrolled two new boys, and she hoped they would get along with the others."

"Perhaps they will begin to think of expanding Keele's—" began the baron, before his niece cut him off.

"Two new pupils! To whom do you refer, Mrs. Terry?"

"The first is from Oxford proper," she answered, "a boy close in age to Gordy and Peter. Mrs. Weatherill says he will do very well—he is content to be led by the others, without being odd or so small or weak that they are tempted to pick at him. The second, I believe, is younger, and I hope he will fit as well. Poor little thing—apparently neither Nixon's nor Magdalen School would take him."

"I knew it!" cried Mrs. Dere, drawing herself up. "It's that Archie Wilson child, is it not?"

"Why—I don't believe I know the name." Mrs. Terry blinked in some surprise at Mrs. Dere's vehemence. "Ought I too?"

"Indeed you ought! We all ought. I was speaking with the Weatherills myself and learned from them that there is a very good reason the other Oxford schools refused him." Her gaze swept the room to ensure she had their full attention before she pronounced ominously, "I'm afraid there is some...irregularity as to the boy's parentage."

"Dear me," murmured Mrs. Barstow, knowing she must interject, for Adela's sake.

"Which is to say," Mrs. Dere kept on, "he is the natural son of somebody. Some dreadful town rake—"

"That is not how Adela phrased it," ventured Mrs. Barstow in her soft voice.

But Mrs. Dere had already turned on the baron. "Sir—surely you cannot approve of this? The Weatherills' school exists only on your sufferance. Therefore, should not they be more select in whom they choose to educate?"

"I'm sure—" Lord Dere began to wind himself up.

"And Mrs. Barstow," Mrs. Dere's golden head whipped back to regard her. "Surely you do not want your son Gordon taught alongside—someone of dubious parentage?"

Poor Mrs. Barstow colored, her mouth working a moment, and then she hazarded a deprecating, "If Gerard and Della think no harm will come of it. There is nothing...catching about illegitimacy, after all. I am certain if the child has—wicked tendencies—that would prove another matter."

Rather than soothing their hostess, Mrs. Barstow's words had the opposite effect, and Mrs. Dere's magnificent bosom swelled. To be thus crossed, in her own (or very nearly her own) drawing room? And look at her uncle sitting there, saying nothing, as usual! What was the world coming to?

"I fear we must agree to disagree, madam," she said curtly. "I am not at all convinced of the advisability of this course. In fact, I have already informed the Weatherills that if this Archibald Wilson starts at Keele's, then Keele's must carry on without my Peter. I will withdraw him. If I must hire another private tutor for him, so be it, but there are certain standards which must be maintained."

"Mrs. Dere—" began the rector.

But the baron's niece had worked herself to a pitch of indignation. "Mrs. Barstow, I understand that, given your own son's place in life and the—regrettable circumstances with which your family has already been connected, you might be less particular about such things, but I have a responsibility not only to my son but to the name and barony of Dere."

Thus must the biblical Joshua have sounded when he thundered, "As for me and my house, we will serve the Lord!" And in the electric silence which fell, probably it was not only Jane Merritt's heart hammering. But it was certainly only Jane Merritt who then sprang to her feet, and it was Jane Merritt's voice alone which rang out.

"I suppose, Mrs. Dere, when you refer to my family's 'regrettable circumstances' and the connections burdening my innocent brother Gordon, you refer to me."

CHAPTER 2

He that toucheth pitch, shal be defiled therewith.
—Ecclesiasticus 13:1, *The Authorized Version* (1611)

Had she been closeted alone with Mrs. Dere while the woman said such things, Jane would think later, she would not have spoken a word in reply. She would have bowed her head and received the reproaches as her due, unpleasant though the experience would be. So to leap to her feet—to defy the formidable woman—she must have been mad. It must have been her mother's stricken face which compelled her. Or the urgent commission they had received from Della the day before. Or the unjust criticism Mrs. Dere leveled at the Weatherills. Or the thought of Gordy losing the daily company of his friend and schoolmate Peter.

It must have been any and all of these things which compelled her.

But—

But.

But if she were honest, Jane admitted she might have borne even those particular slings and arrows in silence.

Heavens—she might even have done nothing if Mrs. Dere said such things in the hearing of only her family and the baron, or the kind and familiar Terrys.

Therefore, let the truth be told, if only in the privacy of her conscience.

The fact was, fearing what the newcomer Egertons might already know of her, Jane could not bear this public pillorying. It was one thing for Mrs. Dere to throw Jane's past in her own face, but quite another for her to do so before strangers.

Therefore: "I suppose, Mrs. Dere, when you refer to my family's 'regrettable circumstances' and the connections burdening my innocent brother Gordon, you refer to *me.*"

Smothered gasps.

Tableau: *The Disgraced before Her Accusers.*

With Jane so suddenly on her feet, the gentlemen had no choice but to rise to their own, as soon as they overcame their surprise. But even as they did so, she felt her mother and Sarah reaching for her hands to—what?—comfort her? pull her back to her seat? Before they could do either, she had crossed her arms over her midsection, more to halt the tremble she felt coming on than to bid further defiance to their hostess.

Mrs. Dere's astonished blue eyes were hard and round as marbles, and she gave a high laugh. "Mrs. Merritt! What on earth? Do be seated. Gracious, what a...display."

Indeed—what a display!

After two long years of saying nothing, doing nothing, in her own defense, lying as low as she possibly could, she now did *this?*

Against a rising tide of doubt and embarrassment, Jane stammered, "I—beg your pardon, madam. But—but—I must ask you not to cast aspersions upon my family. Aspersions which belong, in truth, only to me." She managed this much before sending one swift, encompassing glance around the drawing room, a glance which could not fail to take in the Terrys' dismay and the Egertons' obvious puzzlement.

Wait—their...*puzzlement?*

Yes, puzzlement. Mixed with astonishment. Miss Egerton's brow was creased, her head cocked. And as for Mr. Egerton—*gracious.* The new curate stared at her as if she were a lapdog who had broken into the Hallelujah Chorus.

In this eyeblink, a dozen thoughts crowded her mind.

If the Egertons were so uncomprehending, it could only mean they had *not,* in fact, known to what Mrs. Dere referred. Which meant in turn that Mrs. Dere had not spoken of it to them, and nor had the Terrys. Even Mrs. Lamb at the Tree Inn was exonerated, for pity's sake.

Oh, mercy.

And now she herself had been the one to make a fuss! If she had only kept her mouth shut, the discomfiting moment would have passed, leaving the Egertons to seek an explanation from the Terrys later, in some private setting. But now Jane had left herself no alternative but to explain her bizarre conduct.

These conclusions were the work of a moment before she felt the hot blood drain from her. Her arms fell to her sides, allowing Mrs. Barstow and Sarah to catch at her and draw her down between them, while, awkwardly, the gentlemen resumed their seats as well. Mrs. Terry straightened, in preparation to join the fray, but Jane knew their well-meaning rector's wife often made matters worse with her impulsive tongue. She must rally, then, and quickly. If her story must now be made known to the newcomers, let it be her, for once, to tell it.

"I must beg *everyone's* pardon for my outburst," she began in an unsteady voice, addressing a scroll in the paper on the wall opposite. "It was inexcusable." As was so much she had done, Jane added inwardly.

"You see," she went on, "Mrs. Dere only spoke the truth when she referred to 'regrettable circumstances.' It—it would not be going too far, even, to call it 'disgrace.' That is—I mean—suffice to say, Mr. Egerton, Miss Egerton, if you did not know already—and I suspect now that you did not—the story is simply this: a few years ago, I made a bad marriage, and it exacted a heavy price. I married my husband—without my father's approval—indeed, without his knowledge, even, for my father died just before the—marriage—took place. Which proved to be a mercy because—because the match brought—it brought—undeserved scandal and—and—and *shame* upon my family. You see...the long and short of it is, my husband Mr. Merritt was—soon arrested for debt. He—was imprisoned. In the Fleet. Where he sadly—died—two years ago."

A little gasp escaped Miss Egerton, but it was not the cluck of condemnation for which Jane had braced herself, and for that she was grateful. As for Mr. Egerton, he said precisely nothing, his eyes drilling into her until Jane thought he must soon see out the other side. Mrs. Dere alone moved, her upright posture relaxing a fraction and chin lifting, as if to say, *You see? You thought me unreasonable, but am I not justified in objecting to* such *a family?*

For Jane's part, she hoped not another word would be required of her for the remainder of the evening. Let Mrs. Terry say whatever she liked now, and Mrs. Dere, for that matter. With any luck, the company would henceforth ignore her, and when she returned home she might crawl under the coverlet, never to emerge again.

It was Mr. Egerton who finally broke the silence.

"Mrs. Dere," he said evenly, removing his gaze from Jane at last, "if we might return to our earlier subject, I may have a solution to the problem of little Archie Wilson. I ought perhaps to consult Mr. Terry as well, because—what if the boy were to come to me? To the rectory, that is, to be taught. Then your Peter and, indeed, Keele's entire school would be spared the child's...murky antecedents."

Jane's head shot up. His disquieting eyes flicked to her, sliced her neatly in half, and then returned to Mrs. Dere.

What did it mean? Did he change the subject to rescue her from the distressful situation, or was he simply wishing to pass over the difficult moment? While nothing in his look betrayed sympathy for her, he must know his proposal risked antagonizing the foremost lady in the district.

"Oh, what a splendid suggestion!" struck in Mrs. Terry. She patted her husband's knee. "Do you not agree, Mr. Terry? Yes. A splendid, charitable suggestion, Mr. Egerton."

"I did not think pointing out the obvious facts was *un*charitable," Mrs. Dere sniffed. "I daresay other parents would object to Archie Wilson, if his situation became widely known. Moreover, those who know me would agree I have shown myself tolerant of...aberrations in the past, including Mrs. Merritt's circumstances, with which she has so baldly regaled us."

"I should more accurately have called it a 'peacemaking' suggestion, then," Mrs. Terry amended hastily. "For it would indeed keep the peace to accept this Archie at the rectory. Only consider—our two Tommies, being older, would be in far less danger of having their characters warped by the child's bastardy." Nothing in Mrs. Terry's countenance or tone hinted at amusement as she said this, but Mrs. Dere had known the rector's wife long enough to suspect it might nevertheless be lurking. Before she could make up her mind to speak, however, Mrs. Terry was waving a light hand. "Yes. You rest easy, Mrs. Dere. Your Peter may continue where he is."

"The Weatherills might already be counting on Archie's fees, however," volunteered the baron. It was not the wisest move on his part, for his niece turned on him at once to vent her feelings.

"That may be, uncle," Mrs. Dere rejoined. "But if they were to take Archie's fees, they would perforce be giving up Peter's, if not that of other pupils. Besides, I hope they have not been so foolish as to spend money they did not yet have! That way lies ruin. Indeed, the Weatherills must learn to steward their finances, sir. It has been two years since you gave them the means to start that school with Mr. Keele, and they don't appear in any danger of driving Nixon's or Magdalen School out of business."

Here Frances spoke up. Of all the Barstows, she was the favorite with Mrs. Markham Dere, having been bidden by Adela to win the woman two years earlier. With that goal in mind, Frances had learned to bite her tongue at the proper times and to pay Mrs. Dere the compliments of attention and flattery at others. And what began as stratagem soon became second nature, for Frances found it more comfortable to be liked than disliked, and she managed to bear Mrs. Dere's worst nonsense by the simple method of ignoring it.

"Madam," she began now, "Della and her husband would certainly profit by your counsel, and I will take care to pass it along the next time I see them. It is one thing for the Terrys and Mr. Egerton to accept this boy as a pupil, but the Weatherills have twenty boys at Keele's, and that is indeed another matter altogether! I hope they were guilty of nothing worse than thoughtlessness. Thank heaven you and the baron are always looking out for us."

As Frances hoped, this sop mollified their hostess, whilst also giving the Barstows a minute to swallow any lingering indignation. And perhaps to the relief of all, Wood then entered to announce dinner. The matter was allowed to drop, and it was not until much later, when the company was listening to Frances at the pianoforte afterward, that Mrs. Dere was heard saying to the rector *sotto voce*, "Really, Mr. Terry, before you let your curate take this step, should you not ask the Tommies' families' permission?"

This renewed interference was balanced by another, more kindly inquiry, however, as Mrs. Barstow reported when they were being driven home again: "At our end of the dinner table, Lord Dere told me as quietly as he could that, if Della and Gerard were indeed counting upon little Archie Wilson's fees, I had only to inform him, and he would make good the same."

"Hurrah!" cried Frances. "Three cheers for Lord Dere! Let the Terrys and Mr. Egerton deal with Mrs. Dere, then. So long as the baron does not abandon us, we can weather her storms. And you see, Jane? The worst is over. I never imagined you would meet the enemy in the teeth as you did, but I commend you for it. The next thing you know, you will be attending balls and giving speeches in Parliament."

Jane shook her head. "I must have been mad."

"Well, your madness had method in it," Frances replied. "The Egertons now know the worst, and there's freedom in that. Moreover, Miss Egerton gave no sign of wanting to flee the room, screaming."

"I liked her," said Sarah. "She sat beside me in the drawing room and seemed like a kind, reasonable young lady."

"But what about—Mr. Egerton sat next to you at dinner, did he not, Sarah? Did—he seem horrified?" Jane hoped she sounded nonchalant.

"It would hardly have been courteous of him to mention it," observed her sister-in-law, "but he did not seem unduly aloof. We spoke mostly of how he and Miss Egerton thought they would like Iffley and the rectory."

"I was too afraid to look at him—or indeed anyone as I made my confession," admitted Jane. "I could only tell you how the drawing room wall took the disclosure, which was amazingly well."

Frances laughed, stretching her legs to rest her feet on the seat opposite. "Then I am sorry to tell you that Mr. Egerton did not take it *quite* as well as the drawing room wall. He pressed his lips together, thus—" (she demonstrated in the moonlight from the window) "—and his eyebrow rose, thus, and then he crossed one knee over the other and made his offer to take Archie Wilson."

Which told Jane nothing at all.

Not that Mr. Egerton's opinion should matter more than anyone else's, she counseled herself. But she met so few new people that it was natural for each one to bear exaggerated significance, was it not?

What was *not* natural was that, even when she lay in bed and Sarah had bid her good-night and extinguished the candle, Jane continued to ponder and ponder…Did Mr. Egerton now think of her with disapproval, or did he not think of her at all?

The rectory of the Church of St. Mary the Virgin consisted of an ancient Norman structure enlarged by more recent Tudor accretions. The Terrys and their boarders lived in and principally used the Tudor rooms, as would the Egertons [-when the Terrys departed, but in the interim Mr. Egerton and his sister were given two drafty chambers connected by a narrow sitting room in the Norman portion, and it was to this sitting room, as near to the fire as the chairs could be dragged, that the siblings repaired at the end of the day.

"I confess myself amazed, Philip," said Cassandra, "that you would so rashly involve yourself in neighborhood affairs before you even understood the state of things or each person's position."

He did not pretend to misunderstand her, though he frowned at the glowing embers toward which his booted feet extended.

"You refer to the Archie Wilson controversy."

"Of course."

"You think I ought not to have interfered?"

"Mrs. Terry tells us the Deres are the first family in the parish, and though five minutes' acquaintance with them was enough to show that even the baron goes on bended knee to Mrs. Markham Dere, you immediately went and crossed her, Philip!"

His brow knitting, he watched her working for a minute (his sister's hands were never idle). "I provided a solution," he answered after a pause. "I *helped* her. Now she need not remove her son from Keele's."

"To be sure. You were cruel to be kind," Cassie returned. "You will please understand that when I reproach you, I am wearing my Ambition hat," she explained, "which is usually so snug about your own brow that there is no snatching it off. That's the real marvel, Philip: that you would risk angering the most powerful woman in the parish. It was uncharacteristic of you. You ordinarily always know on which side your bread is buttered."

Her brother shifted in his chair, returning his gaze to the dwindling fire. Something pricked at him. An awareness that Cassie had put her finger on something he was not yet prepared to examine, much less explain. But he only said, "I wonder if any other curate in the kingdom is accused of being such a Machiavelli as you paint me, doing nothing but as a result of calculation."

"Oh, Philip!" she cried, raising her head from her sewing to regard him fondly. "I should not have uttered a word, then, if you really did act from disinterested motives. Because, if you were not my brother, and if it would not have further annoyed Mrs. Dere, I would have leapt to my feet and shouted, *Hurrah*!"

"Heavens, what enthusiasm! Then why reproach me at all?"

"You see," she went on, "all the time Mrs. Dere was complaining and stirring the coals, I had been watching Mrs. Merritt. Really, I could hardly keep my eyes from her because she is so very lovely and yet seemed so...doleful—"

"Hmm. And now we know why," her brother rejoined. "If I had Mrs. Merritt's tale of horror and woe, I would be doleful in company as well, if I even ventured into it."

"Now there you are unkind, Philip! Mr. Terry caught me watching her, and he told me that Mrs. Merritt never *is* in company, if she can possibly help it. She rarely, rarely goes beyond the bounds of Iffley Cottage where the Barstows live, except to go to church. Though of course she must go to Perryfield when she is bid because the Barstows owe everything to Lord Dere. And here I thought you might have shared my pity for her and offered to take Archie Wilson as an act of chivalry."

"Chivalry!"

"Yes—poor Mrs. Merritt being so upset, I thought you might have wanted to relieve her embarrassment. I certainly did."

Egerton straightened in his armchair and began to tug off one of his boots. "My dear Cassie, your compassion is misplaced. It sounds like Mrs. Merritt made a foolish match which ended badly, as foolish matches are wont to do. And if she were never made to feel the consequences of her errors, she might be in danger of repeating them."

To his surprise, his sister straightened in her own chair and scowled at him. "I don't know about that, Philip. While I would agree she made a foolish match, I daresay a hundred equally foolish matches are made every day, with not one in one hundred ending as wretchedly as hers did. For that reason I don't think my compassion a bit misplaced." With a shake of her head, she resumed her sewing. "Why *did* you offer to take the boy, then, if it was neither to assert your independence from Mrs. Dere nor to draw attention away from Mrs. Merritt?"

"Why, I thought it an act of Christian charity," declared Egerton, startled. "Archie Wilson might bear the stigma of illegitimacy, but one cannot choose one's birth, nor should he be blamed for the sins of his father. The best society will ever be closed to him, but with a good education he can make the best of a bad bargain."

"Well, I like that!" Cassie exclaimed. "Archie Wilson is to be excused for his father's misdoings, but Mrs. Merritt must share in her husband's?"

"Of course she must. That is precisely what marriage entails, my dear firebrand. Which is why young ladies must choose as wisely as they are able, with the approval of their family. As she herself confessed, her father objected to Mr. Merritt, so it is not as if the man gave no early signs of unsteady character, signs which she refused to acknowledge. I hope you and my other sisters would never do the same."

"Since no one—respectable or otherwise—has ever shown interest in offering for any of us, you may rest easy on that point, brother," she retorted.

Several minutes of silence followed this remark, and Egerton thought she would leave the matter there. But when he rose, yawning, to excuse himself, his sister had yet one more word.

"Yes, good night, Philip. I will only observe in parting that, as the Lord 'sendeth rain on the just and on the unjust,' I pray that when you are priest to both the 'innocent' Archie Wilson and the 'guilty' Mrs. Merritt, you will show them more equal charity. I certainly intend to."

CHAPTER 3

Ye shall know the truth,
and the truth shall make you free.
—John 8:23, *The Authorized Version* (1611)

When Jane opened her eyes the following morning, something was changed. Not in the bedchamber, to be sure, for there were the familiar cracks in the ceiling plaster, and there was Sarah still asleep beside her, the door to Gordon and Bash's adjoining closet still shut. No, the change was mysteriously in *herself.*

"I stood up to Mrs. Dere," she whispered. "I met strangers and told my story, and—here I still am."

Gingerly she put back the coverlet and slid from the bed, reaching hurriedly for her shawl. It was chilly, but it was not to warm herself that she gave a hop, before gliding across the floorboards in her bare feet and spinning in a circle. What was this feeling? This bubbling up in her soul which threatened to emerge as—as singing!

It couldn't be—no, impossible.

Could it?

That is, could it possibly be...joy?

To think that joy was now so alien to her, so long forgotten that it bewildered her, that she could hardly recognize it when it took hold!

But—yes. This was the feeling she faintly remembered, one which accompanied sunlight sparkling on water; bluebells carpeting the woods in spring; Sebastian and Sarah's wedding day; dancing with her siblings in the Twyford parsonage with smiling parents looking on.

"I told my story, and here I am," Jane whispered again. A few minutes later she was dressed, floating along the passage and down the stairs. She could hear the servants in the kitchen, and she almost laughed to see their surprise when she appeared.

"Mrs. Merritt!" they exclaimed in unison, Irving nearly dropping the coal bucket and Reed poised mid-chop with knife in hand.

"Good morning to you. What a beautiful day it promises to be, though I feel the chill of autumn coming. A morning fire will be welcome, Irving. May I help with that, Reed? I was thinking—Mama and Sarah were speaking the other day of the Cramthorpes, that young Mrs. Cramthorpe was unwell. Might we make up a basket, for Sarah and me to take to them?"

"Mrs. Sarah and *you*, miss?" echoed Reed with unflattering astonishment.

"Yes," Jane returned, waiting to see if her courage would waver, but it held. "Yes. Sarah and I. Because Frances has never liked to go there, ever since she spilled the soup on that one occasion, and old Mrs. Cramthorpe called her 'a great clumsy ox.' Do you remember?"

"I remember," Reed answered dryly. "All my good mutton broth, poured through the cracks in the floor." Though it was not her place to question Mrs. Merritt's inexplicable turnabout—Mrs. Merritt, who could so rarely be got to creep past the front gate!—she intended to discuss this development with Irving at length and to ply the servants over at Perryfield for an explanation.

When the rest of the family rose soon afterward and learned of Jane's intention, they were equally amazed, though even Gordon had the good sense not to ask questions. He was more interested in the agreement reached with

Mrs. Dere, in any event, and drummed a triumphant tattoo on the table with fork and knife when he learned Peter would continue at Keele's. "So much for her! So much for her!" he chanted.

When he was duly reproved for this display and order restored, they turned again to look at Jane.

"I have sat idle long enough," she explained with an apologetic face. "You have all been very patient with me, very forbearing, but after yesterday I see that my…hiding has done no one any good. I have been thinking too much of myself and only myself. You will see I mean to be useful now."

"But are you certain about the Cramthorpes, to begin with?" Mrs. Barstow wondered. "You must not overdo matters."

"I will come with you and Sarah," Frances offered.

"But you don't like old Mrs. Cramthorpe," said Jane.

"I don't," her sister agreed, "but I will come all the same."

While Jane attributed Frances' willingness to curiosity, that did her an injustice. In truth, Frances intended to stand in the gap, lest frank old Mrs. Cramthorpe pop Jane's new courage like a bubble.

Iffley being a modest-sized village, the parish was not overwhelmed with struggling poor, but a few families lived in tumbledown cottages below the watermill, and the three young ladies directed their steps thitherward after breakfast.

The Cramthorpes consisted of the old grandmother, her daughter-in-law, and a pair of young children, boy and girl, who were running about outside when the Barstows arrived, and who did not appear to have bathed or combed their hair in some time. Seeing the basket Jane carried, the children followed them eagerly within, where their grandmother slumped in the rocking chair like a caved-in hillside and younger Mrs. Cramthorpe lay asleep. The air being so warm and close inside, Sarah left the door ajar.

"You again, is it, Miss Elbows and Feet?" barked old Mrs. Cramthorpe, squinting at Frances.

"It's Miss Barstow, yes," answered Frances with a roll of her eyes. "And Mrs. Sarah and my sister Mrs. Merritt."

"Who?"

"You remember me, don't you, Mrs. Cramthorpe?" asked Sarah as she smoothed the bed coverings.

"Of course I remember you!" snapped the old woman. She jabbed a finger toward Jane. "I meant that one."

"I am Mrs. Merritt," said Jane as steadily as she could. "Miss Barstow's next older sister."

"The one who jilted his lordship?"

Jane swallowed. "Er—no. That was my oldest sister Adela. She is married and living in Oxford now."

"Buns!" cried the boy, climbing on a stool to inspect the basket's contents. "Buns and apples!" shrieked his sister. Their clamor provided a welcome diversion, but Jane was aware of old Mrs. Cramthorpe's mouth working convulsively.

When Jane had poured soup into two of the Cramthorpes' chipped bowls, she chose to serve the old woman, only to be rewarded with a triumphant, "I know who you are! You're the eloper who went to prison. If you'd been a daughter of mine, I'd have horse-whipped you."

"Mrs. Cramthorpe!" screeched Frances, elbowing the boy aside to fling herself between Jane and her attacker. "Do try a bun with your broth!"

Sadly, Frances' valor conflicted with the suddenness of her movements. Her limbs tangling with Jane's, Reed's good broth was dashed once again to the floor, splashing the old lady's ankles and streaming across the flagstones.

"Stupid girl!" roared old Mrs. Cramthorpe, almost sitting up straight in her indignation and then bouncing several times in the rocking chair, eyes goggling. "See what you've done! *Again!*" This exercise soon exhausted her, thankfully, and she subsided once more into her customary crumple, but not without her fit penetrating her daughter-in-law's fevered slumber. With a moan, the younger woman rolled over, one arm flopping across the bed and knocking away the bowl Sarah held.

Another wave of mutton broth. Another splash and shriek. More puddles.

So it was this scene—old Mrs. Cramthorpe growling curses, Sarah pressing at the bedclothes to absorb excess broth, and Jane and Frances on their hands and knees swabbing the floor—which met the eyes of the next visitors to push the door open.

"Who's there?" demanded old Mrs. Cramthorpe, peering. "Jimmy, the door blew open. These blockheads didn't shut it all the way."

"It's Mrs. Terry, Mrs. Cramthorpe," the rector's wife replied, tiptoeing from the doorway to a dry spot where the floor tilted upward. "I've come to say farewell for now and to introduce you to Mr. Terry's new curate Mr. Egerton."

Not large to begin with, the Cramthorpes' hovel was positively packed with these additions, though Mr. Egerton lingered in the doorway, bending slightly to avoid cracking his crown on the lintel. Jane was mortified to be found on all fours, presenting her backside to the newcomers, but she had to rise slowly because slipping and going down in a slick of broth would overtop all.

"We've had a mutton-broth deluge," said Frances cheerfully, as if she were frequently found in such circumstances. Tossing aside the rag she held, it landed on the hearth with a sodden *splot*.

"More harm than help, these ones," grumbled Mrs. Cramthorpe. "I didn't even get a taste before it was everywhere but where it should be."

But Mrs. Terry briskly snatched up a somewhat clean rag and gave a few swipes of her own. "What a lovely thought, Barstows, Mrs. Merritt. You see, Mr. Egerton, what an active, benevolent parish you take on? You will not be alone in caring for your flock."

"I *do* see that," he said in his cool way, but his color was heightened. Reaching in his coat pocket, he withdrew a small notebook and pencil. "Have you been long resident in Iffley, Mrs. Cramthorpe?"

"What? What's that?"

"There's nothing wrong with your hearing, Mrs. Cramthorpe," chided Mrs. Terry gently.

The old woman collapsed further under this reproof, and she screwed up her mouth in a pout. "Don't see why you have to go away and leave us to strangers."

"Now, Mrs. Cramthorpe, you know Mr. Terry is unwell himself, and if I do not do something about it, he will not be able to take care of his flock. So be a dear and welcome Mr. Egerton. He's quite conscientious and methodical—"

"Medical? We don't want any of that here!"

"Me-tho-di-cal," enunciated the rector's wife. "I refer to his habit of making notes. I have been taking Mr. Egerton around Iffley this morning to make introductions, and he has been scribbling the whole time, so that he might jog his memory later. You know how my own Mr. Terry will sometimes take to wool-gathering, and when he does, he often forgets little details."

"Hmmph."

"Why, you once called him a 'chuckle-headed halfwit' when he confused you with Mrs. Barbary and asked after your carbuncles."

"I don't have carbuncles!" bellowed the old lady.

"Precisely," agreed Mrs. Terry. "So if you answer Mr. Egerton's questions now and let him record such things, you will prevent such offensive mistakes being made in the future."

While this interchange took place, the Barstow women had been cleaning up after themselves as well as they could, repacking the basket and seeing to the younger Mrs. Cramthorpe and the children, Jane taking advantage of Jimmy's resumed bun consumption to give his smudged face a good wipe and to draw a comb through his hair. Then, to leave the curate and Mrs. Terry more room in which to maneuver, they quietly excused themselves.

Mr. Egerton turned toward the door frame and contracted himself against it to let Frances and Sarah pass, but as Jane followed the toe of her boot clipped an uneven flagstone, causing her to bump the table with her hip. A tin cup clanged to the floor, and when both she and the curate bent to retrieve it, their foreheads met smartly.

"Clumsy as a hog in armor!" squawked old Mrs. Cramthorpe, laughing so hard she nearly tipped out of the rocking chair. Whether it was this jeer or the parson's hand person catching at her elbow, Jane reddened, and he released her the very next instant.

"I beg your pardon," she mumbled, keeping her bonnet brim low to hide her face. If she had been able to look at him, she would have seen that he was scarcely more composed, and he muttered the same reply to the top of her head.

"What did I tell you?" gurgled Mrs. Cramthorpe. "But nothing a good horsewhipping wouldn't fix!" And while this bizarre pronouncement might mean nothing to the newcomers, Jane could not escape fast enough.

No further mishap befell the new curate after the others' departure. That is, no one else knocked heads with him or otherwise made him an outlet for Mrs. Cramthorpe's surliness. He even entertained the children by making hand shadows on the wall while Mrs. Terry saw to the younger Mrs. Cramthorpe's comfort.

"The doctor Mr. Travers had better come and look at her again," said the rector's wife when they emerged some minutes later.

"Look at whom?"

"At young Mrs. Cramthorpe, of course! She is no longer feverish, but she is still lethargic." Mrs. Terry gave him a shrewd look. "Who else would I be referring to?"

"Er—you might have meant the older woman," said Egerton, though as soon as he spoke, he stiffened in surprise. Why—had he just told a lie? Because, in truth, he had been thinking of Mrs. Merritt.

Mrs. Terry lifted a skeptical brow, but she said only, "Sadly, Mr. Travers cannot cure what ails old Mrs. Cramthorpe."

They continued down Mill Lane, Mrs. Terry pointing out other cottages and describing the residents while he recorded the information in his notebook, but when they reached the end she paused, tapping her chin and regarding him. "Do you know, Mr. Egerton, you witnessed something of a miracle at the Cramthorpes'."

"Because the old lady smiled upon us at the end?" he asked. "If it could be called a smile."

"Oh, you may be certain it was," Mrs. Terry returned, almost grinning, "because you will notice she did not accompany it with an insult. Indeed, though you might not believe me, that was old Mrs. Cramthorpe when she is charmed. But no, Mr. Egerton, that was not the miracle I referred to. I meant, rather, the miracle of Mrs. Merritt being back in the world—Mrs. Merritt at the end of her seclusion."

These mentions of Mrs. Merritt's "back" and "end" evoked a memory of the woman's charming posterior as she scrubbed the Cramthorpes' floor, a memory he banished at once, horrified at the direction of his thoughts.

Schooling himself, he managed to reply blandly, "Your husband would agree, for he said much the same yesterday to my sister. Though is something still a miracle if it happens for a second time in as many days?"

"It is not a second time," Mrs. Terry said, "for I suppose she could not escape the Perryfield dinner, considering the Barstows' obligations to Lord Dere. And you must have seen she did not find it entirely pleasant."

"I could not say with any confidence that she found it pleasant at all."

"Exactly."

Who could blame her, with Mrs. Markham Dere picking at her family like that? Egerton thought. But after his conversation with Cassie, he knew better than to voice this. Another vision of Mrs. Merritt flashed across his mind: her leaping to her feet in challenge, hazel eyes sparking and hands clenched. Such fire! Cassie had called her "doleful," but she had not looked doleful then.

After a pause he said, "Is Mrs. Merritt so seldom from home?"

"Very seldom." They had gained the churchyard, but Mrs. Terry held up a hand to stay him before they entered. "One might even call it *never.* Knowing her history now you will understand her reserve."

He gave a slight shudder. "Without a doubt. I must confess, it surprises me that Mrs. Dere is not even more outspoken in her disapproval, considering."

"Well, it *has* been two years," Mrs. Terry said dryly. "Make no mistake—Mrs. Merritt's story was all the talk for a time. This is why I say you have witnessed a miracle. And perhaps Mrs. Dere's provocation had the accidental consequence of goading Mrs. Merritt out of retirement." Shaking her head and chuckling, the rector's wife resumed walking. "And poor dear thing! How does she spend her first day of self-proclaimed liberty? In visiting old Mrs. Cramthorpe and suffering the rough side of her tongue! (Not that Mrs. C's tongue has a smooth side, mind you.) Ah, Mr. Egerton," she sighed, "do take care of our little flock while we are away. We are quite, quite fond of them all."

"I will do my best."

"Yes, I am sure you will, being a conscientious young man. Or you will try. But do you remember in Sterne's *Sentimental Journey,* when Maria says, 'God tempers the wind to the shorn lamb'?"

"I'm afraid I haven't read it."

"You will nevertheless understand the notion, I hope. My Mr. Terry declares he doesn't know a single person who shears their lambs, and I tell him that is not the point. Lest you prove equally obtuse, Mr. Egerton, I will be plain. You are much younger than Mr. Terry and I, sir, and sometimes youth and inexperience might...neglect to temper the wind to the hypothetical shorn lamb. That is, sometimes youth and inexperience are wont to think, *Such circumstances would never befall* me, *a wiser person.* This belief is, however, a false one. And the only cure for such a mistake is, unfortunately, increased age and experience."

But seeing that his expression, though it contained much of polite attention, was devoid of conviction, the good woman gave it up. *He still believes flawlessness possible,* she thought. *At least as it applies to himself.* If her husband were beside her, he would say, "Time must do its work, Mrs. Terry, and you must stop seeking short cuts for it."

Shaking hands mentally with her spouse, Mrs. Terry patted the young curate on the arm. "Well, never mind me. Only say you will make a note of it, good sir, in your book?"

CHAPTER 4

Troylus is the better man of the two...
Oh Jupiter ther's no comparison.
—Shakespeare, *Troilus and Cressida,* I.ii.60 (1609)

Though Sarah and Frances feared such a first essay at re-entering the larger world would drive Jane back into hiding, they were delighted to be mistaken. It was true sudden blushes stained her cheeks as she sat with the family, and true as well that she did not seem inclined to talk much, but when a call at Perryfield was proposed the following day, Jane did not demur, and the day after, when Frances announced she would walk to the Tree Inn, Jane agreed to accompany her.

Secretly, her family rejoiced.

"Of course she must blush, Mama," Frances whispered to Mrs. Barstow when they chanced to find themselves alone. "If you had been there and seen us crashing about! And cross old Mrs. Cramthorpe at her most offensive—I only wish the broth had spilled on her, instead of the floor or the bed. And then for the new curate to find us all mucking and scouring like scullery maids! All that would have been bad enough, but then he and Jane had to strike their heads together as she left." Laughter convulsed her, and even Mrs. Barstow could not prevent a smile, but they soon hushed each other.

"It might have been for the best, Mama. In comparison to such a beginning, any future embarrassments will be mere nothings."

If her family could have seen into her mind—and thank heaven they could not—they might have been troubled anew, however. At least, Jane was. For it was not embarrassment alone which occupied her, nor embarrassment alone which caused her frequent changes in color. As the days passed she found she dwelt less and less on her bungling, and more and more on Mr. Egerton himself. Mr. Egerton as a person. As...a man. And if she had once compared him to her father's lackluster curate, she did so no longer.

No, now, Jane compared Mr. Egerton—to another.

She compared him to Roger.

And if a search had been made throughout the kingdom, it would have been difficult to find two men more unlike.

The Roger Merritt who danced into her life in Twyford had been liveliness itself, bursting with high spirits, always teasing, jesting, flirting. Though he had neither settled prospects nor professional ambitions, his optimism made light of these lacks and persuaded her to make light of them as well. In the dark period wherein the Barstows mourned the loss of father and brother, Roger Merritt streaked across Jane's sky like a comet, and she threw all aside to catch after him.

But a comet trails fire, and fire burns.

When they eloped it was three long days before they reached Scotland and could be married, three long, long days in which Jane's conscience overtook her. "What has become of my daring girl?" her betrothed demanded, impatient with her falling spirits. "I'll take no weakling milksop for a bride." Hardly the words to comfort her.

Nor did matters improve after they were wed, when Jane thought she might hold her head up again. For one thing, she discovered that a Roger Merritt experienced in small doses bore little resemblance to one on whom she must depend round the clock, and he, making this same discovery and resenting it, took to disappearing for hours at a time while she sat alone in strange, dirty inn rooms.

All might still have turned out right, had Roger's rich aunt, whose heir he was, approved the match.

But she did not.

Infuriated by his rashness, she struck him from her will and cut off his allowance, and only then did Jane understand in full her late father's misgivings. For if a Roger Merritt *with* expectations was playful and idle, a penniless one proved an entirely different species.

There turned out to be no core to him, in the end. Nothing to support the structure of his character when the foundation of his aunt's money was removed.

What had followed—well, Jane had dwelt on those memories so very long now that even skirting the painful ground caused her chest to tighten, and she would rub it absently with her fist.

So much for the late Roger Merritt.

Therefore, considering all she had gone through, was it any surprise she could now meet a Philip Egerton and be fascinated? Was it any surprise that, having known Roger Merritt's flaws too well, Mr. Egerton should then carry the day?

Surprising or not, this was the result. This was the cause of her blushes.

Though she had only met Mr. Egerton the two times, the contrast was already plain. Where Roger had been restless as the wind, Mr. Egerton held his vigor in check, like a racehorse waiting for the starter's shout. Where Roger joked and frolicked, Mr. Egerton was serious, almost grave. Indeed, time had not yet revealed whether the man had any humor at all! Where Roger left things to chance, trusting his luck to hold (even when it didn't), Mr. Egerton appeared to do nothing on impulse. And where

Roger's emotions found immediate expression, whether for good or evil, Mr. Egerton kept his passions in check.

If he has *any passions*, Jane thought. The reflection drew a rueful smile. Because she did not doubt that her heedless, younger self would have dismissed the new curate as a starched fellow. Possibly even a prig. Yes, the butterfly who had been Jane Barstow would have lumped Mr. Egerton with the forgettable Mr. Liddell and been hard put to distinguish one from the other. But the wiser and wounded Jane *Merritt*—alas—had no difficulty with it at all.

She foresaw no danger in her meditations; indeed, she told herself it was beneficial to have her faith in good men restored. Moreover, her musings changed nothing because she would never marry again. After the anguish she had inflicted on her family, yielding to further self-indulgence struck her as unforgiveable. And it would certainly be self-indulgent to dream of Mr. Egerton having anything to do with her. He and she may not have begun life as chalk and cheese, but experience had undoubtedly made them so.

It was with this resolution that Jane re-entered the world, submitting quietly to the call at Perryfield (where Mrs. Dere plumed herself on having prevailed in the Archie Wilson controversy) and accompanying Frances to the Tree Inn.

The first sight to greet the sisters was the unsettling one of an urchin hanging upside-down from a branch of the inn's great elm, grimacing and making rude noises. Jane jumped, but Frances threw herself in front of her older sister and held up a threatening finger.

"You come down from there at once, Harry Barbary, or I will fetch Mrs. Lamb."

The boy's lips and tongue produced another unmannerly sound in answer to this address, but he swung himself up out of Frances' reach nonetheless.

"What do you mean, idling in this naughty fashion?" Frances accused. "Does Mrs. Lamb have no work for you today?"

"What's that? What's that? Who wants me?" came the voice of the postmistress from the entrance to the inn. Before Harry Barbary could scramble higher, his employer hastened over with broom in hand and immediately set about with it, whacking and thwacking any part of the errand boy she could reach until he squealed and dropped down from the tree, crying, "I ain't done nothing!"

"That's right, you haven't," rejoined Mrs. Lamb with another swat to his hindquarters, "and us expecting a London gentleman! Where are the things I sent you out for?"

"Here! They're here!" howled the boy, scrambling around the trunk of the elm to fetch several parcels and slinging them at her feet.

"And where's my change, you rascal?"

He dug the coins from his pocket and deposited them in like manner before sprinting for the inn door to escape his mistress' attentions.

"Goodness," said Frances, her lips twitching.

Mrs. Lamb rolled her eyes. "Goodness has nothing to do with that boy! I hired him as a favor to Mrs. Terry because the Barbarys are in great straits, but I'll be blessed if I don't dismiss the creature the instant the Terrys are on their way. It's not my imagination the boy has light fingers, or where have some of my vittles gone? Not to mention the guests complaining of little things missing."

"I suppose the Barbarys are very poor," murmured Jane, "with Mr. Barbary having abandoned them."

Belatedly, the postmistress made note of what would ordinarily have commanded her attention, and her hold on her broom slackened. "Why, Mrs. Merritt! What brings you out on this fine day?"

"A walk," answered Jane, her chin lifting. She was pleased to hear the steadiness of her voice and ignored Frances' pressure on her arm. "Are you indeed expecting a London gentleman, Mrs. Lamb?"

"A real live one!" she declared. "And at any moment, as I expect the express coach from town has already arrived in Oxford."

"But who can this person be?" asked Frances. "We saw Mrs. Markham Dere only yesterday, and she made no mention of anyone important coming to Iffley."

She could not have said anything more calculated to delight Mrs. Lamb, for the woman prided herself on knowing more about Iffley's goings-on than any other residents. With a swelling of her bosom she said airily, "I expect she knows nothing of it, for I only learned of him myself when I received word to reserve a room and 'the largest available'! It's a Mr. Alexander Beck, Miss Barstow. Some rich town swell coming to deliver his...*charge.*" She whispered this last word with a sly lift of her eyebrows, as if it were something scandalous, but when her auditors only appeared perplexed, she added impatiently, "The new boy, of course. The one going to the rectory for Mr. Egerton to teach!"

"Archie Wilson?" breathed the sisters in unison, staring at each other. Had Mrs. Dere known Archie Wilson was somehow connected to a rich gentleman from London when she disdained him?

"That's the name," Mrs. Lamb nodded. "This Archie Wilson is the ward of a Mr. Alexander Beck, but time will tell if 'ward' means what you and I think it might mean." The postmistress here tapped the side of her nose and gave a knowing look.

"Well," said Jane, now applying pressure of her own to Frances' arm, "Mrs. Terry did mention this new pupil. You are indeed quite busy, Mrs. Lamb, if you expect such guests. Therefore Frances and I will be on our way and leave you to it."

Frances waited until they climbed over the stile into Iffley Meadows before saying, "Now why did you have to go and drag me away? We might have learned so many more interesting things about this Mr. Beck or about Archie Wilson."

"I dragged you away because I know too well what it is like to be talked about," replied Jane, "so the least I can do is avoid encouraging the woman."

Shrugging, Frances returned to the enthralling discovery. "Imagine if Archie Wilson's father should turn out to be rich!"

"Indeed," said Jane dryly. "I suspect being the natural son of a rich, important person is an irregularity more easily overlooked than being the natural son of nobody-knows-who."

"Mr. Alexander Beck," repeated Frances. "What a noble name. Well—if he kept his relation to Archie Wilson quiet before, he has let the cat out of the bag now. Telling Mrs. Lamb is as good as printing up a notice and handbills!"

"So it is," Jane agreed, plucking a stalk of saxifrage and twirling it between her fingertips. "In fact, if Mr. Beck does *not* turn out to be Archie Wilson's father, he will have a hard time convincing anyone of it now." She tossed the stem away with a muted sigh. "For instance, I suppose it will be all over Iffley by nightfall that I am disposed to be sociable again, for better or worse."

"How can it be for worse?" asked Frances sensibly. "Seeing you walking about Iffley poses no danger to anyone."

The sisters' ramble took along the marshy banks of the Thames, where they picked blades of grass and made efforts to whistle through them.

"I, for one, am heartily glad you are showing your face again," Frances told her when they tired of this and plumped down to watch the soothing flow of the river. "After Della married, it's been a great bore to go about mostly by myself. You know Mama is always busy with housekeeping and

Sarah with Bash, and Maria is too young, and Gordy is at school, even if he weren't a boy. And if I go over to Perryfield to practice on the pianoforte, Mrs. Dere is sure to join me at some point and treat me like her unpaid companion for an hour or two."

Grinning, Jane prodded Frances' leg with her boot toe. "Poor, poor Frances. Let me make up for lost time, then. What would you like to do that requires my public appearance? Visit the haberdasher? Bring soup daily to the Cramthorpes? Your wish is my command."

"We might walk all the way into Oxford together on occasion when the weather is dry," Frances suggested eagerly, sitting up to tuck her knees beneath her. "It's not above five miles there and back, and then we might visit the shops and the circulating library and even drop into Keele's to see Della. Mama would never let me go so far alone because of all the young men, you know. She says Della can only do it because she is a married woman."

"Very well," laughed Jane. "Oxford on occasion. Good heavens, who knew the pleasures I was depriving you of, all unawares? But come—will the Iffley haberdasher's be enough for today? We can see if Mr. Byrne has any pink calicoes. Perhaps two years ago scarlet would have been more appropriate for me, but I believe now my scandal has faded to pink. What do you say?"

"I say there isn't money for either but looking costs us nothing."

Though Byrne's was a modest establishment, its proprietor stuffed it as full as he could with cottons and woolens, velvets and silks, laces, ribbons, tapes, threads, gloves, and so forth, to the point that even the bow window was partially obstructed with wares.

Having not been inside a shop for so long, Jane gladly lingered with her sister, imagining which items they would choose and for what purpose, if money were no object, but at last Frances settled on a remnant of poppy-colored velvet with which to fashion a new caul to her bonnet.

"I will wait for you in the street while Mr. Byrne wraps it," murmured Jane, when another pair of ladies entered the confined premises. With a nod to them, she edged past and out.

And then several things happened in rapid succession.

The door of the neighboring grocer flew open, and Harry Barbary hurtled out, one hand to his cap as he looked back over his shoulder and the other clutched in a fist, while the grocer bellowed, "Stop that boy!"

Before Jane knew what she was about, she had thrown her arms wide to intercept him, though she could no more have stopped a runaway mail coach than Harry Barbary full tilt. He ran straight into her, his granite head striking her shoulder a powerful blow an instant before the rest of his person, so that she was spun into the street, straight into the path of an oncoming gig!

"Miss!" he bleated, the handful of currants he had filched raining to the pavement, but Jane was dizzily trying to regain her footing.

There was a shouted oath—the clatter of hooves and wheels on paving stone—whinnying—a scream she bemusedly recognized as Frances—and then the wind being knocked from her as something unseen struck her.

The next thing she knew, she was lying on hard pavement, bonnet askew, head whirling. Someone was scrambling...off of her? More racket, more voices. Angry questions. Frightened questions. Somebody whining, "I didn't do nothing!"

"Jane!"

She opened her eyes, and there was Frances' alarmed face hovering over her.

"Jane—oh, thank God! Are you hurt? What's that? Oh! You must be hurt because you're—bleeding!"

Frances' face was joined by the profile of Mr. Egerton—*Mr. Egerton?*

"You there, Harry Barbary," said Mr. Egerton's profile. "Go and fetch Mr. Travers. Yes, the doctor—and quickly." His profile flashed into full face. "Are you all right, Mrs. Merritt?"

"Of course she's not all right!" Frances keened. "She can't talk, and she's bleeding!"

"I can talk," said Jane thickly, her voice sounding very far away, even to herself. "And do stop shrieking, Frances."

"Jane!" her sister screamed in relief. She pressed her cheek to Jane's as she burst into tears, but blessedly this impulse was curtailed by the curate.

"Come, come, Miss Barstow," he soothed, "do not crush your sister further."

Frances obeyed, but then it was Jane's turn to gasp when she saw the vivid blood staining her younger sister. Her gloved fingers rising to touch her own temple, she discovered its source.

"I want to sit up," said Jane.

He held up a hand. "Mrs. Merritt, you might want to wait for Mr. Travers."

"No, I don't think that will be necessary." Tentatively she took stock: her head throbbed, yes, and she felt sore in several places, as if she had tumbled headfirst down the Perryfield staircase, but her bones were intact and her joints in working order.

"No," she repeated. "I believe I am not seriously injured."

"Then take this, please," he answered, fishing out his handkerchief. "Cuts to the head tend to bleed profusely."

She pressed the cloth to her forehead, giving Mr. Egerton her other hand, that he might assist her to stand. "But I don't understand how I cut my head," she murmured, "unless Harry Barbary is secretly a unicorn."

Had she been less dazed she would have marveled to see the twitch of his lips, but his reply was grave enough. "I'm afraid I am to blame, Mrs. Merritt. I threw you to the ground with some violence in my hurry, and you must have cut it on the pavement. But there was no time for gentleness, or else the gig would have made short work of you. It was being driven at rather a reckless speed for our little village streets."

"Who was that, anyway?" demanded Frances. "I blame the driver and that wretched Harry Barbary. I saw it all through the window, and it's true, Jane, you would have been crushed flat as a pancake if Mr. Egerton hadn't happened to be near."

A little crowd was gathering by this point, Frances and Mr. Egerton now joined by Mr. Byrne, the two other customers of the haberdashery, and the grocer, while Mr. Travers approached from one direction with his medical bag and Mrs. Lamb from the other, dragging Harry Barbary by the ear.

"Mrs. Merritt," cried the postmistress over the top of everyone, "The ostler tells me a lady was nearly struck in the road, and then I find Harry hiding under the bar!"

"I didn't do nothing!" wailed Harry.

"You stole some currants from me, you rascal," protested the grocer.

An argument erupted, upon which Mr. Travers said quietly to Jane, "Shall we step into Iffley Cottage, Mrs. Merritt? This is a very public place for an examination. Leave Mr. Egerton here to make the necessary explanations."

She did not need convincing, and tucking her arm under his, she allowed the doctor to lead her and Frances gingerly homeward.

CHAPTER 5

What doth she swound? make meanes for Her recoverie?
—Shakespeare, *Henry VI, Part 3,* V.v.44 (1595)

Y ou!" the two men exclaimed in unison.

The maid Polly paused in her retreat from the rectory parlor, glancing from the visitor to Mr. Egerton and back. The curate was reddening, though with what emotion Polly could not be certain, but he was such a contained young man that *any* strong feeling from him piqued her curiosity.

"You," repeated Mr. Egerton. Then, remembering himself, he gave a hasty bow. "That is, Mr. Beck. Er—may I present my sister Miss Egerton? And I am Philip Egerton, the new curate here at St. Mary's."

"Curate and...rescuer of the imperiled, if I am not mistaken," returned the visitor, making his own bow.

Cassandra Egerton thought this Mr. Beck might be the handsomest young man to whom she had ever been introduced, with his lustrous black hair and impossibly blue eyes. The simplicity and fine materials of his clothing must have cost a pretty penny, moreover, she judged with her experienced seamstress' eye, and then there was the large, gleaming emerald ring he wore. Good-looking young men generally ignored her, so she was caught off guard when this particular one smiled at her. "Did your brother tell you, Miss Egerton, of his derring-do this afternoon?"

Cassie glanced at Philip, only to be as surprised as Polly had been by his high color. "He did say there was a…mishap with a gig driver and—one of our parishioners."

"No, really!—Is she indeed one of your parishioners?" Beck said, one corner of his lips curling in a delighted grin.

"In embryo," admitted Egerton with reluctance. "The rector Mr. Terry goes Monday after I am read in."

"Today, Monday…It's all one." Beck waved away this hair-splitting. "Then you must be doubly glad you were on the spot, Mr. Egerton. It happened so quickly, Miss Egerton! One moment we were trit-trotting down a peaceful lane, and the next, a figure spins across our path! Your brother then shot like a cannonball into the road and bowled away both the young lady and himself."

"Did you truly, Philip?" gasped Cassie, not having heard the incident described so dramatically.

"I hope the young lady was not hurt," said Mr. Beck.

"Not seriously, I don't believe."

"If she is—or will soon be—a parishioner of yours, Mr. Egerton, I expect you know her name and where she may be found," the man persisted. "I would dearly like to call and offer my heartfelt apologies for causing her distress, at any rate."

"That is kind of you, sir," Cassie said, when her brother did not seem in a hurry to reply. "Her name is Mrs. Merritt, and she lives with her family at Iffley Cottage, not five minutes from here. Poor Mrs. Merritt—what a time she has had of it, these last few days! I will certainly call on her tomorrow." She thought Philip would second this suggestion at least—perhaps even insist on accompanying her—but instead his lips tightened.

Mr. Beck was all bland affability. "Will you, Miss Egerton? Perhaps I might plan to arrive shortly after you, then? I would not like to appear at this Iffley Cottage without someone to vouch for me."

She was spared a response by the return of the Terrys at this juncture, leaving the introductions to begin all over again. This was followed by another rehearsal of Mrs. Merritt's near accident, after which the conversation turned at last to what had brought Mr. Beck to Iffley in the first place: the details of Archie Wilson's placement. Such matters once resolved, the dashing guardian made his bows and was shown out again by the maid.

"My goodness what a handsome man!" marveled Mrs. Terry. "Does the room seem warm to you?" She fanned herself jokingly with her hand.

"He is indeed well-favored," Cassie could not help but agree. "And though he may nearly have run down Mrs. Merritt, if he calls at Iffley Cottage, at least now all the Barstow ladies may have a chance to see and admire him."

"Mr. Egerton, did he say before we entered whether Archie Wilson were indeed his natural son?"

"He did not mention it."

"Mrs. Terry," chided her husband.

"It's no use saying 'Mrs. Terry' to me. Now that I have seen the man, the real wonder is that he has not a dozen natural sons to provide for! I don't suppose Mrs. Dere would have objected so vehemently had she known what he looked like. Well! It's a good thing he will leave the boy and go away again, for imagine if such a specimen were to take up residence in Iffley! The gossip and the heart flutterings...I daresay even *I* might have fallen victim to his charms and left you to go to Italy alone, my dear Mr. Terry."

Though not a word they had spoken passed beyond the rectory walls, the village was not long left in the dark regarding Mr. Beck. Mrs. Lamb ensured that, by the following morning, all Iffley knew both of the man's arrival and Mrs. Merritt's near escape. Many families who ordinarily sent servants to the Tree Inn to fetch their post came in person, hoping for a glimpse of the visitor, only to be disappointed that Beck had not yet been seen and had ordered his breakfast sent up.

As a consolation, those with any claim to acquaintance then called at Iffley Cottage, which was how the Egertons required full five minutes to reach the front door from the gate, as they must be stopped and greeted and questioned and conversed with by parishioners just leaving.

By the time Reed announced their arrival, however, only one caller remained with the Barstows, the scholar Dr. Lane, and even he was going. "Again, I am glad to learn you escaped serious harm, Mrs. Merritt," he concluded, his wisp of a beard waving like an overlarge fringe of eyelashes, "and hope to see you on your feet again shortly."

"Thank you, Dr. Lane," she murmured. She had not risen when the Egertons entered and was seated with her back to the window, but Egerton could see she was neatly bandaged, her only other visible injury being a slight swelling and discoloration of the cheekbone beneath her cut. Even this bluish tinge might have been imagined, for her color rose, and before Egerton could wonder at the cause, Mrs. Barstow hurried forward, reaching to take his hand between her own.

"Mr. Egerton, how can I thank you enough for saving my child? Frances told me how quick you were to think and act, pushing her out of harm's way."

"Madam, I am glad I was there," he answered gravely.

"As are we!" cried Miss Barstow. "For it's one thing to be on the spot, and quite another to keep one's head. I was no use at all, I regret to say, screaming and panicking like that."

"It was an alarming situation," he replied soothingly. "Had I had more time to think, I probably would have screamed and panicked myself."

Miss Barstow was not the only one to smile at this unlikely picture, and her mother said, "Please, won't you and Miss Egerton sit a while?"

"You've had so many callers," Cassie demurred. "We would not want to weary Mrs. Merritt."

A twinge shot through Egerton, and he was startled to realize it was annoyance at Cassie. If Mrs. Merritt had already borne the inquisitive visits of half of Iffley, surely she could bear fifteen minutes of them. After all—leaving aside his rescue of her—was he not the family priest, or nearly so? Though he thought he betrayed no outward sign, Cassie guessed his displeasure all the same because she added *sotto voce*: "Beck."

Ah. That was right. If the Egertons tarried any length of time, they risked the threatened appearance of Alexander Beck at their heels. Still, what was the danger of five minutes, or ten?

"We had so many callers that we banished Gordy and Maria, and Sarah took Bash away, all so we would have enough chairs," Miss Barstow was saying. "But that doesn't mean *you* aren't welcome."

"Yes, please do stay," Mrs. Merritt added in turn, coloring in earnest as soon as she spoke. "I am not so feeble that sitting and listening to others converse will dispatch me."

"It's true," her younger sister seconded, adding artlessly, "Jane only minds if everyone stares at her and talks only of her. But it happens that, if you had been present to hear our other callers this morning, Mr. Egerton, you would have heard much of yourself."

"As a matter of fact, Philip was congratulated a dozen times for his valor between your cottage gate and the front door," laughed Miss Egerton, shaking her head at him when he frowned.

"And no wonder! Because the tale grows in the telling," rejoined Miss Barstow, "as does every tale to which Mrs. Lamb contributes, I'm afraid. You are now a full-fledged hero in Iffley, Mr. Egerton."

"My, my," he answered lightly. "Not bad, for a moment's work."

"And I fear Harry Barbary has been painted as the villain," said Mrs. Merritt. Egerton was glad for an excuse to look her way again and to see she was smiling. But when Miss Barstow spoke again, he must turn away once more.

"Harry Barbary *is* the villain, Jane," said Miss Barstow. "If he had not been stealing from the grocer Mr. Linn, Mr. Linn would not have shouted for you to stop him. It is not like you go around every day trying to catch Harry Barbary. And if you had not tried to stop the boy, he would not have run into you and knocked you into the street."

But Mrs. Merritt turned her soft gaze on the curate. "We hear that Mrs. Lamb has dismissed him."

Egerton thought this reasonable enough—Mrs. Lamb could hardly employ petty thieves who might steal from her guests—but the faint pleading in her voice spurred him to say, "I am aware of the Barbarys' struggles and will call upon them, to see what may be done." As proof of his earnest, he withdrew his little notebook and jotted a sentence in it, receiving the reward of a heartfelt, "Thank you!"

But this was to be his only recompense, for here the parlor door opened and the maid cried, "Mr. Alexander Beck!"

The Egertons glanced at each other in sympathetic vexation. Whether by chance or some sixth sense, the man had managed to time his call perfectly to take advantage of their presence!

As for the Barstows, they were scarcely more easy. A day earlier, they would have been amazed to receive a call from a person so wholly unacquainted with them. They knew of the man's expected arrival in Iffley to deliver Archie Wilson, of course, but that could have nothing to do with them. This morning's callers, however, had not left them long in ignorance, falling over each other to announce Mr. Beck's part in Jane's accident, so that his appearance now was not a complete surprise.

"Beck alone again?" Egerton muttered to his sister. "I begin to doubt Archie Wilson's existence." Though he imagined Mrs. Lamb would be glad to supervise the boy, if only to pump him for useful information. *All the better, I suppose. For whatever the woman learns, she will share with anyone who will listen.*

In swept the mysterious Mr. Beck, as smartly dressed and handsome as the day before, and the eyes of the Barstow women widened collectively. On this occasion, however, his countenance was deferential, even solemn. After straightening from his bow, he unerringly sought out Mrs. Barstow to say, "Forgive me for my unbidden call, madam, but my sense of right overpowered the ordinary courtesies."

"Sir," said Mrs. Barstow in her soft voice. (Her daughters guessed correctly that she was wishing Adela were present, for Della always took charge in unpredictable situations.)

Taking a deep breath, Cassandra Egerton did what could not then be avoided, though she felt a stir of resentment. "Mrs. Barstow, if you will allow me to present Mr. Alexander Beck," Cassie began. "Philip and I and the Terrys made his acquaintance yesterday. He is the guardian of little Archie Wilson, of whose advent you have heard. Mr. Beck, may I introduce Mrs. Barstow and two of her daughters, Mrs. Merritt and Miss Barstow."

"Mrs. Barstow," he addressed the matron once more, his gaze not straying beyond the edges of acknowledgement of her daughters, "I come to apologize. I expect you know the role I played, all unintentionally, as the gig driver in yesterday's incident with Mrs. Merritt."

"I do, sir," she replied. "And having heard from all witnesses that no fault whatsoever lay with you, I assure you no apology is necessary."

"Still, it eases my heart to make it," he insisted.

Again he was assured of pardon and asked to be seated, and only then did he allow his eyes to roam daughter-ward. Miss Barstow he examined the precise amount of time allowed by propriety, but Mrs. Merritt's interesting condition warranted a more lingering inspection, one which took in the court-plaster covering her right temple and the surrounding bruising. Given her injuries, her dark hair was merely tied back with a ribbon and then wound in a loose chignon low on her nape—unfashionable, to be sure, but it hinted at her being caught in *déshabillé,* and Beck scrutinized her long enough to make her shrink back.

"Mrs. Merritt," he began, having claimed the open chair beside her, "while I am glad to have your mother's pardon, I would wish to ask yours as well. Believe me when I say I would not have chosen yesterday's circumstances as a way of meeting any person."

Apart from an indeterminate sound in her throat, she made no reply, but she bent her head in acknowledgement, hoping it would suffice and praying Frances would not repeat her comment about Jane not liking attention.

"Does your head pain you very much?" he asked, and Jane fidgeted, disliking the intimacy implied by how quietly he spoke.

To counter this she answered with unusual loudness, "Just a dull ache—hardly worth mentioning. I beg you to think no more about it, sir. I do not hold you in any way responsible, and I would not like it to cloud your—ward's—arrival in Iffley. I hope we will meet him soon."

Her change of subject was too decided for Mr. Beck to ignore, so he graciously left off his murmuring to say, "Yes. I would be delighted to introduce you all to him, but today he is with the inn maid, sorting his belongings before I take him into Oxford. It has been some time since I passed through here, and there are plenty of acquaintances and sights to see again."

"Will...Archie go to the rectory soon?" Jane asked.

Mr. Beck clicked his tongue regretfully. "Much too soon, I am now inclined to think."

"We agreed he would be transferred on Monday," spoke up Egerton to the room at large, "after I am read in and the Terrys have gone."

While everyone would have liked to ask more about Archie Wilson, Mr. Beck's possible paternity seemed to place an embargo on further questions, though Frances ventured, "And then you will return to town, sir?"

"It...had been my intention."

Egerton threw him a sharp look.

"And still is, for the immediate future," resumed Beck. He dismissed this vagueness with an equally vague wave of his fingers. "It has been so very long since I was in the country to do anything beyond a little shooting. How *is* the shooting hereabouts?"

The Egertons being so new they could not answer, even if Philip had been a hunting parson, and what the Barstows knew of shooting could be measured in a teaspoon.

"I'm afraid we don't know," Mrs. Barstow said. "Perhaps, if he were here, Lord Dere of Perryfield—my cousin—might be more helpful, though I do not believe he shoots much anymore."

"All the better, Mrs. Barstow," replied Beck. "For then he likely has more birds than he knows what to do with." His gaze swept the company before landing once more on Jane. "What would you say the chief amusements of Iffley are, then? Assemblies? Card parties? Musical evenings?"

Jane blushed, remembering how she had spent her only years in Iffley doing absolutely nothing which would interest a world-wise man like Mr. Beck, and Frances must have thought the same because she leapt in to say, "Not many assemblies—in fact, none. But there have been a few of the other things."

"We are very quiet here, I suppose," Jane now gathered herself to add. "But I know my sister and her husband in Oxford attend some lectures."

Mr. Beck made a playful face of horror, at which even Jane smiled.

"Lectures? Good heavens. That will never do. Are all the beauty and high spirits of Iffley's young people to molder away in obscurity? What a waste." But before he could say more, steps and voices were heard in the passage, and the remaining Barstows spilled in, the children boisterous and smelling of sunshine and fresh air. Another round of introductions followed, after which the visitors consulted the mantel clock and reluctantly took their leave, adjuring Jane not to rise.

"If we do not see you in church tomorrow, we wish you a pleasant journey back to town," Mrs. Barstow told Beck politely as he bowed to her.

"Thank you, madam. I'm afraid you will not see Archie or me tomorrow—prior engagements in Oxford. But I am grateful once again, for your good wishes and your kindness about the events of yesterday."

To Jane's amazement, both her mother and Frances actually colored and fluttered a little as Beck made his farewells. Steeling herself for she knew not what, she was both relieved and piqued when he left without another look at her. Goodness! Not that it mattered. She would never see him again, most likely.

Turning back, she found the Egertons beside her, Mr. Egerton's clear, clear gaze slicing through her as if she were a transparent jelly.

Miss Egerton said, "Tomorrow and Monday will be very busy, but I will come again, if I may."

"Yes, please," replied Jane, flustered. "But I am not so infirm as all that." To the curate she ought to say *something*, she knew—if only he did not look at her as if he knew Mr. Beck's unsettling effect! "I—I thank you again, Mr. Egerton, for your—assistance."

To this he merely inclined his head, but there was nothing cold in the movement, and she was encouraged to add shyly, "And won't you please let me know if you learn anything of Harry Barbary, sir, when you have the opportunity?"

"Gladly."

Another nod, and then he was gone.

CHAPTER 6

She made her public Re-entry upon this
Stage of human Levities.
—John Kidgell, *The Card* (1755)

Considering her shock and injuries, no one in Iffley would have been surprised by Mrs. Merritt forgoing church that Sunday, but Jane contrarily wanted all the more to go. Not only to hear Mr. Egerton read himself in, but also to say farewell to the Terrys and perhaps catch a glimpse of little Archie Wilson. Moreover, the gig incident had had the unexpected consequence of exposing her to nearly everyone in Iffley at once.

"I daresay I spoke with them all yesterday, and they all saw my bandage and bruises," she mused, frowning at her discolored face in the glass. "Though today, in addition to black and blue, I begin to see some green."

"Just wear my gauze veil over your bonnet, and you may hide in plain sight," Sarah answered, sliding open a drawer at the bottom of the wardrobe.

"Let us hope no other members of the Egerton family will attend," said Jane. "They would be the only strangers present."

There were *not* dozens of Egertons to be faced, in the event—only an older gentleman and two younger ladies who filed into the pew behind Mrs. Terry and Miss Egerton (thus obligating Dr. Lane and family to move back one pew, which forced the Bellews to move back one pew, and so on). As the Barstows always sat in the first two righthand pews with the Deres, Jane found herself directly across from the strangers, and she blessed Sarah's veil for the anonymity it provided. Though the filmy gauze blurred her surroundings, it must do the same for her own features.

The veil stirred as Mr. Egerton swept up the aisle, austere and handsome in his robe and snowy surplice, but once he reached the pulpit she must be satisfied with listening, rather than looking. But listening was indeed a pleasure.

Mr. Egerton read himself in with no hitches. He had a warm, even delivery, as clear as Mr. Terry's if not more so, considering the rector's recent illness and coughing fits. When the curate finished with the Thirty-Nine Articles and his Declaration of Assent, he gave way to Mr. Terry, and Jane's attention strayed. Beneath the cobweb of silk draped over her bonnet, she need not turn her head to let her eyes roam, and she turned them on the strangers.

Conveniently, they must swivel in her direction to see the pulpit, but the nearest young lady went further, draping her forearm across the edge of the pew and resting her chin upon it. She was a pretty creature, clothed in blue wool and yellow kid gloves, with hair the color of new-minted guineas, a rosy mouth, straight nose, and long lashes casting shadows on her rounded cheeks.

The beauty gave a silent sigh and leaned out a tick, craning her neck to peer around the pew before her. A moment onward, she sat up a little straighter, her lips curling into a smile. Her gloved fingertips gave the merest flutter. Fascinated, Jane's eyes traced the direction of her gaze and was not surprised to see it fixed on Mr. Egerton, seated upon the chancel. And that he saw the wave Jane did not doubt, for he himself shifted on his bench and turned his head once more toward Mr. Terry. His exact expression

Jane could not determine through her veil, but the change in posture was enough to tell her the greeting had not been without effect.

Who was she? A sister? A cousin?

A sweetheart?

She had not long to wonder, for when the service ended, the congregation spilled into the churchyard to take leave of the Terrys and to be introduced to the strangers. Such was the hubbub that Jane was free to observe, silent and ignored.

"My uncle Geoffrey Cottrell, my cousin Miss Cottrell, and my uncle's ward Miss Hynde," Mr. Egerton announced, indicating each. Father and daughter Mr. and Miss Cottrell were as alike as two peas, if one pea were male and some thirty years older. Both were tall and angular; both had unruly brown hair (Mr. Cottrell's silvered with grey) and stern features; both regarded Philip Egerton with complacent approval. The new curate then drew chuckles when he attempted to make known all his new acquaintances in turn, the rector or Mrs. Terry prompting him if he forgot a name. The Iffley Cottage family he managed without difficulty, but was it Jane's imagination, or was she the only one he neglected to look at directly?

It is the veil. He knows I wear it because I do not wish to be singled out.

At least, Jane hoped that was the case. Because the alternative was that he did not care enough to look her way. Or, worse, he was not eager for her to know his family.

"If I might have everyone's attention," announced the rector's wife with a clap of her hands, "though I have said my good-byes to each of you over the course of the week, Mr. Terry and I hope you might linger a few minutes for tea and biscuits on the rectory lawn. The Tommies have even organized some games for the children. How fortunate the weather is so fine."

In a short space, Jane found the protective hedge of her family neatly stripped away. The children ran off at once (followed by Sarah in pursuit of Bash); Mrs. Barstow was carried off by Mrs. Terry to advise her on the laying out of the food; and even the reliable Frances was appropriated by Mrs. Markham Dere to second her in some musical opinions.

Jane stood alone.

Consciously she edged closer to one of the tables the maids set out and affected to smooth the cloth covering it, but then she must back away for the trays of French biscuits and Shrewsbury cakes to be laid. Nor did she want to hover there, as if eager to snatch up all the refreshments.

She was about to attach herself to Lord Dere's side as he spoke with some of the Oxford set, when a gentle "Good morning to you, Mrs. Merritt," sounded at her elbow.

Whirling, Jane discovered Miss Egerton beside her. Though the two had not exchanged more than twenty sentences in their brief acquaintance, the sight of the young lady's pleasant, candid face buoyed her. "Good morning, Miss Egerton. I congratulate your brother on his reading in. You must be proud of him."

"Thank you. I suppose I am proud of Philip, but in truth I am more pleased with myself," she laughed. "You see, Philip gaining this curacy is no great surprise—he has had every step of his career planned since he was twelve years old. Whereas to find myself here in Iffley, nearly independent and in charge of a household, all without first being required to marry—that is the true wonder! It may only be for a few months, but I intend to make the most of them."

Miss Egerton's frankness diverted her, so that Jane smiled behind her veil. "I do congratulate you, then. Do you think you will like having the care of three young pupils in the house, in addition to your brother?"

"With four younger siblings, minding younger children is nothing new to me, Mrs. Merritt," she answered, "and the Tommies seem tractable enough. We will see about this Archie Wilson, of course, when we finally meet him tomorrow. But short of him being a second Harry Barbary, I am inclined to think I will be very, very happy in Iffley and that the months will fly by."

"I am glad of it," Jane said. "And you never know. Although the Terrys will return in the spring, perhaps your brother will find another curacy afterward, and you may keep house for him there as well."

"True. Though I believe the likelier next rung on my brother's ladder will be a living of his own. St. Lawrence Church, in particular, as promised to him by my uncle Mr. Cottrell there. And when Philip gets that, then—poof!" She snapped her fingers. "Like Cinderella's coach and footmen on the stroke of midnight, the spell of my freedom will be broken, and I will return to my parents' house."

"But why?" asked Jane. "Might you not continue with Mr. Egerton, even when he gets St. Lawrence Church?"

Miss Egerton shook her head with a rueful smile. "I'm afraid not. For the instant Philip secures sufficient income, he will marry Miss Hynde."

"Miss Hynde!" Jane's gaze flew across the churchyard to where that young lady stood beside Mr. and Miss Cottrell—and Mr. Egerton.

"Oh, mercy—I shouldn't have said that!" cried Miss Egerton, her fingers flying to her lips. "I blame your quietness and reserve, Mrs. Merritt—they lull one into making confessions. No—that is my second error, for it is not fair to lay my indiscretion at your door. But truly I should not have said that, and I beg you not to repeat it."

"I—will say nothing of it," promised Jane.

"Philip would kill me! Why, *she* doesn't even know of his intentions because my brother says 'there's many a slip,' and so forth. But one only has to know Philip a short time before one realizes he always gets what he wants, sooner or later."

Jane felt a cloud of lowness descend upon her, though why she should be surprised or disappointed by the news she could not explain. Only see how dear and sweet and pretty young Miss Hynde was! Of course Mr. Egerton would notice her. Fall in love with her. Set down in his little notebook: "Item: one wife, the purest and loveliest to be had." Nor did Jane believe for a moment that Miss Hynde knew nothing of his intentions—not with the little wordless greeting she had given him in church. No. There might generally be many a slip 'twixt cup and lip, but this cup and this lip appeared a safe bet.

Nevertheless she rallied enough to say more firmly, "Not a word of it will pass my lips, Miss Egerton. I—do know, after all, how unpleasant it is to have private matters made public."

This reference to her own woes reassured Miss Egerton immensely, and she gave Jane a sympathetic smile. "Thank you."

With another effort Jane succeeded in sounding almost playful. "In any event, Miss Egerton—one day you might still have your own household, if you yourself were to marry."

"It's kind of you to say so, Mrs. Merritt. I don't know why it is, however, that there always seem to be a great many more young ladies who would like to be married than there are gentlemen to marry them."

Amen to that, Jane added inwardly. *Especially if one sets aside the unsuitable gentlemen whom young ladies would do better not to marry.*

Although such thoughts usually led straight to Roger Merritt, on this occasion they followed a different path. How lovely it would be, to be an unsullied innocent again, as Miss Hynde was! To have all the world before one, but to be safeguarded from errors such as Jane had fallen into by the love of a good man.

These meditations caused pangs of a different sort, and Jane fell silent as they watched the children darting among the headstones in the churchyard. Miss Egerton proved an easy companion, however, sharing a few amusing anecdotes about some of them which Mrs. Terry had told her.

"I like the Tommies already," she said. "Young boys are always lively, and I suspect they will test us when the Terrys have gone, but they get along with each other, and I think they can be managed. The only question will be how the mysterious Archie Wilson will fit in. Though he can't be that bad, can he? Or we would have heard about it already from Mrs. Lamb. She has had him at the Tree Inn for two days now, after all."

"Mr. Beck did say they would be in Oxford for much of that time," Jane reminded her.

"Of course, but she has let us down nonetheless. She was so prompt to report your accident far and wide, but of Archie Wilson not a whisper!"

"Perhaps because I am a scandalous creature," suggested Jane with the shadow of a smile.

"And a bastard boy is not?" Miss Egerton countered, the humorous lift of her eyebrows taking the sting from her words. "And considering how handsome Archie Wilson's 'guardian' is, Mrs. Lamb has been inexplicably close-lipped about him as well. No, no, all her talk has been of you nearly being killed and of the iniquities of Harry Barbary."

"Miss Egerton," Jane said, "I have been thinking about Harry Barbary."

"Thinking of revenge?"

"Not at all," Jane laughed. "Thinking of what might be done for him. I know there is no parish school, but do you suppose he might be taught to read?"

"Gracious! Do you mean to foist him on my brother as well?" marveled Miss Egerton.

"Oh, no!" cried Jane. "Please do not suspect me of it. He has already agreed to Archie Wilson, and I would not dream of asking him to add Harry Barbary to his schoolroom. I only meant that—what if I were to try teaching him? Sarah and Frances and I already give lessons to Maria and Bash, so I have a little practice with a primer."

"Why, Mrs. Merritt, what a splendid idea!" Miss Egerton agreed, her face lighting with eagerness. "What if we were to do it together? We might gather Harry Barbary and little Jimmy and Anna Cramthorpe and teach the three of them. There is a perfect room in the older part of the rectory which nobody has used in an age—we would be in nobody's way there…"

The two young ladies, almost vibrating in their enthusiasm, had taken hold of each other's hands by this point.

"We must get Philip's permission, of course, and the Cramthorpes' and the Barbarys'," Miss Egerton continued, "but I cannot imagine anyone would oppose the plan."

"Do you think we might start with an hour or two, twice a week?" asked Jane.

"That would be good, and then we might increase it or decrease it, as we judge best. Let me talk it over with my brother. I doubt we will begin this week because I will not want to bother Philip until everything has settled—"

"Absolutely. That is very sensible—"

"Let me call on you in a few days, when he and I have talked—"

"Yes! Oh, yes. That would be delightful. Whenever it is convenient for you."

To have her proposal meet with such overwhelming approval filled Jane with a pleasure she had not experienced for quite some time, a pleasure augmented by the thought that she had made a friend. After her unhappy marriage and long isolation, it was like the sun sailing out from behind thick clouds to bathe her in warmth.

Her elation lasted a full thirty seconds before they were interrupted by the unexpected sight of Miss Hynde scurrying over to them. Dropping a hasty curtsey to Jane, the girl shook her own happy gloved fists and snatched at Miss Egerton's hands just as Jane released them.

"Miss Egerton! Oh, Miss Egerton! You will never guess, so I must tell you. I have asked Mr. Cottrell and Mr. Egerton if I might come for a visit! Martha said it would be making a nuisance of myself because you and Mr. Egerton were seeking to get established, but Mr. Egerton said it would be no nuisance at all, if *you* did not think it would be. So tell me, Miss Egerton, would it? Would it be all right with you? Please? Please please please may I come?"

Philip Egerton's exact words had been, "You would likely find it dull, Miss Hynde. I fear there is little in the way of amusement in Iffley, and I will be much occupied with my parish and teaching duties and Cassie with keeping house."

But Miss Hynde turned pleading blue eyes upon him, urging in a melting voice, "Oh, Mr. Egerton, I promise I would be no trouble at all, and you cannot think what diversion any sort of travel provides a person like me. I, who since the loss of my father have hardly stirred from Cottrell Hall! Everything I have seen of Iffley thus far convinces me of its delights."

As this "everything," to his knowledge, comprised only the Tree Inn and the church, Egerton could not prevent a skeptical smile, but it was his older cousin Martha Cottrell who said in a quelling tone, "What nonsense, Felicity. You've no more manners than a kitten, inviting yourself where you've not been asked and where, I daresay, you would only be in the way. Philip and Cassandra have work to be done and no time for frivolities."

Miss Hynde's face fell, and later Egerton would tell himself it must have been Martha's harshness which overcame his reluctance. Five minutes in Martha Cottrell's company would have even a saint begging for a holiday—how much more one as sweet and playful as Miss Hynde? Therefore he heard himself say, "I suppose, Miss Hynde, if my uncle and Cassie could be persuaded, I would have no further objections..."

The matter was soon settled, Geoffrey Cottrell making the calculation that his daughter's complaints would be easier to ignore (through long practice) than his ward's pouting, and Miss Egerton giving way because she thought her brother wished her to. In her case there was a sigh of vexation to be smothered, for wasn't that just like a man? To invite his potential sweetheart to stay, even though the greater share of entertaining her would fall upon Cassie? Philip might be in love with Miss Hynde, but Philip had work to do, leaving Miss Hynde forever on Cassie's hands.

In this Miss Egerton did her brother an injustice, for when Miss Hynde first made her request, unexpected reluctance made him answer as he did. He ought to have leapt at her suggestion—would it not be a delicious foretaste of future delights, when the two of them would begin married life?

And yet—

And yet he thought he would prefer to establish himself in his new role without such distractions. Miss Hynde's presence would be setting the cart before the horse. It would be premature. After all, he could not be expected to court her when it was not yet time for courtship, but nor could he ignore her, lest she resent his inattention and take a dislike to him. He would have to tread carefully, feeling his way, as if he had not already so much to occupy him!

This, at least, was what Philip Egerton told himself, and he believed it. It did not occur to him that his new parishioner Mrs. Merritt had anything to do with his reluctance. Because Mrs. Merritt had nothing to do with anything, really. He had, of course, looked at her more than once from the pulpit, but she was now a member of his flock, and he had looked at each of them, he was fairly certain. Or perhaps his eyes had been drawn by the veil she wore. What earthly reason was there for it, here, where everyone knew her and had spoken with her only the day before? It only made her conspicuous, and should she not be thinking of things beyond herself in church?

CHAPTER 7

**But I could acquaint you with a stranger piece
of news than any you have heard yet.
—Fanny Burney, *Cecelia* (1782)**

If Mrs. Lamb had failed to do her job properly in the previous two days, she compensated with an announcement so astounding that the village rang with it.

"Yes, it's true," the woman declared to the latest group of curious neighbors, a group which included Jane and Frances. "Greenwood Hall has been let, to none other than Mr. Alexander Beck, who stayed here recently. He has closed with the agent and will take possession on Friday, the first of October."

"What does one man need with such a house, if the child will be at the rectory?" asked one. "Greenwood Hall is second only to Perryfield in size."

"Maybe the child will not board with the Egertons after all," said another.

"Mr. Beck said nothing of removing the boy from the rectory," said Mrs. Lamb decisively. "Maybe he means to have London people down."

"Where will he find enough servants?"

"Maybe he will bring down his London servants as well."

More murmurs rippled through the gathering, though whether at the idea of additional London visitors or the possibility of their own servants being poached was unclear. And though Mrs. Lamb was generous with details of Beck's looks, amiability as an inn guest, what food and drink he requested or praised during his stay, and what the maid thought of his neatness or wardrobe, it was soon obvious to Jane and Frances that there was nothing more substantial to learn, and they resumed their walk.

"Do you suppose Mrs. Markham Dere and the baron have heard yet?" asked Frances as they skirted the upper field.

"Surely. Wood would have told them when he brought the post. Mrs. Dere wouldn't deign to seek further crumbs of information from Mrs. Lamb, but she is likely eaten up with curiosity."

"Let's call at Perryfield, then," Frances suggested. "And then walk home along Wallingford Way, so we may pass Greenwood Hall."

However little Jane wanted to see Mrs. Dere, such a loop would take them past the rectory on the return leg, and she agreed to the plan. Moreover, she had the gratification of seeing she had guessed Mrs. Dere's curiosity correctly, for even before they reached the Perryfield gate they spied her through the gap in the wall, pacing the front lawn.

"Good morning, madam," called Frances with a wave. "We have just come from the Tree Inn, and you cannot imagine the news we bring."

This was just the right note to strike, for then Mrs. Dere could pretend indifference and ignorance. "Indeed? Good morning to you, Frances, Mrs. Merritt. Why don't you take a turn about the grounds with me and tell me about it?"

"It will be told before we are even to the first corner," said Frances, positioning herself between her sister and Mrs. Dere, where she knew both of them would prefer her. "Everyone thought Mr. Beck would return to town after having disposed of young Archie Wilson, but now Mrs. Lamb says he has taken a lease on Greenwood Hall, to take possession on the first of October!"

"Goodness!" said Mrs. Dere with convincing incredulity. "Whatever for?"

"No one can say. He did call at Iffley Cottage briefly, the day after he nearly ran Jane down, and he asked about the shooting in Iffley, so perhaps he comes to shoot."

"He called at the cottage?" This time the surprise was genuine, and Jane detected a note of indignation that Perryfield's preeminence had been overlooked.

"I don't suppose he would have, if not for the accident," Jane spoke up. "After all, we none of us were acquainted with the other."

"When the baron and I came we did not see Mr. Beck," she said, affronted, as if the Barstows might have hidden the man behind the sofa.

"He came later—perhaps an hour afterward," explained Jane. "And apparently he had already met the Egertons, because, as they were present when he arrived, Miss Egerton made the introductions."

"In any event," resumed Frances, applying her usual salve to Mrs. Dere's wounded pride, "I know you disapproved of Archie Wilson, madam—whom we still have not seen, as Mr. Beck did not bring him along—but I daresay if Mr. Beck intends to live at Greenwood Hall, he will certainly hope to know you and the baron. The question is, will *you* wish to know him? I must say, he was a well-dressed, handsome man and seemed courteous enough."

"Hmm."

But the girls could see her mind working. A well-dressed, handsome man who could afford both a house in town and one in Oxfordshire was naturally allowed greater scope for "irregularity" than a shabby, plain, poor one. In fairness to Mrs. Markham Dere, her improved consideration of Mr. Beck was hardly singular.

"We will know him," Mrs. Dere pronounced at last, with a lift of her chin. "It would be unneighborly to do otherwise, and truly, my greater fear was the influence that Archie Wilson's company might have on Peter. There will be no danger to Peter from the adults having social intercourse with the—guardian."

"Very reasonable," Frances concurred, and Jane suspected only a sister would have caught the infinitesimal quiver of amusement in her reply.

"In fact, I suppose as the first family in the district, it behooves the baron and me to host a welcome dinner," Mrs. Dere sighed. "I may count on you to play for us, Frances?"

"Yes, madam."

"I suppose cards might also be fitting."

"He will likely welcome whatever you propose."

More questions followed, similar to those posed to Mrs. Lamb, and though the sisters could not answer them any better than the postmistress had, when they took their leave Mrs. Dere was quite cheerfully planning her reception of the man she had so recently disdained to know.

From Perryfield the walk to Greenwood Hall was an easy one, the road dry but not too dirty, apart from a few passing carts flinging up dust. No wall enclosed the three-storey 17th-century brick-and-stone home, but it sat in a modest park beside a pond, solid, symmetrical, and just visible from the road. It had ever been quiet and deserted the other times they walked by, but this time it was a positive hive of activity. The front door stood open, and the very carts which had passed Frances and Jane were drawn up to be unloaded. A sturdy woman emerged on the step, and though they could not hear her at this distance, it was obvious she was directing the proceedings.

"My word," said Frances. "Do you suppose all these people are sent by the landlord or by Mr. Beck?"

Jane shrugged. "With any luck, one of them will go into the village for something, and then Mrs. Lamb will discover all. Come along."

"He must be very rich, to rent such a house for himself on a whim."

"Or very extravagant."

"And he is undoubtedly handsome."

Jane halted to peer at her younger sister. "You mustn't form a *tendre* for him, Frances. We know almost nothing about him, except that he is somehow responsible for Archie Wilson."

"Why can't I like him?" Frances retorted. "I'm seventeen—the perfect age to imagine myself in love. I don't suppose anything will come of it because he looks a little old. Even *thirty,* possibly. Though, of course, Della was engaged to Lord Dere, and he was at least as many years her senior!"

"Della wasn't in love with the baron," Jane chided. "And even if she had been, Lord Dere might be old as the hills, but he is kind and respectable."

"Why do you say it like that? Do you think Mr. Beck is not? It could be that Archie Wilson is *not* his son, you know. He might have been left on Mr. Beck's hands by any number of people, for any number of reasons."

Jane made a face. "If he was, I think that would be something Mr. Beck would be quick to advertise. No, I'm sorry to say, I suspect Mrs. Dere was right in her initial caution, however willing she is now to put it aside."

"Oh, pooh! I suppose you mean to have him yourself," said Frances slyly.

"Nonsense!" cried Jane, coloring.

"He found you very interesting when he called," her sister persisted. "More interesting than me, at any rate, to judge by the number of times he looked at you or spoke to you, compared to me."

"Honestly! If it had been you he nearly ran down with his gig, I expect you would have come in for your share."

"But really, Jane, you didn't find him attractive?"

Jane's color deepened, but not because Frances had made a lucky guess. Rather, she blushed because it was not the charming newcomer who appeared just then in her mind's eye. But she only said, "Mr. Beck is good-looking enough. But I don't think of him for myself because I will never marry again. Therefore you may trust my impartiality when I tell you he would not make a good match for you."

They continued in thoughtful silence until the lane crossing the fields met with Church Way. Because the trees were still in full leaf, Jane's view of the church was obscured, but her pulse quickened nonetheless, and she forgot all about Mr. Beck until Frances said, "He will cause a stir, you know."

"Who will?"

"Why, Mr. Beck! Who else could I mean? There are quite a few unmarried ladies in Iffley—Sarah, you, me, Miss Egerton, that Miss Hynde person who is coming to visit, *Mrs. Dere,* even...Yes—quite a few unmarried ladies and very few unmarried gentlemen—or at least ones which everyone in Iffley hasn't known for years."

"There's—Mr. Egerton," ventured Jane.

Frances flipped a dismissive hand. "Certainly Mr. Egerton is unmarried, but don't you think it more likely he already has his eye on his uncle's ward, or she on him? Why else would Miss Hynde be coming to Iffley? Therefore we are left with Mr. Beck."

"Well, you may strike Sarah and me from the list of contenders," rejoined Jane, "and I would strike *you,* so that leaves Miss Egerton and Mrs. Dere to fight over him. And Miss Hynde, if she comes to prefer him." She could not prevent a wistful smile at the thought of Miss Hynde choosing Mr. Beck—what would Mr. Egerton do, if his chosen one flitted away?

Frances saw the smile and nudged her with a playful elbow. "Are you thinking of Mrs. Dere losing her heart to Mr. Beck? It would be delightful to witness, wouldn't it? And imagine how pleasant our lives would be if she married him and removed to town!"

"So pleasant," echoed Jane guiltily.

As they drew nearer the church, Jane held an inward debate: was it wrong to want to stop at the rectory? She would like to know if Miss Egerton had yet spoken to her brother about their proposed parish school, but was that the real and entire reason Jane sought an excuse?

It was not, she had to admit. Because it was also true that she had not seen Mr. Egerton for some days. If not for that, she might have been willing to let Miss Egerton call first. Indeed, that was what she and the curate's sister had decided on Sunday, wasn't it? Yes. Yes it was. Biting her lip, she reproved herself, but then it was Frances who dropped the excuse in her lap.

"I warrant the Egertons don't know the news yet," she said eagerly. "Should we stop in and tell them?"

"But they will be busy, Frances," Jane answered, now as willing to avoid the Egertons as she had been hopeful of seeing them a moment before. Such yearnings of hers were reprehensible and therefore must be checked. "The Terrys only left, and Archie Wilson only arrived on Monday."

"And today is Thursday. I say they've had long enough. Oh, don't look like that, Jane! All right, we needn't call, but let's just traipse through the churchyard. We might even peep into the church, that way we could say we were wondering if they wanted us to make some garlands for Michaelmas."

The ruse proved unnecessary, however, for no sooner did they enter the churchyard than they met Miss Egerton on the gravel path approaching them.

"Mrs. Merritt! Miss Barstow. I was just setting out to call at Iffley Cottage," she greeted them warmly. "But now that you are here, you must come back with me to meet Archie and to hear all I have to tell."

Frances tugged on Jane's not-unwilling arm, and the sisters followed, though Frances whispered, "Drat! She already knows. I begin to understand Mrs. Lamb's joy in always being the first to tell."

Jane made no response, being too occupied with maintaining her outward calm.

"This way," said Miss Egerton, beckoning them into the room directly off the entry.

"Behold!" she sang. "What do you think of our new parish schoolroom?"

Jane's delight was unfeigned, for the small parlor had been fitted with a large square table, an assortment of chairs, a shelf holding several books, and a framed blackboard. A faded rug covered much of the floor, and sausage-shaped pillows were tucked at the base of the windows to prevent unwelcome drafts.

"It's perfect, Miss Egerton! Does this mean your brother approves of our plan?"

"Philip says it's a splendid idea, if only Harry Barbary will agree to it. He thinks we won't have any difficulty persuading the Cramthorpes."

"Good thing there are two of you," said Frances, "because then one of you can sit on Harry Barbary at all times, so he doesn't run away."

The curate's sister laughed. "Why, Philip said nearly the same thing—I was just trying to put it in more exalted terms. There's no doubt we will have our hands full, Miss Barstow, but one can but try."

"Shall I speak to the Barbarys, and you to the Cramthorpes, or vice versa?" asked Jane. "I might have better luck than you with the Barbarys because, even if the boy feels no remorse, his mother might."

"We will shake on it," declared Miss Egerton, holding out her hand. "I think Harry Barbary and old Mrs. Cramthorpe are equal bargains, if you ask me. Now come—wouldn't you like to meet Archie Wilson?"

"But wait, Miss Egerton," Frances said. "What of your news?"

"I've already told it," she replied, gesturing at the schoolroom. "But I do wonder if—if you might call me Cassie. I know I'm the curate's sister and that Philip would never go around asking people to call him by his

Christian name, but we at least will be teaching together, Mrs. Merritt, and it would make me very happy if you would."

"Yes, we would like that," Jane answered for them both.

Clapping her hands, Frances gave a little hop. "And—Cassie—this means you don't yet know the other news flying about Iffley!"

"What news would that be?" came a voice from the doorway, causing all three young ladies to start.

For all Frances' delight in being the tale-bearer, she had not pictured her glee being observed by the village priest, and in her confusion words abruptly failed her, leaving her to hum and haw until Jane interposed. "Frances means to say that Mr. Beck has rented Greenwood Hall, a large house not far from Perryfield. But—perhaps Archie has already mentioned it."

"He has not." Even as he bowed, his eyes flicked from Frances to her, and Jane had the idle thought that he gathered himself to do so because he withdrew his gaze almost as soon as it touched on her. Why?

"Archie hasn't mentioned *anything* if he could help it, as you will see," whispered Cassie, mouth twitching. "But isn't that marvelous, Philip? Mr. Beck at Greenwood Hall and Miss Hynde soon to be with us. Your flock increases providentially, like Jacob's."

When it did not appear Mr. Egerton was going to answer his sister's remark, Frances recovered enough to ask, "How soon will Miss Hynde be here? Mr. Beck takes possession on the first of October—next Friday. And Mrs. Dere at Perryfield has come round enough to say she will host a dinner for him!"

"There's a turnabout!" declared Cassie. "Mrs. Dere's decision to embrace Mr. Beck—I speak metaphorically—will relieve her mind greatly about the whole Archie business, I daresay."

"Yes," said Jane, "that is what Frances and I think."

"Miss Hynde will be here by next Friday as well," Mr. Egerton replied shortly in answer to Frances.

"Did you need something, Philip?" his sister asked.

"Thank you, no. I—heard voices and came to investigate."

"May I introduce them to Archie, then? It will be good practice for him, to be made to speak."

"Does he not speak?" wondered Frances.

"See for yourself," said Cassie airily, leading the way from the room. Her brother stood aside to allow the young ladies to precede him, and this time Jane did so without mishap, though she was terribly conscious of him behind her in the passage.

Stop this nonsense at once, Jane Merritt!

A scuffle and a scramble were heard in what Jane thought of as the Terrys' parlor when they entered, but when she peered around Cassie's shoulder she saw the two Tommies at their table, Tommy Wardour innocently consulting an open book and Tom Ellis pointing his pencil with a pocketknife.

"Where has Archie gone?" Cassie asked them, even as they stood to receive Jane and Frances.

Ten-year-old Tommy Wardour gave an unconvincing shrug, but fourteen-year-old Tom Ellis silently pointed under the table.

"What? Good heavens!" Cassie instantly dropped to her knees. "Archie, dear, whatever are you doing down there? Come out at once. We have guests."

This command meeting with neither compliance nor argument, Jane and Frances could not resist leaning down themselves to look under the table. Two great round eyes blinked at them from beneath unruly hair, all belonging to a small boy tucked with his knees to his chest in the farthest corner.

Rueful sympathy rippled through Jane. How many times, after all, since her crushing scandal, had she wanted to do exactly what Archie Wilson was doing, when there were new people or new situations to be faced?

Giving him a tiny wave, she straightened, tugging Frances up with her. "Good afternoon, Tommies," she said loudly, "how are your studies faring?"

The boys answered readily enough, and their conversation succeeded in drowning whatever the Egertons were having to say or do to persuade Archie Wilson to come out.

At last it was accomplished, Frances smothering a giggle when the curate backed out on his hands and knees and rapped the back of his head on the edge of the table. There stood little Archie Wilson, flushed and rumpled and faintly defiant, but Jane recognized it for the shyness it was. His little face transformed, however, as he stared at her, his diffidence fading away, to be replaced by something unreadable.

"Archie," said Mr. Egerton, not unkindly, "these are two of our neighbors, Mrs. Merritt and Miss Barstow. They have a younger brother not many years older than you. Can you say, 'How do you do?' to them?"

The boy mumbled something. Cassie's lips parted (doubtless to urge Archie to enunciate), but her brother gave the smallest shake of his head, and she desisted.

"I'm pleased to meet you," murmured Jane, a little discomfited by the child's intense regard. To hide her confusion, she turned away and resumed talking with the Tommies. While she wondered how Archie would like his guardian taking up residence at Greenwood Hall, it was probably best he receive the news in privacy, and Jane nodded a hint at Frances.

When the Egertons accompanied them to the door, however, she did say on impulse, "Mr. Egerton, I am so pleased that you approve our plan—Cassie's and mine—of teaching Harry Barbary and the Cramthorpes."

"It is a generous one," he said quietly. "Whether it will meet with success only time will tell."

"Yes. Well. Thank you, in any case, for letting us try and for providing the space."

He nodded.

Cassie reached for Jane's hand and gave it a parting squeeze, in her face all the warmth and affection absent from her brother's.

CHAPTER 8

**Ah Ma'am, but as the jack-ass driver said,
there's two can play at that game.
— Henrico Glysticus, *Tears of Camphor* (1804)**

Mrs. Barbary and her four children lived a few hovels past the Cramthorpes, and, if possible, they were equally unpleasant to visit. It was not that Mrs. Barbary was cross and sharp-tongued like the older Mrs. Cramthorpe, it was that, as Frances put it, "One is afraid she will open her mouth and never close it again till the last trumpet."

It was Sarah, therefore, who agreed to accompany Jane the following morning, leaving Frances to oversee Maria's lessons and keep Bash out of trouble.

"I am proud of you, Jane," her sister-in-law said in her gentle way.

"For crawling out from under my rock?"

"For deciding you have done enough penance. You took all the consequences of Roger Merritt's flaws and choices upon yourself, as if they had been your own."

"But, Sarah—in a way they were my own. For Roger had managed to live within his means before he married me—"

"With the allowance from his aunt."

"Yes, but had he never married me, his aunt would never have cut him off and driven him to extremities. So it really was our unwise match and the burden of supporting both of us which led him to do what he did—the debts, I mean. The drinking, the Fleet."

They were outside the Barbarys' cottage now, but Sarah lay a hand on Jane's arm to arrest her. "What you say is true, Jane, but it does not follow that, if he had not married you, he would not have made another match equally offensive to his aunt, with much the same results. That is all I ask you to recognize."

"I should never have run away with him. Papa warned me that Roger was—unsteady."

"That alone was your error," said Sarah. "But none of the rest of what followed. And heaven knows you paid for it, even before you came to us at Iffley." She shivered, remembering how Adela had described Jane's circumstances in the Fleet. "Therefore, I am proud of you for...deciding to hold up your head and to be in the world again."

"Oh, Sarah!"

The two embraced on the doorstep, only to be bumped from it the next instant by Harry Barbary, as the boy burst out the door. He took one look at Jane, eyes widening, before whooping and dashing away.

"Oh, Mrs. Barstow, Mrs. Merritt," Mrs. Barbary cried in her plaintive voice. "What an honor! Oh! Please excuse—everything—how hard it is to keep things clean with so many children—"

"And one of them Harry," whispered Jane to Sarah as they entered.

There was no danger of Mrs. Barbary hearing them, however, for she had not ceased to speak. "—How I wished I could call at Iffley Cottage to say how sorry I was for Harry pushing you in the street, Mrs. Merritt. What is to be done with that boy I can't say, but he'll be the death of me, only I expect he'll run away soon enough as his father did. But until he does, what trouble! I blessed my stars when Mrs. Lamb said she would give him a shilling a week to do things for her, but that didn't last, and then to hear he's been stealing from Mr. Linn—! Currants! Harry doesn't even like currants. It's the mischief he likes, and I can't beat him properly because I would like to see anyone try to manage such a boy when she has three other little ones to look after, and he's so fast to slip away if I reach for my broom—Lolly! Get off of there and let the ladies sit down. I asked Mrs. Lamb if Lolly couldn't go on her errands for her instead of Harry though she's only four, but Mrs. Lamb said she couldn't approve of a little girl running all over Iffley and wasn't it bad enough with Harry out of my sight? Better out of my sight than in, I said—"

"Mrs. Barbary," interrupted Jane, seeing her chance, "it's Harry I've come to speak with you about."

Instantly the tiny woman with her faded hair and pale blue eyes drew herself up. "N-Now, Mrs. Merritt—no harm's come to you in the end, for you to go after my Harry."

"I don't mean to 'go after' Harry, Mrs. Barbary, but rather to suggest he might—"

"Suggest? Suggest he might go to the workhouse?" The woman's voice rose. "Suggest he might deserve more than Mrs. Lamb dismissing him? If I want suggestions, I'll thank you for them! Hoity toity! Coming after my boy—You of all people should know everyone makes mistakes, seeing as you've made more than your share—"

"Mrs. Barbary!" gasped Sarah, seeing Jane flush.

But stopping the woman when she was in a taking was as impossible as putting a tablecloth over an erupting volcano, and tiny Mrs. Barbary sprang up, going red herself and balling her fists. "For what's not paying what you owe but another kind of stealing?" she demanded. "My boy has mischief in him, but he's not the only one! I know where you and your husband ended, before you got freed and came back to Iffley, so it's no use putting on airs with me and coming to tell me my boy harmed you—"

"But I—" began Jane, rising herself and hardly knowing whether she wanted to run away or to push the woman down.

"The Fleet!" shrilled Mrs. Barbary. "I know you were in the Fleet, or as good as, since it was your husband that did it, the not paying—and you think you're better than my Harry? If you ask me—"

"Mrs. Barbary!" Jane almost shrieked, her heart pounding so hard she didn't even feel the hand Sarah put out to steady her. "I have not come to accuse Harry of anything. I have come to say the new curate's sister and I would like to start a parish school. We would like to—teach Harry to read, that is."

Sarah would later say that Jane, in her crisis, succeeded in doing what no one in Iffley ever had: she struck Mrs. Barbary dumb. The woman gawped. Collapsed back on her chair. Failed even to notice that the baby had crawled near to the fire and begun to suck on the handle of the nearly empty coal bucket. (Sarah rescued her.)

"With your permission," Jane hurried on, "Miss Egerton and I propose teaching him at the rectory, say, beginning Thursday after Michaelmas for an hour or two. We mean to ask the Cramthorpes as well. Perhaps Tuesdays and Thursdays at ten? And—if everyone is amenable—we might increase it to a third day."

By this point Mrs. Barbary's mouth was working, perhaps out of sheer habit, but still no sound emerged.

Jane pressed her advantage. "Do you approve of the plan? May we go and find Harry?"

The moment the woman jerked her chin in a nod, Jane and Sarah made their escape.

"Well, that was worse than I expected," said Jane when they were safely up Mill Lane. Such an understatement made the two fall against each other, smothering laughter. But their mirth ended in gasps when Harry Barbary popped from behind a nearby hedge.

"I won't go to gaol no matter what you say!" he declared. "Nor be hanged!"

"That's good news," Jane replied, straightening. "And I have more for you. Because how would you like to go to school, Harry, and to learn to read?"

The boy, whose blond hair and pale eyes brought his mother sharply to mind, stared at her much as his mother had, minus the working mouth.

"The curate's sister Miss Egerton and I would like to start a little parish school," she explained.

"I don't want to go to school."

"You might learn to read, write and cypher."

Harry only made a rude noise which would have had Mrs. Lamb and his mother reaching for their brooms. Turning to go, he took aim with the haw berries he had plucked, pelting a red squirrel until it scurried away, chittering.

"Very well," sighed Jane. "We will try our luck with Jimmy and Anna Cramthorpe. They don't appear overly doltish."

"There you're wrong!" cried Harry Barbary, spinning back to scowl at her. "Jimmy is a great blockhead."

"Oh, dear. We will have to be very persistent and patient then," answered Jane with a shake of her head, "for if he is as stupid as that, it will take a long time to teach him."

"I could learn *ten* times faster than Jimmy Cramthorpe," insisted Harry, snatching at some hawthorn leaves and ripping them to bits. "A *hundred* times."

"My word! That would have been wondrous to see. Perhaps if I tell Jimmy that on Thursday morning, it might motivate him," she mused. "I might say, 'Jimmy, if you are as dull-witted as Harry Barbary claims you are, think how you will astonish the world when you can read and write and do sums! We will have to show you at the fairs like a performing horse.'"

Taking Sarah's arm, she nodded at him. "Thank you for the idea, Harry, and we wish you a good afternoon."

"No Harry Barbary, then?"

Looking up from where she was bent over the primer between Jimmy and Anna Cramthorpe, Jane saw Mr. Egerton in the doorway. It was the first Thursday morning after Michaelmas, and Cassie had gone to fetch cushions to raise Anna in her chair. Holding up their new shared primer and slates for him to admire, Jimmy and Anna beamed at him, and Jane had a dreadful suspicion she was beaming as well.

"Wait and see," she replied, relieved to hear the calmness of her voice. "But I have tried my best."

After patting Jimmy on the shoulder and mussing Anna's hair, he smiled at Jane. No—he *grinned,* eyes twinkling, and Jane felt it to her core.

"You spoke with him, or with Mrs. Barbary?" he asked.

"Both. Mrs. Barbary gave her permission, but Harry was—er—inclined to resent the offer."

"I don't doubt it," chuckled the curate. "Still, your intentions were good."

"I have not given up hope," Jane insisted, her face warming at his approval.

He raised a questioning brow. "You think his mother might persuade him?"

"Oh, no. I fear Mrs. Barbary hasn't any more sway over him than the rest of us. Only Harry Barbary has sway over Harry Barbary. But I attempted to...appeal to his self-interest."

When she did not enlarge upon this, he said, "Ah. I would have liked to hear that conversation, especially if your method works."

"Look!" squeaked Anna Cramthorpe, removing the forefinger she had been sucking on to point out the window.

Their heads turned just in time to observe a vanishing thatch of blond hair and narrow blue eyes.

"Eureka!" laughed Mr. Egerton, dashing from the room to reappear the next instant with Harry Barbary in tow.

"I won't go to gaol!" the boy protested in his familiar refrain as he tried to wriggle from the curate's grasp. "I weren't doing nothing!"

"I'm glad to hear it," Jane said swiftly, "because if you had come for a lesson, I'm afraid there are only two slates. If we had to teach you as well, poor Jimmy would have to share Anna's."

Jimmy unwittingly aided the cause by clutching his slate to his chest. "You heard her! Go away, Harry. They weren't expecting you."

At once Harry stuck out his chin. "Too bad for you, Jimmy Cramthorpe, because I'm here too."

"Oh dear oh dear," sighed Jane. "Well, Jimmy, I'm sorry, but you will have to give your slate to Harry. But perhaps he won't like school," she added in a conspiratorial whisper, "and it will only be for today. I'm sorry."

One corner of his mouth curling as he pressed his lips together, Mr. Egerton released Harry Barbary, who snatched the slate from his fellow pupil and plumped himself down on an open chair.

"That's where the teacher sits," said Anna around her fingers, which she was sucking again.

"I suppose Miss Egerton and I can stand for an hour," Jane said regretfully, now seeing Harry grip the slate with one hand and the chair with the other. She thought—hoped—Mr. Egerton would almost smile at this too, but his brow knit.

"*Will* you be well enough to stand for an hour?" he asked. "Your injured head—I can fetch another chair."

"I'm perfectly well now," she threw back, widening her eyes to indicate, *Hush! Leave this to me!*

Harry's eyes flew to her now bandage-less forehead, from which the bruise, though still discernible, had faded to a sallow shadow. But before he could burst out again with his inevitable "I won't go to gaol!", Mr. Egerton perceived his error. He began backing away. "Well, I had better see to my own pupils, Mrs. Merritt, but I will say our cook Winching made gooseberry tarts for Michaelmas, and I expect anyone who is still here at the end of the lesson would be welcome to one, including you."

"Thank you, Mr. Egerton," she replied, unable to prevent a smile at this transparent bribe.

Cassie reappeared then, her arms laden with cushions. And like the sensible girl she was, she betrayed no amazement at the sight of their newest pupil, saying merely, "Try these, Anna, and you will be better able to reach the table."

The curate left without another word, and the lesson began.

An hour and odd minutes later, crumbs from the gooseberry tarts still sticking to their faces, the children raced away, now chattering with each other, while Jane and Cassie set the room to rights.

"I think," said Jane, straightening Anna's cushions and sliding the chair against the table, "that went as well as we could hope."

Cassie nodded eagerly. "Did you notice that, by the end, Harry stopped pretending he was here upon sufferance?"

"I did, and I think Jimmy and Anna outright enjoyed it. But we had better not get a third slate yet. Let Harry believe he continues to inconvenience Jimmy until he wants to be here for more reasons than that."

Heads together, the two sat at the table planning their next few lessons and eating the remaining fragments of tart until Cassie rested her chin on her hand and sighed. "I do wish Felicity weren't coming tomorrow, though that sounds ungracious."

"Miss Hynde seemed a pleasant person," said Jane cautiously.

"She *is* a pleasant person. It isn't that. It's that Philip and I are establishing ourselves in Iffley, with the Tommies and Archie, with the church and the parishioners. And here you and I are starting our little school. But when Felicity comes, she must be taken into consideration. She must be included. And she is so young! I do not know how well she will be able to entertain herself." Cassie made an apologetic face. "Just listen to me complain! I beg your pardon for it, Jane."

"But surely—she will have needlework and books and music to occupy her," Jane suggested. "And if—Mr. Egerton is—fond of her, he will make time for her, so that all the responsibility for amusing her does not fall solely upon you."

"Possibly," answered Cassie doubtfully, "but I cannot picture Philip dancing attendance upon her, no matter how fond he might be. When we would visit my uncle Geoffrey, my brother seemed more content to sit and admire her than to engage her, if that makes sense."

Jane was finding it too tempting to hope Miss Hynde would prove burdensome, however, and she guiltily began to gather her things.

"Oh, see?" Cassie wailed. "I have horrified you."

"You haven't, Cassie. I only thought you must have much to do in preparation for her coming."

"But you will call, won't you, or will we not see you again until church on Sunday?"

"I don't like to intrude—"

"Then we may call upon you? Because if we may not, what on earth will I do with her following me about around the clock?"

"Of course you may call at Iffley Cottage with her whenever you like," Jane assured her. "And who knows? She and Frances might take a liking to each other. They are nearer in age, and then she could follow Frances around half the time—though that would involve frequent calls to Perryfield because Mrs. Dere can hardly do without my sister."

"Yes!" Cassie clapped her hands. "What a lovely thing that would be. We will certainly call, then. The first moment I catch her stifling a yawn. Well, good-bye. Wasn't it great fun teaching them the alphabet? They might be just scribbles on a page now, but soon they will have meaning! Good-bye!"

CHAPTER 9

**Having now got sight of her face, he exclaimed,
with an oath, that she was an angel.
—Henry Mackenzie, *The Man of the World* (1773)**

After some discussion, the Egertons decided Philip would hire a cart at the Tree Inn to fetch Miss Hynde from Oxford.

"For we can't expect her to walk two miles," Cassie reasoned, "and we would have to hire someone to bring her trunk in any case."

Therefore Egerton found himself driving into Oxford on Friday afternoon, Mrs. Lamb having urged him to keep an eye open for Mr. Beck, "for he's due to take possession of Greenwood Hall today, but I don't suppose I'll see him. A gentleman like that will have his own means of getting about."

"He had the gig," Egerton reminded her.

"That's right! The gig that almost knocked down Mrs. Merritt, but for your quick thinking, sir."

"I was glad to be on the spot," he said for the hundredth time.

But Mrs. Merritt was on his mind as he set out. When he had approved the front room for the parish schoolroom, he had not thought whether it would be advisable for such a person as Mrs. Merritt to be at the rectory so often, when Miss Hynde would also be there. For did he not have a responsibility to both Miss Hynde and to his uncle Geoffrey to guard the girl's innocence and spotless character? It was one thing for Miss Hynde to encounter the likes of Harry Barbary and the Cramthorpes—for "ye have the poor always with you," as was understood—but Mrs. Merritt was not the poor as the Bible understood the poor. She was poor in spirit, perhaps, and poor in means, but not poor in education nor poor in her original station in life.

No—her fatal poverty had lain elsewhere.

She had proven herself, by her own admission, poor in character.

And while Philip lauded her recent attempts to amend her past with good works, there was no denying redemption required more than a few weeks. What then was to be done in the meantime? Should Miss Hynde be warned against her? Be cautioned with Mrs. Merritt's story?

She must, he decided, as he turned into Berrye Lane. Because the alternative—were Miss Hynde to learn the truth through gossip or, worse, were she to mention Mrs. Merritt in her letters to his cousin Martha and Martha to learn the truth—well, the result would be in all respects regrettable.

He could picture Martha's response already. She would undoubtedly write to Cassie (in full knowledge the letter would be read to Philip), reminding her that "evil communications corrupt good manners." And the Egertons would be obliged to defend themselves when Philip was not certain he would be thoroughly in the right. An untenable position. The thought of Martha's imagined criticism provoked an inexplicable surge of protectiveness toward Mrs. Merritt, however, but he was crossing Magdalen Bridge and had no time to analyze his feelings.

Drawing up in the coachyard Egerton tossed the reins to an ostler and jumped down. "Has the Witney coach come?"

"Oh, aye. If you're here for the young lady, she's in the coffee room."

Conscious of his heart beating faster, Egerton pushed his way inside, where, despite the many people seated or milling about, he spied her at once beside the window, hands folded in her lap and a maid guarding her like a dragon its den. This maid said something to her mistress, and Miss Hynde's head lifted at once, dimpling in a demure smile. A bar of sunlight haloed the golden hair peeping from her cap, lighting as well her blue, blue eyes and the rose of her cheeks. More than one head turned in admiration, and he heard behind him a murmured, "What an angel!"

Egerton felt the swell of pride any young man would have felt, to claim the acquaintance of such a vision, but he was nevertheless aware that, barring the maid's presence, the upcoming drive would mark the first time the two of them were ever alone. And suddenly he wished he had made a list of things to talk about or questions to ask. One couldn't simply stare at a girl—especially when one was driving—however angelic she might be.

She waited for him to cross the room, of course, being too well-mannered to wave or call out, but by the time he reached her she was on her feet to make her curtsey.

"I hope you have not been waiting long, Miss Hynde."

"Not at all, Mr. Egerton," she replied. "Has Cassie not come with you?"

"With three pupils at the rectory, the youngest not even seven, we thought it best if she remained. Would you prefer to take some refreshment before we go?"

To his mingled relief and dismay she refused, so there was nothing to do but be on their way.

There was her trunk to be seen to, at least, and then she must be handed up and her maid deposited on the bench in the cart bed and the ostler tipped. Then Egerton must negotiate the horse into the High Street. But when these things were done the work must begin.

"I hope you left my uncle and cousin in good health?"

"Very good."

"And your journey—how was it? Any difficulties along the way?"

"None at all, thank you." She was looking with interest at their surroundings, and Egerton pointed out the Friary, the Physic Garden, Magdalen's gate and tower, the Cherwell.

"What a fine day," Miss Hynde remarked. "September can be hot and dusty, but today is the first of October."

There was no denying either fact, but nor could he think of any ready response.

"I am glad it does not rain," she continued with a charming laugh and a toss of her head. Though it was not a coquettish toss, it made the small curls framing her face bounce beautifully.

Think of something to say! he adjured himself.

"I too," was the meager result.

This drew another laugh from her—perhaps she thought his awkwardness amusing, but it had the happy result of making her take charge of the conversation.

"I cannot tell you how glad I am you and Cassie let me come, Mr. Egerton. Even if you both live very quietly, it will be a *new* quiet from life at Cottrell, if you understand me. And the faces I see will be new faces, and novelty is always welcome. Even the people I met when you read yourself in intrigued me, and I hope to know more of them. Have you any favorites among them yet? There was a little man with a beard like a goat and then one very pretty lady—what was her name? I will have to learn everyone's names again. But she sat across the aisle from me in the church and spoke with Cassie afterward. She had a veil. She was the only one that morning wearing a veil."

"I suppose you mean—Mrs.—er—Mrs. Merritt," answered Egerton.

"Oh, dear! If you are not certain of her name either, I had better ask Cassie before I address her."

"No. I'm certain. It's Mrs. Merritt." Feeling abruptly warm, he ran a finger under his neckcloth, despite it being, as Miss Hynde so helpfully pointed out, the first of October.

"Mrs. Merritt," repeated Miss Hynde. "And was Mr. Merritt there that morning?"

After having worried how he might introduce the subject of Mrs. Merritt's personal history, here it was, and with the gate opened for him. Well, he had asked for it, hadn't he? The opportunity to put Miss Hynde on her guard.

But Egerton had not been prepared for the tightening of his throat or the sudden stab of uncertainty. *Come, man. What are you waiting for?*

Vexed with himself, Egerton swallowed and plunged ahead. "There was no Mr. Merritt there," he blurted. "Because—he's dead."

"Heavens!" cried Miss Hynde, more surprised by his clumsy manner than by the information imparted.

"It's been a couple years now, I think," he blundered onward, deciding he may as well be hanged for an old sheep as a young lamb. "Which is why she does not wear mourning. But I'd better warn you, Miss Hynde, that hers was a foolish, doomed match. Despite her late father's disapproval of Merritt, it seems she eloped with the man."

"Eloped!" she breathed, marveling. "My word. And she looks so sweet and sad! I don't believe it. She really, truly ran away with a man?"

"Er—yes." Miss Hynde might not be blushing at this disclosure, but Egerton was. "Yes. After which scandal and imprudence, Merritt's own family disowned him, leaving the two of them nothing to live upon."

"Goodness gracious." She was shaking her head in wonderment. "Then what happened?"

"Then...because they had no income, Merritt soon ran up debts he could not pay. That is—in short—he was arrested for debt and thrown in the Fleet Prison. She went with him, of course. Mrs. Merritt, I mean. And that was where her husband died. In prison. In the Fleet."

Had Egerton unloaded a wagon of coal on Miss Hynde's angelic head, it could hardly have been more unexpected, and she was for a minute confounded.

"To think!" she murmured. And again, "I don't believe it. What a tale you are telling me, sir! It *must* be a tale—an idle one meant to tease me. And if it is, it is hardly courteous of you."

"It is no tale," he said grimly. "I have told it ungracefully, but it is the plain truth. And I thought you had better know because—Mrs. Merritt and Cassie have engaged to teach a parish school at the rectory a few mornings a week. That is, you will likely see much of Mrs. Merritt, and—and—"

"And you wished to warn me off?" Miss Hynde hazarded.

It was exactly what he wished, he supposed, but for whatever reason it vexed him further to have her name it.

She wasn't listening for his answer in any case, being too amazed. Tapping gloved fingertips against her lips, she shook her head, repeating, "Good gracious! An elopement and—and *prison!* My word. And then he died. My, my, my. How—tragic for them."

"Tragic?" He frowned. "Yes, I suppose it was. But it was a tragedy which could easily have been avoided. The word 'tragic' would be better reserved for the *unavoidable* category of ruin, the sort which arrives through no fault of one's own."

Miss Hynde was young and full of suitably youthful dreams of love, which might explain why she flashed him a look then—one which it would not be a stretch to call *pitying*. Pitying, with perhaps the slightest tinge of distaste. But Egerton was staring straight ahead at the road and saw nothing.

Being a penniless orphan, however, Miss Hynde had long learned to recognize on which side her bread was buttered, and she thus set aside her own feelings now to enter into his (or what she imagined were his). "Goodness," she began again. "How shocking. I see why you chose to share her tale with me. After all, what will your cousin Martha think, to know I will be so frequently in company with such a person? You and Cassie have been very forbearing, I daresay, to receive Mrs. Merritt. Not only to receive her, but to allow her scope for...redemption. But, yes, Martha will be scandalized."

"This is why I felt I should give you warning," Egerton replied through a stiff jaw.

"How I admire the clergy!" she sighed. "Their duty toward their flock, no matter how speckled the sheep, and in the face of possible criticism. Nor would I want to make difficulties for you and Cassie, but I can hardly hide this from Martha, can I? She will disapprove of Mrs. Merritt's unfortunate history as much as you do, you know, and I'm afraid she will certainly write to you to express her opinion. But you will simply have to explain that, at heart, you and she are in perfect accord on the matter. Oh!" she cried, her little gloved hand clutching the seat beneath her, "Careful there, Mr. Egerton—you nearly scraped that hedge. Do you think Martha would go so far as to call Mrs. Merritt a *fallen woman*? I think not—because that is not exactly right, is it? Mrs. Merritt would be a fallen woman only if she and Mr. Merritt had never married, isn't that so?"

"Miss Hynde," interrupted Egerton, when he could bear no more, "you must tell my cousin whatever you like. I would not have you think anything must be hidden. And Martha must be free to have whatever opinions thereon which she cares to. It would be worth mentioning in your letter, however, that Mrs. Merritt is a first cousin once removed of Lord Dere of Perryfield, and the Deres, at least, have chosen to let bygones be bygones."

"Thank you, sir. That is a very good point and a weighty one. It's only that—if you will forgive me for saying so—your cousin Martha can be so very...proper and—strait-laced. I myself am prepared to like anyone you and Cassie like, and indeed I admire you both all the more for overlooking Mrs. Merritt's...youthful indiscretions, shall we say. So I hope Martha will come around to your way of thinking, but I must confess to you, she already had much to say to Mr. Cottrell about you teaching Archie Wilson."

Miss Hynde continued in the same vein, but in truth he was no longer attending, being too disturbed by her disagreeable comparison between himself and his cousin Martha. He and Martha Cottrell "in perfect accord on the matter"? He and Martha Cottrell, whom Egerton would without a qualm have called priggish, prudish, prim? Being likened to her vexed him, and his first instinct was to reject it as nonsense.

And yet—

The cart brushed another hedge, and with effort Egerton relaxed his tension on the reins. It would hardly serve to drive off the road and give Mrs. Lamb more grist to grind.

But truly—was he indeed like his cousin Martha?

Egerton considered himself an honest man, one willing always to acknowledge the proverbial beam in his own eye before he beheld the mote in his brother's, but granting this particular—characteristic—pained him. Yet there it seemed to be, so plain that even the ingenuous Miss Hynde remarked it. He had felt the need to warn Miss Hynde against Mrs. Merritt for the very reasons his cousin Martha would have done so.

Which meant he was, to some considerable degree, Martha-ish.

He was, to some considerable degree, priggish, prudish, prim.

He felt ill.

At the Tree Inn, the ostler climbed into the cart to help them unload at the rectory and return the vehicle, and though Egerton was quick, Mrs. Lamb was quicker.

"Good afternoon, Miss Hynde! You are very welcome again to Iffley. We will be glad to have that cart back shortly, sir, because there are all manner of items to be delivered to Greenwood Hall, now that Mr. Beck has come to take up his lease. Did you chance to see our other new resident when you arrived at the Angel Inn, Miss Hynde? Mr. Beck, Archie Wilson's *guardian*, shall we say? You are not acquainted with him? Ah—somehow, in all the excitement, I thought your earlier visits overlapped, but of course I believe he was in Oxford when you and the Cottrells were here. He's not a man easily to be forgotten—so handsome and fashionable! Oh! On your way already, Mr. Egerton? Yes, well, off you go. Good-bye, good-bye!"

"What does she mean about a lease?" asked Miss Hynde, one hand to her bonnet as they jolted away again. "Is Mr. Beck making another visit, or is already come to take your new pupil away?"

Briefly Egerton explained the letting of the hall, and this time she was silent, not speaking until they were passing Iffley Cottage, where the sight of a little short-haired child playing with a dog in the front garden made Miss Hynde clap her hands in delight. "Who is that, Mr. Egerton? That little boy? It was a boy, wasn't it?"

He gave the barest glance. "Sebastian Barstow. Better known as Bash. The nephew of the Mrs. Merritt we were discussing. Her late brother's son."

"Another 'late'?" she breathed. "That poor family!"

She really did have the compassion of an angel, Egerton congratulated himself. The beauty of an angel, the compassion of an angel—she would be a welcome addition to the rectory. Her innocence and native kindness an example to the village. Yes, let other young ladies learn from her. He would himself endeavor to learn from her, for if he did indeed currently resemble his cousin Martha in the most unappealing ways, perhaps Miss Hynde could shape him for the better.

All these resolutions Philip Egerton made as he drew up to the rectory gate and climbed down, passing the reins to the ostler. And in the ensuing hubbub, where he assisted Miss Hynde and her maid to alight, and the Tommies and Cassie appeared to greet the guest, and the servants wrestled with Miss Hynde's trunk, and Egerton settled the account with the ostler—in all this activity he did not once allow his thoughts to stray. He did not once think of the Iffley Cottage residents or how, while Miss Hynde's eye had been drawn to little Bash and the Barstow lapdog Poppet, Egerton himself glimpsed beyond both these charming figures the open front door, in which was framed Mrs. Merritt in profile, her apron being untied by Bash's mother. Mrs. Merritt, without cap or bonnet, leaving all unhidden her pretty features and lush dark hair.

Mr. Egerton's
notebook

Greenwood Hall

The Rectory

The Golden
Cross Inn

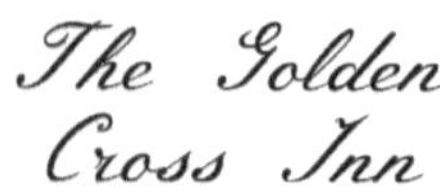

CHAPTER 10

Merry it is in the good green wood.
—Sir Walter Scott, The Lady of the Lake (1810)

Mr. Beck had indeed come to Iffley, for the very next day as the Barstows sat at their needlework a note arrived.

"We are invited to a card party at Greenwood Hall on Wednesday evening," read Jane, to a chorus of indrawn breaths. "At least, some of us are. He addresses it to "The Mesdames Barstow, Mrs. Merritt, and Miss Barstow.""

"See? I am never invited!" complained Maria. "Though I play cards better than you, Jane."

"And I wish you might have my place, Maria," Jane told her. "We hardly know the man, to be invited."

"He better have invited Mrs. Dere, if he knows what's good for him," said Frances.

"But he hasn't met the Deres, I don't believe," Jane answered. "Dear me, he may stumble at the threshold if he invites us without inviting them. After all, there is no reason to curry favor with Iffley Cottage, but every reason to do so with Perryfield."

"Iffley Cottage does boast three pretty young ladies," Mrs. Barstow said with a fond smile.

"Only three? Why do you not count me, Mama?" Maria cried.

"Because you aren't pretty," spoke up Gordon in provoking, younger-brother fashion. It being Saturday, he was lying on the carpet dragging a string to amuse the cat.

"No, sweeting, I did not include you because you are still my darling little girl."

"Yes, you are eleven, Maria," returned Frances, "as you so often remind us. But Mama, shall we go? Mr. Beck is so handsome and dashing!" She elbowed Jane in the ribs here, as if Jane could have forgotten their earlier conversation.

"Perhaps you ought to stay home with Maria as well, Frances," Jane rallied her.

"I do not see how we could avoid going, without giving offense," replied Mrs. Barstow. "And I confess I would very much like to see inside Greenwood Hall. But I do wish we could discover if he invited the Deres. I would hate to be in Mrs. Dere's black book, if it can be helped."

"I could run to the Tree Inn and see what may be pried from Mrs. Lamb," Frances offered at once.

But even if her mother might have condoned such a measure, the next moment Maria called from the window seat, "Here is Miss Egerton with that Miss Hynde person."

Jane's breath quickened. Mr. Egerton's beloved! The fortunate, fortunate girl.

There was not time for further thought, however, for the ordinary sewing must be put away and fancy work taken up; Gordon must scramble to his feet; Maria's cascade of bushy curls must be smoothed.

"Miss Egerton, Miss Hynde, welcome," Mrs. Barstow greeted them. "Won't you be seated?"

"Good morning to you all," said the curate's sister. "How good of you to remember my uncle's ward Miss Hynde. She came just yesterday, but I thought I would walk her about Iffley and remind her of people's names."

"How delighted I am to have so many young people so near," Miss Hynde declared, clapping her hands. "And look at this adorable dog and cat!"

Miss Hynde proved impossible to dislike, for she praised everything and everyone at Iffley Cottage: the family members; large families in general; the pets; Poppet's repertoire of commands, as demonstrated by Maria and Gordy; Bash's limited vocabulary; the ladies' needlework; a magic trick Gordy showed her; the furniture and its arrangement; the prospect from the front window; the convenience and charm of the cottage taken altogether. Within fifteen minutes she had all the Barstows eating out of her hand. Jane alone, in the privacy of her mind, felt a reservation. For, though it might have been her imagination or her too-present consciousness, she could swear Miss Hynde looked at her in a particular way, with a mixture of awareness and curiosity and pity, all rolled into one.

With an effort, Jane fought down resentment, scolding herself as she had done a thousand times in the past two years. If she was infamous in her small way, it was, alas, all her own doing.

"Oh, look, Cassie!" cried Miss Hynde, when Sarah removed from Bash's mouth the card he had found to chew on. "The Barstows received an invitation too! Isn't that from Mr. Beck, now of Greenwood Hall? Archie told us the little shape on the seal is meant to be the Stone of Scone. It's a pun, see? Mr. Beck's family is at the 'beck' of the monarch. We received ours this morning."

The Barstows exchanged looks of renewed concern. Truly, if the Deres were not invited now, something would have to be done!

"We will go," said Mrs. Barstow, "though we are barely acquainted with him. And I hope you at the rectory will as well...?"

"Philip says we haven't any choice but to go," giggled Miss Hynde. "Because Mr. Beck is Archie's guardian. But I am glad of it, and you are too, aren't you Cassie?"

"Philip"? Jane twitched at this use of his Christian name. Were they already so intimate?

"Why doesn't Mr. Egerton want to go?" asked Frances. "Doesn't he like cards?"

"Cassie says he likes whist and quadrille but finds Commerce dull," said Miss Hynde. "And I declare I am exactly the opposite! For Philip is so serious and intent that there is no beating him in games of strategy, while I would rather have a good chat around the table. But perhaps there will be enough of us present that Mr. Beck will have one table for the serious card players and one for the light-hearted."

"Or, if there are three of you, four of us, and Mr. Beck, we might all play a round game like Speculation," Jane suggested. "That might please both you and Mr. Egerton because it involves strategy as well as chatting around the table."

"True!" agreed Miss Hynde, favoring Jane with another of her curious looks. "Will you propose it, or shall I?"

"Oh!" Jane demurred. "I was only speculating myself. I will let the host decide, but if it is whist or quadrille, I will know not to play against Mr. Egerton."

The church was unusually well attended that Sunday, many hoping for a glimpse of both Miss Hynde and Mr. Beck, but they must be satisfied with Miss Hynde alone, for Beck was nowhere to be seen. Jane sat in the center of the second Dere pew, hidden by both Sarah's veil and Mrs. Markham Dere's formidable straw bonnet with full black chip brim. The repeat wearing of the veil caused a frown to fleet across Egerton's features as he ascended the pulpit steps, but she had only worn it to fend off Mr. Beck's possible gaze.

After the service, Mrs. Dere said loudly to the baron, "Uncle, I had thought we would see Mr. Beck before his card party on Wednesday." With lifted brows she consulted the cluster of Barstow dependents gathered around them. "Mrs. Barstow, I assume Mr. Beck issued an invitation to Iffley Cottage as well, in consideration of what is due to those connected with Perryfield."

"He did, madam," replied Mrs. Barstow with a relieved smile at her family. "Are you and the baron now acquainted with the newcomer?"

"My uncle thought it appropriate to call upon Mr. Beck yesterday," said Mrs. Dere, and those in earshot immediately understood this to mean Mrs. Dere had insisted the baron call, and the baron had obeyed. "Lord Dere being first among families in Iffley, it would be remiss to leave such niceties to the last. It would be taken as a deliberate snub."

"How did you find him, Lord Dere?" asked Mr. Chauncey.

"Has he come from town alone or with a party?" asked his wife.

"Did he tell you why he did not intend to come to church?" asked Mrs. Lane, Dr. Lane's wispy beard nodding beside her to second the question.

"I expect Mr. Beck and his friends might have mistakenly attended at St. James in Cowley," ventured Lord Dere in his mild manner. "It is the closer church to Greenwood Hall, though a different parish. It did not occur to me to warn him against possible confusion."

"That must be it," agreed Dr. Lane. "He is probably even now having the matter explained to him by Howe over at St. James."

"Then he did have guests?" persisted Mrs. Chauncey.

"He did. His stepsister Mrs. Rowland and her husband, and a friend by the name of Hardy."

"Stylish sorts, I imagine," said Mrs. Lane, "if they are his town friends."

But judging degrees of fashionableness was quite beyond the baron. "They seemed pleasant enough people."

Mrs. Lane and Mrs. Chauncey looked no better satisfied with this vagueness than Mrs. Dere had been upon first hearing it, and Mrs. Chauncey said with a sigh, "Well, even if Mr. Chauncey calls upon them, I doubt a more adequate description will be forthcoming. How I envy you, Mrs. Dere, being invited to the card party! I will certainly call at Perryfield on Thursday to hear all about it, and in much greater detail."

With such a hum of curiosity in the air, Jane could not help but be infected, and even she began to anticipate the occasion she had once wished on Maria.

When Jane arrived at the rectory on Monday for the next parish school lesson, there were two surprises awaiting her. First, Miss Hynde was perched on a stool in the corner, her workbasket beside her ("Where I will work and hold my tongue and be entirely out of your way"). And second, any budding eagerness Jane felt for the approaching card party was easily eclipsed by Miss Hynde's.

"Oh, Mrs. Merritt," she breathed, sliding from her stool to make her curtsey. "I have been thinking and thinking about what I will wear on Wednesday. I scarcely slept for excitement. Have you decided? What you will wear, I mean. I have never been to a card party and am not even introduced to Mr. Beck, and I dread making any faux pas. Cassie says she will wear her spotted muslin, and I thought my muslin with pale green sprigs, though perhaps that is too spring-like?"

Possessing but few gowns suitable for evening wear in company, Jane said, "Perhaps just my white gown with a blue train."

"With your hazel eyes you would look very pretty in my green sprig," Miss Hynde declared, her head on one side, "but you would have to add length to the hem because you are taller."

Jane was spared responding by the noisy arrival of their pupils, who regarded Miss Hynde with suspicion (Harry Barbary) and awe (the Cramthorpes). But because she indeed did nothing but sew in silence after the lesson had begun, they soon ignored her, and Jane gave her credit for keeping her word.

When the children had gone again, Miss Hynde's tongue loosened. "How very good you both are, to teach them. Very good indeed."

She gave Jane again that look of mingled pity and thoughtfulness which made Jane want to squirm., but Jane said instead, "Would you not find it more interesting and comfortable, Miss Hynde, to sit in the parlor where the Tommies and Archie have their lessons? The Tommies, at least, are more advanced in their studies."

Miss Hynde gave a charming blush, and it was Cassie who replied. "My brother advised her that it might be less distracting if she kept away. Tom Ellis is fourteen now, you understand, and when he saw Felicity, you could almost hear the twang of Cupid's bow…"

"Nonsense, Cassie!" protested Miss Hynde, her color deepening, but she giggled. "That silly boy."

Mr. Egerton had banished his beloved during lesson times? Jane could not help wondering if it was Tommy Ellis alone who found the girl's presence distracting. Perhaps Mr. Egerton feared his own gaze would wander too often to his adored one, making teaching impossible. Or perhaps Mr. Egerton would brook no rivals, even in the form of an adolescent pupil.

Tuesday passed in the same fashion, though when Jane returned home on that day, she was informed by an eager Maria that the Greenwood Hall people had called in her absence. "So now we all know what Mr. and Mrs. Rowland and Mr. Hardy look like, and you don't, Jane!"

"And what do they look like, Miss Superior?"

"Mrs. Rowland is not handsome, but she is so modish one doesn't even notice for several minutes because one is studying her clothing and trimmings," Frances supplied.

"I was frightened of her because she had sharp eyes," admitted Maria, "and when I was pushing up the corner of the carpet with the toe of my slipper—because it was already curling upward, Frances!—she gave me such a look that I didn't dare speak or move until they were leaving."

"So Mrs. Rowland is fashionable and frightening," said Jane with a grimace. "What of the two gentlemen?"

"I thought Mr. Rowland would fall asleep," Sarah chuckled. "His wife had to nudge him with her elbow! And Mr. Hardy did nothing but hang on Mr. Beck's little speeches. Take heart, Jane—there is nothing to fear from either of those two."

"Did Mr. Beck make little speeches?"

"Yes, and he proved as charming as the first time he called," Mrs. Barstow said lightly.

"He asked us our favorite card games, Jane!" said Frances. "There will be thirteen altogether, you know, which means there will be at least one round game, so I nominated Commerce and Speculation, even if Mr. Egerton dislikes them. What do you think?"

"I think Mr. Egerton is courteous enough and certainly old enough to pretend a liking, no matter his true feelings."

"True," her sister agreed. "I don't imagine we would even know he had a preference (or an aversion), had he been present. In fact, he might have been rather put out by Miss Hynde being so frank, but there is no harm in us knowing, is there?"

"No harm at all," answered her mother, "unless we chose to torture the poor man with games he disliked whenever we met him."

This idea amused them all, and the rest of the day passed quickly in refurbishing their gowns and caps for the coming occasion. As Jane stitched a length of lace to the hem of her blue train, she found anxiety beginning once more to outweigh anticipation. For if the hard-eyed Mrs. Rowland disapproved poor Maria turning up the carpet with her toe, how much more might she disapprove Jane's misadventures?

But inevitably Wednesday came, and inevitably the hours passed, and inevitably Reed announced the arrival of the Perryfield coach. The ladies were handed in by the footman Harker to be greeted by the baron and Mrs. Dere, and they were off.

"I defy all Oxfordshire to produce such a lovely and amiable family," pronounced Lord Dere with his old-fashioned grace, beaming upon them. "I will be proud to arrive at Greenwood Hall with you all beside me."

While this drew no more than a cool, "Thank you, uncle" from Mrs. Dere, Jane was grateful for his words. And indeed, his mild eyes meeting hers, she suspected it was more than courtliness which inspired them. *He knows I am all nerves, and he means to encourage me.*

Alone of those beside her, Lord Dere understood—truly understood—what Jane had experienced, because he had seen her in the Fleet with her unfortunate husband. Therefore, alone of anyone in the world save Adela and her husband Gerard, Lord Dere could offer sympathy without arousing Jane's defensiveness. On the contrary, she felt her throat constrict and hot tears rise.

But no—she absolutely could not cry—not when they would be so soon at Greenwood Hall!

Her family guessed enough, however, that Sarah's hand crept across the seat to take Jane's, and Frances began loudly to admire Mrs. Dere's evening dress. These measures succeeded. The tears were beaten back and equanimity restored, so that when they arrived at the Hall and Harker lowered the steps, Jane accepted his assistance with outward calm.

"My, my," marveled Frances, elbowing Jane. For new white gravel had been laid in the drive, and new potted autumn flowers flanked the steps leading to the entrance. Greenwood Hall itself blazed with candles and lanterns.

They were not the first to arrive, for there stood the rusty creaking carriage which every Iffleyite recognized.

"Ah," said Lord Dere, nodding at it. "Mr. Egerton told me on Sunday that Mr. Beck would send the Tree Inn's landau for them. Quite thoughtful of our host." Which only made the Barstows smile because they knew their benefactor could only know such a detail if he had first offered to send the Dere coach.

Extending both his arms, one to Mrs. Dere and the other to Mrs. Barstow, the baron led them toward the steps, Sarah, Jane and Frances trailing after.

CHAPTER 11

**He was...excellently qualified to shine at a round game,
and few situations made him
appear to greater advantage.
—Austen, *The Watsons* (c.1803)**

L ord Dere, Mrs. Markham Dere, Mrs. Gordon Barstow, Mrs. Sebastian Barstow, Mrs. Roger Merritt, and Miss Barstow," announced the
footman at the threshold of the glowing drawing room. Candles burned in
every available sconce and branch, including at the corners of the two card
tables and evenly spaced at the round table. Fresh packs of cards lay waiting
for the company, which was still gathered beside the fireplace.

While Jane's eyes took in the Greenwood party, she was nevertheless
aware of Mr. Egerton standing between his sister and Miss Hynde. *Fine
feathers might make fine birds*, she thought, *but a fine* bird *looks well in
any plumage.* The cut of his coat and the knotting of his neckcloth were
nothing so elegant as those of the town gentlemen, but, unlike Mr. Rowland and Mr. Hardy, Mr. Egerton's figure required no tailor's subterfuges.
Jane supposed Mr. Beck's person was equally noble, being as tall and even
broader of shoulder and chest, but his easiness with admiration reminded
her of Roger—never a good thing.

Her family had described the Rowlands and Mr. Hardy accurately: Mrs. Rowland scrutinized Jane from head to foot; Mr. Rowland blinked drowsily; and Mr. Hardy saw Mr. Beck smile upon her and then smiled upon her himself.

When all had been properly introduced, Mr. Beck raised his hands for their attention. "My dear guests, this occasion is prompted not only by a wish to know my new neighbors better, though that is highly important to me, but it is also intended as a peace offering." Allowing the murmurs of surprise and curiosity to die away, he continued. "Mrs. Merritt, I hope you will forgive the liberty of my sharing the story of our near accident with the Rowlands and Mr. Hardy. It was too shocking a circumstance and my guilty part in it too large for me to forget easily."

However little Jane cared to be singled out thus, she was obligated to respond and did so quickly with a murmured repetition that she had never blamed him for his part in it and therefore bore him no grudge.

"Thank you, Mrs. Merritt," he acknowledged with a bow, "for your generous and repeated assurances. Nevertheless, this evening's little entertainment is my way of making amends. If you will indulge me, I beg you to demonstrate further proof of your pardon by choosing the games we are to play tonight."

Any Barstow could have told Mr. Beck that this public appeal was not at all to Jane's taste—or at least not to the taste of who Jane had become. Nor did it please Mrs. Dere, who felt this slight to her rank, whether Mr. Beck had knocked Mrs. Merritt on her head or not.

But in the panic which rippled through her, Jane kept her head sufficiently to remember Miss Hynde's helpful chatter. "All right, then, sir. As we are one, two, three—thirteen in number, may I propose one table for the serious whist players, one for a lighter game—perhaps casino or vingt-un?—and the remainder at a round game like Commerce or Speculation?"

"Excellent," declared their host. "Entirely well thought out, Mrs. Merritt. And as one final favor, would you please choose your seat and the game to be played at your table? I will humbly join you there, and everyone after may choose for himself. We may change games and places after tea, but do tell us how we are to begin."

A flicker of vexation caused Jane's lips to tighten—must the man insist on joining her table?—but she forced a half smile. And though she would have liked to choose the whist table to observe Mr. Egerton, she did not think her skills would earn his admiration. They might even annoy him, if he were forced to partner her!

Suppose she chose Speculation? *Then there would still be a chance he might play at my table—Miss Hynde said Speculation would appeal to him more than Commerce.* But for this thought she punished herself at once. For heaven's sake, what was wrong with her? The man was already half engaged to Miss Hynde, and even if he weren't he would not think of Jane Merritt in a thousand years!

Thus: "I will choose Commerce," she said quietly. With five at table, that would at least dilute Mr. Beck's unwanted attentions.

Their host rubbed his hands together as if Jane had named his most favorite pastime. "Splendid. And you, Lord Dere? Mrs. Dere?"

The baron chose whist and Mrs. Dere casino and so forth until it was the curate's turn to select his table. With one seat left for whist, Jane was unprepared to hear him say, "Commerce for me."

Sedate, businesslike Commerce?

Surely he only chose it because Miss Hynde had already joined Jane and Mr. Beck, or why would he torture himself? Indeed, his golden-haired angel now glanced up from arranging her ivory fish in neat rows to throw him a perplexed look. While Miss Hynde gave no sign of being besotted with Mr. Egerton yet, Jane thought she surely must be flattered by his willingness to make little sacrifices for her.

Sleepy Mr. Rowland made a fifth at their game, perhaps because it would require the least attention, and Mr. Beck opened the seal on the new pack of cards before passing it to Jane. "Your deal, Mrs. Merritt, but I would be happy to shuffle for you, if you would prefer."

Though his offer was given with no particular, meaningful inflections or looks which Jane would have resented, her reply was cool. "Thank you, sir. I am well able to handle my responsibilities."

"I am glad to hear it," he answered, "for how often is the dealer blamed, when a player dislikes his hand! I remember a time at one of the clubs when two members came to blows—you were there with me, Rowland. Lang accused Partridge of manipulating the deal and called him 'Partridge the Packer.' Shocking business.'"

"I remember," said Mr. Rowland.

"But what is a 'packer'?" Miss Hynde asked, pushing her three-fish stake into the center.

"Someone who arranges the cards to his own benefit," explained Mr. Beck. "In short, one who cheats."

She gasped, her pretty mouth falling into an 'O' as round as her blue eyes as Jane dealt the cards. "And what happened next, Mr. Beck?"

"I leaped up to restrain Lang," he said mildly. "The man was drunk as a wheel-barrow in any case, and for my pains I received an eye blacker than that which you suffered, Mrs. Merritt, if you will pardon my mentioning it."

Jane only shook her head, but her hand trembled.

"I have distressed you!" cried Mr. Beck when she clumsily let one card slip to fall face up upon the baize.

"My—it is nothing," she answered, snatching up the card again. "A bad hand."

"Then why do you not exchange it for the widow?" he pressed, tapping the dummy hand that lay face down in the center. "As the dealer you may, you know."

"Having chosen the game, I daresay Mrs. Merritt is familiar with the rules," interposed Mr. Egerton. His gaze never left his cards, but Jane had the inexplicable feeling he guessed she was not troubled by the memory of her recent accident and injury. As indeed she was not. No—what made Jane stiffen and turn scarlet was Mr. Beck's offhand reference to the unknown Lang drunkenly gambling and quarreling, a scene she could picture all too easily. For how many nights had Roger Merritt spent in just such a manner, in the Fleet Prison taproom? How many times had he then returned to their communal lodging in the early morning, loud and clumsy and speaking cruel words to her?

"I will keep my hand," she said, after clearing her throat.

"Though it is so bad?" asked Mr. Beck, a frown marring his overly handsome face as he leaned toward her.

Fighting an urge to press her first two fingers to his forehead and push him back upright, she repeated, "I will keep my hand."

"Hmm...a deep strategy, Mrs. Merritt." With a sigh and a rueful shake of his head, he slipped out one of his cards and exchanged it for one in the widow.

Play continued, and Jane blessed the very sedateness of the game, for it allowed her to gather herself once more, to school her features and begin to respond more appropriately to the conversation around her. When Mr. Rowland took up a card from the dummy hand, rather than add it to his own silently, he waved it at Mr. Beck. "Three of spades, Beck. Unlucky and worthless. Does it remind you of anything?"

The ladies stared at this veritable monologue from the drowsy man—this speech being longer than all the other words he had yet spoken, put together—but Mr. Beck roared with laughter. "That's right, Rowland.

Trey of spades." Smiling round at the company, he related another incident, this one to do with two Newfoundland dogs in Hyde Park. "Trey—so called by my friend because of the three black marks like pips on his back and flanks—Trey gets in a scuffle with another Newfoundland, this one all black, and Trey prevails. 'Oh ho!' cries McNamara, when Trey has the other dog pinned, 'It looks like my Trey beats your ace!' Well, the other fellow didn't find this joke so amusing as the rest of us, I'm afraid."

"Oh, dear," breathed Miss Hynde obligingly, as Rowland and Beck chuckled, "what happened next?"

Mr. Beck shrugged. "The other fellow threatened McNamara and says he'll knock him down, so McNamara takes umbrage. They fought a duel at Chalk Farm, but nobody was much the worse for it."

"Saw 'em arm in arm t'other day," said Rowland.

"Goodness," Miss Hynde breathed.

Jane saw Mr. Egerton shoot a keen glance at Mr. Beck, and she suspected he thought Mr. Beck's anecdotes too much for Miss Hynde's innocent ears. His gaze dropped before their host was aware of it, however, and he immediately gave the second knock on the table to call for all hands to be revealed.

"Perhaps Mrs. Merritt should remind *you,* sir, of the rules of Commerce," said Mr. Beck dryly, observing Mr. Egerton's two sixes and an ace. "I had not even thought of knocking yet, and my total exceeds yours, Egerton." He placed his own queen, knave, and six down.

Mr. Rowland's sequence of hearts prevailed, and the deal passed to Mr. Beck. Apart from the flashing of his emerald ring, his expert shuffling was done with no air of drawing attention to himself, but Jane remarked it all the same, only to be chagrined when he caught her watching. Though he said nothing, the corner of his mouth lifted, and she looked away.

"How—how do you think you will like Iffley, Mr. Rowland?" she addressed him abruptly.

Mr. Rowland's eyelids, which had been drooping in the interval between hands, flew open. "Iffley?"

"Yes. Iffley. Where you now find yourself."

"Hoping it won't be a thundering bore."

"Milton!" reproved his wife from the whist table, causing her husband to start in alarm. "Speaking of bores, you indeed have the manners of one. The b-o-o-r sort. If you suffer from *ennui* here it will be because you lack resources. You don't read; you don't write; you hardly dance. Here is Alexander providing cards, and if Commerce does not amuse you, you have only yourself to blame, for you chose it."

"I'll swap seats with you, Rowland," offered Mr. Hardy from the casino table. His willingness to abandon his own table was another instance of *lesè-majesté* toward Mrs. Markham Dere which the matron did not miss, and her nostrils flared.

"Nonsense," Mr. Beck interjected smoothly. "We'll change after tea, as proposed. You can't be gallant toward Rowland, Hardy, at the expense of my other guests."

Chastened, Hardy shrank under the reproof and turned back to his fellow casino players while Beck rapidly dealt out the cards.

"I must defend my friend Rowland, Mrs. Merritt," said Mr. Beck. "He would have given much the same answer were he to find himself anywhere but at the clubs or Epsom, so nothing personal was intended. And in addition to cards, I have promised to do all in my power in the way of shooting and dancing and billiards to render the provinces acceptable to him. For what Rowland lacks in manners he makes up for with loyalty to me, don't you, Milton?"

"That's right."

"So if Rowland finds himself rusticating in Iffley at my request," Beck continued, "the more pertinent question would be, why did *I* come down?"

"And why did you?" asked Miss Hynde helpfully, when Jane said nothing.

Examining his three cards, Beck flicked his fingers to pass on the widow. Then he answered, "I have come down to Iffley and rented Greenwood Hall for *love,* Miss Hynde."

"Love!" Miss Hynde gave a blush and a giggle, her eyes meeting Jane's, for lack of any other female player at their table.

But instead of sharing in Miss Hynde's embarrassed pleasure, Jane worried for Mr. Egerton. Although Mr. Beck was not flirting with Miss Hynde, he was not far from it, and that could not be pleasant for the girl's would-be lover. For Mr. Egerton's sake, then, Jane ought to guide the conversation in a different direction.

But the curate did it himself. "Being altogether new here, Beck, you can only be referring to your love for your ward Archie. My sister and I, as well as the two Tommies, have already grown fond of him, and he begins to emerge from his shyness, which was extreme at first."

"That's it," rejoined Beck, "my love...for little Archie." But he said this with a twitch of the eyelid facing Jane, which she prayed was an involuntary spasm and not a *wink.* A spasm could be safely ignored, but a wink must be resented.

She turned her head away to be safe. "I am—delighted--to hear Archie grows more comfortable at the rectory," Jane said sincerely to Mr. Egerton.

"It is early days yet," he replied, "but he begins to see the value of dealing 'aboveboard.'" And then, to her astonishment, Mr. Egerton's own eyelid twitched at her. There could be no mistaking this for anything but a wink, given his punning allusion to Jane finding Archie beneath the table, but she was amazed how differently she received this one! This one caused no surge of indignation—not a bit. This wink produced, rather, a flutter which began in her midsection and spiraled up to her throat.

Swallowing (it was not the sort of obstruction which could be swallowed down, however), she fumbled with her cards, exchanging one almost at random with the dummy hand, with the result that she gave away a king in trade for a four of diamonds.

Though Commerce might be a game with almost no strategy, with such distractions Jane still played poorly, losing the first two of five shillings Lord Dere had insisted on staking each of his dependents. Therefore it was a relief when the servants entered with the tea and the table could be abandoned.

"Darling," murmured her mother, taking her aside, "I had better tell you that we were speaking of London at the whist table, and when Mrs. Rowland learned the baron was the only one to have been in town at all recently, she asked him a dozen questions about everything under the sun: his favorite hotel, which tailor he patronized, whether he had seen so-and-so play thus-and-such at Drury Lane, and on and on. Well, you know Lord Dere had nothing of interest to report on any of those things, so at last she said, 'My dear baron, if you will pardon me for asking, where *did* you go when you were last in London, and whom *did* you see?'"

Jane held her breath during this account, and now she made a pained face, dreading what she knew would follow.

"Yes," admitted her mother. "Exactly. What choice did Lord Dere have? He did try to wriggle out of it. He said he was in town for your sister's wedding, but then Mrs. Rowland must hear where Della and Gerard were married and who married them and who were the witnesses. At last it came out—that you were present, and the reason the Weatherills married in town instead of in Iffley was that they had brought you up to see your husband before he died."

Giving herself a surreptitious thump on her chest, Jane managed to release her breath. "And then, of course, she wanted to know where Roger had been, and why I was not with him in the first place?" she prompted.

"Yes."

Angling herself away a fraction, Jane peeked around her mother's arm to where Mrs. Rowland sat upon the sofa preparing the tea. The woman was occupied with her task, but Jane's heart sank to see Mr. Beck beside her, listening intently as her lips moved.

"It—it could hardly have remained a secret," she whispered, with what little sound she could produce. "And—it is not everyone's fault nor everyone's duty to try to—protect me. It is what it is."

In answer, Mrs. Barstow nodded sadly, pressing her daughter's hands between her own until Jane could feel the warmth through their gloves, and then Sarah and Cassie joined them and they must speak generally.

Now everyone knows, she told herself. *Or will know, shortly.*

But her next thought caught her off guard: *Well, there is freedom in it.*

Good heavens! Was that the case—or was she simply becoming enured to her infamy? Hardened to it?

However hardened she might be, she still hovered by her mother and Sarah, accepting her cup of tea from Mrs. Rowland with a murmured thanks and pretending not to notice the sharp look the woman gave her. Sharp and impertinent.

But Mrs. Rowland's look was soon forgotten when, after some minutes of his guests dutifully conversing and mixing, Mr. Beck tapped a spoon against the tea urn.

"If I may interrupt, we come now to the second half of our evening," he announced, "of which I hereby appoint Mrs. Markham Dere empress." He accompanied this designation with a bow, and Jane saw at once that this belated deference made up greatly for his earlier perceived snub. "Mrs. Dere of Perryfield will choose our next card games, as well as where she will sit, and we will all scramble to accommodate her. This overall honor would have been yours from the outset and for the entirety, madam, if I had not had the misfortune of nearly running Mrs. Merritt down."

Mrs. Dere acknowledged this homage with a nod of her own, her dark-gold hair catching the candlelight, and if she thought (as Jane did) that Mr. Beck overdid everything, she gave no sign.

"Tell us our fates, Mrs. Dere!" he commanded.

When it was done, and just as Jane congratulated herself that she could play vingt-un in peace with neither Mr. Beck nor Mr. Egerton at her table, Mr. Beck passed by to join the players of Speculation.

Bending down on the pretense of having dropped a few counters, he murmured just for her ears, "Are you certain of your game, Mrs. Merritt? Twenty-one is not so easy as it looks. I hear one may lose a lot through not *sticking* in the proper circumstances."

Inhaling sharply at his tone—so different from the respectful one he had used toward her to this point—her wide eyes met his. And there was no mistaking or misunderstanding it this time: his eyelid dropped with exaggerated slowness in an unwelcome, insolent, insulting *wink*.

CHAPTER 12

I have been blown out of your gates with sighs.
—Shakespeare, *Coriolanus,* V.ii.3433 (c.1605)

F elicity, my dear, I *beg* you," said Cassandra Egerton at the breakfast table, after their young guest released her third, prolonged, luxurious sigh. Inclining her head a fraction toward the foot of the table, Cassie tried to remind her of the boys' presence, which Miss Hynde was too apt to overlook.

However little Miss Hynde dwelt upon the rectory pupils, the same could not be said for the Tommies. As Cassie had noted, Felicity's arrival had burst upon not only adolescent Tom Ellis like a *coup de foudre*, but also upon younger Tommy Wardour, and the two lads were apt to stare at her, mouths agape, whenever they found themselves in the same room. They were doing so now as she sighed and sighed and dreamily buttered her roll. At least little Archie Wilson seemed to have kept his head or his heart, whichever it was, Cassie thought with her own inward sigh, or Felicity's conquest would have been unanimous.

But she must take comfort where she could, and Cassie admitted that Philip's continued sensibleness came as a vast relief. Her brother neither sighed nor stared. Perhaps he smiled a little more often, and if Felicity tried his temper as she did Cassie's, he hid it thoroughly. Cassie doubted he had even noticed the girl's sighing.

In this assumption she was mistaken.

Egerton had, in fact, been debating whether to ask Miss Hynde if anything troubled her. She did not *appear* troubled; she appeared happy. Not that that would be any more reassuring.

"I do apologize, Cassie," said Miss Hynde (with a fourth—more abbreviated—sigh). "I was only thinking how very delightful the card party was."

"D-D-D-Did you win?" asked Tom Ellis, this bold effort making all the blood rush to his face.

Miss Hynde blinked as if her cup of chocolate had spoken to her, before rousing herself with a little shake and turning to note his existence. "Why, no, I don't think so. Not a farthing. I may even have lost a few shillings."

"Then why was it delightful?" Tommy Wardour ventured, feeling superior to the older boy because he managed to speak fluently and without turning the color of a boiled lobster. And Miss Hynde even smiled upon him!

"It was...the company," she replied. And if ever a voice sounded like someone hugging herself, it was Felicity Hynde's. Turning her glowing eyes to Cassie she murmured, "Wasn't *he* something?"

"Oh, dear," gulped Miss Egerton, trying her very best not to glance at her brother. Poor Philip! Suppose Felicity's visit led not to her falling in love with him but with Mr. Beck! Not to mention, here sat Mr. Beck's charge not five feet from her. But Archie was young—he likely was paying no attention, or, if he was, he just as likely did not know to whom Miss Hynde referred.

Cassie's second mistake.

"Do you mean my guardian?" piped up that same Archie. This contribution was startling in itself, for, though Egerton had told the truth in saying Archie grew less shy around them, he only meant Archie no longer hid under the furniture. The boy still spoke only when spoken to, when replies could not be avoided.

Miss Hynde's hands flew to her lips, as if she only this moment remembered Archie's connection to Mr. Beck. "Goodness!" she squeaked.

"The ladies always make a fuss over him, my mama once said."

Then Cassie did look at her brother and he at her. Archie Wilson had known his mother? And though everyone at the table would have liked the boy to say more, he went back to the sandwich he had made of cold meat and buttered roll.

Miss Hynde's curiosity overpowered her scruples, however, and she waited for him to swallow before asking, "Were your mother and Mr. Beck well acquainted, Archie?"

The boy shrugged. "I don't know, but Mama wanted money, and he said, what had happened to the money he already gave her? Mama cried a lot, and he gave her more and went away."

"Goodness," breathed Miss Hynde again as two and two made four. She now stared at him as hard as the two Tommies ever stared at her, perhaps trying to trace a resemblance in Archie's round face and snub nose.

Before Cassie resorted to kicking her brother beneath the table to do something or say something, for heaven's sake, he roused himself. "At least hosting his card party was a net profit for Mr. Beck," he said, in a good imitation of nonchalance. "For I believe Miss Hynde was not the only loser. The evening cost me a half-crown. What about you, Cassie?"

"I lost at whist and gained at vingt-un, which left me as I began."

"Mr. Beck was quite skillful at Speculation," said Miss Hynde. "Twice he convinced me to part with my trump card in the hopes of turning up a better, and he even persuaded Mrs. Dere to purchase one of his face-down cards to protect her trump, though she held a knave, and the king had been played in the previous hand. I suppose she had forgotten. But though he carried all before him, I did not mind a bit, for I won something better."

"And what was that?" asked Egerton with trepidation.

"Why, the promise of a ball!" she exclaimed. "Speculation is so noisy that you must not have heard it, but I asked him what other amusements he planned for Mr. Rowland, and Mrs. Dere interposed to say that she intended to have a welcome dinner at Perryfield in honor of all the newcomers. And I said maybe we might have a little music at the rectory—because mightn't we? It would be so easy. Cassie and I could play, Philip! Mr. Beck praised both ideas and said it must be the spirit of Speculation driving him, but he would stake a private ball, if Mrs. Dere would be so good as to help him with the guest list." Clasping her hands, she beamed upon the table at large. "He asked Mrs. Dere if she would lead the ball with him, as she is the first-ranked lady in Iffley—"

"He has certainly guessed who to make up to," Cassie interjected dryly. "Another half hour of this and I suspect so-and-so's influence on Master Peter Dere would be considered an unqualified good."

"Who is 'so-and-so'?" demanded Tommy Wardour.

"We would go to the ball, of course, wouldn't we, Philip?" pleaded Miss Hynde. "Or Cassie and I might, mayn't we, if you are not the dancing sort of clergyman?"

"I am very much the dancing sort of clergyman," answered Egerton, so stiffly that his sister almost giggled in spite of herself. "Even if I were not, I would consider it my duty to my uncle to attend, as you are in Iffley under my aegis."

This unintentional pomposity was no way to win a heart such as Felicity Hynde's, not when she had been admiring the dashing Mr. Beck, and she almost gave a giggle of her own. But she succeeded in disguising this as a species of nasal congestion, quickly pulling out her handkerchief to dab at her nose. "Thank you, sir."

The clock chimed, and Egerton blurted, "Off you go, boys. You may begin the translations I set out for you, Tom and Tommy, and for you, Archie, I left something to copy."

The silver clattered; the chairs scraped; the door of the dining room opened and shut.

"Felicity," Egerton began again, aware of a prickle of dread at the task before him, "I had better say that a little caution regarding Mr. Beck might be in order."

"Ooh—here comes another of your warnings. Is he dangerous too, then?" she asked brightly. "Dear me. First Mrs. Merritt, and now Mr. Beck? Who knew Iffley held such perils?"

He flushed. "Felicity—"

"Yes, yes, I understand. Your duty to my uncle and all."

"Philip means to say that my uncle Geoffrey would hardly look kindly on Mr. Beck's—er—youthful escapades," Cassie tried to help.

"Or Mrs. Merritt's 'youthful escapades,' presumably," returned Miss Hynde, her soft little chin sharpening in unexpected resistance.

"Mrs. Merritt has nothing to do with Mr. Beck," Egerton said shortly.

"Not *yet* she doesn't," sniffed Miss Hynde. "But, if I'm not mistaken, she too might benefit from this warning."

"What do you mean?"

She raised innocent eyebrows. "Oh, nothing at all. Only that I do not think Mrs. Merritt was blind to him, let us say. And though you are not responsible to Mr. Cottrell for Mrs. Merritt's welfare or reputation, does she not still have a claim on you as a member of your flock?" When neither of her companions replied at once, she shrugged. "I understand. Mrs. Merritt I am welcome to know—she and Cassie even call each other by their Christian names—but Mr. Beck I must keep at arm's length."

"Mrs. Merritt poses no danger to you." The curate spoke this through gritted teeth, scarcely able to comprehend where the morning had gone wrong. It was as if a downy kitten had bared her teeth and bit through his skin as he stroked it.

"No danger," she repeated, sliding back her chair and rising. "But suppose I did not choose to keep Mr. Beck at arm's length? Suppose I, like Mrs. Merritt, refused to heed others' warnings?"

Egerton had risen from courtesy, and Cassie's lips parted to express something of her shock at this manner of speaking, but Miss Hynde would not stay to hear it. At the door she said, "I will not be joining your lesson with the children today, Cassie. For my own safety I am going to keep away from Mrs. Merritt and write a letter to Martha. Good morning to you both."

"My!" breathed Cassie, when they were alone. "What on earth? Who knew sweet little Felicity could speak to us thus? That she could think thus?"

A deep frown marred her brother's handsome brow. "It comes as a shock to me as well, Cassie. I made a botch of that. Who could blame her for rejoicing at the prospect of a ball, especially after the last few months spent living with my cousin Martha?" He sighed. "Surely it would have been better to let the precautions wait until we saw a greater possibility of harm."

"Possibly, possibly," fretted Cassie, "but it was not your fault alone, Philip. I started it, but I could not help myself, with Archie sitting there, unwittingly *proclaiming* his mother's relationship with—"

"Yes."

"She will not *do* anything, do you suppose?" Cassie persisted.

"Besides write to Martha, you mean?"

His sister pulled a face. "Let us hope that was an empty threat. Because what would be the point of telling Martha she had been introduced to a—rake and a—a woman like Mrs. Merritt?"

"Don't even speak of them in the same breath," he commanded sharply. "There is a very great difference between one who—feels remorse for her deeds—and another so utterly careless of the world's opinion. It almost makes one want to throw Archie back at him! If it's a matter of indifference to Beck that he kept a mistress or fathered a bastard, why should the rest of us bear the embarrassment or see to the consequences?"

"Oh, Philip!"

But he held up a hand, already shaking his head. "Of course I don't mean that about Archie, Cass. It's not his fault. I'm merely venting my spleen. Yes, we were stupid this morning. We should have simply held our tongues. And we will do so, from now on. We will even have the musical evening she wants, to demonstrate our goodwill. Though we have made her defensive, she has more sense than to feed a *tendre* for the man simply because she has been warned against him."

After witnessing Miss Hynde's unexpected outburst, doubt prevented Cassie from offering any definite assurances, but seeing his lips disappear in an unhappy line, she hastened to say, "If it's any comfort, Philip, even were Felicity to nurture inadvisable feelings for Mr. Beck, he did not seem inclined to reciprocate. That is, I did not think him flirtatious with her."

"That's right," he agreed, some of the tension leaving his shoulders. "It was Mrs. Dere he sought to flatter."

"Yes. Not from any interest in her, I suspect, but in order to seal his social acceptance in Iffley." His sister smiled to see his features relax, only to undo all her work the next moment when she said, "If you ask me, flirtation-wise, Mr. Beck seemed more interested in Mrs. Merritt then either Mrs. Dere or Felicity." Folding her napkin neatly and nodding to Polly, who entered with a tray for clearing, Cassie failed to see the effect of her words. Instead she hurried to the mirror above the mantel to make herself neat. "Heavens! Jane and the children will be here any moment. But do you think, Philip, that out of all that was said there was a kernel of useful truth? Ought I to warn Mrs. Merritt against him?"

Her eyes sought his in the glass, but he was staring at the bare cloth while Polly scraped it for crumbs.

"No," he said at last. "I had better do it. As Felicity remarked, Mrs. Merritt is a member of my flock. Send her to my study when you have finished with the lessons."

Sometime later, his pupils set to their work and a book of sermons open upon his desk, Egerton heard a timid knock. After Felicity's excitability at breakfast, such quietness from Mrs. Merritt should not have caused his pulse to race, but apparently his pulse would do what it pleased. It must be because of the disagreeable task which lay ahead.

"Enter."

"Cassie said you wished to speak with me."

"Yes, Mrs. Merritt, good morning. Won't you sit down? How did Harry and the Cramthorpes fare today?"

A genuine smile bloomed on her face. "They have all learned their alphabet and we began with some simple words: cat, rat, bat, and so on. Harry is the quickest, and when he thought of 'fat' and 'mat' all by himself, even he could not hide his delight." Her gaze traveling quickly over the cozy room she added, "I had thought Miss Hynde might be with you because she did not join us this morning."

"Ahem. Er—no. She had a letter to write." He lay down his pen knife because he was fiddling with it.

"Miss Hynde is so charming, she must have many school friends to write to," she said, folding her hands in her lap.

A cloud fleeted over his brow because Egerton realized he had not the least idea who Miss Hynde's friends were. "Oh. Yes. To be sure. Though she had governesses, not school. And—and you, Mrs. Merritt? Did you go away to school? Or did you have a governess?"

"Neither. My father taught us all himself, along with a few pupils, as you have at the rectory." Biting her lip, she rearranged her hands so that the other was placed on top. "Forgive me, Mr. Egerton, but I would be more comfortable if we—if you—were to tell me what you wanted to say. Perhaps it is my unfortunate history, but I cannot help feeling uneasy in situations like these—waiting for a figure of authority to address me, I mean to say."

"Figure of authority!"

"Yes, of course." Lifting her eyes to his, she said, "You are, in Mr. Terry's absence, our priest, sir."

Suddenly he felt old and bearded and patriarchal. Was this what she thought of him? That, like a warden or offended deity, he sought to punish her for some transgression?

"I did not—that is—let me relieve your mind, then," he stammered. "I have no reproach to make, Mrs. Merritt. Rather—I meant rather to...caution you."

She stared. "Is there something in my recent conduct which alarms you?"

"No," he said decisively. "Nothing at all of that nature."

"What, then?"

"I only mean to warn you against...fostering a—friendship—with someone like Mr. Beck."

To Egerton's knowledge, Mrs. Merritt had had no more to do with Beck than courtesy demanded, apart from being nearly killed by the man's gig; thus he half expected her to blaze up as Miss Hynde had. Even Felicity only accused Beck of flirting with Mrs. Merritt, not Mrs. Merritt of flirting with Beck.

But however out of order his warning had been, Mrs. Merritt did not blaze up. In fact, she diminished.

"I—see," she said, scarcely audible. Egerton could see her throat working. "Thank you, sir, for your...concern, though I assure you from the bottom of my heart that there is no need for it. Not in the least. And—and I hope my continuing conduct will alleviate your fears. It is a hard thing to earn trust again, after one has broken it, but, if my assurances carry no weight now, perhaps they will—increasingly—as others come to know me better. Even as I have come to know myself. Good—good day to you."

Before he could say that—wait—on second thought, perhaps he had been rash to raise the subject, and could she possibly strike the last ten minutes from her memory?—she was gone.

Egerton dropped breathlessly back into his chair as if his legs had been chopped from under him. He felt like a brute. A breathless brute.

It could not have been plainer that she interpreted his warning as mistrust—and hadn't it been? She received it as an aspersion on her character—but—but—wasn't her character as streaked as a tiger's pelt, and all through her own doing?

There was no way such a conversation could have gone pleasantly, but then why did he feel as if it could hardly have gone worse?

CHAPTER 13

She sees defamed Glory, wronged Right.
— Edward Benlowes, *Theophila; or, Loves sacrifice* (1652)

Jane did not walk directly home from the rectory. How could she, when tears threatened and she was most certainly red in the face?

Why should you be surprised? she demanded of herself. *Why should you think a few weeks' acquaintance enough to make him—make* anyone—*forget the past?*

In Mr. Egerton's book, a woman who could fall in love and run away with an imprudent man must ever after guard herself against every passing rogue, lest she repeat her mistakes. In Mr. Egerton's book, Jane Merritt, having proved herself reckless, must be protected henceforth from her own poor judgment. She could not be trusted to have repented, to have grown, to have learned.

As if I could like a scoundrel like Mr. Beck! With his gaming stories and dueling stories and London stories! With his unpleasant friends and his poor Archie Wilson in tow! Roger, at least, was as innocent as he was foolish, until he met with disappointment. Jane ripped leaves from the hedges as she marched past, shame at what the curate thought of her shifting to anger with Mr. Beck. Why did he have to come to Iffley and cause her trouble?

Why did he not stay in London with his ilk, where they might find all the amusement they craved?

Cutting across the Upper Field, Jane seethed and stamped, stamped and seethed, somehow keeping her footing, though the ground was uneven and stubbled after the harvest. She might have wandered for miles, had her ear not caught the sound of riders, at which she halted abruptly. Good heavens! What was she about? She had never walked so long or so far alone since coming to Iffley and had better return home before her mother sent Frances in search.

Turning on her heel, she began to retrace her steps, expecting the sound of the horses' hooves to fade. Instead the riders came onward, leaving the common sheep-way for the very field in which she walked. When they were abreast of her, Jane could not do otherwise than look up, and she was not a jot pleased to see the very Mr. Beck she had been castigating in her mind, accompanied by his toady Mr. Hardy.

"Why, it's you, Mrs. Merritt, on this fine afternoon," Mr. Beck greeted her, touching the brim of his hat. "Hardy and I wondered what young lady would be abroad on her own, but now it all makes sense. After all, a lady, once married, may go where she pleases."

"That's right," seconded Hardy, chuckling. "A lady *once* married."

Jane's reply was crisp. "Yes, indeed. I sought not only fresh air but solitude."

So broad a hint could not be overlooked, and Hardy's foolish smile grew uncertain. He glanced at his friend for guidance, but Jane was already regretting her bad manners. She might not like Mr. Beck (and by extension anyone who flattered him), but there was nothing to be gained by rudeness.

"I was just returning to Iffley Cottage," she resumed, in a softer tone, "and really must be on my way, or my mother will wonder at my tardiness."

To her dismay, her repentance was immediately punished by Mr. Beck dismounting to walk beside her.

"What rotten luck of mine," he said gaily. "When I am driving my gig, I nearly finish you, but when I would like to offer you a ride, that you might be home the sooner, I am entirely gig-less."

As he delivered this sally, Mr. Hardy sprang down on her other side, intending to play the fellow gallant, but his boot landed awkwardly on the uneven ground. Staggering, he lunged for the nearest support, which happened to be Jane's person. Her smaller, lighter person. With a yelp, she nearly toppled over, only to have her other arm seized by Mr. Beck, who gave an equal and opposite jerk, suspending her like a bone between two hungry dogs.

In fact, that was precisely what Jane looked like, in the opinion of Mrs. Markham Dere, who was driving her pony cart along Church Way. Dragging the pony to an immediate halt, the good woman waved her crop and shouted, "Holla there! You! What are you about? Stop that at once, or I will call the constable!"

While the threesome was too far away for Mrs. Dere to identify them, Jane recognized both the pony cart and the voice at once, and what had already been a bad quarter of an hour now received an additional flourish.

"If you will excuse me, gentlemen," she uttered firmly, "I will take care of this." Shaking herself from their grasp, she squared her shoulders and marched in the direction of their inquisitor, because the only alternative to facing Mrs. Dere would be to flee and try to beat the pony cart to the cross-way, but the odds of that were so low it hardly qualified as an alternative. Therefore she accepted her fate, not even looking back to acknowledge Mr. Beck's and Mr. Hardy's farewells, though she was relieved to hear them remount and ride away.

"Why—can that be *you,* Mrs. Merritt?" demanded Mrs. Dere, when Jane drew nearer.

"It is, madam."

"Oh! My word. My, my word." Mrs. Dere pursed her lips, until she remembered she was a handsome woman of a certain age and that pursing her lips might cause lines to form. Then she switched to clicking her tongue ruefully. "You had better climb up with me, Mrs. Merritt, and I will take you home."

"Thank you, madam, but I am nearly there already."

"Climb up with me, Mrs. Merritt. I have something to say to you."

Swallowing a sigh, Jane obeyed, and if she could possibly have spared any pity, she would have felt sorry for the pony Chauncey, who must now pull her additional weight. But no—Jane could only brace herself for another lecture, and Chauncey must bear his own fardels.

She was not a bit surprised when the cart reached the cross-way and Mrs. Dere steered away from the village to follow the common, which in those days had not yet been enclosed. As poor Chauncey was a mere thirteen hands high and plump with easy living, he did not set a thundering pace even when he had only Mrs. Dere to haul, and Jane feared that if the lecture did not begin at once they would have to make the long loop past Perryfield, rather than turning when they caught Church Way again. Therefore, it was she who spoke first.

"Mrs. Dere, I was returning home from a walk, and it was only chance which took the gentlemen across my path."

"Mm," said her companion with aggravating vagueness. An 'mm' like that could mean anything but most likely meant, *If that is your story, it is not a very believable one.*

"I did not ask Mr. Beck—for it was Mr. Beck and his friend Mr. Hardy you saw—to accompany me, nor to dismount and walk beside me," Jane persevered, "but they did so in any event. When Mr. Hardy dismounted, he lost his footing and grabbed my arm, nearly pulling me over. Mr. Beck only took my other arm to keep me from falling. And that is when you called to us."

This drew an "I see" from Mrs. Dere so drawn out that Jane knew she did not see at all. And then poor Chauncey, after his effort to set the heavier cart in motion, heard his mistress' "whoa" and must clop to a halt once more.

Turning on the little bench seat, Mrs. Dere gazed frankly into Jane's face, and Jane felt herself blush though she had done nothing wrong.

"Mrs. Merritt," began Mrs. Dere ominously, "it pains me to say this, but I feel it my duty."

Jane swallowed. Said nothing. Wished herself miles away.

"Though you are a widow as I am, and we are allowed more freedoms than are generally accorded to young unmarried ladies, I think it unwise to...court gossip by wandering alone in places where you might come to grief. Why—for an instant there, I thought you were some foolish young miss taken up by kidnappers! What else was I to assume, when I saw you stumbling around, grappling with strange men?"

"Grappling"!

"Madam! This is Iffley—hardly the Seven Dials," Jane could not forbear saying.

She regretted it at once, for Mrs. Dere shut her eyes for a long moment against such horrors. "Mrs. Merritt," she resumed with a sad shake of her lovely head, "your familiarity with the—rougher—parts of London far exceeds mine. I hesitate to remind you of the dreadful incidents and places in your recent past—"

"I need no reminder of them," Jane broke in, feeling her temper rise in spite of herself. "And the closest I ever came to the Dials was to ride in a hackney coach along Oxford Street into Holborn. You must pardon me—I referred to the place only in jest."

Perhaps because Mrs. Dere herself was not so familiar with town, either the good or the unsavory districts, or because she still resented the baron taking Jane and her older sister shopping and to meet the bishop of London two years prior, she passed over this.

"My point being," she rejoined, "a woman with your experiences can never be too careful to…shield and preserve what remains of her reputation. Mr. Beck is handsome and amusing, I grant you, but I would counsel you especially to be on your guard—"

"Pardon me," Jane interrupted for the second time, her hands now balled into fists as she pictured wresting Mrs. Dere's riding crop from her and whacking her over the head with it, "but you may rest easy on my account. I have no interest whatsoever in Mr. Beck—or anyone, for that matter—so your warnings, though I'm certain they are kindly meant, are wasted upon me. But—again—I thank you. Now, if you don't mind, I think I will climb down and continue homeward."

While Jane's words might have been polite enough, there was no mistaking the sparks in her eyes, and Mrs. Dere naturally took umbrage. This miss who was no better than she should be—this—this runaway creature who had married the worst sort of blackguard—a girl who might not know the Seven Dials but who certainly knew the inside of the Fleet Prison!—did such a person dare to give *her* such a look! It was not to be borne. She was Mrs. Markham Dere, niece by marriage to Baron Dere and mother of the heir, a lady of spotless reputation and high character. And were her pearls of wisdom to be trampled upon by this ungrateful, unrepentant, unredeemed, un-*anything* slip of a person? Why, if not for her fondness for Miss Frances Barstow (and her son Peter's for Master Gordon), the whole family at Iffley Cottage might be tossed in the Thames, for all Mrs. Dere cared.

And while Mrs. Dere might not have spoken a single one of *her* thoughts aloud, neither could Jane mistake the outraged lift of her eyebrows and iron stiffening of her person. And Jane too thought of her sister Frances and brother Gordon and every other Barstow dependent on the goodwill of the baron and Mrs. Dere. And admitted bitterly to herself that—truly—in the last analysis, what had Mrs. Dere (or Mr. Egerton, upon reflection) said to her which she had not, at some time, said to herself?

"Mrs. Dere," Jane began again, calling on all her strength to say the words, "I have been rash, and I ask you—to pardon me. I wish you would believe me, that you can never reproach me more harshly nor thoroughly than I have reproached myself, but I hope you will understand it is less easy to bear when coming from another."

To Mrs. Dere's everlasting credit, despite her own vexation, she could hear the sincerity in Jane's speech now and even admitted, *Well, if I had as many blots on my conscience as she has, I daresay I'd find it mortal unpleasant to remember, day and night.*

Taking as deep a breath as Jane had, she replied, "Yes, I can see that. But I've spoken my mind now, so I will try to refrain in the future from touching upon the subject, except to say, *do* be careful, Mrs. Merritt. And there is no need to go off in a huff. I will drive you." Here she clicked her tongue at Chauncey, tapping his rump with her crop, and the good little pony lumbered into motion again.

"I had just come from calls at the Cottage and rectory when I saw you, Mrs. Merritt," Mrs. Dere continued, "because I invited you all to the welcome dinner. We will have quite the giddy whirl in the coming weeks, for that charming Miss Hynde informed me that the Egertons intend to host a musical evening. Did Mr. Beck happen to mention a date for the Greenwood ball?"

"He did not. Really, madam, they came upon me a bare minute before you saw us."

"All right, all right," Mrs. Dere said placatingly. "I intended to call at Greenwood Hall next, in any event, and, if the gentlemen are still out, perhaps Mrs. Rowland can tell me."

True to her word, no more unpleasantness passed Mrs. Dere's lips than was usual in her company, and Jane was shortly home again to pretend delight in all the proposed gatherings. But it was much longer before she felt any peace after such a tumultuous morning.

It was only the following day, as she sat at her work, that she heard her mother say, "Frances, whatever are you working on? We promised Mrs. Dere those shirts for the poor basket."

"Oh, Mama," she protested, "I have made two shirts already, and if you all are sewing them as well, it's not as if Iffley is overrun with poor people."

Sarah leaned over to inspect the fine white muslin in Frances' lap. "That is very pretty lace you are adding."

"Thank you. I intend to sew a new ribbon over the waist as well, and then, *voilà!* A new gown for the Perryfield dinner. I'm afraid I will have to wear it again for the ball, but perhaps Jane might let me borrow her blue?"

"Certainly," answered Jane, sewing steadily, "because no one would notice if I turned up in a tarpaulin."

"One person might notice," her sister replied.

"Do you mean Mrs. Dere?" asked her mother.

"Oh, right—two people might notice, then," Frances amended. "But I meant Mr. Beck, Mama."

"Frances thinks Mr. Beck looks at me," explained Jane, more to make short work of the subject than to enlarge upon it. "Which, if true, makes no difference whatsoever. Frances and I decided he must either flirt with Miss Egerton, Miss Hynde, or Mrs. Dere to amuse himself."

"*You* decided," retorted Frances. "Though he did not seem keen at the card party to get started with any of them. And, as for me, Mr. Beck hardly remarked whether I was alive or dead! Which was so tiresome because I would very much like to be flirted with."

With her mother and Sarah on hand, Jane need not issue any further warnings about Mr. Beck's unsuitability, and it was some balm to her soul to see Frances flare up under persecution.

"I didn't say I wanted to marry him, Mama!" Frances huffed. "I only said I wanted to be flirted with. Honestly, what a fuss. If Miss Hynde over at the rectory dared to admire Mr. Beck or sew fresh trimming on her dress, I daresay she would not be rapped on the knuckles as hard as I have been."

Even to this Jane contributed nothing, though she could not help agreeing inwardly, *No, but only because Mr. Egerton saved all his knuckle-rapping for* me.

CHAPTER 14

Tut, tut, thou art all ice, thy kindness freezeth.
— Shakespeare, *Richard III*, IV.ii.2605 (c.1592)

Though she had not done anything wrong, for the days following her double chastisement Jane reverted to her earlier habit of keeping to Iffley Cottage. The parish school lessons could not be avoided, but on those days she ensured her arrival coincided with that of Harry Barbary and the Cramthorpes, and she escaped home as soon as she could, making excuses when Cassie invited her to linger. Nor could church be avoided, but there Jane persisted in wearing Sarah's veil and clinging to her sister-in-law like a barnacle to a ship's hull. When the Deres or Cassie and Miss Hynde called at the cottage, Jane was found in the parlor with the rest of the Barstows, but a visit from Mr. Beck and Mr. Hardy she escaped by dashing upstairs and pleading a headache.

"Mr. Beck was sorry to hear you were unwell," Frances informed her with a roll of her eyes when Jane stole back down. "And he hopes you will recover in time for the Perryfield dinner. You will, won't you? Or do you intend to dodge that too?"

She did not.

When the Dere coach drew up before the house the next Thursday, Jane took her place within, though she was startled to learn from the Perryfield footman that they would also be picking up the Egertons and Miss Hynde.

"Mr. Egerton said he could ride up with Ogle so there would be six in the coach," said the second groom Harker.

"Thank goodness the rain stopped," Mrs. Barstow returned as she moved closer to Jane to make room for Sarah on their bench, "or Mr. Egerton would have had an uncomfortable time of it."

Sarah agreed, but Jane fought a ridiculous twinge of envy for Ogle. The rain had indeed stopped, leaving a clear and sparklingly cold night for a drive. How lovely it would be to sit beside Mr. Egerton under the stars, the warmth of his person as solid and reassuring as his character. Apart from at a distance in church, she had not seen the curate since their uncomfortable parley, though he had never been far from her thoughts. Lucky Miss Hynde, to have such a heart as his waiting there, hers for the claiming!

If Miss Hynde shared this opinion she hid it well, however, beaming at them as she climbed in a minute later and crowing, "How thoughtful of Mrs. Dere to place all these blankets and bricks! Aren't you glad you aren't a gentleman, so you don't have to offer to take the outside seat?"

On her mettle after Greenwood Hall's card party, Mrs. Dere had ordered more lights than usual, the windows casting a glow upon the drive and the landau already standing before the entry. Jane, too, was prepared and almost glad to see Beck's party had preceded theirs. For she intended to put on a show of her own. A quiet, decisive one which would lay to rest the fears of the interfering. She would not be rude if it could be avoided, but nothing in her words or manner would encourage Mr. Beck. If the Mr. Egertons and Mrs. Deres of the world could never approve of Jane Merritt again, at least she would give them no future grounds for *dis*approval.

This design was tried at once, the moment she removed her wraps in the entrance hall.

"Mrs. Merritt," cried Mr. Beck with an elegant bow, "I need not ask if you have recovered from your headache, for your blooming looks speak volumes."

"Thank you," she told his left ear. To her vexation, she felt her face warm, but it was only because Mr. Beck's remark drew looks from those nearest, among them Mr. Egerton. Whether he too thought her blooming was impossible to say, for his expression was impassive and his look lasted no longer than an eyeblink.

Frances looped an arm through hers, whispering mischievously, "If I stay close to you all evening, Mr. Beck will have to address me too. Love me, love my dog."

Had Jane wished to ensnare Mr. Beck, she would have been quite frustrated, for Mrs. Dere seated her where she imagined she would come to the least harm: between Lord Dere and Mrs. Barstow, and across from the somnolent Mr. Rowland. Indeed, maintaining a steady flow of talk at their end of the table proved impossible, and they must seek further down, where Mrs. Dere, Mr. Beck, and Mrs. Rowland talked enough for all. Frances must have been happy, for being Mrs. Dere's favorite, she was placed at the woman's left hand, immediately across from Mr. Beck, but with true Frances instincts, she knew her patroness would frown upon any attempts to address the man, and she kept fairly mum. Mr. Egerton sat halfway along the table, flanked by Mrs. Rowland and Miss Hynde, and while Jane would have been surprised if he conversed at any length with Mrs. Rowland, she was equally surprised to see how little he and Miss Hynde spoke. Indeed, Miss Hynde spent much of the meal looking past her would-be suitor and tuning her silences, her smiles, her murmurs, and her chuckles to whatever Mr. Beck was saying or doing.

Jane could not call it a successful mingling of groups, and after a while she gave an inward shrug and turned her metaphorical back on them, spending the remainder of the time putting quiet questions to the baron and answering his.

When the apple tart was consumed the ladies rose, leaving the gentlemen to their port and politics, but in the drawing room Mrs. Dere assured them the wait would not be long. "I told the baron we would have some music with our tea or hear poetry read, so he was not to dawdle, and I certainly do not want the dining room to reek of smoke when they are done."

"Philip doesn't smoke, for one," his sister Cassie offered.

"And the baron rarely," agreed Mrs. Dere. "Though he keeps a box of cheroots to offer guests."

"Alexander and Hardy and my dear husband will make short work of those," Mrs. Rowland said dryly. "The dining room curtains at Greenwood already smell like a chimney sweeper's soot sack."

This was not reassuring to the mistress of Perryfield, and she cast a fretful look toward the drawing room door, as if debating whether to drag the men off by force.

Frances had taken a seat at the pianoforte and was turning over the sheets of music. "Do you never worry, Mrs. Rowland, that Mr. Rowland will fall asleep when he is smoking and set fire to the house?"

"Pah. Rowland always wakes up when the women go. He says it's the shrillness of female jabbering he can't stand. He must drowse in self-defense."

But poor Mr. Rowland's period of alertness was cut short that evening, for Frances was only halfway through her second piece when the doors opened and the gentlemen entered. Their appearance was so sudden that Jane was caught out, alone upon a settee because Cassie had risen to inspect the baron's bookcase. And then, before she could rise herself, Mr. Beck streaked across the room to drop down beside her.

"What a delightful air, Miss Barstow," he called over to Frances. "Pray continue, and do not let our entrance interrupt so charming a performance."

"Yes, yes, my dear," the baron seconded. "It has been some months since I had the pleasure of hearing this piece."

Without a word Frances obeyed, leaving the rest of the gentlemen to dispose themselves about the room and providing Mr. Beck with a cover for whatever he might choose to say to Jane.

He wasted no time.

Propping an immaculately tailored elbow along the back of the settee, he leaned toward her to murmur, "How abruptly you left Hardy and me, Mrs. Merritt, when we came upon you walking."

Jane edged away on the pretense of brushing a fleck of something from her skirts. "I would not have wanted Mrs. Dere to think me in any danger," she replied.

"Ah, but it was not *you* in danger."

Refusing to understand him, Jane gave an "mm" worthy of Mrs. Dere and fixed her eyes on Frances' back. Which did not prevent her from noticing they attracted almost equal interest as the fair piano-player. Mrs. Dere watched them surreptitiously. Miss Hynde watched them in her own attempt at stealth, but her lips pouted. Mr. Egerton watched them with not the least attempt at disguise, one brow lifted.

Familiar resentment flooded her. *I am doing* nothing *wrong. I was sitting here first, and I did not choose this place so that he might join me. My conscience is clear.*

"You will not ask me why I am in danger," sighed Mr. Beck. "Heartless creature."

Then Jane looked at him, temper still pulsing through her. "I do not ask you, sir, because this sort of talk is distasteful to me, and I wish you would forbear."

A muted chuckle twisted his mouth. "You quite fooled me at first, Mrs. Merritt." Giving an impatient click of her tongue, she turned away again, but it did not dismay him. "When I first met you—after our near accident—I told myself, 'Alex, there is the sweetest, most innocent rose—or, at least, as innocent a rose as a widow may be. Her very guilelessness perfumes the air. Her clear and artless gaze—'"

Whipping open her fan, Jane began to wave it furiously, as if his objectionable attentions were a miasma of coal smoke requiring a hurricane to be dispelled.

"But I have since learned," he continued, unperturbed by any atmospheric phenomena, "that your show of innocence is just that—a show. In fact, you have for some years been rusticating here to live down your notoriety, have you not?" Another mocking sigh in her ear, and Jane twitched to feel it brush her skin. "You must not think I reproach you with these things, Mrs. Merritt. Quite the contrary. I actually prefer women who know what they are about, and it took me entirely by surprise to find myself drawn by the opposite. Therefore, to discover I had come upon a paradox, two in one, embodying simultaneously innocence and experience...I declare, I am at your mercy."

"Then go away!" she hissed, driven beyond self-control. "If you are at my mercy, go away and leave me alone."

"That, alas, is the one thing I cannot do, even to please you."

Frances' second song mercifully ended here, and Jane sprang up to applaud, her fan falling to the carpet. "That was splendid. Just splendid."

Her younger sister stared at her, mortified that now everyone must affect similar enthusiasm for the modest sonatina, the gentlemen all on their feet, clapping politely.

"It was indeed," declared Mr. Beck. His heartiness was a balm to Frances, but he ruined it the next instant by turning to Jane and urging, "Might we prevail upon you next, Mrs. Merritt? I am at your service to turn your music or to accompany you with my voice."

And then Jane lied, out and out.

"I couldn't possibly," she answered. "Our little dog Poppet—I was playing with him and got him too stirred up, and he inadvertently bit my finger." She fluttered her gloved hand. "Therefore it has been somewhat stiff. But if you sing, sir, might one of the other ladies accompany you? I am certain I speak for all when I say it would be a treat to listen to you."

Mrs. Dere, Mrs. Rowland, and Miss Hynde all spoke over each other to volunteer, with the result that the latter two politely yielded to their hostess. With a proud lift of her chin, Mrs. Dere strode to the instrument, leaving Mr. Beck no alternative but to bow and follow.

Jane could have laughed in triumph at his fleeting grimace, but she permitted herself only the tiniest smile as she bent to retrieve her fan.

The settee gave a bounce as a vexed Frances dropped onto it. "Whatever made you call such attention to me?" she grumbled when the music resumed.

"I'm sorry, sweeting, but I had to get away from him and his unwanted attentions."

"Ah, that we all should suffer so! Doesn't he have an excellent voice, though, to go with his excellent person?"

"Handsome is as handsome does," replied Jane grimly. Even to her sister she could not repeat Mr. Beck's odious insinuations. That he should claim to like her better, for the things which she would prefer to forget! The things which caused her such grief, then and now. And to dare to mention "women who knew what they were about," as if Jane would take pride in being of their number!

If she disliked the man before, she detested him now, and brusqueness in her dealings with him no longer struck her as something to be avoided.

Surely people without courtesy were less particular about its absence in others?

"In any event, Frances, don't leave me alone the rest of the evening."

"I didn't mean to leave you alone then," her sister replied, "only the gentlemen returned sooner than I expected. No, no. I will cling to you faithfully."

However little pleasure his own singing brought Mr. Beck when not accompanied by the lady of his choice, his performance won general approbation. Miss Hynde, for one, listened as if it were a matter of life and death, leaning forward, eyes intent, hands clasped to her bosom. Egerton noticed, of course—he could only pray no one else did, for the girl was so artless. Though the man sang very well, any possible enjoyment Egerton might have derived was spoiled by Beck himself. What havoc the man was wreaking among Egerton's female acquaintance!

Egerton did not fault Miss Hynde for being fascinated by Beck. Young innocent that she was, it was only too natural that she be overwhelmed in her first encounter with a handsome, dashing London rake. It would be odd if she were not.

It would only be natural as well if jealousy of Beck were to gnaw at Egerton, but he felt miraculously intact and unharmed, and he could not help but feel complacent. *The man is not worthy of my jealousy.* Perhaps he might feel differently if Beck showed any signs of reciprocating Miss Hynde's foolish *tendre*, but he did not. Indeed, Beck hardly seemed to realize Felicity existed. If anything, his attentions were all for—had all been for—

It's disgraceful. Has he no respect for her and what she has endured?

From across the room Egerton's gaze had returned again and again to the pair, observing with rising indignation Beck's inexcusable leers and leans and murmurs. Mrs. Merritt's answering coolness, however—obvious to Egerton though he could not hear a word spoken—deserved praise. She alone of the ladies present appeared untouched by the man's charm. Most unexpected, considering her history.

Their last conversation having ended in mutual dissatisfaction, Egerton could not resist this opportunity to restore harmony, and when the tea was prepared and she rose to fetch her cup, he made haste to cross paths with her.

"Mrs. Merritt, I am sorry to hear of your injury," he began.

"My injury?" she repeated, her brow knitting. Her fingers drifted to her forehead. "But it's been better for quite some time now."

"I referred to Poppet biting your finger," he explained.

"Oh. That." Inexplicably she went crimson. "Er—thank you. It is nothing."

Smiling he said, "Perhaps not, but you have suffered more than your share of injuries lately, and I would have liked to hear you play." Not that he would have delighted in watching Beck turn pages for her or sing love songs while casting flirtatious, melting looks, but this assertion was true in the main.

"Mm," she returned vaguely. "Perhaps on another occasion."

When she retreated a step, intending to return to her seat, Egerton heard himself blurt, "Mrs. Merritt, if you would permit me to say...I fear I displeased you earlier, when I cautioned you toward a certain person. But I see my solicitude was unwarranted."

"As I said at the time." She spoke in such a muted voice that he had to bend his head to hear her beneath Beck's showy booming.

"Yes," he agreed, "you did say there was no need to worry. And that you hoped, with increased acquaintance would come increased trust. You were very right to say so, Mrs. Merritt, for so it is. I see, from your conduct, that you are in no—further—danger. Your...suspicious attitude toward him is—is praiseworthy."

Gladly would he have groaned and rapped his forehead with his knuckles at this awkward speech. Was it just his imagination, or was he becoming more priggish and affected by the hour? The very personification of *par*sonification? Why could he not simply say he had been misguided, assuming her past actions dictated her future choices? Why could he not simply say she had been right, and he had been wrong?

When she replied at last, his heart sank at the coolness of her manner.

"'Approbation from Sir Hubert Stanley is praise indeed,'" she quoted dryly, and had any of her family overheard, they would have delighted in this flash of her former sauciness. "If you will excuse me, Mr. Egerton..."

"A moment, Mrs. Merritt." His hand reached for her of its own accord, stopping just short of her forearm. "That—was not how I intended to sound. Officious and—presumptuous—I mean. As you observed last time, I may be your family priest in Mr. Terry's absence, but that need not make me a—a—a—a downright ass."

His reward for this humbling of himself was instant pardon and a smile which lit her face, warming him from tip to toe.

If this is the power of forgiveness, Egerton thought, *I may have to err again.*

Much later he was to wonder, if they been alone and without witnesses, what more might have been said or done?

For no more could be said or done in the moment.

Beck roared to his conclusion; Mrs. Rowland approached to refill Egerton's cup; Miss Barstow appeared at her sister's side and never left it again; and Egerton himself, with a stifled sigh, resumed his place beside the angelic Miss Hynde.

CHAPTER 15

'Tis but the shadow of a wife you see,
The name, and not the thing.
— Shakespeare, *All's Well That Ends Well*, V.iii.310
(c.1616)

Harry, what have you got there?"

The cluster composed of Harry and Jimmy and Anna's heads broke apart. The Cramthorpes' hunched shoulders and averted eyes bespoke guilt, but Harry grinned with mischief.

Jane held out a hand. "Let me have it."

"Now, now, miss."

"Let me have it."

With a shrug, the boy produced a crumpled piece of paper and placed it in her hand. "We were trying to *read*, miss, as you taught us."

"This doesn't look like the primer or the Bible to me," answered Jane, glancing down. "Oh!"

Snickers engulfed first Harry, then Jimmy.

In large, rounded script was written: "Alexander Beck. Mr. Alexander Beck. Mrs. Alexander Beck. Felicity Beck." These combinations were framed by drawings of hearts, vines, and flowers.

There was no question of the children having written it—they could barely copy the letters from the horn book. But did they understand what it said?

"Where did you find this, Harry? It clearly does not belong to you."

He swung his foot, kicking at the table leg. "It was on the floor."

"Of our schoolroom?" Jane asked incredulously.

Harry gave a slow shake of his rumpled head. "No...I saw it when I came back from the kitchen where Miss Egerton said I might go for some bread and cheese."

His teacher's eyebrow rose to indicate her opinion of this likely story. As if Miss Hynde would drop such a thing in the kitchen! It was far easier to imagine Harry Barbary making a few detours through the rectory and snatching up whatever caught his eye.

"Are you going to tell Miss Egerton, miss?"

"Perhaps." Jane wished Cassie were there now to manage the situation, but with the musical evening to take place later that same day, she had left the day's lessons to Jane. "In the future, Harry, you must leave everything just as you find it, or Miss Egerton will no longer allow you to wander through the house."

"But what does it say, miss?" demanded Harry incorrigibly. "Is it a love note?"

"It does not concern you, at any rate," Jane replied, folding the paper and tucking it in her sleeve. "Let us continue with our reciting. Anna, you begin..."

If the children managed to learn anything in the remaining minutes, Jane deserved no credit for it, her mind being occupied. Occupied with what had *not* been written in Miss Hynde's script. That is, there had been no "Philip Egerton. Mr. Philip Egerton. Mrs. Philip Egerton. Felicity Egerton."

It was none of her business, of course, whom Miss Hynde loved or did not love, and while Jane would not allow her conscious self to dream of Mr. Egerton, she was human enough to feel a guilty pleasure in Miss Hynde *not* dreaming of him.

But if everyone was so intent on warning Jane against the danger posed by Mr. Beck, should not Miss Hynde be equally on her guard? Especially if, unlike Jane herself, the girl was eager for his attentions.

With a shiver Jane remembered her younger self, and how she had been warned by her father against Roger Merritt. It served no purpose in the end, *that* Jane proving so flighty and blind and headstrong, but perhaps Miss Hynde would be more biddable.

And the warning should be given now, while Mr. Beck did not think of Miss Hynde, lest when he grew tired of Jane's indifference his efforts turned to the latter young lady for amusement.

Cassie will know what ought to be tried.

"Very well, children," she announced, absently cutting off Jimmy's recitation, "that will do for today. We will resume on Monday. Be sure to practice writing your alphabet—you might do it on a windowpane or in the air or by drawing a stick through dust, even. And repeat your verse so that you may tell it to Mr. Egerton next week."

"I could write the alphabet in a book with a pencil," said Harry Barbary, and had Jane not been distracted, this remark would have aroused her suspicion. As it was, other than a fleeting hope he had not come by these items through robbing the grocer again, she merely replied, "So you could. Goodbye. Goodbye."

The moment she heard the rectory door shut and their shouts and footsteps receding through the churchyard, Jane went in search of Cassie. Avoiding the drawing room, where she heard Miss Hynde singing and playing, and the curate's study, where she expected Mr. Egerton and his students had retreated, Jane peeped into the kitchen.

"Good morning, Winching. Have you seen Miss Egerton?"

Bobbing a curtsey, the cook said, "Not for a quarter hour, Mrs. Merritt, but she said she was going to arrange flowers for the drawing room."

She would just have to pry Cassie away, then.

Sure enough, when Jane entered, she found Miss Hynde at Mrs. Terry's old Zumpe square piano and Cassie placing fronds in a vase.

"Jane! Have they gone? What do you think? I haven't as many flowers as I would like, this late in the year, but these look well, do they not?"

Miss Hynde halted on a jangling chord, whipping around to favor Jane with a chilly nod.

"Please, don't let me interrupt. Cassie, the vases look lovely, but may I speak to you a moment apart—about Harry Barbary?"

"That sounds ominous," chuckled Cassie, laying the remaining fronds aside and following Jane from the room as Miss Hynde turned slowly back to leaf through her music.

In the dim passage, Jane thrust the paper in her friend's hand. "On one of his exploratory jaunts through the house, Harry found this. I caught him showing it to Jimmy and Anna, though none of them could read it. But, from the...embellishments they guessed at its import."

Squinting at the writing, Cassie drew a sharp breath. "Oh. Oh, dear. Oh dear oh dear."

"I leave it to you to deal with, Cassie," Jane whispered, "only I feel duty-bound to say that—that I do not believe the man in question to be—the sort of person a young lady ought to—set her heart upon, if it can be avoided—He is not—"

"How dare you!" screeched a high voice, and then there was Miss Hynde among them, red and snatching at the paper. "How dare you read my personal things! How dare you take what is private and discuss it behind my back?"

"Miss Hynde!"

"Felicity!"

The girl burst into tears of embarrassment and rage. Crumpling the note in her fist, she then shook that fist at Jane. "Has no one ever told you not to read private correspondence? But I suppose a person like you hasn't any scruples! You ought to be ashamed of yourself, Mrs. Merritt!"

"Miss Hynde," gasped Jane, shocked at both the suddenness and the vigor of the attack, "I did not—it was not—I did not mean—"

"And how dare you cast aspersions on him?" Miss Hynde's voice rose, her whole person shaking. "How dare you—you *impugn* another's character, when you—when you—as if you were one to talk! As if you were one to sit in judgment! Why, I should—"

"Miss Hynde."

In such a rumpus, Mr. Egerton's tread had gone unheard, but the sound of his level, firm voice cut through the tension and clamor at once. The three young ladies fell apart, Jane having to steady herself against the wall, her knees like water.

Cassandra was the only one in any condition to speak, and while she had no desire to take sides against the girl who might one day be her sister (as unlikely as that was beginning to appear), nor to be caught between potential lovers in a quarrel, her native honesty could not be denied.

"Brother, it seems that Harry Barbary picked up a scrap of paper, which Mrs. Merritt then confiscated and showed to me—"

"After she read it herself," sobbed Miss Hynde.

"The writing upon it concerned Felicity's private matters," Cassie went on. "Therefore she was...distressed."

"Miss Hynde," Jane finally schooled herself enough to say, "I understand your—discomfiture. But—I had to look at it, in order to know what should be done. One of the reasons I chose to give the note to Cassie was that she might decide what to do, if anything. I knew you would not like anyone—to have seen it, and I thought to spare you that knowledge by drawing Cassie apart—"

But Miss Hynde only cried the harder, covering her face with both hands and fleeing, a task more easily done with one's eyes open, for she ran straight into the wall and then the door jamb (adding insult to injury) before getting safely away.

"Mercy," muttered Cassie.

"Mercy," her brother repeated with a low whistle.

Cassie threw him a grim glance. "You had better let me take care of this, Philip. It will be less trying for her."

"If you think so," he answered. "If it helps, you might tell her that I do not ask to be told the contents of the note. I warrant she'll think the fewer people who have seen it, the better."

"That's for sure. Though I daresay you hardly needed this straw to know which way the wind blows." Blowing out a breath, she turned toward the stairs. "'Bye, Jane. See you later this evening."

When Cassie was gone an awkward little pause fell.

"I—believe I will go home now," said Jane.

"You're white as a cloth," he replied. "Perhaps you had better sit down a minute."

"No, thank you. I'm perfectly well."

But when she released the wall, she swayed and might have slid to the floor, had Mr. Egerton not caught her by the upper arm.

His grip made short work of her pallor. Heat shot up her arm from where he held it, from arm to shoulder to breast to neck to face, and when she inhaled sharply, her eyes meeting his, she found his countenance as suddenly scarlet as her own.

It was over in an instant. He released her as quickly as if she were a burning log he had shifted by hand, and Jane was equally flustered. She must leave. Be gone—before he guessed the cause of her agitation! Retreating, she collided with the wall as clumsily as Miss Hynde had, before fleeing, praying her face had not been read as easily as the girl's note.

Philip Egerton. Mr. Philip Egerton. Mrs. Philip Egerton. Jane Egerton.

Hours later, when dinner had been eaten and darkness fallen, the Iffley Cottage family made the walk to the rectory for the musical evening, Jane finding comfort in the safety of numbers. Not only the adults had been invited on this occasion, but also Gordon and Maria, to their delight. Thus surrounded by a hedge of five Barstows, Jane did not suppose either a tiresome Mr. Beck or a still-angry Miss Hynde could come near her, not that she was thinking overmuch of either of them.

No, she thought only of Mr. Egerton. Mr. Egerton, from whom she must now also hide, metaphorically speaking, until she succeeded in quashing the painful emotions welling up. Who would have thought she could lose her heart again, after all the disasters which had befallen her?

The real question is, how could I not lose my heart to him, worthy man that he is?

But worthy or not, he would never think of her in a million years, and therefore she must forget him. She must endure the next few months until the Terrys returned, and then Mr. Egerton would go away, never to be seen again.

One could not give up someone who had never belonged to one, but it still cost Jane many a pang to think she must relinquish even the possibility of friendship with him.

But she must.

Because the morning had been a very near thing, and what would happen if he were ever to discover her secret?

Jane almost thought she would rather return to the squalid shared quarters she occupied in the Fleet Prison than suffer Mr. Egerton to gaze on her with pity and dismay. Still harder to bear would be his chosen bride's certain triumph—but how could Miss Hynde feel otherwise, after Jane had inadvertently had her at such a disadvantage?

But would Mr. Egerton still court Miss Hynde, marry Miss Hynde, when she bore feelings for another? Or was he not aware? Though Cassie had implied he could guess the contents of Miss Hynde's note, what if he could not? Or what if, once cautioned, Miss Hynde conquered her tendre for Mr. Beck, just as Jane intended to conquer her affections for Mr. Egerton? Miss Hynde was young and susceptible to charm, as Jane had once been, but Jane could not suppose Miss Hynde would remain blind long to a man of Mr. Egerton's quality beneath her very nose. Indeed, Jane firmly believed she herself would not have been swept away by Roger Merritt had there been someone better with whom to compare him.

Surely before too long the scales would fall from Miss Hynde's eyes, and then—ah, then—then Jane would have to bear watching them smile upon each other and bear hearing their engagement announced. And Mr. Egerton's hand would clasp Miss Hynde's arm, not for fear of her collapsing, but simply because he rejoiced to call her his own.

At least nothing Jane feared had yet come about, for when the Barstow company entered the milling drawing room, Miss Hynde stood beside neither of the Egertons. Instead she leaned on her instrument, showing Tom Ellis a piece of music while he gazed on her, stupefied, as if he had sustained a blow to the head but not yet fallen over.

Mr. Egerton Jane dared not look at, but she was nonetheless aware of him at all times: where he stood, whom he greeted or chatted with, whether he looked at Miss Hynde (he did not, nor she at him). Mr. Egerton and Miss Hynde might be fated for each other, but there had at least been no éclaircissement since the morning. Reprehensible or not, this last observation could not but soothe Jane's spirits a little and bring a half smile to her lips.

"You are complacent, Mrs. Merritt," came the unwelcome voice of Mr. Beck, accompanied by his equally unwelcome person directly before her, blocking all else from view. "What mysterious source of joy brings the rare boon of a smile to your lips?"

Honestly. Were there women who appreciated such nonsense?

"I look forward to the music, sir."

The man put a hand to his breast and bowed, as if she had paid him a compliment, and too late Jane realized it might be understood as praise of his singing at Perryfield. "Do you—sing again tonight, Mr. Beck?"

"As you guessed, Mrs. Merritt, I do indeed. At the Perryfield dinner Miss Hynde asked me in particular if I would lend my modest talents to our little entertainment. Did she not ask you as well? I do not mind telling you how determined I am to hear you perform. She has not asked. I can see from your expression that she has not. Mrs. Merritt, I here give you notice that I intend to lodge a petition for you to be included."

Given Miss Hynde's feelings toward both Mr. Beck and Jane herself, this was the last thing Jane wanted, and she was obliged to affect a wheedling tone. "I thank you, but I beg you might defer this wish, sir. I know how carefully both Miss Hynde and Miss Egerton have planned this evening, and I could not forgive myself or you if we were to spoil things."

Another elegant bow. (Jane resisted a childish urge to bring her knee up to meet his broad forehead.) "I cannot refuse you, Mrs. Merritt, when you ask so sweetly. But in return, would you grant me the second two dances of the Greenwood ball? I must give the first to Mrs. Dere, as is due her rank, but if you would honor me with the next..."

With a reply barely more formed than a grunt, Jane conceded, thanking God the next moment when Cassie clapped her hands for everyone's attention and bade them be seated. Stupid Mr. Beck of course looked right and left for where he might find a chair next to hers, but she had foreseen this and glided away to take the place saved for her between Frances and Sarah.

Miss Hynde was a clever and charming musician, Jane had to admit, choosing pieces which displayed her voice and skills to advantage. And when Mr. Beck joined her in a duet, a hum of admiring murmurs arose. Jane thought Mr. Hardy might burst with esteem for his friend, and even Mr. Rowland started awake at one particularly pleasing harmony and muttered, "Fine, fine. Dashed fine."

Jane allowed herself just one peep at Mr. Egerton, to gauge his response. Did he too hear the whispers calling Mr. Beck and Miss Hynde a handsome couple, whose performance was "dashed fine"?

He was at his most severe, sitting straightly, mouth thinned. He did hear the others, then, and he did not like it.

Unconsciously, Jane mirrored him, her own person straightening and mouth thinning. Yes, she understood. Jealousy was, of all emotions, the most unpleasant. And Mr. Beck was, for all his shortcomings, a good-looking, eligible man who might easily steal Miss Hynde, if he chose to.

Again she wondered if he knew the contents of Miss Hynde's note, and if he did, if he had spoken to her about it. Did he frown now because his beloved scorned his warning, or did he frown because he could not help but fear the loss of her?

There was no way of knowing, and Jane dared not study him longer.

Miss Hynde and Mr. Beck were followed by Cassie Egerton, who played twice as well for a fraction of the attention and approbation. If Jane had not made such a spectacle of herself at Perryfield applauding Frances' performance, she would have been tempted to do so now, because it was so unfair, but instead she promised herself she would certainly take Cassie aside and tell her at the first opportunity.

CHAPTER 16

Charity and beating begins at home.
— John Fletcher, *With without Money* (1639)

October turned to November, and on every tongue and mind in Iffley was the Greenwood ball. Even those with no hope of an invitation expected to derive good from the occasion, especially the shopkeepers, the tailors and dressmakers, and the stables of the Tree Inn. And many who lived in Oxford during term time planned on returning to their Iffley homes in order to attend.

"You must all come to Perryfield to practice your dancing," Mrs. Dere insisted. "I declare, it has been so long since I attended an assembly or ball that I won't know my left foot from my right when Mr. Beck leads me to the top of the room."

The Barstows answered the summons, of course, but it was no hardship because they too feared rustiness, and a happy Mrs. Dere made life easier than an unhappy one. A happy Mrs. Dere granted precious items like surplus ribbon, lace, and satin to trim their gowns and caps, as well as the loan of pendants, bracelets, jeweled combs, and rings. This largesse extended even to Jane, to whom she presented a lace cloak only slightly crumpled with damp ("but that will make it hang more softly").

"Thank you, Mrs. Dere," Jane replied, trying to hide her surprise and bracing for the sly stab of the knife which often followed.

Sure enough, it came.

"I must praise you for your conduct of late, Mrs. Merritt," Mrs. Dere pronounced, watching magnanimously as Jane shook out the cloak and ran an appreciative finger over the double-press point lace edging. "Unlike that foolish Miss Hynde, you have not thrown yourself at the head of Mr. Beck, no matter how handsome he may be."

"There is no danger of that, madam," replied Jane quietly.

"*I* would throw myself at his head, Mrs. Dere," declared Frances with the boldness of a favorite, "only I suspect Mr. Beck would duck, and I should go flying clear over."

"How you love to tease me," returned Mrs. Dere fondly, "but if I am not mistaken, it is your sister Mrs. Merritt whom Mr. Beck has his eye upon."

With an effort Jane managed not to wring the lace in her hands. "I don't know about that, madam."

"Indeed? Has he not spoken words to that effect when he whispers to you in gatherings?"

"Mrs. Dere, Jane cannot be blamed for—" began Mrs. Barstow, driven to defend her most vulnerable child from this attack, but it was Jane herself who interrupted her.

"He has," she admitted, "but I have told him that I do not like it. I cannot help having to answer him when he addresses me, nor could I think of an excuse to refuse to dance with him at the ball, but be assured I take no pleasure in it."

"Are you certain he does not tempt you at all, Mrs. Merritt?" probed Mrs. Dere. "Such a dashing man of the world. Was not your Mr. Roger such a specimen?"

"He was," Jane allowed with reluctance.

"And Mr. Beck has the advantage of money."

"Money or no, it is all equal to me," Jane insisted. "Miss Hynde is welcome to him. *Anyone* is, though I too would advise Frances to look elsewhere. I have no designs on him—not now and not ever. I have learned my lesson."

Her earnestness proved persuasive. Mrs. Dere even favored her with a nod of belated approval. "Very good, Mrs. Merritt. How does the saying go? 'That man must daily wiser grow, whose search is bent himself to know.'"

Mrs. Dere's maxim, however useful a reminder it might be to the general populace, was by this point second nature to Jane. Who else had more time to know herself? Who else had more cause to wish herself wiser?

And what she had learned about herself might be summarized in a short list:

1. Contrary to what novels taught, it was possible to be in love more than once in one's life.

2. Love could be doomed for myriad reasons.

3. Resisting love was a hundred times more difficult than yielding to it, and which was ultimately more painful remained for her to discover.

4. The good thing about having been unhappy for two years was that, when a new cause for unhappiness appeared, everyone still blamed the old cause. Which was accurate in one sense, for the new cause stemmed directly from lingering consequences of the old. And,

5. She rather liked teaching.

This last finding provided welcome variety to her darker meditations, and to her amazement it was Harry Barbary she particularly enjoyed. For while the Cramthorpes were diligent pupils, it must also be recorded that Jimmy was rather dull and Anna rather scatter-brained. But Harry—Harry was clever. And, still better, Harry was curious.

"Miss—how do I write my name?" "How do I write your name?" "How do I write like the writing in the note?" "Why does the alphabet look different in your writing than in the hornbook?"

While Jimmy and Anna still took pains to form their letters, Jimmy with his tongue between his teeth as he wrote and Anna producing virtual hieroglyphics, Harry was soon capable of a legible—if not an elegant—running hand. Jane began to have visions of the boy becoming a useful member of the community. Why, instead of stealing from Mrs. Lamb or Mr. Linn, if they could be brought to pardon his past sins, he might become a worthy assistant to them! An errand boy who could read directions on letters or tally columns of figures.

Yes, Jane rather liked teaching.

So it was something of a shock the very morning of the Greenwood ball when Harry brought a sheet of paper to her with some of his new writing on it. He waited to produce it until Cassie had stepped out with Anna to clean her dripping nose.

"Look, miss," Harry said.

"Oh, no, what have you got this time, Harry? Where did you find it?"

"This is mine!" he protested. "I've written a sentence about you, but you tell me what you think of it."

"A sentence! Goodness. But where did you get this piece of paper, Harry?"

"I found it somewhere," he said without a blush.

Frowning, Jane considered pursuing this further, but her eye fell upon the writing, and she at once forgot about the paper's provenance.

"'Mrs. Merritt,'" she read under her breath, "'deserving of charity for her ill-advised marriage.'"

"Oh, ho!" cried Harry, bouncing on his bench with eagerness. "I worked out some of it! 'Deserving' because it was like 'desert,' like 'our fathers did eat manna in the desert,' but 'charity'—I didn't know what 'c' and 'h' are together."

"They usually make a 'ch' sound," Jane replied automatically. "As in 'church' or 'change.'"

But her heart was hammering. If Harry did not even know what he wrote, he must have copied it.

"Harry—where did you see this sentence?"

For the first time, he looked wary, but he wiped his features blank and nipped the sheet from her fingers. "I can't rightly say, miss. But I wrote it down in hopes it said something better. I hoped it said you deserved something better. Like having your hand shook or your cheek pinched."

But Jane was adding two and two and making four.

"Harry—some time ago, you mentioned writing the alphabet in a book with a pencil."

"Did I?" He sounded easy, but Jane noticed Jimmy Cramthorpe suddenly hunching lower at the table and feigning deep interest in his work.

"You did," she answered. "And I thought it odd at the time but soon forgot about it. How do you happen to have a book at home, or a pencil?"

"I didn't steal it from Mr. Linn!" he declared. "I—I found it. Them, rather."

"Like you 'found' the note with the hearts and flowers the other day?" (Jimmy by this point was hunching so low Jane thought he might do better simply to crawl under the table. But there was no use interrogating the younger boy because Harry would no doubt make him pay later for any tale-telling done now.)

"...Maybe..."

"They must be returned at once," she commanded. "I—will not ask where you found them, the book which contained this sentence and the pencil which wrote it, but you must put them back."

"Now, miss, are you going to peach me?"

"No. I am not." It was the entire truth. The very last thing in the whole world which Jane wanted to do was to march up to Mr. Philip Egerton, his stolen book of parish notes in hand, and inform him that Harry had shared its contents with her. And the *second* to the very last thing in the whole world which she wanted to do was to discuss it further with Harry Barbary.

"But this must stop. Promise me, Harry, or I will tell Miss Egerton and leave it to her what should be done."

Considering where he had found the items and how much he liked his time at the rectory, Harry would prefer not to cross its current mistress. "I promise," he said.

"Then we will say no more about it."

The lesson continued; Cassie and Anna returned; the lesson ended.

"Winching has bread and butter for you in the kitchen before you go," Cassie told them as they scraped their chairs back.

Harry threw one glance at Jane, each understanding the other, and then he dashed from the room.

Cassie seized Jane's hands and twirled her in a circle. "There, that's done, and now we have the ball to look forward to. I know you don't want to dance with you-know-who, but at least you have a partner for two sets. What if nobody asks me but Philip? I will insist he stand up with me twice, then."

"Nonsense," said Jane, going rather red. "Mrs. Dere was counting all the gentlemen who would be present, and she thinks the numbers will be very even."

"That's a mercy. I believe Lord Dere sends his coach for us after they have picked you up, so Philip may freeze again in the outside seat. If the chill renders him clumsy, have no fear, Jane. Dancing with Felicity and me will limber him before we send him your way."

But it was not Mr. Egerton's possible clumsiness Jane feared.

It was facing him again, now that she knew how he looked upon her. Now that she understood each of their previous encounters in this new light. Not the light of courtesy or kindness or understanding. Nor the light of growing friendship.

No. A different light altogether. A crushing one.

"Deserving of charity."

If Greenwood Hall had put its best foot foremost for the card party, for the ball it positively dazzled. In addition to candles and lanterns, swags of autumn and hothouse flowers garlanded the entry and ground-floor windows.

"My word!" breathed Miss Hynde as the Perryfield coach drew to a halt, patting the silk rosebuds in her own hair. "It quite puts one to shame."

Somebody had to demur, but with Mr. Egerton perched with the coachmen outside it fell to a chorus of Barstow women to insist that, no, no, she looked lovely. Miss Hynde probably could have spared Jane's approbation, but she fluttered prettily and thanked them before Harker opened the door and unfolded the steps.

Miss Hynde was not the only one looking lovely. While Jane wore no rosebuds in her hair, Frances had insisted one of Mrs. Dere's cast-off ribbons be wound throughout, this one a rich red to complement Jane's dark tresses. A second of these ribbons, her only other adornment, enwrapped the high waist of her muslin gown beneath Mrs. Dere's lace cape. All the rest which pleased those who saw her—her eyes, her regular features, her pleasing person, the color which flooded her cheeks—was simply Jane herself.

"Mrs. Merritt."

Jane had unwittingly stood where Mr. Egerton must spring down, so they could not avoid looking at each other, but she dropped her eyes nearly at once to the gravel as she made her curtsey. His gaze lingered however, taking in her tout ensemble, before Cassie and Miss Hynde took an arm on either side, that he might lead them to the entrance.

"He must have invited additional London friends," murmured Sarah beside her, "because I doubt Iffley holds this many people."

In spite of herself, Jane was awed. Daunted, even.

Had she truly spoken curtly to this glittering society man? What a dunce he must think her! Who was Jane Merritt but a country nobody, whose only venture into the greater world ended in disgrace. Who was she to resent his flirtations? Flirtations which certainly meant nothing to him, which cost him nothing. The very fact that Jane took umbrage at them only emphasized her naïveté. But how else could she respond? Flirting with him in turn was unthinkable.

I must keep my temper. If I neither encourage him nor amuse him by firing up, he will soon weary of the sport and turn his attentions elsewhere. This has only gone on so long because I foolishly played into his hands.

Along with pretending Mr. Egerton did not exist, this would make her second unbreakable resolution, and Jane hoped fervently she would have more success with this one. Greeting the hosts was the first hurdle, as Mr. Beck stood beside the Rowlands and the inevitable Mr. Hardy to receive his guests. With a peep at her mother and Sarah, Jane pasted what she prayed was a copy of their unsmiling-but-serene expression across her own features. She made her curtsey. Her gaze skimmed across the London party without a hitch, and then she was free to follow her family up the stairs.

On the first floor, lines of smoke-darkened portraits stared at the transformation of their long gallery into a ballroom, with musicians tuning their instruments on a raised platform at the near end and tables holding light refreshments at the other, doors along the length opening onto a passage lined with rooms for cards and the supper.

The gathering throng buzzed with anticipation, and acquaintances were pounced upon as if after a long absence, though most of the conversation consisted of praise of their surroundings. Kind Lord Dere asked each of the Barstow ladies and Jane for a dance, saying, "At your convenience, my dears. I will always be found here, so if you ever find yourself without a partner and would like to dance, you need only come and tell me."

"May I have you for the first, then?" asked Frances at once. "Unless, Mama, you would like to be first."

"Goodness, no, child," Mrs. Barstow laughed. "I know you are dying to dance, so how could I be happy if you had no partner? But when you have done your duty by us, dear baron, you must promise me you will then do whatever you like."

He bowed in acquiescence, but his smile was so tranquil that Jane knew he thought his duty no burden. It was this sweetness of his that emboldened her to say, "Lord Dere—would you mind dreadfully if I asked you to ask Miss Egerton as well? Cassie feared only her brother would, and you will find her a charming partner."

"It would be an honor. Only bring her to stand by you, and if I look in danger of going unclaimed by one of you, I will ask her at once."

It was a comfort for Jane to know she would have at least one respectable partner with whom she need not tread upon eggs. And indeed, she should also consider herself lucky that, if she had to dance twice with Mr. Beck, at least she would have done with it early.

Would Mr. Egerton consider asking her to dance an act of charity? Jane did not know, and she was afraid that wishing he would hardly accorded with her resolve to forget him.

"Mrs. Merritt, if you are at liberty to open the ball with me, I would be glad of it."

She turned to find Mr. Hardy at her elbow, though why he should be there was a puzzle. As if he guessed her bemusement, he said, "Beck told me to keep an eye on you and make sure you had a partner."

Biting the inside of her cheek, Jane managed to swallow her indignation, though inwardly she fumed. Keep an eye on her, indeed! What business of it was his if she had no partner? The impudence of the man! As if being singled out for Mr. Egerton's pity were not bad enough—now Mr. Beck must hover over her in possessive care?

Fortunately nobody noticed her vexation, moving as they all were to find their partners. Jane placed her hand upon Hardy's arm (perhaps a trifle more firmly than the occasion called for) and allowed him to lead her out. But when he headed for the top of the room where Mr. Beck and Mrs. Dere stood, her pressure grew heavier, dragging on him.

"Come, come. Don't be shy," said Hardy.

"I'd prefer to be further down," Jane insisted. "It is easier to keep the figures in mind with a few repetitions before we have to change from first to second couple, or vice versa."

"Good point. Very well. Here?"

"Here" had its own drawbacks, being but three couples below Mr. Egerton and Miss Hynde. But at least the latter were also beginning the dance as a second couple, so that with any luck Jane and Mr. Hardy might never be in the same foursome with them. It did mean, however, that Jane would have to make a greater effort not to look in their direction, since the figures would require her and Mr. Hardy always to face toward them as they traveled up the room.

Mr. Hardy, being free of similar conditions, was already twisting to peer up his side of the set, no doubt to catch Mr. Beck's eye and indicate all was arranged to a wish.

So be it, Jane thought. With the number of couples standing up it would be, at most, twenty minutes of her life.

The music began, and she stepped forward to clasp Mr. Hardy's hand.

CHAPTER 17

—Grandmamma, what great teeth you have got!
—*That is to eat thee up.*
And saying these words, the wicked Wolf fell upon Little Red
Riding-Hood and eat her all up.
— Robert Samber, trans., *Histories, or tales of passed times.*
***With morals. Written in French by M. Perrault* (1741)**

Jane blamed Mr. Hardy for wasting her efforts when their dance ended. She had succeeded marvelously, sailing through the patterns without once letting Mr. Egerton creep beyond the periphery of her vision and forgetting all about Mr. Beck. She had even succeeded in enjoying herself, for, despite his failings, Mr. Hardy danced creditably and spoke just enough to banish awkwardness.

But, alas, when the dance ended and he straightened from his bow, he took Jane's hand and said, "Let me deliver you to Beck, who tells me he has claimed the two next."

Objecting to being handed over like a parcel of goods, Jane resisted. "Thank you, but I would like to return to my mother's side."

"Your mother's side? Pooh! You're no fifteen-year-old girl, Mrs. Merritt. Come."

He tugged; she stood firm. The other dancers leaving the floor flowed around them, except for Mr. Egerton and Miss Hynde.

"Good evening again, Mrs. Merritt," said Mr. Egerton, adding with a nod, "Hardy."

Jane made the mistake of looking straight at him because how could she help it, if he popped up before her? She hadn't had time to prevent it, and her heart gave a little electric jump. The buff of his silk waistcoat brought out the gold streaks in his brown hair, and in the folds of his neckcloth a peridot studded his tie-pin, the stone gleaming like a third hazel eye.

"Would you do me the honor of standing up with me for the next dance, Mrs. Merritt?"

"Oh, I like that, Mr. Egerton," said Miss Hynde tartly. "Would you rather I find my own way back to Cassie?"

"Felicity, of course I would see you back first—"

"She can't dance with you next," blurted Hardy. "Already got a partner."

"Mr. Hardy, I also have a tongue and am perfectly able to answer the questions put to me."

"The third dance, then?"

"She's got a partner for *both*, Egerton."

"Mr. Hardy, for heaven's sake—"

"The *same* partner, matter of fact—here he comes."

Seeing Beck shouldering his way toward them, Mrs. Dere on his arm, Jane stuffed down a groan of frustration. And she should not have been sorry when Mr. Egerton muttered, "Another time, perhaps," and moved off with Miss Hynde, but she was. And she should not have let Mrs. Dere's look, half-approving and half-remember-what-I-said-to-you-ing, vex her, but she did. Therefore the smile she turned on her new partner was forced and did not reach her cheeks, much less her eyes.

Some gentlemen would have hesitated, to see their fair partner regard them thus, but Beck considered it all part of the game, and he grinned at her enough for two people. "Shall we, Mrs. Merritt?"

And before Mrs. Dere could complain of ill-usage as Miss Hynde had, the faithful Hardy sprang into the breach, crying, "Mrs. Dere, I dare not believe your hand unclaimed for the next, but if I should be so fortunate...?"

She would leave all the talking to him, Jane vowed.

But this being the second dance of the evening, far more pairs were joining the set, so that the lines stretched nearly the length of the gallery. Thirty minutes, if not longer, she calculated. And she had promised him *two* dances! A solid hour in each other's company.

As Mr. Beck said nothing himself, only regarding her with bright and annoying curiosity, as if to see what the wild animal he had captured might do, Jane had time to take herself in hand once more.

I must be courteous and impervious to provocation. Because he would—here she blinked at her flash of insight—*because he would then find me dull!* And the key to ridding herself of Mr. Beck must surely, surely lie in being dull. Had he not confessed as much, when he first called at Iffley Cottage? The man was always in search of amusement. Let Jane smother him in *ennui*, then! Yes, let her make the best use of the hour ahead.

"What a faithful lieutenant Mr. Hardy is," was her humdrum opening.

"What? Oh, Hardy. Yes. Somewhat of a dull dog, but loyal as one. What he lacks in sparkle he makes up for in tenacity." They cast outward, and when he led her back up he pressed her hand, but she ignored it utterly.

"How did you meet him?" she asked.

"School. When we were boys scarcely older than Archie." He shrugged the topic away, now raising one eyebrow at her and twitching his lips in what she supposed he thought a tempting manner. She merely blinked at him, and then he must wipe his expression blank before he crossed with Mrs. Lane.

"Speaking of Archie, how does he like his new situation?" was her next attempt. "Do you never think of having him at Greenwood Hall with you?"

"Never. How chatty you are tonight, Mrs. Merritt. But while I daresay most people enjoy speaking of themselves, I myself am perfectly devoured by curiosity about *you*."

This caused the first break in Jane's serene exterior, and she answered a trifle too quickly, "Indeed? Well—how unlucky—because it happens that I don't like to speak of myself either." At least, not with the Alexander Becks of the world.

"Then we must take turns bearing the onus," he replied. "But to demonstrate my good faith, I will confess to you that I do not prefer, in fact, to be under the same roof as my ward. It is a sign of growing wisdom, do you not think, Mrs. Merritt, always to prefer the bright, unsullied future to the errors and pitfalls of the past?"

Startled, Jane was late to cross with Dr. Lane on her diagonal and had to fly at him to keep up, causing the Oxford don's wispy beard to bob in alarm. She flashed him an apologetic smile, but her mind was on her partner's words. Was this finally an admission from Mr. Beck that he was, in fact, Archie Wilson's father?

The foursome went in circle (Mr. Beck administering another hand squeeze), and then Jane and her partner progressed up the room.

"You ask me no questions," Mr. Beck observed.

"It—is not my place to inquire into another's past errors and pitfalls," said Jane.

This drew another grin from him. "Never say you are losing your courage, Mrs. Merritt! While your earlier escapades no doubt brought you some notoriety, in some quarters they only rendered you more alluring."

"So you said earlier," she answered curtly, feeling her grasp on her temper slipping.

"And have you nothing to say in return? Mrs. Merritt, having proven yourself a woman of few compunctions, I have been not only drawn to you, as I have made clear, but my London acquaintance would marvel to witness my patience. At first I hung back, believing you a true innocent. But when I learned your story, my patience abandoned me, as did any desire to indulge you in these shows of pretended modesty. Admit it—don't they also begin to pall for you?"

"Shows of pretended modesty"? "*Shows*"?

Like tinder at the application of a match, Jane's self-command went up in flame, and it was all she could do to shut her eyes, lest lethal beams shoot out of them. Mr. Egerton's penetrating gaze was child's play in comparison, though, as a matter of fact, the progression of the dance had brought Mr. Egerton and his partner looping back down toward Jane and Mr. Beck, and the curate's keen eyes did indeed catch the flash in Jane's before she hid it.

"Mr. Beck," she said in a shaking voice, opening her eyes again, "I believe I would like to sit down."

Instead of appearing chastened, there was a gleam in his own blue eyes. "Ah. To be sure. Can you manage one more time through the figures? At the bottom of the set we may slip away with no harm done to the other couples."

She was too overset to remark his use of "we" and merely nodded. She even felt a degree of gratitude and relief to hear him make the necessary excuses: "Pardon us—the exertion and heat of the room—I will certainly speak to the servants about opening another window—" And poor Jane was still innocent enough to think that, as he led her away through one of the doors, across the passage, into the library, he would leave her there in peace to recover.

Not so.

Scarcely had he directed her to the sofa by the fire than he took hold of her upper arms and pulled her against him, hair gleaming, teeth gleaming, eyes gleaming.

"What are you about, Mr. Beck? Release me at once!"

"Come, come, Mrs. Merritt," he purred. "There is no audience here, to appreciate your little act."

"It is—no—act!"

"Mm...I rather like the struggling, though."

His grip on her was so tight that Jane's wriggling and writhing availed her nothing, and he was too close to kick, though she managed to stamp once on his boot before he wrapped her fully in his arms, pressing her against his full length.

"I will scream, sir!"

But this only drew a chuckle. "If you think to compromise me by doing so, I warn you that I am not overcareful of my reputation. Your first adventure ended badly, but why not try again, my dear? We might have a good deal of fun, and I can at least promise you won't end penniless in the Fleet. Ask Archie's mother, if you doubt me."

By this point tears of helpless rage filled Jane's eyes. "Do me the honor of believing me, sirrah. I can do nothing to change the past or my ruined reputation, but I would never, never, *never* accept your disgraceful offer, not if it were the only thing between me and eternity in the Fleet! Never, never, ne—"

But Mr. Beck, blinded by his past success with other women and determined to possess this lovely creature despite her tiresome protestations, could stand no more. With a groan of desire and conquest, he smashed his lips to hers, swallowing up her never-ending "nevers."

"Mm...mm...ah...mm...Aaah!" The man's noisy enjoyment quite drowned Jane's squeals, even while he held her locked, and his mouth pressed so hard she feared he would knock her teeth into her throat. He kissed and kissed and kissed her, if kissing it could be called. Roger had certainly never assaulted her like this, even at the last, when in despair and in his cups.

Mercy—when would it end? Did he not need to breathe? She herself thought she would faint shortly. Well, perhaps that would be for the better. She was so little a participant in this activity that he might not even notice her absence.

Only a sound of near thunderous loudness could recall Mr. Beck to his senses, but the sound did, at long last, come.

"What—is—the—meaning—of—this?" bellowed the too-familiar voice of Mrs. Markham Dere. And Jane prayed it wasn't a sign of growing shamelessness that, when her unlikely savior broke the spell, between feelings of horror and relief, relief was uppermost.

Mr. Beck lifted his head, releasing what remained of Jane's poor lips but not loosening his hold on her person. And after his onslaught, Jane did not think she could straighten her neck to save her life, but she managed to turn her head a little, both to see Mrs. Dere and to deal with the horror portion all in a lump.

But the lump proved greater than imagined. For Mrs. Dere was not alone. She was accompanied by Sarah Barstow (not a problem), Lord Dere (also not a problem), Mrs. Rowland (probably not a problem because Mr. Beck's ways would not surprise her), Miss Hynde (this might be where problems would begin), and Mr. Egerton (a problem from top to bottom).

"What has happened?" asked Mr. Beck, not at all dismayed. "Has the music stopped? The house caught fire? What brings you all here, when there is a perfectly good ball in progress in the other room?"

When no one had a ready answer to this lazy impudence, he nodded toward Mrs. Dere. "But that was discourteous of me, Mrs. Dere. You asked a question. I know you have been widowed several years, but what you just interrupted was, in fact, lovemaking."

"It was not!" protested Jane, but through her bruised and numb lips this emerged as "Iff waff wah!"

Then several things happened at once: Mrs. Rowland thoughtfully shut the library doors; Miss Hynde burst into tears, covering her face; Mr. Egerton stepped forward, jaw set and hands balled in fists; and Lord Dere quietly moved in front of the curate, raising a hand.

"Mr. Beck, unless we have interrupted a proposal of marriage—and an acceptance—I demand an explanation," the baron said in his quiet, steady way.

Then her assailant did loose Jane, leaving her to collapse onto the red velvet sofa when her knees failed to support her, and he turned to address Lord Dere. Beck might be a reprobate, but rank was rank and the questions of a baron not to be waved away.

"Lord Dere, I recognize Mrs. Merritt is a cousin of yours, of sorts. But she is also, like many of your dependents, a widow and fully of age. Therefore, whatever...amours...she pursues are now her own concern."

"I am not pursuing any amours! (Uhm nuh puhsuh unnamuss!)" protested Jane, beating on the back of the sofa. Mr. Beck's hold had cut off the blood flow to her extremities, and her arms felt like felled trees. Still—her sentiment was obvious to those who knew her, even if she could not attack her attacker or enunciate her denunciations. Seeing this, Sarah Barstow slipped around the baron to take Jane gently in a protective arm.

"My dear uncle, Mrs. Merritt is under your protection, and that man must be made to offer for her," insisted Mrs. Dere to the baron. "Whether she be of age or not, she cannot be discovered in such a—a state without an accounting! To fail to do so would be an insult to the name of Dere. As if we have not endured enough opprobrium from *certain quarters,* as you well know. To heap yet more disgrace upon this family would be intolerable! Not to be borne!"

With his palms held up ruefully, Mr. Beck sighed. "But I make no offer, my lord. I have not; nor do I intend to."

If mortification were a crevasse, Jane was certain she would never be able to climb out of this one. Which was worse? To be found in a compromising situation with the wretched Mr. Beck, or to hear him refuse utterly to be compromised?

As slowly and intelligibly as she could, Jane said, "I will not marry him," emphasizing her words by cutting the air with her hand, which was now prickling with pins and needles.

"She won't marry him," interpreted Sarah.

"There," said Mr. Beck with an ironic little bow in Mrs. Dere's direction. "What can be done? Even if I were not so incorrigible a devil, the horse cannot be made to drink."

However much Jane might resent being compared to the proverbial horse, she and Mr. Beck were in perfect agreement on the matter. She crossed her blockish arms in front of her and shook her head decisively. It might cost her her tenuous rapprochement with Mrs. Dere, but better that than being forced upon a man who did not want her and whom she positively despised.

Sputtering and I-never!-ing, Mrs. Dere hardly knew where to direct her outrage.

"Come, Mrs. Dere," coaxed Mrs. Rowland. "You see there is nothing to be done. Why don't we all return to the ball before our absence is noticed, and this little imbroglio becomes more widely known?"

"I am going nowhere unless Mrs. Merritt returns as well," she declared. "She must be kept under my eye, or we must leave at once!"

"But you cannot go," Mrs. Rowland wheedled, "not when your departure with Lord Dere would signal an end to the ball. Imagine a ball ending after just the first two dances! It would be a catastrophe and would lead to such talk that everyone would demand an explanation."

Though Jane wanted nothing more in the world than to climb back into the Dere coach and go home, even she saw the logic in Mrs. Rowland's argument.

"I will come with you, Mrs. Dere," she said carefully, rising. "I have nothing further to say to...this person."

"You will come with *me,* Jane," the kindly baron pronounced, extending his arm to her. "You might give me that dance you promised me."

She took it, blinking back tears and grateful that no one but he could feel her tremble. Outrage had fueled her through the dreadful scene, but as it began to leak away, despair took its place.

"Sir," she murmured, "surely you will believe me when I say I did not invite Mr. Beck's attentions."

The baron tilted his head toward her, and Jane feared he could not understand her through her bruised lips. Must she say it again, and more loudly?

"I did not want to kiss him," she tried again, glancing back to see how closely Mrs. Dere followed. "You must believe me! I told him I wanted to sit down, but I did not think he would stay with me, much less—come at me—like that."

"I believe you."

"Oh!" Her relief at having one ally made the lump in her throat swell.

"But you must tell me what to do, Jane," he said. "If that man has insulted you, I must take measures to address it."

Instantly Jane was shaking her head, picturing the silver-haired baron challenging young, virile Mr. Beck to a duel and being senselessly injured—or worse, slaughtered! If she had already wronged her family and this good man by running off with Roger Merritt, she would not now add to her tally of misfortune.

"No. No, please, sir," she urged, her voice husky. "Let it be forgotten, as much as it can be forgotten. The only person in that room who might tell of it would be Mrs. Rowland, but she would only tell her husband or Mr. Hardy. There would be no purpose in telling any new Iffley acquaintances. Please—let it be buried in oblivion."

Her companion heaved a sigh. "Such conduct only continues because it is allowed to continue. Against my better judgment, I will obey you in this, Jane. But if he insults you again, I cannot overlook it."

In answer, she merely lifted his hand to her cheek in gratitude. There would never be another insult, for she had no intention of ever being alone with Alexander Beck again.

With this vow in mind, she raised eager eyes to his. "Sir, perhaps there is one way we might assist in this all blowing over..."

CHAPTER 18

You counsel right, my friend.
— Oliver Goldsmith, *An history of England: in a series of*
***letters from a nobleman to his son* (1764)**

Such had been the drama of the scene in the library that, when Miss Hynde burst out crying, no one had attention to spare the overwrought girl, and she had soon choked and sniffled herself into silence.

Egerton, certainly, had no thought for Felicity's distress, being too occupied with his own.

If distress was the word for it.

Did distress involve internal roiling and boiling, like lava forcing its way to a volcano's mouth? Did it encompass wanting to seize Beck by his neckcloth, to hurl him bodily from the window? If it did, then Philip Egerton was distressed.

What could Mrs. Merritt be thinking, going aside with the likes of Beck? What did she suppose would happen? Could she have sought it? Welcomed it? And to think she had told him, Egerton, so recently that Beck was nothing to her!

And he might not have known any of what passed, had Cassie not seen Felicity slip from the ballroom. "Better see what she is up to, Philip," she hissed, "because I did not like the look of it."

He wished he had not followed Felicity. Then he would not have witnessed what he witnessed. Any of it.

Nor could he believe Lord Dere was going to let Beck go unpunished! Had Egerton been Mrs. Merritt's protector, he would not have stirred a step before he flung Beck's roguery in his face, let the consequences be what they may.

But he was not Mrs. Merritt's protector.

Nor her brother, nor her husband.

There was nothing to be done therefore but to swallow his wrath as best he might.

Mrs. Rowland, giving Beck a nudge with her elbow, whispered something to him, to which he shrugged and strode away without a second glance. The woman gave an exasperated sigh, throwing Egerton a deprecating glance, as if to say, *Rascals will be rascals!* before following their host.

He was left alone.

Alone, with nothing to do but to school his features into politeness again, that he might return to the ballroom.

Only then did Egerton hear a sniff.

With a start, he wheeled to discover its source, having just enough presence of mind not to exclaim, "Felicity!" as if he had forgotten her very existence, which, in fact, he had.

The girl sat nearly swallowed up in a plush armchair, staring gloomily on vacancy, the tracks of dried tears lining her cheeks. The firelight caused her golden hair to glow like a nimbus, and Egerton thought she looked like a broken-hearted angel.

"Felicity?" he said gently.

She raised blank blue eyes to his. "What."

"Are you all right?"

No answer, but he saw the smooth column of her throat work.

"Can I fetch you something? Or can Cassie?"

"Philip—" Her head jerked up suddenly. "—You saw what I saw."

A tongue of wrath flared up again at this reminder, and he hesitated before replying. "I did."

"I suppose she is very beautiful."

"What do you mean?"

"That Mr. Beck should kiss her," she said dully. "And so ardently."

Egerton was silent.

"Some men prefer dark hair to light, you know," she continued, plucking at her skirts to make them drape more smoothly. "And I suppose some men prefer hazel eyes to blue, though I had always heard blue the more praised."

"Felicity—"

"Or it could be that she...lured him here and proved too tempting to resist." She heaved her own sigh. "A person with experience such as Mrs. Merritt has—she knows how best to manage such things. And I suppose she wants another husband, but it can't be easy to find one who will overlook her...what she has done."

To hear his own fears and musings spoken aloud did not improve his mood.

"Felicity, you had better forget what you saw here just now," he answered in a tight voice. "My uncle would not thank me to know you had been exposed to—such things—while under my care."

"But how can I forget?" she almost wailed. "I will never forget! Not that you would understand—you being the way you are."

For the second time he asked her, "What do you mean by that?"

She sniffed, producing a handkerchief and blowing her nose without any attempt to be dainty. "Oh, I daresay you understand me, Mr. Egerton. You might even take it as a compliment."

"Take *what* as a compliment?"

She stared at him, and for the first time her wide blue eyes struck him as brisk, rather than sweetly candid.

"Oh, you know," she rejoined, a touch impatient to make irrelevant explanations when her world was crumbling. "I mean that you're—sensible. Wise. Upright." She tossed the adjectives at him like coins to a beggar who had drawn too near. "Reserved. Parsonic. Not a bit like—him—Mr. B—" More tears welled, and she blew her nose again.

Egerton found himself sitting across from her, though he did not remember moving. "This...is what you think of me, Miss Hynde?" If it was—and it was obvious she did not mean her words as compliments—how could he possibly win her?

Moreover, was this—equally dismaying—the *general* opinion of him?

But here she lost patience. She was only eighteen, after all. "Why would I have said it was what I thought of you, if it was not what I thought of you?" she demanded, waving the hand which clutched her now-sodden handkerchief. "And I will add that, if you hope to be a really effective parson, you might try not to talk about yourself when presented with someone in *despair*!"

Reddening with consciousness, he straightened. But he grasped at the tail of her speech for rescue. "Really, Felicity—despair? You didn't know the man existed a fortnight ago!"

"That is precisely what a—a person like you would say," she retorted, now hammering the arm of her chair with her little fist. "You don't believe in love at first sight because you've never experienced it—never felt it! Why, I doubt you've ever felt love at second sight, either. Or third sight. Or hundredth!"

"That is neither here nor there!" he answered, his own voice rising with his temper. "Felicity, Cassie and I have a duty toward you, which was why I warned you against Beck. And now, having observed what took place in this room a few minutes ago, you see the validity of our concerns—"

"I see he is a passionate, ardent man," she cried, now crossing her hands over her breast and shutting her eyes, "and I see also that everything I have been told is wrong and the novels are right. To win a passionate, ardent man, one has to be passionate and ardent oneself." Opening her eyes again, she shook her head. "I looked at Mrs. Merritt. She was embarrassed to be discovered *in flagrante*, yes, but she had gone with him willingly—I *saw* her do it because I saw them go." Another heavy sigh. "Mr. Beck has never once thought of me or looked at me, with her around. Being birds of a feather, they flocked together, while I—I did not exist."

Miss Hynde was not the only one on whom enlightenment was dawning. Egerton felt as if his beloved were metamorphosing before his eyes—and indeed she was, in a sense. She had been an innocent schoolgirl before coming to Iffley, and though she had not done anything so dramatic as to fall from grace, certainly her eyes had been opened. And who could Egerton blame for this predicament but himself? But how could he have guessed that she would fall in love so quickly with a man like Alexander Beck, or that she would think Mrs. Merritt's conduct something to be taken as a pattern?

The damage must be mitigated.

It had been a bad idea to let Felicity come to them. It had been un-planned and thus unprepared for.

She must return to my uncle and to Martha's supervision.

"Felicity," he said. "Let us go back to the ballroom now, or we will be missed. Cassie will be concerned."

But in answer, her head whipped around, favoring him with a decidedly un-angelic scowl, her reply emerging in—well—it could only really be called a snarl: "Oh, go away, Philip. Do!"

He had not been wrong about Cassie growing concerned, for when he emerged from the library into the passage, he almost collided with her.

"Brother—what has happened? Where is Felicity?"

Placing a finger to his lips, he drew her away, crossing the passage again to enter the card room. There, after a glance to assure himself none of the old men playing at whist would overhear them, he told her briefly what had passed between Beck and Mrs. Merritt and the aftermath.

By the conclusion, Cassie had both hands pressed to her lips, her eyes round.

"So would you agree with me?" he pressed. "Given how dangerous it would be to her heart and well-being if she remained, wouldn't the proper course be to send Felicity home again to my uncle?"

"Oh, Philip."

"Or am I being too sensible, wise, upright, reserved, and parsonic?" he added ironically.

Her hands dropped. "What? Whatever are you talking about?"

"*She* called me such, in comparison to Beck." He gestured with his head back toward the library. "Compared to his 'passion' and 'ardor,' in particular."

His sister made a pained face, reaching for his arm to comfort him. "How could she? How could she be so...blind? I am sorry for it, Philip. I know how you care for her."

Cassie spoke nothing but the truth, as he could always expect from her. But as the realization sunk in—that Miss Hynde not only did not care for him, but she preferred this...blackguard!—he was nevertheless aware that the blow had not felled him.

He was still standing.

His brow darkened, however, for what would this mean for his plans? Was it the positive end of them, or only a delay? Would Miss Hynde come to her senses? And if she did, was she not now something of a tarnished idol?

"Parsonic," murmured Cassie. "Is that even a word?"

"If it is, it is not meant to be flattering. But that was probably the worst of the lot she threw at me."

"Oh, Philip," said his sister again.

Laying his hand over hers, he pressed it before pulling free. "Now, now, Cass. No more pitying me, or you will make me cry," he teased. "I will do my own pitying, thank you. But no more beating about the bush. Only tell me, *is* it right to send her home?"

"Yes. Yes, I suppose we had better. And if that makes me parsonic too, then so be it. But Philip—I must say a word on Mrs. Merritt's behalf. Because Felicity is surely mistaken to say Mrs. Merritt invited that man's attentions!"

For whatever reason, Egerton did find balm in Cassie's earnestness, and the darkness of his brow lifted a touch. "That may be, but if Felicity insists on assuming and admiring the—what shall I say—the worst interpretation of Mrs. Merritt's conduct, it is another reason to remove her from the latter's influence."

"Mm-hm." Cassie studied her brother thoughtfully. For he did not sound like a man whose heart lay in pieces. Rather, he sounded much as he had when Mrs. Barbary told him her husband had returned just long enough to steal her money and spend it on gin. That is, he sounded like a parish priest with a burden to carry.

Parsonic indeed.

"I will find the right time to impart the news," he continued. "Tomorrow, I suppose."

"No, no. You had better let me do it. And the sooner the better. If she is as wild as you say, she might try to make a scene with him tonight."

"Heaven forbid! We must keep her away."

His sister grinned. "I will tell her all her weeping has made her look like she has a bad cold. She should avoid him then. In fact, if I begin with telling her she is going back to Cousin Martha, it will likely bring on even more tears."

"It won't be a pleasant task. And I still feel I ought to do it."

She blushed. "But you can't, Philip! At least, not if you wish to marry her. She will be angry and—suppose she should...guess your intentions? She might then...question your motives or—or—accuse you of being jealous."

Instead of blushing as hotly as she, he almost chuckled. "Look at us, trying to protect each other. Well, perhaps you have a point."

"Yes, I do."

"Fine. The shortest cut falls to you. And I will take another task upon myself."

"What task is that? Surely you don't mean to speak to Mr. Beck!"

She shrunk from the sudden glitter in his eyes (then he *was* jealous, after all!), but he only said through tightened lips, "No, I don't mean to. It's Mrs. Merritt I will speak to."

"But—why? What will you say to her? I told you she could not have invited his attentions."

"Never you mind, but I do have a pastoral duty toward her."

And with a muttered thanks, he left her.

Despite the numbers of dancers swirling through their final figure, Egerton had no trouble picking out Mrs. Merritt and Lord Dere, and he was glad to see Beck at the far end of the gallery in conversation with other guests.

Intercepting them as Lord Dere led her toward Mrs. Barstow, he executed a hasty bow. "Mrs. Merritt, might I have the honor of the next dance?"

He could see the swelling of her bruised lips had begun to subside, but that hardly made her more intelligible when she accepted in such low tones. The baron, however, beamed upon him, clearly crediting the parish curate with a good deed in partnering his forlorn dependent.

"Very good, Mr. Egerton. Jane, I happily bestow you upon your next partner, who will have the added good fortune of taking you to supper afterward."

Supper! Egerton's mouth popped open before he could prevent it, and his astonishment did not escape Mrs. Merritt. She took care to make herself understandable this time: "You need not escort me to supper, Mr. Egerton. I will sit with my mother."

Courtesy dictated he make heartfelt protests to her suggestion, and Egerton did, but judging by her color and lowered gaze, Mrs. Merritt was not persuaded of his sincerity.

Such a beginning did not augur well for what he had to say to her, and they passed the first few minutes of the dance in silence, apart from Egerton having to apologize to the woman on his diagonal when he forgot to cross with her until she was almost upon him. *Pay attention, man!* And was *he* trembling, or was it Mrs. Merritt? For when the figures required him to take her hand, he had the memory of a butterfly landing on him as a boy, and how he had tried so hard to stay motionless that he ended in quivering head to toe.

It was plain that he must say what he had to say to her before he could be at ease in her company. And plain as well that she must be expecting unpleasantness, or why should she avoid his gaze and say nothing? Well—she might be embarrassed, he supposed. Hardly inconceivable, considering how he had last seen her, wrapped in Beck's arms as the rogue nigh devoured her face. Egerton's own gaze dropped to her tender lips, and he swallowed.

"Mr. Egerton, please!" frowned Mrs. Diagonal again when he failed to move. He leaped out of her way, begging her pardon—no—*babbling* her pardon, and something miraculous happened.

Mrs. Merritt giggled.

It was not in the least a mean-spirited giggle, but rather a spontaneous sound he had never heard from her and suddenly wished he might hear again.

And feeling his embarrassment evaporate, Egerton responded with a grin of his own. "Perhaps a little more practice would not have been amiss. Cassie did advise it."

As quickly as it had come, Jane's smile faded. "Yes. Mrs. Dere invited us to Perryfield to practice, or else I certainly would have been rusty. It has been so long since I danced."

He bent to catch her eye again. "And see how effective your practice was—you have not missed a single step, while I have missed several. But was the good lady so harsh a task-mistress?"

Jane shook her head. "No, of course not. Only—" she broke off as the figures separated them briefly, but when they came back together she did not complete her thought.

"Only what?" he prompted.

"I do not want to sound ungrateful, when she has been so good to my family. The very ribbons I wear are her lendings!"

He nixed the first response which came to mind: "And very nice ribbons they are, too." She would receive this as flattery, which he suspected she would dislike. Instead, thinking to surprise another smile from her, he said, "But let me guess: the ribbons came with an equally generous measure of condescension?"

It worked. Mrs. Merritt's dimples came and went. "I did not say that."

"You did not have to. I am getting to know my parishioners, you see. And understanding people's foibles is part and parcel of the job."

"Ah, but talking of one person's 'foibles' to *another* person surely isn't," she observed with a twitch of her lips.

His hand flew to his throat in mock dismay. "You have me there, Mrs. Merritt. You have 'broken my teeth with gravel stones' and 'covered me with ashes.'"

Another giggle met this, and Egerton began to swell with complacency at his success.

But then a shadow chased the sunshine from her features. "It seems you understand. She has our interests at heart, Mr. Egerton, but—that is not always a comfortable situation. Not when—not when one has...acted against those same interests. I needn't explain to you—"

Egerton could picture exactly the form Mrs. Dere's "condescension" had taken; no doubt she had encouraged Mrs. Merritt to be on her best behavior at all times, and no doubt Mrs. Merritt had bristled up just as she had when *he* encouraged her to do the same, inwardly, if not openly.

And now they were within a heartbeat of him repeating the offense! Because he must, for Mrs. Merritt's own sake and for Miss Hynde's.

He put it off some minutes, telling himself that, if he were to annoy his partner now, there would be no escaping from each other. Whereas, if he annoyed her at the end of the dance, she might insist again that he return her to Mrs. Barstow, and he might yield, to their mutual satisfaction.

But at last, as the figures took them to the top of the room, nearer and nearer where Beck still stood surrounded by a little court of admirers, and as Mrs. Merritt grew visibly stiffer, looking anywhere but Beckward, Egerton could postpone it no longer.

"Mrs. Merritt," he blurted, "at the risk of giving you pain, there is one thing I must say."

"Then—must you say it?" she asked, tugging at the tops of her long gloves in agitation.

"Yes. I am sorry. I—do not blame you for what I—what we all—witnessed a half hour ago, but I feel it my duty to say you should avoid going with certain people to...isolated places. Not only for your own safety and reputation's sake, but also for the—example it sets to others."

"Others?" She hung, mid-figure, before stumbling into motion again.

"Yes. Others who are perhaps more...innocent and thus vulnerable. Er—that is—Miss Hynde. I refer to Miss Hynde. The example it sets to her." Which was a stupid thing to add because who else could he mean but Felicity? Certainly none of the other witnesses—the baron, Mrs. Dere, the younger Mrs. Barstow, or Mrs. Rowland—not a one of them was in danger of being seduced by Beck.

But when, for better or worse, he had bumbled through his speech, Mrs. Merritt met it with a look every bit as wild as Felicity's had been, and Egerton steeled himself for reprisals. Good heavens, what an evening. Would she too hurl adjectives like missiles at him? Batter him with qualities she despised? Pulverize him with "parsonic"?

But Jane Merritt was no eighteen-year-old miss.

She said nothing. Thought much, but said nothing.

Her cheeks flaming with color, he could almost see her pulse beating in her throat, and she ripped her gaze from him, training it on the floor (where Egerton was amazed it did not blister a channel through the wood). When the steps of the dance obligated him to take her hand, she did not even bend her fingers to his but woodenly let him carry hers as if it were a relic upon a pillow.

And at last, after the suddenly endless dance wound to a close and she rose from her curtsey, features blank, she said only in an equally blank voice, "Thank you. Now will you please take me to my mother?"

CHAPTER 19

**Fare thee well! I'll never hold
communion with thee more:
But from the day-book of my
dearest friendship I'll cross thee out.
— Joseph Reed, *Madrigal and Trulletta* (1758)**

Keele's School in Oxford consisted of adjoining buildings in Cornmarket Street near the town hall. One contained the pupils' schoolrooms, hall, and library, as well as the kitchen and buttery, while the other held studies for Mr. Keele and Mr. Weatherill, the boys' dormitories, the Weatherills' living quarters, and several small parlors. In the coziest of these Mrs. Gerard Weatherill and her sister Jane sat one morning the week after the Greenwood ball.

"I wish you might stay with us for months," sighed Adela, drawing her needle through the delicate muslin in her lap. "Apart from the cook and scullery maid, I am surrounded by the male sex, from ages six to sixty. There are female callers, of course, but those short little quarter-hour spells hardly count."

"Another time I will," Jane promised. "But I cannot leave Miss Egerton much longer to deal with Harry Barbary by herself. Even a ten-day absence meant four entire lessons where she must manage both his mischief and the schoolwork. And she has not written to me, which tells me she does not want to say how difficult it has been."

No one had written, in fact, though Jane had been in Oxford six days already and had sent two letters herself to Iffley Cottage and a thank-you to Lord Dere for his help in sending her. The silence made her uneasy. Not that she feared the Barstows were unwell—rather she feared they had matters to tell her which they struggled to put down on paper. Matters like *what was happening with Mr. Beck* or whether word of Jane's latest calamity had spread.

Adela knew the whole story by now, of course, the only bit held back being the bit Jane held back from everyone—her ill-fated affection for Mr. Egerton. And Adela being Adela, she furiously took Jane's side, now counting the unknown Alexander Beck a mortal enemy. Adela had also taken it upon herself to send a secret note to the baron, begging him to smooth Mrs. Dere's ruffled feathers regarding the incident—not as small a request as it sounded, since no doubt Mrs. Dere's feathers were exceedingly ruffled on this occasion, and even if they had not been, the baron so rarely stood up to her.

Lord Dere's reply was now tucked in her pocket. In characteristic fashion, he timidly assured her that he would try his best, but more helpfully he enclosed several banknotes, for "would it not lift Jane's spirits to take her shopping…?"

"If I only have you four more days, let us go out and walk the High Street," announced Adela, laying down her work. "You must find trinkets for Frances and everyone, and I will show you that calico I like, from which we might make matching dresses. What fun! Hooper the maid usually comes with me for propriety's sake, but I had much rather it be you."

A couple hours later, books and ribbons, gloves and stockings were all inspected and chosen, along with a Jacob's ladder for Bash and a fox-and-geese board for the whole family. The calico, moreover, was pronounced so fine they purchased enough for Maria as well.

"Oof! We might as well drop our parcels at the Angel Inn," suggested Della when they were finished. "Their boy can deliver them all to Keele's, and we may take refreshment in the coffee room."

Crossing the bustling inn yard, Della disappeared into the coffee room to claim a table, while Jane waited at the counter to arrange for the parcels. So constant was the opening and closing of the inn door throughout, that Jane did not bother to glance over. Not until she heard someone call her name.

"Why, Miss Hynde!" she exclaimed, amazed to see the young lady before her, wrapped in a dark wool traveling cloak. "Whatever are you doing here?"

The girl's round blue eyes narrowed unmistakably, and her nostrils flared. "What does it look like? I am going home. Or back to Cottrell Hall, at any rate, on the Witney coach."

"But—why should you go? Is Mr. Cottrell or Miss Cottrell unwell? You have only been a few weeks in Iffley."

With a sharp glance over her shoulder, Miss Hynde seized Jane's elbow and hurried her aside. "Let us go where we will not be interrupted."

Over Jane's startled questions, Miss Hynde dragged her along one of the passages and thence into an alcove where the Angel Inn stowed a variety of umbrellas, walking sticks and one unmatched boot.

"Miss Hynde, what can you possibly have to say which could not be said more comfortably in the waiting room?" Even as she asked, Jane's heart began to hammer. Was it about Mr. Egerton? Could the girl somehow have guessed—?

"I am glad to encounter you here, Mrs. Merritt," declared Miss Hynde. "I have learned there is nothing to be gained by holding my tongue, but you left Iffley so soon after the ball that I could not put my learnings into practice."

"Your learnings?" asked Jane with increasing trepidation.

"Yes. Since I am going and will never see you again—nor anyone else I care to see—" Miss Hynde continued, almost on a sob, "Not that I care to see *you*—I intend to speak my mind. Because it is *your* fault, Mrs. Merritt that I am being sent away."

"*My* fault? Miss Hynde, I do not have the pleasure of understanding you."

"Don't you? Then I will explain. I say it is your fault I am being banished. It is terribly unjust, and I have told Mr. Egerton so. But I am nevertheless being sent away all because you are so—promiscuous and unscrupulous and—and—and—"

"Promiscuous?" gasped Jane, unable to prevent herself from parroting the girl yet again. If not for the alcove wall enclosing them she might have crumpled to the floor in astonishment. Could Mr. Egerton have dared to call her such a thing, or did it originate with Miss Hynde? "How—dare you, Miss Hynde!"

"You eloped, didn't you?" the girl retorted. "Ran away with a man before you were married to him." Crossing her arms over her chest, she said loftily, "Mr. Egerton told me."

"But I did marry Roger—as soon as we could," whispered Jane. Despite everyone under the sun knowing her story, the knowledge that Miss Hynde had it from Mr. Egerton pierced Jane through. "And he—was the only one."

"The only one *yet*," Miss Hynde choked. "If you had not been caught with Mr. Beck, would he not have been another? That's why you ran away to Oxford—because after what happened at the ball, Iffley was too hot to hold you. Admit it—you may as well, for you'll never see me again either. Admit it!"

But Jane was rallying. While she had never thought or tried to evade punishment for her foolish match, seeing it only as her due, what happened in the Greenwood library was another matter altogether, and she would be confounded if she took the punishment for Mr. Beck's transgressions!

"I—admit—nothing," she pronounced therefore, straightening to her full height (which was at least three inches taller than her accuser). "I concede nothing. You are entirely mistaken, Miss Hynde, and I was not a willing participant in what you witnessed."

Few who knew Jane Merritt in Iffley would have credited the existence of this version of her, an avenging fury with head held high and eyes blazing, but Miss Hynde was not a bit surprised. For who but a creature of fire and allure could capture the heart of the dashing Mr. Beck? Therefore it was not overawe which finished Felicity Hynde, nor that she was persuaded Jane spoke the truth (she was not). Rather it was that she was only eighteen and felt a failure and was being banished to the tender care of Martha Cottrell.

She burst into tears.

"Miss Hynde—Miss Hynde!" cried Jane, utterly perplexed. Her own temper faded in the face of this storm, and, after scrutinizing the girl a moment to assure herself the fit was genuine, she patted her shoulder. Miss Hynde only sobbed harder.

"Miss Hynde, do calm yourself," Jane pleaded. "You will be overheard." It had been sheer good fortune no one had yet passed their alcove, but Della would surely come in search soon, and, now that Jane came to think of it, Miss Hynde could hardly have come to the Angel Inn by herself, which meant—

"I don't care!" wailed the girl, even more loudly than before, if that were possible. Jane's hand itched to cover Miss Hynde's open mouth, wide as a starving baby bird's. "I don't care who hears me or sees me! What does it matter now? Everyone is so cruel to me. I, who have done nothing to deserve anything. *You* run away with one man and kiss another, and nobody does anything; whereas *I*—"

They were on familiar ground again, but this time Jane only rolled her eyes and tried to gather Miss Hynde to her. If the child could not be hushed with reason (and if murder was not allowed), perhaps a partial smothering against Jane's shoulder would serve?

But this made matters worse, for Miss Hynde resented the embrace as much as she resented the universe's favor toward Jane, and she began to struggle mightily, wriggling and trying to twist her face away from the wool-cloaked shoulder, uttering, "Let me go! Let me go at once, you—you—hrmmffy—"

The next instant, Jane was wrapped in iron bands and flung into the dimly-lit passage, carrying Miss Hynde with her. The girl's head struck the wall before Jane knew what was happening, so that, when she released her in horror, Miss Hynde slid down the papered and wainscoted wall to the floor.

Then all was confusion.

"Have you got him, sir?" demanded a gruff voice. "Ruffian! Brigand!"

"It's not a *him*, it's a *her!*"

"Felicity!"

"Mrs. *Merritt*?"

"Jane?"

"You know this person?"

"Whatever are you doing here?"

"What happened?"

"Let go of me, Mr. Egerton." This last came breathlessly from Jane herself, having recognized his voice and worked out who had seized her from behind to clutch her as tightly as ever Mr. Beck had.

She was obeyed with a muttered apology, and as all the exclamations were being repeated, the whole huddle tumbled into a parlor the inn host opened for them. He was a burly man trussed in a gold-buttoned coat who frowned upon such disturbances of the Angel Inn's peace.

I am a half-clogged drain, Jane thought wearily, *drawing every bit of surrounding scandal to collect at my edges.*

Except she doubted half-clogged drains attracted as many onlookers as she did, for in addition to the inn host there was a waiter from the coffee room, an ostler, both Egertons, Adela, and a few other strangers who must have been drawn by curiosity.

Miss Egerton took charge. "Ah," she said, clapping her gloved hands together once. "Here is the very young lady we were searching for," she said, indicating Miss Hynde, who had thrown herself in a chair and buried her face in her arm. "And we need not have worried, for she was in the company of—a mutual friend. But thank you all for your assistance in the search. You may go now."

"Wasn't acting like a mutual friend in my opinion," grumbled one of the strangers, pointing a finger at Jane. "If she's a friend, why was that one crying and screaming?" Another jab of the finger, this time at the huddled Miss Hynde.

"*Are* you all right, miss?" whispered one who must have been Miss Hynde's maid, bending over her.

The young lady pushed her away without looking, mumbling, "Oh, *do* go away, Robertson. I wish everyone in the whole wide entire world would take himself off and leave me alone."

Robertson stood her ground, but the strangers had no more excuse to remain, and they reluctantly withdrew, the ostler pausing to announce in an apologetic tone, "Coach for Witney goes in five minutes."

That made Miss Hynde kick at the carpet, while her maid risked her mistress's ire again. "Hadn't we better get you cleaned up, miss? You look a right mess."

"What does it matter how I look?" she snapped. More whispered urging followed, however, and eventually she sat up, turning her back on the rest of them and allowing Robertson to make repairs.

Jane gave the Egertons and her sister a rueful glance, not surprised to find them all looking to her for an explanation. As if the sound of her voice wouldn't cause Miss Hynde to fire up again! Stifling a sigh, she said, as quietly as she could, "Mr. Egerton, Cassie, may I present you to my sister Mrs. Gerard Weatherill? Della, this is Mr. Terry's curate Mr. Egerton and his sister Miss Egerton. And—er—Miss Hynde."

"Aren't we Miss Prim and Proper?" jeered Miss Hynde.

"Felicity," said Mr. Egerton in a cutting tone Jane had never before heard from him, "you are welcome to give your account—quickly—of how you came to be...grappling...with Mrs. Merritt in the passage, but I must ask you to mind your manners."

"Don't speak to me as if I were a child!" she flashed at him. "I am tired of everyone's hypocrisy. You are banishing me, as if I had done anything wrong, so I disdain to make explanations. Let *her* tell you whatever she pleases. It's plain you'll believe her, instead of me. Come, Robertson, or I will miss the coach. Cassie, you have been kind to me—at times—therefore I wish you well. Good-bye."

The girl stormed out before the Egertons could respond, but when the door slammed behind her, Cassie said, "Philip—we cannot let her go on these terms—what will my uncle say?"

"Given how vexed she has been with us this past week, these might be the only terms available," he replied grimly. "But I will see her off."

Cassie followed his departure with troubled eyes before turning to Adela. "Mrs. Weatherill, I am sorry we meet under these circumstances, but be assured we are honored to make your acquaintance. Perhaps Jane told you—Miss Hynde—the young lady who was so...overwrought just now—is the ward of my uncle. She has been visiting us in Iffley for several weeks, but I am afraid it has ended badly." She sighed. "The only comfort—not a very comforting comfort—is that my strait-laced cousin Martha will say we are doing the right thing."

She had no sooner finished speaking than the door opened once more, to admit a defeated Mr. Egerton.

"Has the Witney coach already gone?" asked his sister.

"It will in the next minute," he answered heavily, "but Felicity was clear that if I did not go away at once, she would make another scene."

"Oh, dear." Cassie crossed to pluck sympathetically at his sleeve. "Let us pray she will understand why we do this, as she grows and reflects upon—her time with us. She may even thank us eventually, Philip."

Which Jane interpreted to mean, "Don't lose hope—you may still one day win her!"

"But what on earth was happening, Jane?" Adela rounded on her sister. "Am I the only one who does not understand what I just saw with my own eyes? However did you come to be in the passage—wrestling—with her?"

Instead of replying straight away, Jane's hand flew to her mouth, and she sank into the chair Miss Hynde had vacated. Heavens—what was wrong with her? And something must indeed be wrong, or how else to explain the *something* which felt suspiciously like—like a laugh!—threatening to bubble up from her throat?

She must be mad! she thought, as she stuffed it down. Or it was hysteria, brought on by relief, now that Miss Hynde was gone. Or it was because there was a point after which horror toppled over into absurdity, and that point had been reached.

What was there to hide, in any event? These three people already knew everything which happened at the Greenwood ball. And no matter what Jane told them now, Della would continue to love her and Cassie to like her. As for Mr. Egerton, well, he already thought her past hope, so what further harm could be done?

Spreading her hands wide, palms up, she cleared her throat and tried to master herself.

"I'm afraid Miss Hynde has been—nursing some resentment toward me," Jane began, "and when she saw me she—er—led me away to that alcove to speak her mind. I did not know you were sending her back to Cottrell Hall until she told me, but if I understand aright, she—blames me for what she feels is a punishment. An injustice. That is—she thinks it unjust that *I* was the one found—being embraced by Mr. Beck—but *she* is the one being shipped off."

"But you didn't ask Mr. Beck to kiss you!" declared Adela hotly.

"We know that, Mrs. Weatherill," Mr. Egerton rejoined. "As Felicity noted, we did not believe your sister did anything wrong, other than, perhaps, to put undeserved trust in Beck's character. You may rest easy on that point."

Jane stifled a sigh. Why was it that any crumb of praise which fell from Mr. Egerton's table made her want to hug herself? Or hug him? Being Mr. Egerton's charity case was not so different from being his pupil, she imagined.

"But Felicity unfortunately could not be persuaded that Mrs. Merritt did not—invite Beck's attentions," he went on, "Beck being a big handsome fellow whom many find charming."

"She thought no woman could possibly resist him," explained Cassie.

"All right, then," said Adela, regarding her sister steadily. "Miss Hynde blamed you, Jane. But please explain the grappling!"

"Miss Hynde began to cry," Jane resumed. "I tried to comfort her, but she...objected to this. I suppose because she saw me in the light of a rival. It must have felt...patronizing. She grew louder, instead of quieter, and I panicked. I—er—pressed her against my shoulder. Not hard enough to do her any injury, of course."

"You smashed her face into your shoulder?" asked Adela.

"Only to—assist her—in quieting herself!" Jane pleaded. "Truly."

A silence followed this speech. One so complete that Jane could hear her own pulse. Surely, if the Egertons did not condemn her for being kissed by the loathsome Mr. Beck, neither would they condemn her for attempting to calm Miss Hynde—even if doing so had only made matters worse?

She peeped at Adela, but Adela was determinedly staring at the mantel. And for very good reason, for when her sister felt her look and ventured to meet it, Jane saw by the sudden pressing of Della's lips that she was trying very hard not to laugh.

Instantly Jane looked away, for she knew from long experience that, if she and her older sister once gave way to giggling, there would be no end to it, and then what would Mr. Egerton think!

But the curate was occupied with passing the brim of his hat through his fingers, round and round, round and round. And Cassie—Cassie sat unmoving, staring at the fire, until at last she thumped her breastbone with her fist. Once, twice. Then a high-pitched note was heard—faintly at first.

Jane blinked at her friend, whose shoulders hunched as the note gained in loudness.

"Stop," choked Mr. Egerton. "Cassie."

But his sister shook her head helplessly, and Jane saw with amazement Mr. Egerton's own shoulders hunch.

"Poor Felicity!" gasped Cassie.

In the end it was the Egertons who gave way first, Cassie breaking forth into a scream of laughter, to be joined by her brother's roars, and it was a mercy all around that the Witney coach was by then well out of earshot.

CHAPTER 20

A rich Rogue now-a-days is fit Company for any Gentleman; and the World, my Dear, hath not such a Contempt for Roguery as you imagine.
— John Gay, *The Beggar's Opera* (1728)

The day Lord Dere's carriage would fetch her home, Jane's first and only letter arrived from Iffley.

Perryfield
Iffley

12 November 1802

Dear Mrs. Merritt,

Although the baron informs me you will return home to-morrow, I could not allow you to do so without warning, as we had this morning a most surprising conference with one of our neighbors from Greenwood Hall, specifically Mrs. Rowland. (Mr. Rowland was also present, but as he said nothing but Good Morning and Good-Bye, I will pass over him.) Lord Dere and I had not seen Mrs. Rowland since the night of the ball, having sent only a bare note of thanks afterward, for reasons you will guess. Nor did we see any of the Greenwood party in church, for we suppose they continue to worship in Cowley (if they attend church at all). The baron has continued much affronted by the liberties Mr. Beck took with you, but I do not need to tell you he received the visitors with a courtesy they did not deserve.

After the niceties were dispensed with (including some teasing on her part, that no one at Greenwood Hall was informed you had left Iffley, and they were left to learn it when they called at the cottage), we discovered Mrs. Rowland's sole purpose in coming to Perryfield was to sing the praises of Mr. Beck and to see how we took it. In brief, Mrs. Merritt, I suspect Mr. Beck's interest in you continues and can only conclude that, having now made this interest clear to the baron through his go-between, he may even be contemplating making you an offer! What other conclusion can be drawn, astonishing as it is?

When she had gone, I told the baron as much, and while he hemmed and hawed in his usual fashion, he implied that he would oppose any match. I, however, think an honorable offer worthy of consideration for a woman in your position. Given the events of the past, it is not likely you will receive another, if you will pardon me for saying so; therefore this one is not to be refused lightly. If ever the incident of the ball were to become more widely known, coupled with your actions of recent years, your reputation would sink still further, possibly never to recover. Thus, whatever Mr. Beck's past mistakes (and you must be the first to agree no one is without mistakes), if he plans to reform now, why should you not be the beneficiary?

I trust you will give the matter all due consideration. Please give my compliments to the Weatherills.

With sincere affection,
Alice Dere

Such a letter robbed Jane of speech, both for its content and its advice, and when Adela saw her sister go alternately red and white and red, she knew it would be useless to ask for an explanation.

"May I read it, Jane?"

Wordlessly Jane thrust the paper at her and then propped her feet up on the fender because what was the use of being ladylike, when everyone seemed to have decided she was no longer a lady?

"Oh! Oh, my word!" sputtered Adela when she recovered the power of speech. "If Mr. Beck weren't so dreadful, it might almost be worth marrying him, so you might have the power to tell Mrs. Dere to mind her own business! Though I marvel at the flexibility of her conscience. It swings like a pendulum, tick tock. Tick: Archie Wilson's company would corrupt Peter Dere. Tock: never mind, let us welcome Mr. Beck to Iffley society. Tick: oh no, he won't do after all, if he is going to kiss people at balls! Tock: never mind again, he's perfectly acceptable because he offers marriage. It's enough to make one giddy." She clicked her tongue at her sister. "Don't look like that, dearest Jane! Absolutely no one but Mrs. Dere will encourage you to accept him, if he really does ask."

"Mm," said Jane. Removing her feet from the fender, she subsided on the knobby sofa, burying her face in the upholstery.

"Mm, what?"

"Mm, she does have a point. No one will ever propose to me again."

However much Adela would have liked to contradict her sister, the plain truth was Adela had mournfully said almost those exact words to her husband Gerard more than once. On this occasion, however, she compromised by saying stoutly, "To marry such a one as Mr. Beck would be worse than never marrying again."

"Poor Lord Dere," was Jane's next, unexpected remark to the sofa cushions. "He probably hoped, when he took in Mama and all of us, that at least we would all grow up and be married, and he might only be left with Mama, but now look! It will be Mama and me and possibly Sarah, forever and ever."

"Nonsense," retorted Adela, though admittedly without her usual conviction.

"And one day the dear baron will die, and then what will become of us? Mrs. Dere will be so grudging of our dependence that life will be hard to bear."

Practical Adela had of course already thought of these things, and she said, "Surely good Lord Dere will provide a little legacy, and possibly even a life-lease on the cottage. He knows Mrs. Dere's nature as well as we do."

But Jane wasn't attending. "Thank heavens Frances and Maria grow prettier every day," she mused. "And Mrs. Dere favors Frances, so perhaps she might help her to catch a rich husband, and we may all become our future brother-in-law's dependents."

"Not all men are unsympathetic," murmured her sister, now following her own thoughts just as Jane pondered hers. "Some might understand and forgive what has gone before, especially when the wrongs committed were done in youth." Adela imagined some anonymous older, wiser gentleman who might enter her sister's life at some point—perhaps a widowed father of a future Keele's pupil? Adela would invite Jane for a longer visit, then, one which might coincide with the father's comings and goings. It was not that Mr. Philip Egerton did not enter Adela's mind despite his relative youth, but Jane had told her of the curate's intentions toward Miss Hynde and thus disqualified him. (And while Della might wonder at Mr. Egerton's preferences, that was neither here nor there.)

But this was no time to dream of embryo future husbands for Jane—not when Lord Dere's carriage would be at Keele's within the hour, and both sisters must shake off their reverie to pack Jane's belongings.

"Perhaps Mrs. Dere is deceived, and he has no intention of making an offer," Adela said as she lined a box with paper to carry Jane's purchases.

"Indeed, it would be out of character," agreed Jane hopefully. "Mrs. Rowland might have been sent to Perryfield for a different purpose altogether—to determine if the baron took umbrage at Mr. Beck and to mollify him if he had."

"Exactly. And Mrs. Dere cannot be angry with you if you do not accept a proposal you do not receive, so all will turn out."

"Yes, Della," said Jane, crumpling the clean shifts in her arms in her eagerness to be persuaded. "After all, why should Mr. Beck want to marry me, when he never has wanted to marry anyone before?"

Adela might have added that other pretty faces were easily found, not to mention pretty faces with damaged reputations, and Alexander Beck had never offered for any of *them*, but she kept her counsel and instead folded Jane in a hug.

Jane's determined optimism lasted until she was handed into the Perryfield landau by Harker and the door shut behind her. It being a blustery day which threatened rain, both covers had been raised, and she was alone.

"If I were Adela, or if Adela had been in my situation, she might have married Mr. Beck," Jane told the empty seat opposite her. "For though he would make a wretched husband and will probably keep a mistress and father more Archies, if he pays off the mistresses and educates the illegitimate offspring, would he not be even more generous to his lawful family? Mama and Sarah and Frances and Maria and Gordy and little Bash would then be made secure for life, even after the dear baron dies and leaves all to Peter Dere and his mother."

But Jane was not her sister Adela, and perhaps if Lord Dere had been rascally like Mr. Beck, even Adela could not have found it in her heart to marry him. Jane Merritt being Jane Merritt, she could only resolve for the hundredth time to watch herself and do all she could to avoid further injuring her family's well-being.

She alit at Iffley Cottage to be wrapped in as much warmth as if she had been gone a twelvemonth. Sitting with Bash on her lap, flanked by the dog and cat, she answered all their questions about Oxford and the Weatherills, distributed her gifts to general delight, and said, yes, she did know about Miss Hynde's early departure and had in fact seen her at the Angel Inn. More details on that last would have to wait, for in the first pause Gordon burst out with, "Jane, is it true? Peter says you're going to marry that Mr. Beck person."

His female relations turned on him reprovingly for his tactlessness, and only when the chorus died away did Jane stammer, "Mr.—Mr. Beck hasn't asked me."

Her younger brother made a face at this evasion. "But supposing he does, Jane."

"Then—no. If he does, no. Certainly no."

"That's what I told Peter," said Gordon. He gave his family a playful scowl. "And you all needn't have jumped at me, when you wanted to ask the same thing."

"We knew without asking that Jane would not want to marry him," retorted Frances.

"I didn't know that!" cried Maria. "But why shouldn't you, Jane, when Mr. Beck is rich and handsome and feels bad for almost killing you!" (Suffice to say, Maria had been considered too young to be told of the Greenwood ball incident.)

Again Jane felt the unaccountable giggle bubbling in her throat, and she buried her face against little Bash's plump, sweet-smelling head to hide it. "Well, I can't marry him out of pity."

"I'm sorry we didn't write to you while you were gone," began Mrs. Barstow. "We didn't want to alarm you."

"Because Mr. Beck and the Rowlands and Mr. Hardy came to call in your absence," Frances took up the thread. "Purportedly to talk about the ball, but really they didn't stay long when they learned you had gone away to Oxford. Then they only wanted to know when you would return."

Although none of this surprised Jane, her good humor flagged perceptibly.

"And then Mrs. Dere told me Mrs. Rowland also came alone to call on them at Perryfield," Frances added.

Heaving a sigh, Jane set her little nephew back down to toddle around. "Yes. Mrs. Dere wrote to me about Mrs. Rowland's visit. And if she told you about it, Frances, you likely have told everyone—and Mrs. Dere has clearly expressed it in Peter's hearing—that she would approve the match. If any offer is forthcoming, that is, and despite the baron not being persuaded of the fitness of it."

"And why should he be persuaded?" her mother asked. "Lord Dere would not overlook roguery simply because it was plastered over with money or a handsome face."

"But what has Mr. Beck done?" asked Maria plaintively.

No one answered her, but Sarah, who had taken up her little boy and held him at his request to see out the front window, gave a gasp. "He is coming! Mr. Beck!"

What a scramble followed! Mrs. Barstow would have sent the younger children away, but Jane begged everyone please, please to stay (a request seconded by Maria and Gordon), though Frances pointed out that there simply wasn't place for one more person to sit if they *all* remained, and then everyone must find work to occupy their hands, and Bash's face must be wiped and his hair tidied.

"Mr. Beck," announced the maid Reed, opening the parlor door on a family all tranquilly laying aside sewing, embroidery, schoolbooks, or the fox-and-geese board to rise and make their salutes.

Jane herself had lunged for the narrowest chair in the farthest corner of the room, one with arms she might grip to hide any trembling, and when she made her curtsey, nodding vaguely toward Mr. Beck's knees, she perched in her chosen seat and took up her work again. That is, she took up Maria's clumsy little sampler of a cottage surrounded by...trees(?) above floating swans(?), for it had been Maria she expelled from her place. Poor Maria had miscounted her satin stitches in the pinwheel border, so that some pinwheels swelled like sails before the wind and others drooped as if becalmed. In any case, Jane quickly threaded an embroidery needle with blue floss and began filling a corner of the cottage with petit point stitches.

Mr. Beck was not to be deterred, however, by her show of busyness. After making easy chit-chat with Mrs. Barstow for a minute, remarking on the fox-and-geese game Gordon and Maria engaged in, and patting Bash on the head and praising him to his mother, he picked up one of the unoccupied chairs and carried it to place beside Jane's.

"What a pleasure to see you again, Mrs. Merritt. How did you find Oxford? Is it not odd that a place just minutes away by carriage can feel like an entirely different world?"

She completed her stitch.

So he was going to pretend nothing had happened, then? Two could play at that game.

Jane murmured appropriate responses, albeit cool ones, and continued her embroidery with such diligence that Beck was obliged to feign interest in her work.

"What idle dogs we men are, in comparison to you ladies! Here I sit, empty handed, while you all work and work, doing everything so skillfully." Leaning over Maria's sampler, both to find something specific in it to praise and to draw still nearer to Jane, the sight of Maria's lopsided pinwheels and lumpish trees checkmated him. "Oh!" he said. "How—er—fanciful."

Jane heard, rather than saw, Maria swell up, preparatory to explaining her work, and she quickly answered, "Thank you. It's Iffley Cottage and the—some of the…trees nearby. And these—" pointing at the swans which were possibly also frogs "—are local fauna."

"Marvelous," Mr. Beck uttered, recovering. He slapped his knees to simulate enthusiasm. "Nothing you do, Mrs. Merritt, has its equal, to my eyes. Therefore—I wonder if I might speak with you…apart."

"My goodness," replied Jane. "Having only just returned to my family, I am loath to be away from them. And our cozy cottage hardly permits private conferences—I daresay you wouldn't want to force everyone to abandon their comfortable seats."

"Certainly not. We might walk in your charming little front garden for just a few minutes. You will be back to your—embroidery—before you know it."

Biting back a sigh, Jane made quick calculations: the sooner she heard him, the sooner it would be done with, and at least walking with him before the house and in view of the road would preclude him forcing more unwelcome kisses upon her. Moreover, there would be fewer eavesdroppers out of doors, unless Reed or one of the Barstows chose to open a window and apply an ear to the gap.

"Very well," she answered crisply. "Let us walk there." Chin raised, she tossed aside Maria's sampler and rose, smoothing her dress and marching away before Beck could scramble up himself to offer his arm.

"Mrs. Merritt, I have offended you," he said when they were alone and pacing the frosted grass.

He had, and she was not in the mood to deny it, so she said nothing.

"At the ball, your beauty overwhelmed me, and I acted thoughtlessly on what I believed to be your invitation."

"It was not an invitation," said Jane. "It was my own naïve thoughtlessness." She turned before they reached the dormant flowerbeds, that they might stay in sight of the front windows. "I would never like such a scene repeated, Mr. Beck. Never."

"Nor shall you!" he declared, whirling to stand in her path, gloved fist on hip, dark eyes flashing and tousled locks tousling. (One part of Jane's brain remained detached enough to think Frances would enjoy this show, for, in appearance at least, Mr. Beck embodied the hero of a romantic novel.)

"My friends think me a fool—save Hardy," continued Jane's admirer. "My stepsister Mrs. Rowland, in particular, claims I have been taken in—but she admits you play your cards well, Mrs. Merritt."

Jane's bosom swelled with indignation, but before she could find words Mr. Beck's momentum carried him onward. "Mrs. Rowland says any woman who has seen what you have seen and done what you have done should content herself with attracting a worthy man's attentions, whether they be honorable or otherwise. She grants you your superior looks, you understand, and your connection to Lord Dere, to save you from a less exalted fate—and she violently opposed my doing more for you, but—ah, Mrs. Merritt! I am a man under a spell, from the moment you rose from the pavement after I nearly knocked you down with my gig. Then *I* was the one knocked down, you see, metaphorically speaking. I, Alexander Beck, who have never been ensnared by any woman, though many have tried. I had fallen, never to get up. And when you kissed me—"

"I never kissed you!" flashed Jane when she choked down some of her fury. "I never did! *You* kissed *me!*"

"—I knew all was lost, and I must have you, whatever the price!" Snatching her hand, he clutched it to his manly breast as he dropped to one knee. "Say you will have me, Mrs. Merritt! I offer you my hand and heart, my name and all my worldly goods. Only say the word and all I have is yours!"

"Get up, Mr. Beck," she hissed, tugging in vain to free her hand. "Get up. You will regret this folly, and we had better forget it ever happened."

"It may be folly, but I embrace it passionately," he returned, giving his dark locks another enchanting toss. "I only regret having angered you at the ball, so that you must make this show of reluctance now. Not that it does not have its own, contrary appeal. In fact—"

In fact, the contrary appeal proved too much again for Mr. Beck's minimal self-control, and he sprang at her like a wild beast from the brake, smashing his person to hers and his devouring mouth, yet again, to her close-shut one.

CHAPTER 21

**His virtue, such as it was, could not stand
the pressure of occasion.
— Ann Radcliffe, *The Romance of the Forest* (1791)**

Y et once more the overmuchness of Mr. Beck pressed fully upon Jane, reducing her scream of fury to a muffled "mm-ee—mm," unheard above his own ardent groans and murmurs and thwarting as well her attempts to bite him. She could only pray her family was indeed watching from the front window, and that someone—anyone—would burst out to interrupt.

Frances did not fail her.

The front door flew open with a bang, her younger sister bellowing, "There you go, Bash! A perfect day to play out of doors. Go find your auntie Jane." She gave her nephew a push, but the little boy only gawped in puzzlement still holding his Jacob's Ladder, having just been scooped up from the carpet two seconds earlier. It required the appearance of his mother the next moment, his coat in her hands, to rouse him, but then he toddled off as fast as his plump legs would carry him.

As Frances intended, Mr. Beck released Jane upon hearing they were no longer alone, but only to an arm's length, and he lifted his voice to say in the cold, carrying air, "Shall you tell them, Jane, or shall I?"

"Yes, Mrs. Merritt, do not keep us in suspense," another voice rejoined, equally loud but considerably brisker. "Do tell. Am I to bestow your vicar's blessing?"

And there—oh, heavens! Why was she so mercilessly, unceasingly, inexplicably *cursed*?—at the cottage gate stood Mr. and Miss Egerton, his hand on the latch and his sister's on his arm—one might almost have thought—to restrain him.

For one so young, Jane's life held more than its share of Worst Moments, but this one shot easily to the upper ranks. It was so ridiculous that she could hardly comprehend it. Why must Mr. Egerton forever and always be catching her in compromising situations, and why must all of them be directly traceable to Mr. Beck, whom Jane had never once asked or wished to love her?

It's not fair, Jane seethed, as Miss Egerton loosened her hold and allowed her brother to open the gate. *It's not fair, and I simply won't stand for it. I don't care what he thinks—his estimation of me could not be lower, at any rate, nor my reputation worse. I will tell the truth. Because it is either that or to throttle Mr. Beck right here, right now, with my bare hands.*

"She is speechless," began her would-be lover, beaming upon his new audience and swelling like a rooster about to issue the morning's first, triumphant, cock-a-doodle-doo. "But I cannot keep silent. Rejoice with us, for the lovely Mrs. Merritt has consented to be my bride."

Bash alone received this news with equanimity, giggling when the dog Poppet jumped at him and sent him plopping down on his backside. Sarah and Frances stared, mouths falling open. Perplexity furrowed Miss Egerton's brow. And Mr. Egerton—well—Jane had seen statues less stiff.

All this she took in in an eyeblink, and then she forced her (newly) bruised lips into speech. At least she had practice in this now, and knew to speak slowly and exaggeratedly, to make herself understood.

"That…is not so."

Mr. Beck chuckled ruefully. "She is right to correct me, and I accept it with all humility. Good practice for a man who hopes soon to be married. As my darling points out, she has *not* in fact accepted me yet. She had no chance because I could not withhold further—heh heh—further proofs of my affection."

"Your...proofs," replied Jane with painstaking clarity, "only delayed my inevitable refusal. And I beg again never to have them or your offer repeated."

The Barstow ladies sagged in relief, but it went unnoticed because all eyes were on Mr. Beck, whose smile faltered. "But—my very dear Jane—"

And despite her resolve to speak the truth, the whole truth, and nothing but the truth, so help her God, Jane wavered as well. Honesty might be her goal, and his persistence might compel her to make herself very, very clear, but perhaps she had overstepped into cruelty. Whether she had or not, Mr. Beck's crestfallen features could not fail to operate on her. Therefore she said more softly, "I am sorry to tell you in this manner, but you would not listen."

Giving him that inch, however, encouraged him to take an ell, and Mr. Beck lifted his square jaw, determined to hurl himself once more unto the breach. "You object because I did not apply first to Lord Dere or your mother for your hand."

"I—what? No, sir."

"Then you object because I alluded to your sullied past," he persisted, "instead of consigning it to oblivion and flattering you."

A flush rose up her neck. "Mr. Beck. I have never denied what I have done. Any part of it. Not to you, nor to anyone. Your mention of it in this context was not chivalrous, but neither was it the deciding point. I thank you for your offer, but I—decline it. Whole-heartedly and—and—permanently."

There was no mistaking her this second time, and the fact that he had indeed mistaken her now made matters worse. For now Beck was the one turning scarlet, the hands which had gripped her so tightly gathering in fists. That she would speak to him so dismissively—Alexander Beck, no mean prize in the matrimonial stakes—and in the presence of others!

"Augusta warned me of this," he sneered.

"Augusta?" echoed Jane, drawing back from the glitter in his eyes.

"Augusta," he snapped. "Mrs. Rowland. She could not understand why I should throw away my name and fortune on 'a country miss with nothing to boast of but country manner and country ignorance.'"

"Now, see here, Beck," interjected Mr. Egerton, released from his spell of paralysis so fleetly that Jane startled. The curate was suddenly between her and her rejected suitor, his own face in Beck's, eye to eye and nose to nose. "There's no call for insults. You have spoken your piece, and Mrs. Merritt has given you her reply."

Undaunted in the face of this challenge, Beck not only held his ground but narrowed the distance between them another inch. "Stay out of this, Egerton. It does not concern you. You would have done better to keep on walking, rather than nosing into something so obviously private."

Standing behind him, Jane could not see the curate's face, but she heard his hesitation. A hesitation which acknowledged that Beck had made a fair hit.

"I might have," conceded Egerton, "but—Mrs. Merritt being a—vulnerable member—of my flock, I thought it my duty—"

Beck's features twisted so derisively the onlookers were amazed to see his handsomeness dissipated. Even Frances, though her *tendre* for the man had suffered a reverse after the Greenwood ball, wondered at the transformation.

"Your 'duty,'" Beck mocked. "How keen you are to do your duty, Egerton, when there is a pretty young lady involved! I daresay, had you caught me making love to Mrs. Barbary or Mrs. Dere, you would have thought twice before interfering."

The Barstow ladies could only thank Providence Mrs. Dere was not at hand, to hear herself mentioned in the same breath as Harry Barbary's mother, and perhaps the conjunction explained why the curate went as red as his antagonist.

Perhaps, perhaps not.

"Watch yourself, Beck," he answered, each word dropping like a stone in an icy pond. "If you wish to attack me, pray leave Mrs. Merritt and my other congregants out of it, or—or—"

"Dear me—or what?" sneered Beck. "Or you will excommunicate me? I'm no churchman, but I don't believe you have the authority, humble curate that you are. You had far better run along and leave the grown-ups to settle this matter. Only look at you, standing there huffing and puffing! You heard me. Go on, then."

Now, however much a man like Philip Egerton might honor the cloth and find satisfaction in his chosen profession, he was nevertheless but flesh and blood beneath that cloth, and there was only so much that flesh and blood could be asked to bear. This London coxcomb had been nothing but a thorn in his side since his first appearance in Iffley, when he nearly killed Mrs. Merritt! And now—after Egerton had graciously taken on his "ward" Archie's tutelage, and after Egerton had banished his own would-be sweetheart because Beck had driven her out of her head—this scoundrel had the impudence to taunt him? To tell him to take himself off, while he, Beck, harassed Egerton's flock however he liked?

With a roar that even his sister had not heard from him since he was a young boy, Egerton launched himself at Beck, only their nearness preventing them tumbling to the ground.

Shrieks rent the autumn air as the men grappled, each struggling for the most effective grip as they shoved and shouldered, alternately gaining and giving ground, boots sliding and kicking up clumps of grass and soil. Cassie Egerton was calling her brother's name, whether from fear or to recall him to his senses not even she knew. Little Bash screeched, jumping up and down, trying to catch at the gentlemen's coats in excitement, before wailing in rage when his mother snatched him away. Iffley Cottage emptied out, and before Jane could say Jack Robinson a dozen people drawn by the noise lined the low stone wall of the front garden, and there was Harry Barbary of all people swinging on the gate!

"Hurrah! Hurrah!" whooped the incorrigible youth.

The two men were too evenly matched in size and strength for one to prevail easily, and where Egerton's fury cost him any cool-headedness, Beck underestimated his opponent's abilities.

Altogether, Jane thought later, the tussle could not have lasted longer than a minute before it was brought to an abrupt close, not by one or the other's victory, but by the unexpected clarion call of Mrs. Markham Dere: "What in mercy's name is happening here?"

Magically, they broke apart. Beck swiping the back of his hand over his mouth and Egerton rubbing his knuckles. The latter's eyes flicked to Jane's, where she stood with her fingers pressed to her lips, before turning with every other gaze to face the chief lady of Iffley.

And it would be no exaggeration to say that every heart present sunk yet a few degrees more when none other than Mrs. Lamb the postmistress was spied over Mrs. Dere's shoulder, Harry Barbary's sleeve in her grasp and her nose twitching.

Now the whole county will hear of this! Jane despaired. Unlike the incident at the Greenwood ball, which had been witnessed only by a trusted few, this could not be hushed up.

But fear of (yet another) scandal took second place to Jane's anxiety for Mr. Egerton and his part in this.

Mrs. Dere has no power over him, Jane assured herself. *She cannot dismiss him. Mr. Terry would have to do that, and he is in Italy now.*

But no sooner did Jane decide this than she thought of bishops and how bishops might be applied to, and how Mrs. Dere was precisely the sort of woman to apply to one. Jane could imagine the letter and the interview. She could even hear Mrs. Dere complaining of the unfitness of "brawling clergymen"—she would use that phrase, Jane supposed. Never mind that Mr. Beck had provoked Mr. Egerton! And Mrs. Dere thought Mr. Beck a suitable person to marry?

All these thoughts streaked like lightning through her mind. For his part, Mr. Beck did not seem inclined to make explanations, merely grinning lopsidedly despite his gashed lip. But next to her she heard Mr. Egerton draw a deep breath.

"Mrs. Dere," blurted Jane before he could speak, "Mr. Egerton came upon my—my—my interview with Mr. Beck and—he—er—misinterpreted what he saw." Wait—had she just told a lie? She had. For it had not been a misinterpretation on the curate's part—he had assumed (and she had confirmed) that the embrace was forced upon her—

"He was a-kissing her," declared Harry Barbary, pointing at Beck and back at Jane, "and then the priest and him had words, and then the priest goes for him."

"That will do," said Mrs. Dere quellingly. Or, in a tone which quelled ordinary folk, but on Harry it had no discernible effect.

"I knew Mrs. Lamb would want the long and short on't," he answered with a shrug, to which the good proprietress of the Tree Inn felt obliged to retort, "That's all you know, boy!"

With a swish of her cloak, Mrs. Dere passed through the open gate into the front garden to take a prominent stand between the actors in the scene and the audience. "Mr. Beck," she addressed him loudly, "I trust you have an announcement to make, which will render all clear and seemly?"

His lopsided grin widened to reveal more glistening teeth, and he shot Jane a glance full of equal parts challenge and revenge. "I can't rightly say, Mrs. Dere. In these cases, doesn't it always depend on the...lady's answer?"

Jane blanched.

She understood him.

Despite her earlier refusal, if she now declared to the world that she was engaged to marry him, he would let it lie and there would be no scandal beyond an indulgent shaking of heads and clicking of tongues that the young people should seal their bargain in so public a fashion.

But if she told the truth...

And I told myself I would. Come what may.

How could she do otherwise? She could never, never marry such a man. Each new revelation of his character only repelled her further. But if she told the truth, Jane suspected he would be a terrible enemy to have. Spiteful. Vindictive. Possibly dishonorable. Oh, if only he would go away and pursue some other woman—one who would gladly receive his obnoxious attentions!

All eyes were fixed upon her, awaiting her answer, and Jane folded her arms, taking hold of her elbows for courage.

"Of course, such matters are private," she began, relieved to hear the unsqueakiness of her voice, "concerning only the parties involved."

"Should have thought of that before making a public spectacle," muttered someone from the crowd at the gate, to be seconded with approving murmurs. "Not every parson would take up arms for you when he saw such doings."

For once Mrs. Markham Dere's majesty came to Jane's aid, for she leveled a glare at the assembly, and they fell silent.

Clearing her throat, Jane soldiered onward. *The truth.* Still, the less said, the better.

"Mr. Beck did indeed make me an honorable offer—which I then refused." Ignoring the general approbation, quickly followed by the general gasp, she wound up hastily. "He—er—pressed his point, and that was when Mr. Egerton intervened. So, that is all there is to be said. If you would excuse me..."

"You might have beaten Mrs. Dere down with a feather, she was so confounded!" Frances reported an hour later, when her mother finally permitted her to knock on Jane and Sarah's bedroom door. Jane lay across the coverlet, a pillow over her head and her face turned toward the wall. "I'm afraid things aren't going to be pleasant for us," she continued, sounding more eager than dismayed, and hugging her knees to her as she sat on the bed. "Why Mrs. Dere wouldn't even *look* at me when I tried to speak to her—she just turned on her heel and marched away. She slammed the gate so hard it stuck, and Mr. Beck had to vault over it a minute later. Miss Egerton could hardly be expected to do the same, of course, so Mr. Egerton and Irving had to work at it for some minutes until they could wrench it open again, though I kept saying they might go out the back door, if they were in a hurry."

When Jane said nothing, her younger sister tried to see it from her perspective and concluded that, on balance, she would not be particularly interested in the difficulties with the gate either.

The door creaked open, and Frances saw her mother peek in, a question in her eyes. When Frances shrugged, Mrs. Barstow entered, to sit beside her second oldest daughter and lay a hand on her ankle.

"Darling," she said, "this is not your fault. It is so horribly unfair that you, who have been such a model of good conduct since—since you came back to us. It is not a bit just that you should have to suffer because of Mr. Beck's wrongdoing."

At this, Jane rolled over heavily and raised red-rimmed eyes. "But don't you see, Mama? It *is* my fault. That wretched Mr. Beck—he told me—several times—that he felt free to take liberties with me because of what I had done and seen. Because of my history, I mean. He thought I was being missish to object. Being false. He only offered to marry me because I resisted him, and I suppose that made me interesting."

Mrs. Barstow pressed her lips together, giving Jane's ankle another squeeze. "I am so very sorry."

Jane sighed, heaving herself to a sitting position and clutching the pillow to her stomach. With her dark hair loose and her dress rumpled, she looked quite wild. "No, Mama. *I* am the one who is sorry. And now Mrs. Dere is doubly furious. Firstly because I refused Mr. Beck against her express wishes, and secondly because I involved the family in yet another scandal."

"*He* involved the family in yet another scandal," insisted her mother, Frances agreeing with a vehement nod.

"Well, whoever did it, it doesn't matter. She is angry, and this time there will be no containing the story, not with Mrs. Lamb and half of Iffley there as witnesses."

"I will smooth it over, given some time," Frances assured her stoutly. "You lie low, Jane, and when Mrs. Dere has calmed down she will allow me to explain. It's only a matter of time. A month, maybe. Possibly two. After all, she warmed to you within six months of your first coming to Iffley, even after Della had put her in a temper, and this second time will go easier."

Smiling sadly, Jane thought how nonchalantly Frances could speak of lying low for months. But Frances had not already done so for two long years. Unlike her sister, Frances had not just experienced the sweetness of beginning to live again after so long a dormancy.

"Perhaps I might go and stay with Gerard and Della again," Jane suggested. "Mrs. Dere and everyone else might forget the fuss sooner if I am not underfoot. And though I cannot imagine Mr. Beck would ever call again, if I am in Oxford I might go for walks with little danger of encountering him."

Her mother colored and made a placating face. "Certainly you might go again, but perhaps not straight away, darling. If—if Mrs. Dere did not want her son Peter in company with Archie Wilson, she may make objections to him seeing you at school."

Too soon Jane saw the truth in this, and while she shoved down the self-pitying wail which threatened to escape her, she could not help her lip trembling. After a minute, she managed a nod.

Yes.

She would hide away from the world again, keeping out of sight within the walls of Iffley Cottage, not venturing farther than the back garden. For however long it took Frances to wheedle Mrs. Dere back into good humor and for the storm to blow over.

She owed her family that much.

CHAPTER 22

How should the sons of Adam's race
Be pure before their God?
— Isaac Watts, *Hymns and spiritual songs* (1707)

Christ Church Cathedral
Oxford

14 November 1802

Mr. Egerton,

Recent alarming reports of your involvement in an altercation have reached my ears, reports unbecoming a priest and a fellow of Christ Church. Please write to me at once with an explanation and consider this a warning against the loss of your temporary curacy.

With sincere goodwill,
Rt Revd John Randolph

Iffley Rectory
Iffley, Oxfordshire

16 November 1802

My dear uncle,

I was grieved to hear that your ward Miss Hynde continues to resent the abbreviation of her visit to us, but your agreement that it was for the best gives me much peace. Indeed, I assure you, sir, the protection of Miss Hynde's reputation and innocence could not have been more important to me than to you. You may have guessed the reason for this, uncle, though I have never yet spoken of it.

In short, I had thought in the fullness of time to apply to you for Miss Hynde's hand in marriage. Whether she herself guessed this I do not know, but after her time in Iffley I cannot not say I am at all confident I might one day win her. If she has opened her heart to you or to my cousin Martha, you might best advise me. That is, if Miss Hynde suspects my sending her away was motivated by jealousy, and if she now lives in expectation of an offer from me, tell me at once, and I will do the honorable thing sooner, rather than later, though I imagine she would refuse me in her current mood. If you and Martha do not *believe she has divined my intentions, however, I would prefer to wait, not only to give her time to forget Mr. Beck, but also until I am better situated to support a wife and family.*

I anxiously await your reply.

Please give our love to Martha and our compliments to Miss Hynde.

Your loving nephew,
Philip Egerton

Cottrell Hall
Oxfordshire

18 November 1802

My dear nephew,

I advise you to put Miss Hynde from your thoughts. If she has any expectation of an offer from you, she has said nothing of it. Nor would I recommend that you act precipitously, making an offer when none is required. Furthermore, as her guardian, I would be loath to approve a match where there was so little to live on as a modest fellowship and temporary curacy.

Your loving uncle,
Geoffrey Cottrell

And who could say how long he could maintain even those, Egerton thought gloomily. He had replied to the bishop's note, of course, and after five days of silence could only hope that no news was good news.

"What does my uncle say?" asked Cassie, when the Tommies and Archie had been excused to the schoolroom. She had recognized the hand on the letter as soon as Polly placed it beside her brother's plate, and though Philip had not shown her the one he sent to Cottrell Hall, he had discussed it with her, and she had been on tenterhooks for him while they waited for the reply.

He tossed it across the table. "Read for yourself. You may do so in less time than it would take to tell you the contents."

And while Cassie found this to be true, she went thrice through it, hiding behind the sheet of paper until she might school her expression. Her uncle Cottrell was always terse, but *this*—! What good would it do for her brother to receive the bishop's pardon, if he still lost Felicity?

Carefully she folded the letter and slid it back across the cloth. "It is very short, even for my uncle."

"He does not waste words," agreed Philip.

Worrying at her lip, she stopped with an effort. "What—will you do?"

"Do? In regard to Miss Hynde? Nothing, it appears."

He frowned, but it was not a frown of unhappiness so much as one of meditation.

"But Philip! Will you so easily abandon...all your plans?" When he did not respond, Cassie busied herself with collecting crumbs from the tablecloth and depositing them on Archie's plate. "Or do you only mean to postpone them? Perhaps my uncle only meant to say, after all, that since Mr. Spacks has not yet given up the ghost and made the living available, and since Felicity is angry with you—with us—why not set your plans aside for the moment?"

Unfolding the letter again, her brother scanned it once more. "I suspect your interpretation is an optimistic one, Cass, for I do not read encouragement of my suit here."

"Because you haven't the income yet! He makes no other objection, Philip."

He considered this, drumming his fingers on the sheet of paper. "No, but he might easily have said something like, 'wait until the living is yours.' I wonder if he is having second thoughts about promising it to me."

At this she gasped. "But he *did* promise it to you! Even if my uncle disapproves of you marrying Felicity, he would not be so lost to honor as to rescind his offer of St. Lawrence Church! Why, it is one thing if he will not approve of you marrying Felicity and another altogether if he deprives you of the means to marry at all!"

"Mm."

The clock chimed, and Cassie knew he must go to join his pupils, but she reached a hand across the table to halt him. "Wait, Philip. There's no help for it if you are determined to be discouraged, but—are you? That is...unless—unless *you* have changed your mind?"

His gaze met hers sharply. "Why do you say that?"

"I mean—I mean—unless you decided, on second thought, that you and Felicity wouldn't suit."

"Why should I decide that?" he asked.

His sister heard the mild challenging note in his question, but she loved him too well to mince matters. She tried to downplay the seriousness of her next words, however, by beginning to stack the empty dishes. "Oh, I don't know," she said dryly. "It isn't as if you and Felicity grew particularly close in her short time here. If anything, her visit rather injured you in her esteem. Not that I expect her feelings for Beck to endure long, with nothing to feed them, but the fact that she could admire such a person does not say a great deal about her judgment."

"It speaks to her youth," was his quick reply. "There is no denying Beck is a dashing fellow, one more apt to win favor than a clergyman. She—would not be the first to be swayed by a man's charms into acting foolishly."

Though he did not name names, Cassie's thoughts unconsciously followed his. "Very true. And if Mrs. Merritt is anything to compare with, Felicity will be improved by the experience."

"You think Mrs. Merritt improved by her...mistakes, then?"

"Of course I do," she answered. "Surely her Roger Merritt could not have been any handsomer than Mr. Beck, and Mr. Beck is far wealthier, yet she was not at all tempted on this occasion, despite his attentions. That shows hard-won wisdom. And repentance. A truly silly girl would fall again into the same errors."

"Mm."

"Oh, don't grunt at me, Philip! Moreover, look what her wisdom is costing her—this time she has resisted a match *against* the wishes of arguably the most influential person in her family's life. You must have seen how Mrs. Dere was stone and ice to the Barstows in church on Sunday."

"I was too distracted by Mrs. Dere being stone and ice to me," he joked. "I'm afraid she blames me in equal measure for the failure of her plans, as if I had counseled Mrs. Merritt to refuse Beck! I warned her against him, I admit, when I suspected him of merely flirting with her, but I had nothing to do with her rejection of his proposal—"

"But surely, had Mrs. Merritt consulted you, you would have been equally against her marrying such a man!" pressed Cassie. "After what we know of his relation to Archie! Barring a miracle, I do not think he would make any woman a good husband. Certainly he will not be a faithful one."

Her brother's gaze fell to the tablecloth, and the thoughtful frown reappeared. "No. If Mrs. Merritt had asked my opinion, I would not have had her marry him."

"I am glad to hear you say it. I would think little of your own wisdom if you had. Poor Jane! She will need our kindness now, between Mrs. Dere's anger and this new scandal. The younger Mrs. Barstow told me at church that Mrs. Merritt will not be venturing from Iffley Cottage for the time being. In fact, her sister Miss Frances will be taking over the parish school with me."

"Not venturing from Iffley Cottage?" he echoed.

"For heaven's sake, Philip—you heard all the chatter on Sunday. As if she hasn't endured more than her share of staring and pointing, talking and whispering."

"At the risk of exciting your wrath, I persevere in saying—and she would agree with me—that Mrs. Merritt had only herself to blame for that initial period of staring, pointing, talking, etc. when she came to Iffley. And the fact that there is a *second* uproar is, I'm sorry to say, directly attributable to there having been a *first*."

His sister only shook her head at him. "Oh, Philip, how blind and pitiless you are."

He stared at her. "Blind? Pitiless? What on earth?"

"Blind and pitiless," she repeated. "If you cannot see—I mean—if you don't realize your part in it all. Especially since it was you who—made this mole-hill into a mountain!"

"My dear sister, I haven't the least idea what you are talking about."

"Haven't you? I am talking about you getting into that tussle with Mr. Beck! If not for that, who besides we and the Barstows would even have known that he tried to kiss her again? And none of us would have said a word, just as we didn't say a word after the Greenwood ball. But because you couldn't keep your temper, the matter went on—long enough to attract Harry Barbary and Mrs. Dere and Mrs. Lamb and all Iffley! Yes, Philip, I assign the shares of blame differently. I consider the misfortunes Jane will now have to face—to be largely attributable to *you*."

Astonishment silenced him, and in that silence she added with uncharacteristic spite, "And then, while she is shamed and talked about, *you* receive pats on the back and admiration for your 'manly chivalry' (apart from the bishop's note, of course, but even that reprimand I suspect to have been *pro forma*). Therefore, unless you apply equal ruthlessness to your estimation of Felicity Hynde, I will consider you all-around unjust."

When he recovered his voice, he demanded, "Am I wrong, Cassie, in thinking you are not overly fond of my uncle's ward?"

"Me?" she cried, blushing and already beginning to regret her rash speech. "I—I—If you love her, Philip, and tell me she will be my sister, I will love her with all my heart. Meanwhile, I am not *un*fond of her."

"Saints preserve us from such lukewarm fondness, then," he took refuge in teasing. But his color was high, and he pushed back his chair, rising. "Very well. If I have so contributed to Mrs. Merritt's wrongs, I will seek her out at the Cottage, Cass. The least I can do is to apologize for making things worse for her."

Egerton did not fulfill his promise immediately when the day's lessons were finished, however. The truth was, the morning had upset him, and despite the little jokes he had made to his sister and despite the icy rain, he set out on a long walk, the wretched weather in keeping with his mood.

So must Hercules have felt, when he lopped off one head of the Hydra, only to have two sprout in its place! As if the Miss-Hynde situation were not sufficient trouble for the day, Mrs. Merritt's woes must also fall to him?

Let us take things in order, he counseled himself, absently splashing through a puddle. Which meant he must begin by thinking about Miss Hynde.

Felicity, rather.

Was it hopeless with her, or not? How was Egerton to interpret his uncle's letter?

Geoffrey Cottrell did not say his nephew was to put her out of his mind *forever*; nor did he say he would continue to withhold his blessing after Philip gained the living of St. Lawrence Church. The overall tone of the letter, however, could hardly be called encouraging. Was Geoffrey Cottrell merely writing in his usual curt manner, or did he intend to forbid his nephew permanently?

Two months ago the puzzle might have tortured him. Yet today it did not.

And the fact that it did not made him far more apprehensive.

Had Miss Hynde lost her luster in his eyes?

At the least her conduct had dispelled his blind enchantment.

She was pretty as ever, to be sure, still golden like an angel in her looks. But had an angel ever such a temper? Was an angel ever so undiscerning? Did an angel ever yearn so stubbornly for something so...worthless? To have attacked Mrs. Merritt out of jealousy! To envy Mrs. Merritt's unsought power over Beck!

At his reading in, among other articles, Egerton had assented before the congregation to Article Nine, "whereby man is very far gone from original righteousness, and is of his own nature inclined to evil," but it was one thing to assent to a general truth and another altogether to apply it to one's beloved. Though he would not have said it aloud, Philip had believed in his heart that, where mankind might incline to evil, dear Miss Hynde surely only inclined to kittenish naughtiness, pet-like peccadilloes.

Moreover, Philip had called Miss Hynde "young" when speaking of her to Cassie, as if the flaws now made manifest were common to youth. But while youth could explain some of what he had seen, it could not explain all.

The truth was, to this point Philip had always considered innocence—Miss Hynde's innocence in particular—a synonym for purity. Or, at least, "purity" of the pureness available to mortal beings.

But what if this was not correct?

What if—what if a young lady's innocence indicated no more than that she had never been put to the test?

Halted by the shock of his thought, he stood motionless for some time, attracting the regard of sheep huddled under nearby trees to escape the rain. They studied him through their unsettling rectangular pupils, but Egerton was too disturbed to notice.

What if the clearness of Miss Hynde's eyes demonstrated no more than the innocence of untested youth, and was by no means a window to an immaculate, untainted core?

It would mean—horrible thought—that there was ultimately no difference between a Mrs. Merritt and a Felicity Hynde, except that the former had been tried and had failed, while the latter's moral strength remained untested and therefore unknown.

However disturbing this conclusion was to him, he was conscious of an equally disturbing corollary: he was relieved that he had not yet told Miss Hynde of his feelings.

Why? Why should relief be uppermost? And why should that relief be so sweet it contrarily made him unhappy?

If I am relieved, it must mean I do not *want to marry her after all.* But that was nonsense. Felicity Hynde had been his object for several years now, and was he to abandon his pursuit at the first obstacle? If he did, what would become of all his plans, when each stepping stone led logically to the next in the path?

At last the rain ceased, and Egerton found himself in St. Nicholas Road before the Minchery Farm, his boots and the hem of his greatcoat muddy. The farm had once been a small priory of Benedictine nuns, suppressed centuries earlier under Cardinal Wolsey, and though the long principal building was now used as a farmhouse, it was still possible to observe traces of its former life as a chapter house and dormitory. When less preoccupied, Egerton would have admired the ancient stonework encasing the coupled windows and imagined the size of the cloister-garth, but on this occasion he did not even spare a glance, merely turning on his heel when he caught sight of it to retrace his steps to Iffley.

He must be honest with himself, he thought. If only to himself.

It was just as well that his uncle disapproved the match at present. Because, lack of money aside, at present neither Egerton nor Miss Hynde were of the proper mind to make it a success. If it would ever take place, Miss Hynde must conquer both her feelings for Beck and her resentment of Philip, and Philip must learn to love Miss Hynde *in toto*. That is, foolishness, temper, and all.

Either that or sacrifice his long-held plans.

This was as far as introspection and an hour's walk could take him before he reached Church Way again and the Iffley Cottage gate. While nothing had been resolved, and he must wait on time and chance, Egerton felt his peace restored. Toward Miss Hynde and his uncle, at least.

There remained his interview with Mrs. Merritt. And, to judge by the acceleration of his heart and sudden tightness of his collar, he must be less confident of this particular outcome.

Squaring his shoulders, Egerton opened the gate.

CHAPTER 23

A throbbing conscience spurred by remorse
Hath a strange force.
— George Herbert, "Storm" in *The Temple* (1633)

He found the older Mrs. Barstow alone in the modest front parlor of Iffley Cottage.

"Why, good afternoon, Mr. Egerton," she greeted him, her eyes flitting to his rather damp greatcoat. (He had carefully scraped his boots before knocking.) "You find me alone because the young people were desperate to be out of doors when it stopped raining. I wonder you did not see them. They have gone on a walk."

"All of them?" he asked, wondering if his sister had been mistaken, and Mrs. Merritt had kept away from church for some other reason.

But no. Mrs. Barstow flushed, holding up her palms. "Well—all but my dear Jane. She—she—er—"

When she did not finish her sentence, he said gently, "I came to speak with her particularly, Mrs. Barstow. To apologize for my part in last week's to-do, that is. Will she see me, do you think?"

She hesitated, her brow furrowing in thought.

"Perhaps I had better start with you, madam," he added. *In for a penny, in for a pound.* "My sister Miss Egerton told me very emphatically that I made a bad situation worse—far worse—the other day by letting Mr. Beck provoke me. But while I seem to have been universally forgiven my loss of control, Mrs. Merritt…still feels the burden of others' misconduct." She was staring at the carpet by this point, but Philip persevered. "And for this injustice to her, Mrs. Barstow, which is therefore an injustice done to your entire family, I beg your pardon."

If only it might go as well with Mrs. Merritt, for her mother's politeness thawed into affection. Beaming upon him, she impulsively took his hand between both her own and pressed it. "Thank you, Mr. Egerton, for your words. They were not necessary—Mr. Beck alone is to blame—but they are deeply, deeply appreciated. I will pass them on to Jane."

It was his turn to color. "I thank you as well, Mrs. Barstow, but do you not believe she will see me? Selfishly I want to ask the forgiveness of the chief person I have wronged. And she too might like to have someone say she is not at fault."

"You are right. Yes. You are right, Mr. Egerton." Giving his hand another squeeze, she released it. "She is walking in the back yard. She too longed for fresh air. If you go through the kitchen…"

Egerton had never seen the back yard of Iffley Cottage, and he found it a more serviceable area than the front garden. Here were several sheds and a work-house, as well as a kitchen garden now barren but for cabbages, potatoes, and squashes. The fruit trees espaliered against the brick walls would provide ornament in spring and fruit in summer but this late in the year were leafless, as were the large mulberry trees in the center, encircled by stone benches. Flagstone paths wound throughout, widening in one central place to a small terrace. And it was on this terrace that the bottom of a ladder was placed, the top leaning into the branches of the tallest mulberry tree. On the third step of this ladder Mrs. Merritt poised on tiptoe, her back to him, peering (Egerton surmised) over the brick wall into the street.

A passing carriage muffled the sound of his approach, so that when he reached her he found it necessary to clear his throat. "Er—Mrs. Merritt."

With a guilty start, she whipped around to see who addressed her, but the sudden movement sent her foot skating off the wet ladder rung! Down she pitched, and if not for him instinctively throwing out his arms, she would surely have injured herself. And though Egerton's frame was solid, few people can catch an unevenly distributed burden of eight-odd stone without repercussions, and he crumpled to the terrace in turn.

"Oh, Mr. Egerton!" she cried, trying to disentangle herself. "Have I hurt you?"

He did not answer straight away, nor move—he was taking stock. Not only of the awkward way he had landed on his hip or the throb which told him he had also hit his shoulder, but of the warmth and softness and disturbingly pleasant weight of her person atop his. Never mind that her elbow jabbed him as she struggled up, or that a lock of her hair brushed against his lips. When she did manage to wriggle off of him, he felt strangely bereft.

Slowly, he sat up, unable to prevent a wince when his hip protested.

"I *have*," she fretted. "I *have* hurt you. I am so sorry."

"It's—nothing," he grunted. "But perhaps if you would help me up..."

Putting much of his weight on his good leg, he draped an arm over Mrs. Merritt's shoulders to bear the rest. She in turn placed a spread hand to his chest and leaned her head into him to keep them balanced as he halted over to the nearest bench, a delightful journey despite the discomfort, and he had the mad wish that the bench were a mile further off. But it was not, and with muttered thanks he dropped heavily onto it.

"Please pardon me for surprising you. Your mother told me you were out here."

Her hazel eyes had been fixed on his face, but now they fell to the pavers. "It—wasn't only surprise. It was half guilt, I'm afraid."

Although she didn't see his grin, she could hear it. "Guilt? Good heavens. Did I catch you peeping at something?"

But her head hung lower. "The world. You caught me peeping at the world. Or our little corner of it."

It all came flooding back to him then. The scandal. Her retreat. Her unjust punishment. And with the knowledge came the obligation he had laid on himself. In an impulse to provide comfort (a wholly pastoral one, he hoped) his hand lifted in her direction, levitating an instant above the bench, before falling back again.

"Yes. Mrs. Merritt. I hoped I might have a word with you."

Again her limpid eyes rose to his, a gleam of rueful humor in them. "Have away, sir. I have no other plans for the afternoon."

"Well, it seemed fair to ask. I hear you have placed yourself under house arrest, so you could hardly avoid me if you wanted to."

Another gleam. This one hinting at mischief. "Ah, but I could now, having crippled you, or at least having slowed you down. If I don't like your conversation, I can skip into the house and leave you to limp or crawl back as you may."

The changes in her mood, alternating between light and dark, fascinated him, and before he thought he said, "You are playful, Mrs. Merritt."

At once she shrank, and Egerton could have kicked himself. "I know," she murmured. "It's inappropriate under the circumstances, but I seem doomed to impropriety." She shook her head slowly. "Roger. My elopement. The debts. The imprisonment. The Greenwood ball. The Angel Inn. Mr. Beck again."

"No—" his own hand rose and fell again. "I did not mean to imply your amusement was inappropriate. At all. I rather liked it. In fact, I have come to say precisely the opposite. And if I had known you blamed yourself for the Angel Inn as well, I should have come sooner."

Making a vague sound in her throat, Jane wrung her hands. Then, making up her mind, she straightened, shifting suddenly on the bench to face him.

He was not the only one who could do good deeds, she had decided.

"Yes," she said. "About the Angel Inn…I am sorry Miss Hynde was so angry with me. And that we made such a scene. I am sorry as well that she should be so misled by Mr. Beck's character and—handsomeness. But I want to assure you, Mr. Egerton, that—away from him—he will fade from her memory and—her heart with time. I truly believe it. That is to say, there is no danger that she will—fall into the same errors I did. Especially now that she has been removed from my—bad example—as you put it at the ball—"

"Mrs. Merritt, that is not what I—"

"Therefore—" she hurried on, "you need not fear for her. And…I know, in time, she will certainly—that is, she could not help but—but come to recognize your…vast superiority."

Color flooded his face. His lips parted.

Jane went red herself at his response. Oh, heavens—did she really just say what she said? That she thought him superior? *Vastly* so? Oh—why did she not think before she spoke? Because he had surprised her—he had surprised the admission from her. Oh oh oh! *Why not be done with it, then, you ninny,* she berated herself. *Why not simply throw yourself at his feet?*

She was almost panting in her distress, which only increased her mortification. And then she made matters even worse by inhaling sharply—so sharply she knew at once she had given herself hiccups, and her hands flew to cover her mouth.

"You—take great interest in Miss Hynde's—the state of her heart," he fumbled. "And the state of my own."

"Forgive me," she croaked, feeling the urge to hiccup increase as she tried to stifle it. But when could hiccups ever be stifled? Like murder, they would out.

"It was not my *PLACE* to mention such—such *PER*sonal matters." The loud spasms only made the situation more awful, and Jane thought she must be heard in Cowley.

Politely, he made no acknowledgement of her embarrassment. Perhaps he was too embarrassed himself. "Who told you I wanted to marry Miss Hynde?" he asked, his voice low as if to compensate for her racket.

"*OH*, dear. I should not have *SAID* anything. I hate gossip, of course. It is—not my concern whom you *MARRY*." Clapping her hand over her mouth once more, she shook her head vehemently, holding her breath and hardly knowing if she was about to laugh or cry.

Egerton was scarcely less distressed, perspiration breaking out on his forehead despite the November chill. The initial delight which darted through him—Mrs. Merritt thought him superior to Beck?—was chased away the next second when comprehension set in. Wait—Mrs. Merritt knew he wanted to marry Miss Hynde? But how? Had she guessed it, or had someone told her? And if Mrs. Merritt knew, how many others did? Would those others include Miss Hynde?

Worse, what if it were Miss Hynde herself who told her?

"Who told you?" he asked again.

Saying a little prayer that he would not be vexed with Cassie and waiting for a hiccup to pass, Jane whispered in a burst, "Your sister mentioned it once. By accident. Only to ME and then asked me not to say anything, which I HAVEN'T." Back went her hand over her mouth, and she held another breath.

"Ah." Any annoyance he might have felt toward his sister for her indiscretion yielded to relief that the tale-teller had not been Miss Hynde.

They were silent a minute. Another carriage passed in the street. Tentatively, Jane released her breath, crossing her fingers that her hiccups had passed.

"Please don't be upset, Mr. Egerton," she began again, thankfully with no embarrassing spasms. "With Cassie. It was very early on, when Miss Hynde and your uncle and cousin came for your reading in. She has never talked of it since, to me or anyone, I am certain. And—if anyone else guesses at it—and I am not saying anyone has—but if they were to, it would only be idle talk. Because you are a single gentleman and Miss Hynde such a—lovely girl."

"Mm." (If Cassie had been present, she certainly would have told her brother again not to grunt.)

In her determination to be honest where possible, Jane had praised Miss Hynde's undeniable beauty rather than to list the young lady's more doubtful qualities, but it cost her all the same, and she assumed her companion's wordlessness stemmed from blissful contemplation of said beauty.

She assumed wrongly.

It wasn't Miss Hynde's appearance Egerton pondered, though it was the only part of her he admired as much as he used to. He was considering the rest of Mrs. Merritt's remark. Because she was right, of course. Others would have come to the same conclusion about him and Miss Hynde themselves, Cassie or no Cassie! For the Egertons to invite a single and singularly pretty young lady to the rectory—of course everyone must think they did it either to marry her off or to earmark her as Egerton's own.

And if *everyone* must think that, how could Miss Hynde be an exception?

Which presented his uncle's letter in still another possible light: could Miss Hynde have hinted to Martha or to Uncle Geoffrey that Philip intended to ask her, and that he had better not try?

There was no way to know. But one thing was clear. If everyone expected him to make an offer for her, including Miss Hynde herself, notwithstanding her possible refusal, was he not now honor-bound to make that offer?

With sinking heart, his posture slumped, causing his shoulder to twinge. Absently, Egerton rolled it.

Noticing his dejection, Jane could not help wanting to lift it. "Don't distress yourself, Mr. Egerton," she soothed. "If Miss Hynde is—displeased with you at present, it may only be because she is young, and as a young person, she wants to make choices for herself, even if you might think they are bad ones. They are at least *hers*, and therefore preferable in her mind to having—someone—interfere—to keep her on the straight and narrow. At her age I daresay I thought much the same thing." In her eagerness she laid hold of his sleeve, bending to catch his downturned gaze. "Truly, sir. Miss Hynde will come to love you. If my own experience has taught me anything, it is that she will learn to value the true over the flashy."

A line had appeared between his brows as he listened to her, and his eyes sharpened into their customary keenness. Abruptly Jane shut her mouth and removed her hand, certain he read her unspoken thoughts. Springing up, she ran nervous fingers along a twisting mulberry branch, picking at the moss tufted in the cracked bark. *Jane Merritt, you fool! Having got away with your other confession, do you push your luck? The man already considers you his parish charity case—do not give him cause to pity you for worse reasons.*

"You asked for a word with me, sir," she blurted, turning in time to see him struggling to his feet. "Oh—please—you needn't get up. It was only—I was restless. You wanted to speak with me, did you not? And I would guess it was not about Miss Hynde. Having already caused you—er—physical discomfort, let me not add to my sins by wasting more of your time."

"It was no waste," he murmured, but he gladly sank to the bench again. He would have wondered again at the fluctuations of her mind, if his own had not been too full to dwell on them. He touched his forearm, where he could still feel the warm imprint of her hand.

"Yes. Let me come to the point, Mrs. Merritt. You have been so candid, so frank this afternoon. I will try to emulate you." He hesitated. "I wish...I wish you might sit down again. I will not take much longer."

Without a word she obeyed, her skirts fanning out to brush against his leg. But this time she wrapped her arms tightly about herself.

"I came here to apologize. I should have thought of this myself, but I'm ashamed to say it was Cassie who pointed it out. That I contributed to your most recent woes by letting Beck nettle me and flying at him as if—as if I knew no better than Harry Barbary. Cassie says, had I not done so and drawn things out, not a soul in Iffley would have known of Beck's latest—insult—and I fear she is right."

"Oh." It was not so much a sound Jane made as a shape with her lips.

"And for my lack of self-control, you are paying the price." He gave a mirthless chuckle, shaking his head. "Beck outrages you, I make a fearful row, and it is somehow *you* who must hide your head. It isn't fair, Mrs. Merritt. Not in the least."

Her mouth worked again, but then she pressed her lips together fiercely, afraid she would break down.

"Mrs. Merritt," he said gently, "as both your priest and—I hope—as your friend, I intend to make this better. I will explain things to the baron and Mrs. Dere and even stroll past the Tree Inn before the week is out to have a 'casual' chat with Mrs. Lamb. Which is altogether more effective than an advertisement in the *Oxford Chronicle*, you will surely agree."

Then Jane did cry and laugh at the same time, but the tears made her eyes shine, and the smile she turned on Egerton made him think the bargain well made.

"Oh—thank you, Mr. Egerton. *Thank* you. But then—are you not afraid of having some of the scandal redound to your disadvantage?"

Removing his hat to rake long fingers through his hair, he grinned at her. "The injustice continues, I'm afraid. Because apart from a reprimand from my bishop, what drove you to retreat behind these walls only covered me in glory. I refer to martial glory—most unusual in my profession."

"Despite there being no clear winner?"

His grin widened, and he looked almost boyish. Harry Barbary indeed.

"How very kind of you, Mrs. Merritt, to judge I held my own. But no. When one is a curate, victory in warfare is not required. The attempt is enough."

"And Cassie did not scold you for attacking him?" she asked shyly.

"If she did I have already forgotten. There are six of us Egerton offspring, after all, so violence is nothing new under the sun. Don't tell me you Barstows never quarreled and tussled, though there was only one boy among you."

Dimpling, she replied, "We did when we were younger. If you count hair-pulling and name-calling and kicking."

"I most certainly count those things."

"Della—my older sister—and I were the guiltiest, I'm sorry to say."

"Dear me. Next time I will let you handle Mr. Beck yourself."

At this her eyes flashed fire. "If there *is* a next time, I *will!*"

"Mercy," he said with a mock shudder. "To show my repentance, and for Beck's own safety, perhaps I should warn him when he returns from his shooting trip."

"Has he gone away?" Jane asked eagerly.

"He has. And taken his train with him. He did not tell me himself, of course, but he kindly sent word to Archie Wilson. Not that Archie would know whether his guardian were in Iffley or Iceland," Egerton added frowning.

By that Jane understood that Mr. Beck had not been in the habit of visiting his ward at the rectory. She felt sorry for the young boy—assuming Archie minded—but not sorry enough to wish Beck would ever return.

"So there we have it," said Egerton, slapping his palms on his knees. "In another day, two at the most, I will have made my rounds through the village, and then I hope 'thou shalt shine forth, thou shalt be as the morning.' Give me your hand, Mrs. Merritt, as proof of my pardon, and promise me you will come out again to bless all Iffley."

Color washed across her face, but she complied, turning toward him on the bench. He took her hand in his firm grip, playfully giving her arm a single pump to seal the bargain. But then the pleasant sensation of her little slender fingers took him by surprise, and he held them a second too long, every ounce of his blood seeming to rush to the spot where they joined, while the contrast of her downcast dark lashes against her scarlet cheeks roused something like alarm in him.

Yes—surely it was alarm or embarrassment which made him say in his most sensible, business-like voice (as he would think back on it later, cringing), "Well, then! That's one pastoral duty accomplished. A few more to go. All in a day's work."

No sooner did the stiff words pass his lips than he saw her mental retreat, as clearly as if she had drawn shut a curtain.

"Yes," she agreed softly, rising, removing her hand from his without undue haste. "This task being accomplished, you may proceed to the next on your list. I thank you again for your time. Good day, Mr. Egerton."

CHAPTER 24

**New ways I must attempt,
my groveling Name To raise aloft.
— Dryden, translation of Virgil, *Georgics* iii (1697)**

One thing was certain: having occupied such a prominent and enduring position on the list of Mr. Egerton's pastoral duties, Jane vowed she would never have call to appear there again.

There would be no more scandals.

She had been clear and public in her refusal of Mr. Beck, but even if the infuriating man was tempted to try his luck again, Jane would thwart him. She would refuse every invitation where he might be present. That failing, she would rope herself to another family member so he could never again inveigle to get her alone.

Furthermore, she would banish Mr. Egerton from her own heart and mind. For what was the use of his continuance there? He was still going to marry Miss Hynde eventually, and he viewed her, Jane Merritt, as simply one of the more troublesome members of his temporary flock. Pooh. A fig for Mr. Egerton!

If only her unruly thoughts would not keep straying to him. To how much she had been enjoying their unexpected conversation in the back garden. To the memory of his arms catching her, and the feel of his firm person between her and the stone terrace. To his playful handshake which had made her believe they might become friends. Only to have him then ruin it all! To call her his "pastoral duty," and in such a tone!

It did not occur to her until many hours later, when she lay awake beside Sarah, that Mr. Egerton might have said what he said, and said it in the way he said it, as a kindness to her. That he might have read or guessed at her feelings in her blushes and her awkwardness and had then put her firmly in her place for her own safety.

Worse and worse and worse.

But all the more reason for her to set a brave face upon it.

And she would. She was three and twenty now. *Not* a child anymore. Not even who she had been a few years earlier.

Jane did not plan to avoid the curate as she avoided Mr. Beck, however. That would prove nothing, either to him or to herself. No. She must go about her business. Return to her usual activities, including teaching the parish school with Cassie, so that Philip Egerton would understand he was nobody in particular to her. He would think he had imagined her confession—if he had indeed imagined anything. She would be courteous and collected and completely, completely at ease.

And lastly, she would patch things up with Mrs. Dere. She would court the woman as assiduously as Frances had, cost her pride what it might. As Frances herself observed, one only had to make a grand effort to begin with, and then one might slack thereafter, with only occasional puffs to the woman's importance.

Jane gave Mr. Egerton three days to make his promised efforts, and then she and Frances set out for Perryfield, deliberately passing the Tree Inn.

Sure enough, the postmistress Mrs. Lamb burst through the door into the yard with a pitcher of water which she dumped at haphazard on the nearest flowerpot. "Good morning, Mrs. Merritt, Miss Barstow! How nice to see you again, Mrs. Merritt. I see you are well."

Jane decided to let that pass. "Thank you."

"Do you suppose the Greenwood Hall party will return to Iffley soon?"

"I haven't the least idea."

"An interesting letter Mr. Beck will find when he returns…if he returns," Mrs. Lamb said, with a lift of her eyebrows and a significant nod at Jane. But Jane could see Mr. Egerton had done his work for the nod was knowing, rather than insinuating. "The hand was not so fair, nor the spelling—'Ifley' with one 'F,' mind you! And Greenwood in two words."

"Could you tell who—" began Frances, before an elbow in her midsection made her break off. Nimbly she resumed with, "Of course not. In any event, if I didn't know better, I would suggest the letter came from our brother Gordon. His spelling is laughable at times. Good-bye, Mrs. Lamb. We go to call on the baron and Mrs. Dere."

When they were out of earshot Frances said, "What a splendid spy Mrs. Lamb would make! It's almost too bad about the peace, isn't it, or we might suggest she be sent to France to send regular reports home. She would know what Napoleon was up to before he did himself."

Wood the footman led them to the morning room at Perryfield where Mrs. Dere was at her correspondence, but the sound of their voices soon drew Lord Dere from his library to join them.

"Mrs. Merritt, I cannot tell you how glad I am to see you abroad again," he beamed upon her. "Mr. Egerton explained all to us. Quite a conscientious young man. It is a great relief to have Mr. Beck away for the present, if he will persist in such misbehavior."

From Mrs. Dere's rigid posture, Jane knew there was still work to be done, but she had expected it. For Mrs. Dere to acknowledge Mr. Beck's failings would entail acknowledging her own mistake in recommending the match—a bitter pill to swallow. But Jane was determined to gild the pill, if she could.

"I daresay, sir, if Mr. Beck had not heard such stories of me to begin with—stories which were all unfortunately true, he would not have tried the things he tried," she murmured.

It was well done, and at this show of humility (accompanied by Frances' most sorrowful look and regretful nodding) the matron unbent a fraction. "Yes, well," she sniffed. "As the bard says, Mrs. Merritt, 'The purest treasure mortal times afford is spotless reputation.'"

"Just so," agreed Jane, tucking her hands beneath her so that she would not clench them. "I have learned too well that a spotted reputation is an invitation to further mischief. I—blame myself. Thoroughly."

"Nonsense," said Lord Dere roundly. "If a rogue forces his attentions uninvited on a young lady—be her reputation what it may—there is no excuse."

"But Mr. Beck did make an honorable offer, however inadvisedly he went about it," insisted Mrs. Dere. "A good marriage might save such a person. Why, I know any number of young men who were going astray or who had gone astray, who were then improved by a good marriage."

Ordinarily such a pronouncement would have silenced the baron, but he was quite put out by Alexander Beck, and it gave him the courage on this occasion to disagree with the mistress of Perryfield. "That may be, Alice, but I am grateful it need not be our Mrs. Merritt plucking him back from the precipice."

Much as Jane would have liked to hug him for this defense of her, she saw Mrs. Dere stiffening again and hastened to interpose. "Mrs. Dere, I did want to consult you. Because it will be quite awkward when the Greenwood party returns—if they return. What would you recommend, to make things smooth again?"

"I have thought on this," she answered, somewhat pacified by this appeal, "and even discussed it with Mr. Egerton when he called. He said it was fortunate in the end that nobody at Greenwood Hall attends church, for there was one meeting avoided! But we must either all cut the man—cut the whole party—or we must arrange for some general occasion to be held the instant they return, in order for everything to be set on a new footing—one which is polite but distant. They must understand there will be no more private calls, nor private parties among us."

Frances clapped her hands and voiced the eagerness Jane felt. "And? And, Mrs. Dere? Did you think of anything?"

"It was Mr. Egerton who did," admitted Mrs. Dere. "He proposed a gathering at the church where all the pupils would give recitations—Bible verses, quotations, poetry. Even the parish pupils would participate, if you thought them capable, Mrs. Merritt. We would invite the congregation, but Mr. Beck would come, one imagines, to hear Archie Wilson."

"But did Mr. Egerton think Archie Wilson could be brought to recite?" wondered Jane, remembering the little boy beneath the table.

"It hardly matters," Mrs. Dere shrugged. "The point would be to get Mr. Beck there and to get past the initial awkwardness. If you approve, Mrs. Merritt, you and Frances had better go next to the rectory to work out the plan, for the Greenwood party may return any day, and it would be better if the invitation were sitting in the tray when they did."

The idea of seeing Mr. Beck again was dreadful, but there was no avoiding it, and he could hardly bother her in a church. Whether Harry Barbary could be got to behave in church as well, however, Jane couldn't say, but what could she do but approve the scheme? At least it would all be got over at once, and better to be thought a failed schoolteacher than a failed gentlewoman.

After staying a little longer to see the new books the baron had ordered and the latest specimen in his insect collection, Jane and Frances went on their way.

"There," said Frances, as they proceeded arm in arm back the way they had come. "Doesn't your heart feel lighter, to have got that over with? Mrs.

Dere was almost reasonable. With a little more kneading and wearing down she'll be as tender-hearted as the baron."

Jane surprised her younger sister by stopping in the road to look full in her face. "Frances, thank you. If Mrs. Dere is almost reasonable, it's because of your efforts these past few years. Della and I have helped wear her down with our misadventures, perhaps, but *you* have done all the good. The kneading and the buttering and the puffing up."

"Goodness. You make her sound like a cottage loaf," replied Frances, but Jane could see she was pleased to have her efforts recognized. They resumed walking, but after a few steps Jane stopped again.

"And Frances, forgive me, but I must ask: you don't still care for Mr. Beck, do you?"

"Pooh!" said her sister, blushing and tugging on her again. "I never did *care* for him, Jane. I only liked him and thought him handsome, and that is not the same thing. It wasn't as if I dreamed of running away with him." But at that she gasped and covered her mouth. "Oh, Jane, I didn't mean—you and Roger."

But Jane waved this off, too glad to hear she need not be anxious for Frances. As for Roger Merritt—she would rather no one else knew how infrequently she thought of him anymore! She wasn't a bit like her sister-in-law Sarah, sometimes still wistfully poring over their lost brother Sebastian's letters, but then Sebastian Barstow had been a far worthier man than poor Roger.

"Still," Frances rejoined, "it was a blow to my self-regard, to learn I could be put in a flutter by someone who turned out to be a cad. It meant I was no better than a Miss Hynde—except that I did not attack you out of jealousy. There is Miss Hynde, with a perfectly good man to marry—at least I assume Mr. Egerton wants to marry her—but she wanted Mr. Beck! It's all quite discouraging. I plan to be much more sensible next time, however. I won't pay a jot of attention to a fellow until I have subjected him to a thorough inspection in which he proves himself to be sensible, gentlemanly, and respected by all who know him."

Suppressing a sigh, Jane thought this exactly described Mr. Egerton, but there was no time to do more than steel herself, for they had reached the churchyard. And even then she did not have the few steps to the rectory entrance for further preparation, for there stood the curate with the sexton outside the church, pointing up at one of the windows.

"Ah, Mrs. Merritt and Miss Barstow," he said when the sexton trudged away, "what a pleasure to see you abroad."

"Those were exactly Lord Dere's words," Frances laughed. "Did you all settle on them together?"

"Nothing of the kind!" But he colored and looked at Jane. "But...you have seen Lord Dere?"

"Yes. And Mrs. Dere and Mrs. Lamb, to boot," said Jane with assumed calmness.

"And having seen Mrs. Lamb, that takes care of everyone else," added Frances drolly.

"It is thanks to you, Mr. Egerton, that I have ventured out again," Jane told him.

"Yes, well—I wanted to help, as you know. As we discussed." He studied her, his lips parting once or twice, as if he wanted to say something but thought better of it. Then, with an effort, he turned to Frances. "Miss Barstow, I am sure your sister must have told you how I felt responsible for making a mountain out of a molehill. Well—not precisely a molehill, I suppose—bigger than that—but making a mountain out of a mountain lion, perhaps."

Bemused by his uncharacteristic babbling, Frances answered, "Oh, I daresay the incident was already bigger than a mountain lion without your part in it," she replied, trying to humor him. "What would you say to a Russian mammoth? You made a mountain out of a mammoth."

"A mammoth, then. In any case, I apologized to your sister and have tried to set things right."

"And so you have," said Jane. "For which I thank you. But we seem to be talking in circles."

"So we are. Circles." He ran a finger under his neckcloth. "Right."

What ails him? Jane wondered. In comparison to his discomfiture she was downright at ease! "In any event," she tried again, "we have come by because Mrs. Dere shared your suggestion of holding a recital, and I heartily approve, although—are you certain you want to include the Cramthorpes and Harry Barbary in it?"

The practical question seemed to give him firmer ground to stand upon. "We had better, I think. Not only because I am certain you and Cassie (and you, Miss Barstow, on several occasions) have made excellent progress with them, but also because—if the parish pupils were not included—some others—might question why you chose to attend."

"Ah," breathed Jane. "I see. Yes. That makes sense." Indeed, heaven forbid Mr. Beck think she came for no other reason than to see *him* again!

"So perhaps—just have them practice whatever you think them capable of. It needn't be long. Something they already know which might be done right off, that we might announce the recital the instant the Greenwood party returns."

For a few minutes they discussed possible pieces and a likely order for the program, and Frances went to wander among the headstones, humming absently.

It was not until she disappeared around the south side of the building that their conversation flagged and the first awkward little pause fell. Jane instantly stiffened in spite of herself. She blushed, fidgeted, and was about to declare her intention of going in search of Miss Egerton, when he blurted, "Mrs. Merritt—to return to our first topic, your thanks notwithstanding, I think when I left you at Iffley Cottage, you were not pleased with me."

Oh, this wasn't fair! The very last thing in the world she wanted to talk about was the blow it had been to her, to be called a "pastoral duty"! Doing so would only lead to a weakening in both her façade and her resolve, and Jane decided she would have none of it.

"Not a bit of it!" she therefore replied with determined brightness.

He straightened, plainly surprised by her energy. "Er—I am glad to hear it. Though I couldn't help but think I might have offended you—"

"Offended me?" she interrupted with even brisker briskness. "Heavens, no! How could I possibly take offense, sir, when you have been so...charitable. That is to say, so industrious in wanting to set things straight. Zeal and charity! What more could be wanted in a curate?"

For whatever reason, her own zeal silenced him. He stood there, lips pressed together and brow darkened, and Jane, having so emphatically told him exactly how far and no farther she thought of him—hardly knew what to do next. An inexplicable urge to apologize—to *comfort* him—fleeted through her mind, but she stamped upon it, figuratively speaking, casting about for something else to say so they didn't just stand there, but her mind was wiped clean as a slate. His wasn't much better, and they might have stood there till world's end if Polly hadn't popped out of the rectory door with a carpet and willow beater.

Both giving themselves a shake, they began to speak over each other without either being much the wiser, but it had the happy result that Jane continued to the rectory and Mr. Egerton disappeared into the church.

"Did you see my brother?" was almost Cassie Egerton's first speech, after the niceties had been dispensed with. "He set the boys at their lessons and then said he was going for a walk."

"He's over at the church," said Jane. "And yes, we did." Briefly she explained their morning calls. "I thanked him, Cassie, for you doubtless know his part in it all. And I spoke with him about the recital."

Expecting her friend to have much to say about what the Cramthorpes and Harry Barbary could or could not be called upon to repeat before strangers from memory, Cassie only frowned in distraction. "He received a letter from my cousin Martha Cottrell. I was going to ask him if I might read it as well, but he locked himself in his library. I grant you, Martha's letters are not generally thought delightful, but I could not help but be curious about Felicity..."

"Have you heard nothing since she returned to Cottrell Hall?" asked Jane.

"What? Oh—not really. Come, let's go into the schoolroom and make our plans."

In politeness they could not insist on pursuing the subject, but when Jane and Frances were walking home, Frances said, "You saw that, didn't you? How Miss Egerton blushed and changed the subject about Miss Hynde? I'll warrant they have heard something, but she is not at liberty to say. How frustrating! Surely it's something to do with Mr. Egerton and Miss Hynde getting engaged, but we will have to wait and see. In the meantime, I am quite *infected* with curiosity!"

CHAPTER 25

I have lived to change my mind,
and am almost of the contrary opinion.
— John Duncombe, *Letters by several eminent persons de-*
***ceased* (1719)**

Martha Cottrell and her cousin Philip had never been close, though they were the nearest in age. "Nearest" was relative, however, Martha being ten years older and more inclined to treat him as an older sister would a much younger brother.

Her letter, therefore, had been typical: superior, with a hint of reproval, and Philip might have dismissed it with a shrug as was his usual practice. It need not be given at length. But on this occasion, one particular passage troubled him very much.

"Cousin, I have frank words for you and trust you will not take them amiss after all the years of affection between us. I guessed your intentions toward Felicity some time ago. Though I have always thought her a harmless, giddy creature, I recognized the powerful persuasion her looks would have on the male sex and quite expected her to return to Cottrell Hall an engaged young lady. And while I thought it would be wiser for you to wait until you secured the St. Lawrence living before you spoke, I realized you would likely not be able to resist her constant and immediate presence. Imagine my surprise, then, when she returned to us still single!

"While she has never confided in me, she speaks with regrettable unreserve to her maid, and you know how servants will talk. In short, I have learned of her feelings for this third party and her resentment of you for separating her from him. All well and good, Philip. I do not write to you to criticize this course.

"I write instead to warn you, though I daresay many would call me a disloyal daughter. For one so clever as you, will you guess it with just the one phrase, or must I spell it out, to my shame? I had thought my father long resigned to widowerhood after ten years, but I fear his eyes have been opened to Felicity's charms. If you could see how he spoils her, in attempts to cheer her! And worse, in her anger at your "treatment," and in her jealousy of some "horrid woman," she relishes my father's indulgence!

"Therefore, Philip, if you intend to marry her, you had better come at once and make your intentions known to both her and to my father. In her present mood she will likely refuse you, but you need not let that stop you, and it is far more important that you open my father's eyes. I do not say he will give way to your wishes, nor that it will not create some touchiness about the living (hopefully temporary), but it might check his foolish impulses. Do come, Philip, and claim your own."

Ever since he read this at the breakfast table and shut himself in his library to escape his sister's questions, Egerton had been thinking in notes of exclamation.

His uncle Cottrell and Felicity Hynde!

It was unthinkable. Why, the man must be fifty, if he was a day! And poor Martha, who had been mistress of Cottrell Hall for ten years—to fear being supplanted by an eighteen-year-old girl and supplied with a half-score of half-siblings, thirty years younger than herself! Indeed, how much of Martha's concern was for him, Philip, and how much for herself?

Surely Miss Hynde would not want an old husband, he thought, *no matter how resentful she might be of her circumstances or how indulgent Uncle Geoffrey might be. This is all more cry than wool.*

But when he thought of stern, serious Martha Cottrell, he could not so easily dismiss her words. His cousin was given neither to exaggeration, nor to agitation. If she thought these things—thought them so strongly that she took up pen to write them out in black and white and to urge him to come—it must be bad.

It must be real.

And yet, if everything was falling apart—his marriage plans, his career plans—then what was he still doing here, sitting at Mr. Terry's desk in the rectory? Why was he not dashing for the Witney coach, portmanteau banging against his leg? How could he possibly explain his inaction?

Pushing himself away from the desk he began to pace the room, brow furrowed and hair soon rumpled from dragging his hand through it.

But the conclusion he had been avoiding would not be dismissed.

I don't want to marry Felicity Hynde any longer.

It was that simple.

That simple and that complicated.

He was relieved she was gone. He did not love her any longer. Nor did he want to learn to love her again, take her for all in all. He did not want to wait for her to grow wiser—if such a thing could be assumed. And he certainly did not want to offer for her now, when she did not even like him and he could not even say if he liked her!

How had this revolution in his feelings taken place? Yes, his idol's feet of clay had been exposed by her unreasonable infatuation with the unworthy Beck—Felicity's feet of clay and Philip's own naïveté in thinking her an angel. He was embarrassed to remember it now. With her stubbornness, blindness, and temper, Felicity Hynde was no angel. But, perhaps even more discomfiting, Philip began to admit possibly no woman was.

That was not all.

Even compared to the rest of her faulty sistren—and here Mrs. Merritt appeared in his mind's eye—Felicity was lacking. What prevented Felicity from becoming a Mrs. Merritt but opportunity? And how would Felicity have survived disgrace, poverty, imprisonment, loss? He could not help but think she would not have. That instead of being supported by inner steel and guided by her conscience to learn and to grow and to do right, she would have collapsed. Collapsed into shrill bitterness and blame, blame which encompassed everyone but herself.

No indeed, he would not take the Witney coach.

He would write a sympathetic but firm reply to Martha advising her that his uncle Geoffrey must take his chances. It would not be the first time an old man made a fool of himself for a younger woman, and if Felicity should accept him (this Philip considered with an incredulous shake of his head), well, half the world would call her prudent. She might even end in being happy. Geoffrey Cottrell was a respectable, well-situated man and a far better gamble than the likes of Alexander Beck.

Poor Martha. But Felicity would not be an unkind stepmother to her, especially if Martha did not cross her.

And if Philip did not cross his uncle, why, the living of St. Lawrence Church might still be on the cards one day, though he grinned to think of Felicity sitting between his uncle and his cousin in the front pew.

Such was the partial conclusion Philip Egerton arrived at by the end of an hour, and being a man of action, he scribbled a note at once to his cousin Martha and escaped to post it at the Tree Inn, all the while congratulating himself on his increase of wisdom and narrow escape. *There is no guarantee Felicity will ever gain wisdom, but at least I have learned a lesson.*

This complacency lasted throughout his conference with the sexton about repairs to the northwest window. That is, it lasted until his eye caught Mrs. Merritt and Miss Barstow entering the churchyard. Then and only then did the rest of the truth fall upon him, much as the biblical house fell upon the Philistines when vengeful Samson took hold of its pillars.

It was not that the sun sailed from behind the clouds to illuminate Mrs. Merritt in a striking manner. Nor did he hear the strains of an angel choir or any flourish of trumpets—that would be impossible with Closter saying in his loud, nasal voice, "We'll have to have the craftsman from Oxford who worked on the windows of St. John's, but in the meantime I'll stuff a rag or summat in there."

Who could say then what crushed Philip Egerton like the metaphorical load of masonry, except that perhaps when the blindfold of Felicity Hynde was finally ripped from his eyes, for the very first time he could truly see.

See what had been before him for who knew how long: Jane Merritt, the sum total of her, and—more alarming still—see the state of his own heart.

Oh, mercy.

No wonder Beck hounded her.

It was not simply that Mrs. Merritt was lovely, though she was certainly that. Lovely, from the wings of her dark hair to the tips of her toes. Lovely, from her clear hazel eyes which regarded the world with such apprehension to the tender mouth which Beck had not been able to resist.

It was more than that. It was that very vulnerability of hers, which called out his protective instincts. Yes, she had been weak and thoughtless in her earlier years, but flouting the world's conventions had brought punishment, and this she had borne with patience, not attempting to excuse herself or to blame others. Unlike Miss Hynde.

But never mind Miss Hynde because then Mrs. Merritt and Miss Barstow were before him, and Egerton must remember how to string words together. Afterward he suspected he had failed, but he couldn't be certain because his erratic heartbeat had given him the sensation of being enclosed in a drum during the entire conversation, fists thumping on the drumhead until he thought surely one of the young ladies would comment upon it.

When they had gone, Egerton released a heavy breath, propping one hand against the dank, cold stones of the church to keep himself upright. Like a householder discovering he had been swindled by his most trusted servant, Egerton could only demand helplessly, *How long has this been going on?*

Had it been since he spoke to her in the back garden of Iffley Cottage?

No—longer than that. Else why would he have been provoked by Alexander Beck's taunts into attacking the man? Suppose he had caught Beck kissing instead, say, Mrs. Sebastian Barstow, the brother's widow. Philip would have been surprised, of course, and disapproving of the display—but would he have done more than muse at how still waters ran deep? He could not imagine the same wrath surging through him, as it had when he found Beck forcing his attentions on Mrs. Merritt for the second time.

Was it only the second attempt he resented? Was that when he had begun to...care for her?

His breathing shallow, Egerton continued to follow the thread, tracing it back and back, his color coming and going.

Because—yes, it must be confessed—he had wanted to thump Beck that first time, too, at the Greenwood Ball.

When the cold of the stones seeped through his gloves, Egerton swung open the church door and slipped inside. If anything, it was even colder within, but at least there would be no witnesses to his meditation. He stole into the vestry nevertheless, dropping onto a wooden bench and leaning his head back against the stoles, surplices and robes hanging there.

Heavens heavens heavens.

The world was turned upside down. For if he loved Mrs. Merritt, could he possibly…marry her? Take *such* a wife to himself? There might be other clergymen in the kingdom married to widows, but he doubted another could be found in all Christendom married to such a one as *she*—one who eloped with her first husband and shared his imprisonment in the Fleet!

Never in all his imaginings for his life had Philip foreseen such a possibility, and never never would he have imagined himself giving it any consideration. He, who had dreamed of a sweet innocent across the table at meals, sewing in a neighboring armchair in the evenings, and gazing attentively at him from the front pew! Well, Mrs. Merritt was attentive enough in church, he thought with a self-mocking grimace, and seemed to sew as skillfully as the next young lady.

The real question was, how could he possibly *not* marry her? How could he possibly, having never been in love before, do absolutely nothing with the tempest roiling inside him? And if he could not bring himself to marry her, he equally could not stand by and watch her marry another. Not that he feared for her and Beck, but there would be someone eventually. How could there not be? Whenever Beck was got rid of, there would never be another scandal attached to her name, and her original sin would continue to fade into ancient history. Then indeed someone would come, someone who snapped his fingers at her past and remarked only her beauty and intelligence, her kindness and family feeling.

I might marry her in five years.

He rejected this as soon as it occurred to him. While five years might suffice for Mrs. Merritt's figurative spots to fade, there was the problem of the Inevitable Someone coming along and snatching her from under Philip's waiting eye.

But more to the point, he did not think he could wait five years. Five springs, summers, autumns, and winters before he held her in his arms and made her his own? Impossible. He could not. He could—not—wait.

When this realization burst upon him, Egerton actually groaned aloud and leaped to his feet to pace the small room.

It seemed he had already made his decision, then.

He loved her. He intended to have her. Would she have him?

Not that he could ask her yet, when he had nothing to offer but a temporary curacy. Moreover, asking her—engaging himself to her—might even prevent him securing something more permanent. It was something of a checkmate, a nonplus: win a wife—such a wife—and exclude himself from the means to support her, or risk losing her by waiting until he found employment.

I can hint in the meantime, however. I can befriend her. Try to win her. So that if the Inevitable Someone comes along, she will not be tempted by him. Or would she? How did Mrs. Merritt feel toward him? The only thing Egerton was willing to venture was that she was at least not attached to anyone else. Nor did she seem to *dis*like him, which was more than could be said for Beck.

"I will play my cards as well as I can," he told the hanging vestments. "Who knows what may happen before the Terrys return? My uncle may be engaged to Felicity by then and in a good humor. Secure of St. Lawrence Church, then I might ask her. Or, if my uncle fails me, I will look about me for another position."

"Did Mrs. Merritt find you?" he accosted his sister at dinner that day. "Have you discussed what the Cramthorpes and Harry Barbary might recite?"

She had been watching him surreptitiously, wanting to ask about Martha's letter but uncertain how to proceed with the boys present. "We have, yes," Cassie replied, "and we will tell them tomorrow." Her gaze swept over the Tommies and Archie. "And all of you? Have you chosen some lines to recite?"

"Will my mama come?" demanded Archie. The little boy's unprompted speeches were still rare enough that neither of the Egertons chided him for speaking first, before Tom Ellis could get his words out.

"I don't know, Archie. But certainly your guardian Mr. Beck would be welcome to invite her."

Cassie smiled at him for this neat evasion, but she sobered soon enough when Tom Ellis said, "And—Miss Hynde? Might she return to hear us?"

"I'm afraid not, Tom. She is...much occupied at Cottrell Hall."

The young man's shoulders sagged, and a pang of sympathy surprised his tutor. Yes, yes, love too easily ended in disappointment. And how wretched to be powerless over if or when one would see one's beloved!

The mere thought made him impatient to see Mrs. Merritt again, just to assure himself of her existence and to suffer the unpredictable zigzags of his heart. That was all. Just to call upon her and look at her and hear her voice. Under the present circumstances, he would allow himself no more. But it would be better than nothing.

In supposing this would suffice, Egerton could be forgiven for failing to take into account his own nature. That is, having discovered his regard for Mrs. Merritt, and having never before been in the throes of a passion, he failed to understand that love had a mind of its own. Love, in fact, was not something to be placed on a shelf or under glass, to be taken down from time to time and inspected. Nor was he, a man in love, the sort to sit idly by, content to let it simmer untended, as a cook would a humble chowder.

CHAPTER 26

**Seek not temptation then, which to avoide Were better.
— Milton, *Paradise Lost,* ix.364 (1667)**

T hat's right, Harry," Jane said with a nod of approval. "You learned that so quickly I daresay we should give you a longer passage."

"I agree," came a voice from the doorway. "Well done, Harry, and well done, Mrs. Merritt and Cassie."

Jane was grateful she was bent over Harry's slate, that she might have a moment to compose herself. What was he doing here? He had never come to their classroom after that first time.

Reading a different reason in her hesitation, Harry peeked up at her and hissed, "It's all right, miss. I put it back. The little book. Long ago. I put it back."

And then Mr. Egerton crossed the room in two long strides, pausing to feign interest in Anna's misshapen letters and Jimmy's open primer. The two Cramthorpes shrank from this unwonted attention, but Harry nonchalantly slid his slate closer to his schoolmates and was rewarded with a "Is this your hand, Harry? Your writing comes along rapidly."

"What brings you here in state, Philip?" asked Cassie, tapping Jimmy and Anna's shoulders to make them sit up straight.

"Just seeing how our program fares," he answered. "Please, proceed."

Of course his presence ruined everything. Anna could not be brought to speak above a whisper. Jimmy forgot every third word and required Cassie to prompt him. And Harry was determined to show off, shouting, rather than reciting, and bouncing in his seat. When Jane finally gave a tiny frown and murmured admonishment, he exclaimed, "What, miss? Is my 'havior 'ill advised'? Don't I deserve charity?"

Wishing she could sink into the floorboards, to have Harry Barbary parrot Mr. Egerton's note about her *in the man's hearing*, Jane clapped her hands. "That will do for today. You are dismissed. Practice your pieces, and, unless the recital takes place before Monday, we will see you then."

The children scrambled away, but instead of going himself, Mr. Egerton lingered. No—that was not the word for it. "Lingering" implied aimless lounging, as if he merely leaned against the wall and looked out the window. But though he neither paced nor drummed his fingers, Jane was aware as she had always been of the pent-up energy of the man.

Glancing uncertainly from one to the other, Cassie said at last, "I was going to speak with Winching about refreshments for the recital...if you will excuse me."

"Yes," replied Jane, "I was just going, myself. Good-bye, Cassie, Mr. Egerton."

But when she was in the passage she heard rapid steps behind her and turned, her heart speeding, to find him behind her.

"Er—Mrs. Merritt, if I might have a word...?" He gestured back the way they had come.

This is about his notebook! That dratted Harry had to taunt him by quoting from it, and now I must answer for it.

With an outwardly placid nod, Jane returned to the schoolroom, the skin on the back of her neck prickling with awareness of him behind her.

After shutting the door and leaning against it, he ran a hand through his hair. It being December now, he no longer had any sun-lightened streaks, and Jane thought it made him appear serious, more clerical.

He cleared his throat. "Won't you sit down? You probably stood for the entire lesson."

Drawing out Harry's chair she complied. That boy! What if he had *not* returned the notebook? She would not lie for him, but then the question would come, why had she not told Mr. Egerton of the theft?

"Mrs. Merritt." Leaving the door, he strode toward where she was seated, only to veer off at the last second as if he had struck an invisible barrier. This ricochet sent him off toward the window, where he knocked twice on the panes and picked at something stuck to them before whipping around on his heels to stare at her, jaw clenched.

This was all too much for Jane's guilty conscience. Her lips parted in spite of herself to admit the Episode of the Stolen Notebook, only to have the impulse checked when Mr. Egerton suddenly lunged at her!

"Mrs. Merritt," he blurted, dropping to his knee. "I—you—I—would—" Breaking off, he swallowed. Shut his eyes briefly and then opened them again, his chest rising and falling quickly. "That is, Mrs. Merritt—will you marry me?"

She could not have heard him right. Her incipient confession utterly forgotten, Jane stared with all her eyes, and those instruments would have popped from her head, had they not been attached anatomically to the rest of her.

"Will I—*what?*"

He had gone crimson, and he wobbled, having to clutch the corner of the table to steady himself. "I said, would you m-marry me," he repeated.

"But—but—sir—what can you possibly mean?"

Swallowing, he took a slow breath before saying, "I—meant what the words usually mean. Though I apologize for the abruptness of them. The clumsiness. That is, I meant, will you do me the honor of becoming my wife?"

Sagging against the back of the chair, conflicting thoughts tore at her, chief among them confusion and disbelief. Marry her? Why should he want to marry her? He wanted to marry someone else, or so she had been told. Was his offer real? Was it made from disappointment or—again—his cursed charity?

Hauling himself back up, Mr. Egerton simply stood there, either unable or unwilling to say more. Instead he watched the parade of emotions alternately shadowing and lighting her features.

Jane licked her lips. Could he possibly expect her to answer so bald and sudden a question? What if he was not even serious? Or had gone mad, which she was not confident enough to rule out. One thing she knew—she could not continue to sit if he was going to loom over her. She needed to meet him on her feet, as an equal.

Scraping back the chair, she rose, her chin lifting. But the rapid hammering of her heart made her head light, so that she was forced to grasp the chair back like an encouraging hand.

"But—what about Miss Hynde?" she managed.

He looked as bewildered as if he had never heard of such a person.

"Miss *Hynde*?" he repeated.

"Yes. Miss Hynde. Your uncle's ward." As if he could have forgotten. "I—had thought you were going to marry her—remember?"

There was a long pause. So long that Jane wondered if she had said the words or only imagined them. He seemed to weigh and dismiss various replies, and in the end all that emerged was, "It's very likely she will marry my uncle, her guardian, Geoffrey Cottrell."

Jane had not foreseen this! Why on earth would the girl marry her guardian, after having been so taken with Mr. Beck? Even if she had given up on that rogue, wouldn't her attentions be more likely to fall upon someone nearer her own age, her admirer Mr. Egerton? Unless she still blamed the latter for separating her from the former.

There was no more time to wonder over the workings of Miss Hynde's mind, however, for Mr. Egerton waited and watched, now apparently thinking he had sufficiently explained himself. But he had not, for Jane had a thousand more questions.

He advanced a step, and her grip on the chair tightened. "Ah. I see. I did not know that. Are you—terribly heartbroken by—her decision?"

"If I were terribly heartbroken, would I be offering for you now?" he asked, coming still closer. Jane could swear heat radiated from him, a summer sun.

"I don't know," she answered with determined honesty. "I don't know you well enough to say. Therefore, you see, I did not expect this, sir."

To her surprise, his face cracked in a rueful, apprehensive grin. "To be honest, I didn't either. I'm afraid I've been very impulsive. Not that I am often impulsive, but I am—am—"

"A man of action," Jane finished for him. "That much I did guess. And I suppose that characteristic sometimes manifests itself as impulsiveness. Do you…wish to retract your words, then?"

"Retract? No!"

"But—apart from Miss Hynde marrying somebody else—can't you at least give me one other reason why you should wish to marry me? This is all so sudden I cannot comprehend it."

His grin widened, and he hung his head like a naughty schoolboy. "Aren't I wretched at this? I am. Of course. Of course any fool would know this is not the way to go about it. You are right to question my motives, if not my sanity, Mrs. Merritt. But I declare, if I hadn't already made up my mind to ask you at some point, I would have held my tongue. But I *had* decided I would try, in the vague, indeterminate future, so that when I saw you here today—in the moment—I couldn't help myself."

That was evidently not the only thing he couldn't help, for even as Jane shook her head, still waiting for him to give his *reasons*, he caught at her free hand and pressed it between his own. Neither wore gloves, and the swiftness of his deed, combined with the sensation of bare skin meeting bare skin, robbed her of words.

She should have been outraged—she had been when Mr. Beck tried this sort of thing, after all. When *he* did it she had wished he might be blown up by a cannonball, she was so furious. But to her horror and fascination, Jane discovered Mr. Egerton's assault was nothing like Mr. Beck's. For on this occasion, not one spark of outrage kindled in her.

Not one. No—on this occasion, she felt something altogether different.

A humming.

A melting.

A...shivering.

"Jane." His voice was hoarse. His grasp tightened, and she felt the pad of his thumb stroke the inside of her wrist. Once. Twice. Her eyelids shut of their own accord.

Oh, *heavens*. Where would this lead?

It was not a question which would be answered that day, however, because one thing, and one thing alone, saved Jane from being carried away: Experience. The fact that, one fateful time before, she had allowed herself to be transported by a man's magnetism, whirled away in giddiness and passion, to end with her life dashed upon the rocks.

Therefore.

Therefore, drawing upon a hard-won strength even she had not known she possessed, she snatched her hand from his grasp and withdrew to the far side of the table, choking out, "Better not."

"Forgive me," he said at once, his hands dropping back to his sides. "I don't want to be—didn't mean to be—Beck—to you."

"It wasn't that. But I—I demand that you answer my question," she insisted, breathless. "After all, I am hardly the sort of person curates dream of marrying. If anything, I would have expected you thought of me as...a case for your charity. Like—like a Cramthorpe or a Mrs. Barbary." Would he deny it?

He held up his palms. "Jane—Mrs. Merritt, rather. It would be a falsehood if I said, even to flatter you, that I did *not* consider you in the light of charity when we first met. Not the charity owed a Cramthorpe or a Barbary, say—that is, not requiring hams and jams and such—but in need of...kindness and...encouragement. That you might live a more—shall I say—a more blameless life than you yet had."

Defensiveness reared its head inside her, and Jane wished with everything she had that she might throw his "more blameless life" back in his teeth, but alas.

"Thank you for your honesty," she said through tightened lips. It did not make her feel any better that she knew she would indeed feel grateful for it later, when she calmed down and had time to reflect. Because he had made a clean breast of it. He had not tried to deny or disclaim what she knew to be written in black and white in his little notebook. In fact, it was she who had been somewhat underhand by concealing that knowledge.

"You thank me for my honesty, but you don't like me any better for it," he observed, now crossing his arms over his chest. "I do not say such things to wound you but because you asked, and I respect you enough to tell you the truth."

"Mm."

Uncrossing his arms, he laid his palms on the table and leaned toward her. "And it would be fair of you to acknowledge that my 'charitable' attitude toward you differs markedly from the one I hold toward the Cramthorpes and Barbarys."

Apart from another little sound in her throat, Jane made no response.

"To be specific," he pursued, "I am not, for example, asking for the hand of either of the Mesdames Cramthorpe, nor of Mrs. Barbary. You ask my reason for proposing to you. It is—" he paused at this last barrier, having never before spoken such words to any living being. "It is that you have...made away with my heart. I cannot even say how or when, whether you stole it at first sight or carried off portions bit by bit, but the deed is done. *Has* been done, though I was too dull-witted to realize it until—"

He broke off, but Jane had unconsciously drifted closer around the edge of the table, as if following the thread of his words. "Until—?" she murmured.

"Until—yesterday. When I learned Miss Hynde might marry my uncle. Instead of anguish, I felt only relief and could not account for it. And then, when I saw you in the church yard, I understood." Somehow he was beside her again, his breath brushing her skin. "Jane. Beautiful, marvelous Jane. Say you'll be mine, darling. Quickly."

Her hands were once more in his—both of them—her pulse leaping, and she thought, as her head fell back and her eyes closed, *Surely this is not wrong, to give way to this! He will be my husband.*

Then his arms were around her, his head bending to hers and their lips meeting. Oh! Meeting and pressing—urgent, hungry.

"Say it, then," he commanded against her mouth. "Say you'll marry me."

"Yes," whispered Jane, her arms winding around his neck. "Yes, I will marry you."

What paradise, to love and be loved by so good and respected a man! How could heaven so smile upon her, to overlook her transgressions and send her another, worthier person to love?

It was her tears which finally returned them to earth, tears which had no element of grief but which were all joy and gratitude. But even such tears are made of water and salt, and Egerton at last pulled back, laughing and dabbing his tongue at his lips. "Have we been caught in a rain shower? What is this?"

"I'm sorry! It's that I'm so happy," she joined his laugh, even as more tears spilled, and she tried to push him away an inch, that she might retrieve her handkerchief.

"Oh, no, you don't," he said, clutching her closer and kissing her again. "I'm not letting you go yet."

"But—Philip! We're both wet! We will be a sight to see."

"I'll kiss the dry bits, then." Which he proceeded to do, his mouth traveling from her ear to her brow to her hair. "What about your neck? Do you suppose it's very wet?" he murmured. "I had better see for myself. My dear Jane, your throat has the most enchanting hollow…"

Then Jane was good for nothing again, which was why it took some time for the words spiraling dreamily into her awareness to penetrate.

"…Our little secret for now."

Her eyes snapped open.

Feeling her stiffen abruptly, Egerton raised his head. "What is it? Did you hear something?"

"What did you say, Philip? Just now. About a secret?" She had gone strangely pale.

"Don't look like that, my dearest! Do you feel unwell? Poor thing—I've kissed all the breath out of you."

But Jane twisted from his grasp. "What did you say?" she asked again.

He blinked. "I said—until I have secured my next position, it would be better for our engagement to be our little secret." He reached for her again, but she retreated. "Come, Jane. What is it? Can you possibly think I will not keep my promise?" When she didn't immediately reply, he gave a short, mirthless laugh. "Even Roger Merritt kept his promise to you. Would you not grant me the same trust?"

"It was—you used Roger's very words," she uttered faintly. "It startled me." Pulling out Anna Cramthorpe's chair, she sank into it. "Of course I trust you, Philip. Only—why do you want it to be a secret?"

He drew out Jimmy's chair, that he might sit beside her and take her hands again. "Listen to me, Jane. I do not suggest secrecy from any impure motive, but rather from a practical one. You know the Terrys will return in the spring, and when they do I will have no income to offer you. Even my paltry fellowship will end when we marry. Therefore I will need employment. My uncle once promised me the living of St. Lawrence Church in Cottrell, but not only does the incumbent cling most sensibly to life, but, with the whole marrying-Miss-Hynde business, I cannot depend on my uncle's continued generosity. He might resent my having once thought of her, for instance, or she may object to such a gift falling to me. You understand. But you need not fear—I have other connections, to which I intend to apply, and something will surely present itself, though it may be a little while."

"I do understand your situation and the need for delay," Jane assured him, "and thank you for explaining it. But, again, why must our engagement be secret?"

His color rose, and for the first time that morning, his eyes avoided hers. And then she knew.

Without him saying a word, she guessed it all. Guessed it all, and wished she might crawl under the earth.

"Dearest Jane," he said, "you know how people are. Think of ones like Mrs. Markham Dere. Think of how *I* was, before I knew you better. If I were to suggest myself as a candidate for various positions, it might be best—more prudent, as it were—if some of the more...doubtful elements of your past were not...subject to scrutiny. Not only might the sharing of your story arouse prejudice, but it would doubtless cause you pain."

"And *you* pain," she said in a low voice.

"I?"

"My past causes you pain."

Sputtering, he released her hands to clutch at a hank of his hair. "Jane—of course your past causes me pain. Because it caused *you* pain."

"It's more than that," she insisted, half hating herself for wanting to force admissions from him. "You would wish none of it had ever happened. Roger. My elopement. Debt. Disgrace. The Fleet."

"Don't *you* wish it never happened?" he returned. "Don't you wish, Jane, you might wake to find that part of your life a dream? Wait—don't cry. You have caught me off guard, and I have spoken foolishly. Listen to me: I say, not only as your friend and would-be husband, but also as your priest, that nothing in the past is to be regretted if it is learned from. And certainly nothing is to be regretted if it has shaped you into the kind, compassionate, *dear* creature that you are. I only mean that, if we are ever to have the means to marry, the less said about all that the better. Do you understand me?"

She nodded. "Yes. I understand."

After blowing her nose in her handkerchief, Jane tried to repair her appearance, and though Egerton would gladly have rumpled her again with his caresses, her pensiveness held him in check.

"I must go," she said. "Everyone will wonder what became of me."

He caught her by the sleeve. "One last kiss. To seal our secret."

With a look he could not read, she darted at him, putting light fingers to his jaw and the most fleeting of kisses to his cheek.

And then she was gone.

CHAPTER 27

Don't you see December in her face?
— William Cartwright, *The ordinary: a comedy,* i.ii.8
(c.1643)

J ane did not have to feign illness when she arrived at home. Her mother took one look at her pink nose and pink-rimmed eyes and said, "You have overtaxed yourself, my dear. Why don't you go and lie down?"

The bedroom she shared with Sarah had one small window facing north, which meant it was dim and cool in the summer and dim and cold in the winter, and the thrifty Barstows usually dispensed with heating the bedchambers during the day and spent their time in the cozier parlors. On this occasion, however, Jane found the lamp lit and Sarah at their little dressing table.

"Oh, goodness! Jane," said her sister-in-law, quickly folding up a letter and returning it to its packet. "Bash was napping, and I—I—"

And she was rereading Sebastian's letters. Jane did not need Sarah to finish her sentence. Instead, smothering a sigh, she gave Sarah's shoulder a squeeze and threw herself on the bed, wrapping the coverlet about her.

"Are you unwell?"

"I will be fine," she answered, "with a little rest."

"Did you have your hands full with Harry Barbary?"

"Somewhat."

"All right, then. I will leave you in peace. Bash should sleep at least another hour in there." Securing the bundle of letters with its ribbon, Sarah stowed it in the drawer, but leaving the candles burning at Jane's request, she slipped out.

Not being the least bit sick nor accustomed to napping, Jane stared at the ceiling.

He loved her and wanted to marry her! She should have been floating around that very ceiling, singing and grinning like a madwoman. She should have been seizing her family members to dance them around the room. But she could not do any of these things.

Because her engagement was a secret.

Jane groaned. A secret. How she hated that word! How she had hated it ever since Roger. And now, in what should have been a crowning moment, to have the man she adored again say the wretched word, again enjoin her to secrecy! To hiding and slinking, to whispers and furtiveness. Roger had insisted on secrecy because what he proposed was shameful. But Philip asked for it because he was ashamed of *her*.

Throwing off the coverlet, Jane sat up, hugging her knees close, as if to hold herself together. Oh, if only his kisses were not so delicious and the tributes he paid her so tender, so intoxicating!

Because it was not that she did not see the reasonableness of his request; it was that she did.

If he must hide me in order to marry me, he should not be marrying me.

The thought stabbed her, and she buried her face against her knees. *He should not have asked me. Not yet. Possibly not ever.*

And then: "No more secrets," she said aloud, barely above a whisper.

But her voice strengthened as her resolve did.

"*No more secrets.* No more scandals. I have finished with that part of my life, and I do not want ever to be hidden or made to feel ashamed of myself again. If marrying me will bring him or his career in the church down, he had better not do it. I wish—I wish I might be a credit to my husband. But if that is not possible, I wish at least not to shame him."

She was shaking, but she struggled up from the bed to sit at the same dressing table where she had found Sarah. Here were not only hairbrushes, combs, pins, powders, and lotions, but also paper and a wooden pencil.

It might have been the hardest thing she had written in her life. But no—writing to her family to say Roger was in prison had been worse.

When it was done at last, Jane folded it carefully and tucked it in her sleeve. She would sleep on the matter, but if she felt the same in the morning, she would find some way to send it to him.

Fortune favored her, if fortune it could be called.

"How pale you still look, my dear," said her mother the next day. "Perhaps you should go back to bed." But when Jane insisted she was perfectly well apart from restless sleep, Mrs. Barstow relented. "Very well. I will leave you in peace. Perhaps then you might go with Sarah or Frances to the Cramthorpes? I have some mince pies and soup for them."

Frances begged off, so it was Sarah and Jane who set off with the food and Sarah and Jane who met Mr. Egerton as they emerged again half an hour later. (The call lasted longer than usual because the younger Mrs. Cramthorpe wanted to thank Jane for her teaching and the older Mrs. Cramthorpe to criticize it.)

"Mrs. Barstow, Mrs. Merritt," he said with alacrity, his features lighting as he lifted his hat to them. "You here too? What an unexpected pleasure."

"My mother had some things for them," Jane replied, flustered by his nearness. But her resolve had indeed survived the night, and she fumbled at her sleeve. "And—and the Cramthorpes insisted on hearing Jimmy and Anna say their pieces twice over. I—have written them down for you. Won't you look them over and—and tell Cassie if you would make any changes?" Jane told no falsehoods. She had deliberately added the recital verses to her note because it was the only excuse which came to her. Still, she could not bring herself to meet his eyes, for fear she would give way.

Puzzled by both her insistence and her evasiveness, he accepted the folded paper, his fingertips just brushing hers. "Thank you, but I am certain whatever you and Cassie have chosen will do very well."

"Still, do look it over as soon as you have leisure," Jane urged, now adjusting her sleeve and taking Sarah's arm. "I—would feel much better if you did."

"Though no doubt you will learn the selections as soon as you enter," put in Sarah with a twinkle, "for I am sure Jimmy and Anna will be made to perform for you as well."

Before he could answer, Jane was hustling her sister-in-law away, calling over her shoulder, "Good day to you!"

"My word," Sarah said breathlessly as Jane tugged on her. "What is your hurry? Mr. Egerton looked like he didn't know what to think."

"Never mind Mr. Egerton."

"Don't you like him, Jane?"

"Of course I like him. Oh, gracious—here comes Mrs. Lamb as fast as her legs can carry her. I don't suppose there's any avoiding her."

There was not, but at least the postmistress was brief. "They've come back!" she panted before she had quite reached them. "The Greenwood Hall set. Wiley saw Mr. Beck's coach take the turning. What do you think of that, Mrs. Merritt?"

Had Jane not just done something so momentous as break her secret engagement of less than a day's standing, this news would have discomposed her greatly. As it was, she hardly cared, much to Mrs. Lamb's disappointment.

"Is it so?" said Jane. "Then the children will have their recital very soon. Thank you, Mrs. Lamb. And if it was the curate you wished to tell next, you will not find him at the rectory, but rather calling upon the Cramthorpes. Good day."

Watching Jane go, he might have read her note there and then, before he even set foot in the Cramthorpes' cottage, but he too saw Mrs. Lamb's approach and quickly tucked his darling's message away before ducking inside. But not once in the next twenty minutes, when he too must hear Jimmy and Anna recite, and he too must be hunted down by the post-mistress to deliver her news, did he forget the little folded paper in his possession.

Could it be a love note? The mere thought of one was enough to make him interrupt old Mrs. Cramthorpe and finish her complaining sentence for her, with hasty promises that whatever trifle had vexed her the Sunday previous at church would be addressed at once.

But if it was a love note, why had she been so pale and withdrawn? Why had she run away as if she might catch leprosy from him? It might have been embarrassment, of course. Or fear that she might give something away if she remained in his presence. The explanation did not satisfy his wandering mind, however, for in the fleeting glance she gave him there had been a hint of sadness. Of stoicism. If this was to be her outward manner during their secret engagement, Egerton thought he would have to spend half his time inveigling to get her alone.

At last, when both the Cramthorpes and Mrs. Lamb were dispensed with (the latter with assurances that, yes, the recital invitation would go out directly), Egerton returned to the rectory, shutting himself again in his library and praying to be left alone.

The writing was small and neat but not always easy to read because of the many places where his beloved had made errors or changed her mind and resorted to the India rubber.

It was no love note.

Mr. Egerton,

After much pondering, I have concluded that I must end our arrangement. While I am deeply sensible of the honor you do me and thoroughly understand your reasons for secrecy, I find I cannot ever again consent to such a scheme. Despite all I have done and deserved, I confess I cannot bear to be taken on sufferance, nor to enter a match where I am considered so much the inferior partner. Forgive me my pride and my change of heart. I wish you all happiness and every good blessing.

There followed no signature, but only the list of the children's recitations.

In his first year at Oxford, Philip had plummeted from a first-floor window after a night spent skylarking. He had landed hard on the grass below, winded and dazed, miraculously having broken no bones.

This felt like that.

Mrs. Merritt—his Jane—no, *not* his Jane, no longer his Jane—had flung him down with the same ease as gravity, and Philip experienced once more the painful suffocation and shock. If her letter had been written in Hittite he could not have struggled more to understand it.

She "ended their arrangement"?

She cast him into outer darkness yet wished him, in the same breath, "all happiness and every good blessing"?

His first instinct was to rush to Iffley Cottage and plead for her to reconsider. How could they have gone from those thrilling, ardent kisses—which he had not been able to put from his mind more than a few minutes at a time—to *this*?

I should not have insisted on secrecy. It wounded her. I will march over directly and ask her again and tell her we will shout our engagement from the rooftops.

But then the old problem reared its head of how he would support them. For better or worse, his darling Jane's scandals trailed her faithfully, and she could escape them no more than she could her own shadow.

The answer, old boy, is that you should not have asked her yesterday in the first place! You should have held your tongue until you had something secured already, and then none of this would have mattered.

With a groan, he thumped his forehead slowly with his fist. Fool! Idiot! Because he could control himself no better than Beck, he had ruined everything.

But did she love him? She must, surely she must, or she would never have kissed him and let him kiss her. She had not willingly kissed Beck, after all. Therefore, though she had not said the words, she *must* love him.

And if she loves me, she will wait for me.

He would write his letters seeking employment. He would find his next position. He would crawl on his belly to his uncle, if it would do any good. And then, the instant he found something, anything, he would fly to Iffley Cottage and ask her to consider him again.

And in the meantime, however long that meantime might last, he would treat her like the queen of the world.

Yet no sooner did Egerton make this vow, than he could not help but qualify it. She would be queen of his heart, yes, though of course her past could not be undone. He could not pretend her shadow did not exist, but he would henceforth graciously cease to refer to it, if it could possibly be avoided. And it could, once he had a benefice in hand.

With this renewed determination, Egerton set immediately to work, writing five letters that very hour, and when they were done, he decided to post them at once and then reward himself with a call at Iffley Cottage.

Because he should certainly demonstrate to—Mrs. Merritt, he supposed he had better call her again—that he understood her reasoning, yes, but also had no intention of giving her up permanently.

"I say, aren't you a busy man, Mr. Egerton," remarked Mrs. Lamb. "Nearly as busy as all of them over at Greenwood Hall. Another letter came for Mr. Beck that was as ill-spelt as the last. Did I tell you about that first letter? Oh—must you be going already? Good-bye, good-bye! These will go out with the very next post."

When the maid Reed announced him at the cottage, the usually crowded parlor was empty, save for the youngest daughter Maria, the toddling Bash who was teasing the dog—and Mrs. Merritt.

"Where—is everyone?" he asked in surprise. Not that he was sorry to find her nearly alone, but it was so unusual he did not at first trust his eyes.

"Baking mince pies!" declared Maria, springing up. "All but Gordy, who ran over to Perryfield, and Jane because Mama says she needs rest, and I, because someone must watch Bash. Do you smell the pies? I was only allowed one from the first batch because they were for other people, but Mama says these new ones are for the rectory and for us!"

"They smell delicious."

"I will tell Mama you are here," the girl announced.

"No—don't," Jane and Egerton said in unison.

"Don't let me disturb everyone's work," he added. "I won't stay. I only came because—because—"

"You came to approve my note," Jane finished for him. "Of the children's recital selections."

"…Yes. That's it." He felt a banging against his knee and looked down to see Bash rapping it smartly with his Jacob's ladder. Bending to give the little boy's head a pat, he went on. "I don't know if 'approve' is the right word, however. Perhaps 'acknowledge with great reluctance' would be more fitting. Great, *great* reluctance, bordering on…anguish."

She absorbed this in silence, but her little sister frowned. "Mercy, Jane, what have you picked for them to recite?"

"Nor do I consider this a final word," said Egerton. "It is, for *now*. I will not lose hope, unless you tell me I should."

Maria stared from one to the other, but her sister merely pressed her lips together and twisted her hands in her lap.

"Tell me, Mrs. Merritt," he pressed. "Should I...lose hope?"

"I cannot say more than that you—and I—are entirely free," she whispered. "To say otherwise would be no different than if—my note—had not been written, or had not been sincere."

Maria thought the curate not very pleased with this answer, for he looked darkly at her older sister for a full minute. Then, gently disengaging himself from Bash, who had wound around his boots like a cat, he rejoined, "Very well. Freedom all around. I will only say *my* freedom will be spent in the pursuit of my unchanged desires. Good day to you."

When he had gone Maria flew to Jane. "What did it all mean?" she demanded. "Was that truly about the recital, for if it was you are all taking it much too seriously. Perhaps Anna and Jimmy might prefer a poem from Mother Goose instead of Bible verses. The one about the old man with the calf is easy enough, and so is 'Bow wow wow, whose dog art thou.'"

But her sister perplexingly covered her eyes with her hands for a moment before taking up her sewing again and stitching as if for her life. "Thank you, dear," she murmured. "If he asks again, you can suggest them."

CHAPTER 28

**'Lydy,' says his Lordship, ''tis your
Picture to the utmost Resemblance.'
— John Shebbeare, *Lydia, or Filial piety* (1755)**

After all the planning and plotting of the Iffley community, in the
end the students' recital never took place. When Egerton did eventually remember to send the invitation to Greenwood Hall, it was politely declined. Even more surprisingly, the entire Greenwood party kept to
themselves after their return. While they had never attended service at St.
Mary the Virgin, in the following days neither were they seen in the village
or riding about the country. And even those who had declared they would
certainly not call at the Hall after the tenants returned were affronted when
no attempts were made by the Hall to call upon *them*.

"What can it mean?" demanded Mrs. Dere in the churchyard after the
morning service. "If they mean to hide away from society, why return at all
to Iffley?"

"Perhaps Mr. Beck is too ashamed of his conduct," suggested Mrs. Lane,
peeping behind her to ensure neither the curate nor any of the Barstows
were within earshot. "I did not expect him to show his face here, at any
rate, however much I would have liked to see Mrs. Merritt cut him. And

imagine poor Mr. Egerton, if he had had to deliver his sermon with that man in the pews!"

"Poor Mr. Egerton indeed," whispered Mrs. Bellew in an even lower voice. "Do you not think he has been out of spirits?"

"He has, he has," agreed Mrs. Lane eagerly, the circle of ladies unconsciously contracting, and heads leaning in. "Everyone has noticed. Why, Mrs. Lamb said to me—"

"Mrs. Bellew, surely you are not going to repeat that woman's idle gossip," scolded Mrs. Dere, but her reproof was half-hearted.

"I—well—no, but it happens that I quite agree with what she said," floundered Mrs. Bellew. "Which is, he has been low *ever since Miss Hynde departed*. He held up in the immediate aftermath, but as time passed, his depression increased." Then, with a mischievous smile at the mistress of Perryfield she added, "But Mrs. Lamb did tell our maid Jemima one interesting titbit when the girl went to have the ale jugs refilled. It was nothing important, most likely, but..." A shrug.

Mrs. Dere would not stoop to take the bait, but thankfully Mrs. Lane did. "Bother, Matilda! Do finish your sentences, instead of throwing out lures."

Appeased, Matilda Bellew dropped her pretense of indifference. "Very well, then. Mrs. Lamb said a letter from Cottrell Hall came for Mr. Egerton yesterday, and now Mr. Egerton has hired a horse to ride into Oxford this afternoon!"

This was met with muted gasps and unanswerable questions: "Do you suppose he wrote to his uncle and offered for Miss Hynde?" "Why should he go to Oxford?" "If he goes to meet his uncle, why does his uncle not simply come to Iffley?" "Should we ask Miss Egerton what she knows?"

Curiosity won the day, but when Cassie was applied to, she could say no more than, "My uncle has business in Oxford with his lawyers tomorrow morning and asked Philip to meet him there. What about neither he nor I know." Both had guesses, but she refrained from adding this. They would all just have to wait and see.

Though she was wrong as to the cause, Mrs. Bellew did not miss the mark in observing Egerton's lowered spirits. How could he help but be low, despite his resolve not to despair of Mrs. Merritt? In the week which had passed, he had already received three responses to his letters, and none offered employment. If anything, his income threatened to diminish, for, in addition to declining the proposed recital, Beck wrote tersely that he would be withdrawing Archie from Egerton's tutelage after Christmas to send the boy to school in London, and would Egerton be so kind as to inform him?

Much as the shy child had grown on him, and much as he feared Archie would not like the change, Egerton could not be sorry for it, if it meant Beck also meant to return to town.

But even heavier on his heart than his unpromising career aspirations lay Mrs. Merritt. She seemed determined to avoid him. If he happened by when the parish lessons were ending, she chose to walk home with the children. If he called at the cottage, she sewed quietly beside her mother or made some excuse to leave the room. In church she kept her eyes lowered. With the recital idea abandoned, he had no excuse to ply her with notes or questions. Even a highly-anticipated dinner at Perryfield proved a frustration, as he got no more from her than polite phrases, and, try as he might, he could never catch her eye.

It could not be borne.

Did she no longer love him, or had she never loved him at all?

Had she kissed him simply because she liked kissing? It was more than she had granted Beck, truly, but it was not enough for Egerton. Not nearly enough. So, yes, depression had settled on him, depression and uneasiness.

When his uncle's note came, it was as cryptic as his earlier letter, offering no reason for his summons. It likely concerned Miss Hynde, but he couldn't muster any curiosity and only hoped she and Martha would not be there.

The sun had just dipped below the horizon when Egerton rode across the Pettypont, past Magdalen Tower and the Physic Garden into the Oxford High Street. He would have preferred to walk, but knowing he could not leave Iffley until the afternoon service was ended left him little choice. He had been further delayed, moreover, by delivering the news to Archie Wilson.

"You understand what I am saying, Archie? At the end of the month, you will leave us to return to London, to a new school your guardian has chosen. We will be sorry to see you go, for you have been a good pupil and well-behaved lad."

"My mama is in London," said Archie, his features lighting. "Then I will see her all the time."

For the boy's sake Egerton hoped so, though if Archie was illegitimate and his mother...no better than she should be, it was hard to say whether proximity could be considered a benefit of the removal.

"She loves me very much," said Archie, more to himself than to his tutor, "and no one is as beautiful as my mama. Not even Mrs. Merritt."

This last bit jarred Egerton, whose thoughts were never very far from Mrs. Merritt to begin with, and he felt a surge of fondness for the child, remembering that Archie alone of the rectory boys had seemed to prefer Mrs. Merritt to Felicity Hynde.

Passing the Angel Inn, Egerton almost smiled to remember his last visit there, when he dragged Mrs. Merritt out of Miss Hynde's clawed reach. Miss Hynde's temper—what a display! With the rumpus Felicity made, he had not even been able to enjoy the sensation of holding Mrs. Merritt close. Those working at the Angel might have forgotten the incident by now, but Philip had not, and he was glad his uncle Geoffrey had chosen the more fashionable Golden Cross Hotel on Cornmarket Street.

Ordinarily the High Street would be thronged with dons, duns, noblemen with their tutors and servants, gentlemen commoners, more humble commoners, servitors, and dreaded proctors on the lookout for miscreants to pull from taverns. But there were considerably fewer now because the Michaelmas term had ended the previous week. Egerton had spent many years among them all, first as a gentleman commoner and then as a fellow of Christ Church. He had not got into any more scrapes than the average undergraduate and far fewer than many, but it all seemed long ago now, and none of them paid any attention to the sober clergyman in his black coat riding by on an unimpressive nag. When the Terrys returned, would he have any choice but to don his old gown and rent a mean garret near the college? What had been perfectly sufficient a few months earlier now struck him as unendurable, and Egerton shuddered. How could that life possibly compare to the new vision which had replaced it, one of a snug vicarage quickened by the presence of his beloved Jane?

Jane.

Like a tongue probing an aching tooth, he returned to the problem of Jane. In good moments he told himself she loved him but avoided him because their separation was painful. A comforting thought, even if it changed nothing in their circumstances. In bad moments—well, in bad moments he thought he meant no more to her than Beck had, and that she had kissed him for comparison's sake, or for amusement. Since she would not let him get near again, there was only one way of learning the truth: to ask her again when he could engage himself to her openly. And when, oh *when,* would that be? A year from hence? Two? *Five?*

But as Egerton reached the Carfax and clicked his tongue to his hired mount, he little knew how close his deliverance loomed. As the poet Cowper put it, "God moves in a mysterious way, His wonders to perform," and that mysterious way lay just inside the courtyard of the Cross Inn.

Compared to the Angel, not a fraction of the coaches arrived at or departed from the Cross, but nor did the Cross boast the Angel's spacious yard. The narrow courtyard of the Cross was entered under an archway and was only wide enough for a single coach or wagon to turn around in, but it being Sunday, Egerton did not expect much of a squeeze. He dismounted in the street, however, to save himself ducking under the arch, and led his horse in by the reins.

Walled in on every side, the courtyard was lit only by two hanging lanterns and whatever light seeped through cracks in the window shutters. Which is to say, it was a dim place on a winter evening and made much more so by the elegant coach drawn up before the entrance, blocking what light the lanterns threw off. The coach had its own pair of globe lamps, of course, and a servant lad held a torch for the ostlers and stablemen, and it was by this lesser and uncertain light that Egerton saw a sight which stopped him dead.

At first he thought he must have been thinking so hard about her that he willed her into existence. For there stood Mrs. Merritt beside the coach, her back to him, her bonnet hanging down by its straps and her dark hair half tumbled. That is, there stood Mrs. Merritt, being thoroughly, willingly and reciprocally kissed.

By Alexander Beck.

For there was the gleam of the man's emerald ring and there the particular angle at which he bowed his head to reach her lips.

Presented with this sight for the third time in as many months, Egerton—well—it must be stated that then Mr. Philip Egerton, fellow at Christ Church and vicar of St. Mary the Virgin in Iffley, thoroughly disgraced himself.

As Hex Wexham, ostler, age fifteen, would tell the story a hundred times in the next several days, "There we were, loading the baggage, like, for the gentleman and his sweetheart, when there was this great roar, and next thing you know, some madman lays hold of the gentleman's collar and slings him across the court and then throws hisself on top, bellowing something about there'll be no eloping while he's got breath in him! And the other man starts swearing and yelling, and then they're rolling about in the muck, and everyone is screaming, especially the sweetheart. She's a-screaming, 'Alex! Alex! Call the constabulary! Help! Help! O Alex! O Alex!'" Hex's audiences particularly loved when he did the sweetheart's voice accompanied by her hand-wringing, so it was no surprise that portion of the tale grew longer and more elaborate in the retelling.

"'Oh, help!' she cries. 'Alex, my darling own, set upon by ruffians at the very door of the inn! What is the world a-coming to?' She was fit to break your heart, she was, so pretty and so wild, and that must be what acted on the madman because all of a sudden his head whips around to look at her—*snap!* And he goes all still like a statue—"(here Hex would hold perfectly still longer and longer for effect) "—and then *crack!* the gentleman Alex lets the madman have it in the jaw! Down he goes, moaning and groaning, and we all woke up like and ran over to pin his arms and legs till the constable came.

"The gentleman Alex gets up, his eye all swole and wiping off his mouth because the attacker got him good, and he calls for Ed with the torch so he can see what was what. Then he says, thick-like, like he's got a mouthful of porridge, 'Edgeton, you lunatic. What is the meaning of this? You oughtter be locked away in Bedlam.' And we're all sitting on this Edgeton fellow, but he says, 'I thought she was someone else you were a-kissing and eloping with.' And the gentleman Alex throws back his head and laughs *ha ha ha!* 'I know who you thought it was, you fool. They do look a lot alike, don't they? That's why she caught my eye in the first place, lovely Mrs. Mer—' But then the man on the ground lets out another roar: 'Don't you be saying her name in public! Don't you be dragging her name in your mud!' And the gentleman Alex lets out another *ha ha ha* and says, 'Looks like you're the one in the mud, Edgeton. Let Mrs. M be our secret, then.' And the sweetheart hangs herself around his neck and starts screeching, 'Who? Who is Mrs. M, Alex? Who are you talking about?' but he just puts his hat back on and stuffs her in the coach and gets in himself. So I say, 'Sir, don't you want to wait for the constable?' But he flips me a half-crown and says, 'You talk to him. You saw it all.' And then he bangs on the roof for his coachman to go. And the last thing he does, he opens the window and yells, 'Enjoy your time in gaol, and I hope never to see you again.'

"When the coach was gone, Edgeton just lay there. He asked if a Geoffrey Cottrell was come yet, and I was for keeping mum, but Ed went and said he wasn't. And then Edgeton says we must send for Dean Jackson or Barnes the Censor Thingummy of Christ Church because, he says, 'Though I wear no gown, I am a fellow of there,' but then the constable comes, and we go through it all again, and *he* says, 'Oh, no, you hothead. You can tell these things to the gaoler,' and off he marches him!"

In essentials the faithfulness of Hex Wexham's account was admirable, though he could not answer either of the two questions every auditor posed: (1) If the gentleman Alex was not eloping with the madman's sweetheart, who *was* he eloping with? And, (2) then who was the madman's mysterious Mrs. M? In his defense, with Beck gone and Egerton hauled away by the constable, Wexham had no one to consult for answers, so he eventually made up his own guesses, which the reader will be spared.

Egerton had plenty of time to dwell on the affair and to come to his own conclusions, however, during his confinement. As dark nights of the soul went, the city gaol's dank holding cell provided a fit setting, as did the two companions who shared the space, both thankfully too stupefied with drink for conversation.

Beck had called him a lunatic and a fool, and Philip could not blame him. What could he say in his own defense? He had discovered his Jane beside a waiting coach sharing an eager embrace and had leapt to the conclusion that, for the second time in her life, she was eloping with a worthless rogue! Which meant his own kisses meant nothing to her, that her seeming repentance was a sham, and her supposed rejection of secrecy and avoidance of him mere ruses, meant only to throw Egerton off the scent while she plotted with Beck. Wheels within wheels.

With the volcano of rage, hurt and jealousy within him threatening to blow sky high, he had again flung himself on her "lover," and all was going swimmingly, as revenge attacks went, until the screams of the lady finally penetrated his fury.

Screams which did not belong to Jane Merritt.

Screams which belonged, instead, to some other woman Philip had never before met and who, when he saw her face in the light of the coach lamps, was like a copy of his beloved made too quickly—the mouth looser, the nose shorter, the eyes rounder, the bosom more exposed.

Just remembering his idiocy made him groan again. And yet—as he sat there, jaw aching and limbs stiffening, odorous muck drying on him in crusty patches, he was conscious of a thread of something entirely different running through it all, like a vein of gold-flecked quartz traced through granite. Because all through his regret and mortification and his fear of what might happen next ran that precious thread, winding in and out. A thread of—could it be—?

Joy.

Pure elation.

Because Jane had *not* eloped again.

Jane was still his Jane, or would be, if he could manage it. Oh, Lord. However *would* he manage it now? Because now, this time through his own doing, marriage with Jane retreated even further out of his reach. The Bishop of Oxford would be obligated to take action now, grace having failed, and now Philip would also have to face the college's dean Jackson or his deputy, *Censor Theologiae* Barnes. When they heard of his scandalous conduct, he did not doubt he would lose his fellowship as well as his temporary curacy, if he were not voided from his affiliations with Christ Church altogether.

How ludicrous was it, that he had wanted to hush up his Jane's spotty past, only to out-spot her so lavishly! He, who apparently only required the spur of jealousy to metamorphose into a hot-tempered menace to social peace.

Now it would be she who was ashamed of him, for heaven's sake.

A mirthless laugh escaped him then, loud enough that his sodden companions in woe raised bleary eyes. But he broke off and sprang up when the gaoler's footsteps approached.

"Was there any response from Christ Church?" he asked. "I am a fellow there, and my discipline will be handled by the college, rather than the city—"

"So you said," interrupted the unsympathetic man. There had been enough friction between town and gown over the years that Egerton's peremptory demand only irked him. "And no. Term's over, you know, so I wouldn't count on anyone rushing to save you. Probably all off visiting. No word from your supposed uncle at the Cross Inn either," he added, anticipating Egerton's next question.

What on earth had happened to Uncle Geoffrey? Why would he arrange to meet his nephew and then neither come nor send word? Of course, he might have sent word to the rectory, and if he had, Cassie no doubt supposed her brother would learn for himself when he came to town.

"I must send another note," said Egerton. "To my sister in Iffley. She will be anxious when I do not return. My good man, be so kind as to bring me paper and pen, and you will be well paid."

"A coin for me won't do you any good," replied the gaoler, taking the one offered nonetheless and drifting away to fetch the items. "You'll need more than that to pay your fine if you don't want to sit in there until the next Assizes."

CHAPTER 29

**The fortune of the day was quickly changed.
—William Robertson, *The history of the reign
of the Emperor Charles V* (1769)**

T he Barstows were gathered in the Perryfield drawing room, listening to Frances at the pianoforte as Mrs. Dere prepared the tea, when the footman Wood reappeared only a minute after having deposited the tray.

"Er—Miss Egerton is here, madam," he announced.

"Here? *Alone*? How peculiar. Well, show her in, Wood."

Cassie hurried in, still cloaked, bringing with her a rush of cold air. "Do forgive my imposition, Lord Dere, Mrs. Dere, but I did not know where else to turn!"

A clamor of questions swallowed her, after such a dramatic beginning, even while Lord Dere led her to the fire. "You must tell us all about it," he murmured, "when you have warmed yourself."

"Thank you, sir, but I am afraid my news cannot wait," she cried, her voice breaking into sobs. The suspense was dreadful to her listeners, and knowing this, she did her best to master herself, scrubbing at her eyes with one of the many handkerchiefs offered her. Jane was at her side, gripping her arm in a manner which would have been comforting, had it not been almost painful.

At last the curate's sister choked out her story. "I-I do not know all the details—the messages I received by express were very short. But my brother went to meet my uncle in Oxford, though my uncle could not come after all—but Philip doesn't know that because he had already gone. That was one of the messages—the other was that—that Philip—he was there and—and—and—somehow he became involved in a—a violent altercation!"

Another volley of gasps and exclamations met this, but it was Jane's voice which rose above the others to pierce Cassie's ear, even as her grasp tightened. "Dear God! Is he hurt?"

Even in Cassie's distress Jane's heightened concern struck her, as it did the others, more than one of whom turned to regard her.

"I do not know if he was injured," Cassie replied, easing her arm from Jane's iron fingers. "But I think he could not be—not seriously, in any event—or surely he would have mentioned it and asked me to send for a doctor."

"What did he tell you, then, my dear?" asked the baron calmly. "Why did he not simply return to Iffley?"

For a moment she could not answer as her throat worked and a second handkerchief was resorted to. But then: "He—could not come back, sir, because—because—he was arrested and taken by the constable to the city gaol!"

Then it was Mrs. Dere's turn to shriek. What was the world coming to? The curate of her own parish church, to be arrested! It was the end of everything!

Unruffled by his niece-in-law's outburst, Lord Dere persisted, "Was the—other person—arrested as well?"

"I—don't know. My brother's note was only two lines. He only said he had been in an altercation and was then put in gaol for disturbing the peace, and could I—could I please come or send someone to—to pay the fine, so that he could be released until—until he need appear in court to answer the charges. Lord Dere, I did not know where else to turn! I went first to Iffley Cottage, but Reed said everyone was here."

Lord Dere was already striding to his locked desk, even as Mrs. Dere wrung her hands and Jane wobbled on her feet. "We will go at once. Frances, if you would be so kind as to ring for Wood again. Harker and Ogle must ready the coach. We will take the Barstows home and proceed directly to Oxford." Having secured several banknotes in his pocketbook, he hesitated a moment and then looked at Jane. "Jane—forgive me for mentioning this, but it must be said. Mr. Egerton does not name his—er—opponent, but one possibility would be our neighbor Mr. Beck."

"Yes," she said, scarcely audible.

"If Beck is there, do I have your permission this time to threaten him?"

Mrs. Dere let out another shriek, and she rushed to take him by the sleeve. "You cannot, sir! At your age! Think of your family. Think of little Peter, if we were to lose you. I forbid it."

Gently, he detached himself. "Alice, I do not mean to threaten him with violence, if it can be helped, but rather with the force of social opprobrium."

"'If it can be helped'?" repeated Mrs. Dere. "No, sir, I will not allow it! Why should you—or, indeed, Mr. Egerton, for that matter—jeopardize your own well-being and reputation to—to—if Mrs. Merritt will understand I mean no offence—to defend what is already *past remedy*?"

Her normally serene and patient brow darkening, Mrs. Barstow drew herself up once more to repel this attack on poor Jane, but before she could speak, the baron raised both his hands.

"Alice," he said, as quietly as ever, "I give you your head in most everything at Perryfield, and I do not resent it, for you do a fine job as mistress. But in matters of gentlemanly honor, you must give way to me. I will brook no argument. Nor do I agree with you that Jane's story is past remedy. If not for Beck's uninvited impositions on her, not a person in Iffley could fault her conduct in the past two years, nor doubt her true remorse."

Silenced, Mrs. Dere crossed her arms tightly over her bosom and was reduced to *looking* the daggers she felt, but Jane could have kissed the baron's feet. He extended a hand to her. "Since this so nearly concerns you, Jane, would you care to come with Miss Egerton and me to Oxford? You will not see Beck, of course, but you will know what has occurred as soon as it can be told to you."

"Oh, *yes*, sir," Jane accepted with tears in her eyes. "Yes, and thank you!"

The many bells of Oxford were tolling nine when the gaoler reappeared.

"Aren't you the lucky one," he said, shaking his key ring. "Who needs the dean of Christ Church or the Censor Thingummy? Come on, then. Out you come."

Egerton raised his head from his hands. "I'm—free?" However had Cassie managed it?

"Free to go now, but you'll appear when the magistrates sit, or so your friend the baron has sworn. Sworn and paid your fine."

One of the drunks scrabbled at his ankle, jeering, "Ooh, a baron!" but Egerton dazedly shook him off.

"Philip!" sobbed his sister, flinging herself at him when he emerged. "Your lip! Your—your clothes! What happened?"

"Not here, my dear," said Lord Dere behind her. "He will tell us all in the coach."

"Lord Dere, sir," began the curate, "I must thank you and assure you that—"

"Yes, yes. Tell me in the coach, young man."

Apparently when one was a baron, one expected things to be resolved quickly, for the Dere coach waited just outside, the horses' breath smoking in the night air.

It was not only the vehicle which waited. When Hoskins unfolded the steps and opened the door, who should Philip glimpse within but the last person in the world he expected and, at the same time, the one he most yearned to see?

"Jane?" he gasped, her Christian name escaping his lips before he could think. But she had cried, "Philip!" just as Cassie had, her eyes taking anxious inventory of his condition.

Hearing Miss Egerton suck in a breath at these unexpected familiarities, the baron said, "Ah ha. There is more to the story, it appears. Well, into the coach, all of you."

But when they were closed in and rattling along the High Street, with the baron and Jane sitting across from him and the glow of the occasional lantern sliding across her beloved face like a caress, Egerton hardly knew where to begin. He wished he might take her upon his lap and lay her head against his chest while he told her everything. Everything. But short of ejecting his rescuers from the carriage, that was impossible.

Still—where to begin?

Lord Dere helped him. "Miss Egerton informs us you were in an altercation."

"Forgive me for telling the Barstows and the Deres," Cassie interposed hastily from beside him. "I had no idea what to do, Philip, or who to ask. You know we haven't any extra money lying around the rectory."

"I know. It's all right, Cass." With a wrench he tore his gaze from Jane to face the baron. "Sir, yes, I am sorry to say I was in another tussle and—again—I was the one who initiated it."

"Was it—Mr. Beck?" ventured Jane, and he was glad of an excuse to look at her again. But this was the hard part—the awful part—and how he would rather have confessed it to her alone!

"It was," he admitted.

"Well, for pity's sake, Philip," protested his sister. "The first time you attacked him was bad enough, though everyone later said you did the right thing. But what will they say now, if you are going to throw yourself at him whensoever he crosses your path? What will the bishop say this time, when he learns of it? And the dean of Christ Church!"

"I was not without provocation," he said shortly, his nostrils flaring. "I had my reasons—though I was mistaken. I admit that. You see...when I rode into the yard of the Cross Inn, I saw Beck's carriage. You know how it is there—the light isn't very good because it's so narrow. Beck was there, accompanied by a woman with her back to me. He—they—were embracing. I thought they were eloping."

Cassie threw up her hands. "So? He's a scoundrel! Let him elope with whomever he pleases. You cannot defend every woman in Christendom."

But it was Jane who said in a low voice, "Was it—that you thought I was the lady?"

He hung his head. "I did. She had dark hair and your—ahem—your shape. I suspect it was Archie Wilson's mother. You remember how Archie took to you? You must have reminded him of her, at least in appearance."

Though she said nothing, he saw her swallow, her expression pained, and her unspoken reproach knifed through him. He couldn't bear it.

"Forgive me," he whispered. "Jane. Forgive me. Of course you would never. Would never again. Not with him, nor with anyone. I was a fool. Jealousy swallowed me whole. I have no excuse, except that...I lost my mind."

"If I'm not mistaken," said Cassie slowly, looking from one to the other "your mind is not the only vital organ you've lost."

"That's right," her brother answered steadily, his gaze never leaving Jane. "I've lost my heart, too. Lost it who knows how many weeks—months—ago. And I wanted to marry Mrs. Merritt, though I had no right to ask because I had no income to speak of. But because I seem unable to master myself, where she is concerned, I asked her anyway and said we could keep it secret for now." His voice cracked, and he leaned his elbows on his knees to hold her lowered gaze. "Keep it secret! Lest she harm my chances of securing a benefice." With a rueful chuckle, he shook his head and sighed. "I need no assistance there, it seems—in harming my chances, I mean."

"The two of you are engaged, then?" asked the baron.

Egerton's mouth twisted. "We were. For a few hours. Until Jane's conscience smote her, and she told me she could no longer submit to secrecy or deceit. So...no. We are not engaged. Which means I had no right to assault Beck, even if he had been absconding with her. Jane," he said again, leaning farther, "say you pardon me—because 'I believe; help thou mine unbelief!'"

A tear traced a glistening path down her cheek, and with trembling lips she murmured, "I pardon you, Philip. I do."

So rapt and intent were the lovers that Lord Dere and Cassie felt decidedly de trop, but Egerton was contrarily glad of their presence. Let the world know, now.

Sliding from the cushioned bench, he angled himself so that he might drop to one knee, laughing when the carriage jolted and nearly sent him tumbling.

"Jane, won't you be mine, before all the world? What little income I have from my fellowship and my curacy will not be mine through the end of the week, I daresay, but if you will wait for me, we will see what the future still holds for one miscreant and one reformed miscreant."

"Oh!" squeaked Cassie, clapping a hand to her mouth. "Philip, I quite forgot—your note saying you were thrown in gaol quite blew it out of my head!"

Nobody heard her the first time, for all was tumult in the coach. Jane had thrown herself at the curate, laughing and crying and making the carriage rock alarmingly. Lord Dere laughed along with them, tucking his legs up to be out of their way and urging Philip to "give her a kiss to seal the bargain, my lad."

But when order was restored, and Philip had given Jane not one kiss but rather a half dozen, and she had kissed the baron and Cassie in turn, and the baron and her betrothed had exchanged places in the coach, Cassie tried again, giving her brother a hearty thump on the knee.

"Philip, do listen! Because yours was not the only express I received today. Did you not wonder what happened to Uncle Geoffrey?"

"I was just relieved he was not there to witness my imbroglio," he grinned. "No doubt he would have refused to pay my bail."

"Do be serious," she begged earnestly. "My cousin Martha sent an express to say Uncle Geoffrey must delay coming to Oxford because the vicar Mr. Spacks had a stroke of palsy, and they feared for his life!"

This got his attention, all right, and he left off stroking Jane's hand to gawp at his sister. "A...stroke of palsy?"

"Martha says it happened when Uncle Geoffrey and Mr. Spacks had 'words.' It seems Mr. Spacks did not wholly approve of my uncle marrying Miss Hynde next Sunday, and Uncle Geoffrey flew into a temper, and then Mr. Spacks had his fit!"

"Heavens."

"But you see what it means, don't you, Philip?"

"I hesitate to say it, lest everyone think us vultures."

"We are certainly that, I suppose, in considering the implications," agreed Cassie. "But wishing Mr. Spacks long life will not make it so. What is done is done, and now, even if he were to survive, he could not possibly carry out all his duties. He would need a curate!"

Her brother frowned. "In any event, I don't know if my uncle still wishes me to have the living—or if he will after he hears about today's misadventure."

"I will speak with him," declared the baron, slapping his knees. "Have no fear. I will explain all and vouch for your character. I know the Bishop of Oxford as well and will intervene there if need be."

"Would you truly, sir?" Egerton asked, as Jane reached to press the old man's hand and hold it to her lips. "It is too good of you. Jane and I would be so grateful, for your word would carry much weight with them, as would your rank, frankly, with my uncle."

"And you didn't tell Uncle Geoffrey that he shouldn't marry Felicity, did you, Philip?" asked Cassie anxiously. "Because then Lord Dere might say what he liked, but my uncle might still be angry with you as he was with Mr. Spacks."

"No," he answered, remembering his note. "Quite the contrary. When Martha wrote to us last time, I knew I would never marry Miss Hynde. Therefore, I encouraged him, in so many words, to 'have at it.'"

"Hurrah!" cheered his sister. She clapped her hands and nearly fell in Jane's lap when she leaned across to hug her just as the coach clattered to a halt. "Well, my dear Jane, whether it be in the coming months or five years from now, I will rejoice to call you my sister. You see? Secrets are not altogether bad things. You two have been very sly, but I am not the less happy for it."

EPILOGUE

**I thank God all is tranquil again,
after many fears and alarms.
—Mary Delaney, The autobiography and
correspondence of Mary Granville (1755)**

Everyone agreed: the marriage of Mr. Geoffrey Cottrill to Miss Felicity Hynde was a scandal.

Not because Miss Hynde was young enough to be Mr. Cottrill's daughter—that bit was a tale as old as time—but because of who performed the ceremony and the whole way in which it came about.

The old vicar, poor Mr. Spacks (and he was never, after his death, referred to as anything but "poor Mr. Spacks"), died within a fortnight of his stroke of palsy, a stroke for which many blamed his argument with Mr. Cottrill. The wedding was then postponed, but Mr. Cottrill's stern daughter Miss Cottrill let it be known that it awaited only the appointment to the living of Mr. Cottrill's nephew Mr. Philip Egerton. Well and good, but Mr. Egerton's appointment, in turn, awaited his own replacement in his temporary curacy and "the clearing of his name" in the quarter sessions at Epiphany! What sort of vicar required his name to be cleared in court?

That Mr. Cottrill should first kill poor Mr. Spacks and then name as substitute his criminal nephew—?

It was a marvel the bishop would permit it, but rumors flew that Mr. Cottrill was not Mr. Egerton's only influential friend.

"My cousin the lawyer in Oxford says a baron pulled wires and spoke in his defense," sniffed one parishioner, only to be hushed when Miss Cottrill's beady eyes turned toward them.

As if all this were not enough, by the time the scandalous nephew arrived in their village, he brought with him his equally scandalous bride, if "bride" were the appropriate term for a widow who had eloped with her first husband and ended in debtor's prison.

"But he had to marry somebody," hissed another congregant, "for I hear Mr. Cottrill stole Mr. Egerton's own first choice for a bride."

"No!"

"Yes."

"And who could a violent criminal persuade to marry him then, but someone who herself had no reputation to speak of?"

"True, true."

It was all too, too much, and there were many who said that, though they could not escape the payment of their tithes, they would never set foot in St. Lawrence Church again under the circumstances.

But with time curiosity proved more powerful than outrage, and when the February morning of the new vicar's reading-in and Mr. Cottrill's wedding arrived at last, there was not an empty pew in the little church.

Despite being a pardoned criminal, the new vicar was handsome and well-spoken enough, and he bore himself calmly as he joined his nefarious uncle to his own would-be sweetheart in holy matrimony. Nor could any immediate fault be found in Mrs. Egerton, who sat quietly at the end of the first pew, watching her husband with shining eyes.

When the service was ended, moreover, and the wheat thrown at the newlyweds, the new vicar and his wife met every single member of their flock, and the little details they already knew about them showed pains had been taken to learn their names and situations.

"Why," said one to another as they left the churchyard, "they are the most decorous scandalous people I have ever met."

"Just you wait," answered the other. "Everyone can behave himself for one morning, but time will tell, and then there will be plenty of meat for tittle-tattle."

Sure enough, the first occasion came only a half hour later, when the sexton returned to make things tidy and to lock the vestry. Morton was unobtrusive by nature, "but those two might not have noticed a thunder-clap," he reported later to his wife.

For when he slipped into the back of the church, "there were the vicar and his wife a-standing by the pulpit, and him kissing her within an inch of her life and her giving him a Rowland for his Oliver. Then, when they finally come up for air, he says, 'Happy?' and she says, 'Never happier.' And he says, 'Kiss me again, then, my darling Mrs. Egerton,' and off they go again. Never seen anything like it in all my born days, but I got out of there, quick like."

Despite this shocking beginning, however, which Mrs. Morton shared throughout the village by sundown, Mr. and Mrs. Philip Egerton soon settled into their new church and new home and surprised everyone by living a life as quiet and unscandalous and blissful as any which had yet been known in all the realm.

THE END

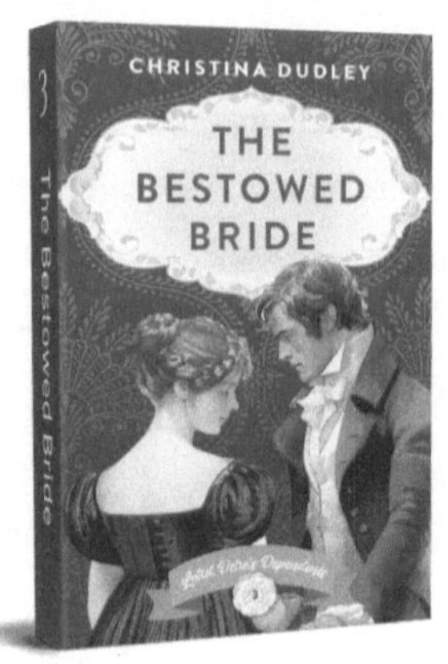

Read Sarah's story next in *The Bestowed Bride*, the third book of the Lord Dere's Dependents series.

THE HAPGOODS OF BRAMLEIGH

The Naturalist
A Very Plain Young Man
School for Love
Matchless Margaret
The Purloined Portrait
A Fickle Fortune

THE ELLSWORTH ASSORTMENT

The Accidental Servants (prequel)
Tempted by Folly
The Belle of Winchester
Minta in Spite of Herself
A Scholarly Pursuit
Miranda at Heart
A Capital Arrangement

PRIDE AND PRESTON LIN

www.christinadudley.com